BLACK MARSH

DEUCE MORA MYSTERY #5

JEAN HELLER

1

—————

*C*hicago . . . Night

The night began quietly enough in downtown Chicago, an area that encompassed the Near North neighborhood above the Chicago River and The Loop south of the river. The Loop was so called because beneath Chicago's busy downtown streets lay a labyrinth of rail tracks. They carried commuter train lines into the center city, then looped around and went out again. The trains were known collectively as The El because most ran almost entirely above ground on elevated tracks. Only in The Loop did they dive into the subterranean world. The Loop neighborhood boasted many of Chicago's finest restaurants, stores, and theaters. Michigan Avenue, nicknamed by the Chamber of Commerce as The Magnificent Mile, ran a straight north/south line down the middle of the city. Just to the west Rush Street ran in a parallel line of some of the trendiest shopping east of Rodeo Drive in Beverly Hills. The area smelled of money and privilege.

This night, it would smell of death.

Chicago Police Training Officer Louis Cassell and Patrolman James Weldon had been touring the area since their shifts began six hours and thirteen minutes earlier. Cassell drove; Weldon worked the radio. He had used it only three times since they came on duty, twice to check in and once to check out for lunch. Cassell had eight years on the force, Weldon fewer than four months. Cassell didn't much like the younger man. Weldon tended to talk too much and claim to know too much. He had been assigned to ride with Cassell only two months out of the academy after he and his first training officer had a falling out. His relationship with Cassell was moving in the same unhappy direction. Cassell was supposed to bring Weldon in line and smooth out his rough edges. He didn't feel that he was making much progress.

Cassell didn't trust his young partner's judgment. The kid was prone to unnecessary violence, bad tactical decisions, and didn't take criticism well. Earlier in the evening he had jumped out of the squad car at a traffic light and hassled a man waiting in a delivery-only zone for his girlfriend to get off work at the Crate & Barrel store on Michigan Avenue. The guy had stayed in his car with his flashers on and wasn't causing any problems. Nobody was delivering anything at that time of night. Weldon rapped hard enough with his nightstick on the driver's window that he might have broken it had Cassell not ordered him back to the squad car. Cassell asked the driver what he was doing, was satisfied with his answer, and told him to move on as soon as his girlfriend showed up.

The two cops hadn't spoken to one another since. Cassell would file a report on the incident after shift.

It was now moving past three a.m., and the squad car was patrolling a part of the Near North Side that made Cassell uneasy at night. Chestnut was a nice street. Upscale condos, restaurants, theaters, parks, Michigan Avenue and Rush Street, the Oak Street Beach, and Northwestern Memorial Hospital all within walking distance. But the eastern-most blocks that ended at Lake Shore Drive were badly lighted, an open invitation to drug dealers, muggers, robbers, and carjackers operating in the gloom.

The hour and the current weather conditions had swept most people off the streets. Winds off the still-frigid waters of Lake Michigan fingered among the downtown buildings in search of pedestrians to harass. While the calendar said it was late May, thermometers said it was forty-two. The "feels like" temperature was thirty-eight. Snow flurries swirled on the winds and melted as soon as they hit the ground. South of Chicago, spring was firmly entrenched, but in the city, winter refused to give up.

Weldon and Cassell saw the two men at the same moment. They walked south from Mies Van Der Rohe Way toward Chestnut. They wore crossover trainers, dark pants, and gray hoodies with the hoods pulled close around their faces against the wind and snow. One spotted the police cruiser and pointed it out to his friend. Their pace quickened. They continued down Van Der Rohe Way, across East Pearson Street behind Water Tower Place and then into the Seneca Playground Park. They were headed for Chicago Avenue where the Northwestern University Chicago campus sprawled over acres of land and offered a multitude of places to hide from the authorities.

"Pull over," Weldon told his partner. "Need to check out these two creeps."

"They're not hurtin' anyone," Cassell said.

"They're wearin' hoodies," Weldon replied.

"So what?" Cassell snapped. "That ain't a crime. If I was out in this weather, I'd be wearin' a hoodie, too."

Weldon wouldn't let it alone and Cassell finally relented. "Call in and find out if there've been any complaints up here tonight about two guys in hoodies."

"We can check 'em out ourselves," Weldon insisted.

"Do what you're told, kid," Cassell snapped. "Now."

Dispatch reported there had been no trouble calls in the area all night.

Weldon wouldn't be stopped. "Pull over and ask if they need directions," he said.

Against his better judgment Cassell did as Weldon demanded, pulsing the siren, and telling Weldon they were getting too close to racial profiling for comfort.

"That's bullshit," the younger cop said. "You can't identify them by race when you can't see their faces."

Cassell didn't have a good answer, but he did have a bad feeling.

When the two hooded men entered the park, Cassell ran out of pavement and couldn't follow. If they wanted to question the men, they would have to give chase on foot.

"Open the trunk," Weldon yelled. "Lemme grab a shotgun."

"No time," the senior man replied. "We'll lose 'em. Use your Taser, if you have to."

Cassell unholstered his own Taser. Weldon pulled his Glock. Cassell found it a dangerous harbinger that his young partner always went for the most lethal weapon on his belt. They'd had words about this before. Now they closed the gap between them and the hooded men. Although the two hooded men had done nothing obviously illegal, their skittish behavior seemed to warrant the police interest. Still, Cassell didn't like it.

"Police," Cassell yelled. "Stop. Get on the ground and put your hands behind your heads. Do it now!"

Instead, both suspects turned and faced the officers. Under the street-lamp Cassell IDed both as Caucasian. He breathed a shallow sigh of relief. One had something in his hand. Cassell couldn't identify what it was. Weldon would say later he thought it was a gun.

"Lay the weapon on the ground," Weldon ordered. "Do it now."

Weldon stopped and drew a bead on the man. Cassell continued until he was only a few feet from the suspects. Cassell recognized the item in the taller man's hand as a cell phone.

"Don't shoot, James," he yelled to his partner. "It's a phone."

As Cassell pointed his Taser at the man with the phone, three shots blasted open the night. The man with the phone fell to the ground, hit by a bullet in his thigh.

The remaining suspect panicked.

"Don't shoot," he pleaded. "Please don't shoot."

Cassell hit him with a Taser burst, and he went down.

Cassell was on him in seconds and cuffed his hands behind his back. He turned his head and saw Weldon walk to the wounded suspect and stare down at his body on the grass. He raised his gun and fired again at point-blank range, hitting the suspect twice in the gut.

"What the fuck are you doing?" Cassell demanded. "Call the lieutenant and a bus. The hospital's only a block away."

Instead, he saw his partner pull up a pant leg and draw a small gun from his ankle holster. Weldon used a surgical glove to place the gun inside the wounded man's right hand.

"Well, shit!" Cassell said. "You carryin' a throwdown piece, for Chrissake?"

Instead, Weldon glared at the older man. "Just shut up," he said. "You didn't see nuthin'."

Cassell walked over to the man Weldon had shot. He felt for a pulse at the carotid artery and found one, though it was thready. Weldon's first shot hit the femoral artery, and the wounded man was bleeding out. Cassell called for an ambulance himself.

"Go back to the unit and wait inside," he told Weldon. "If you move, I'll shoot you." It was an idle threat. But this time Weldon didn't argue.

Both suspects survived to get to the hospital, but the shooting victim had to be placed on life support. Doctors said he wouldn't survive.

The other suspect shook off the effects of the stun gun and cried for his friend. He kept repeating, "Why? Why did you have to shoot him?" The gunshot man, not much more than a kid actually, had not been armed. Cassell told their lieutenant that the gun found beside his body was Weldon's throwdown. Weldon denied it, but nobody believed him. He'd already developed that kind of reputation.

A very brief investigation validated the tased kid's story. Both young men were medical residents at Northwestern on their way to the hospital to support colleagues overwhelmed by new patients coming in with a Covid-19 variant. When they crossed paths with Cassell and Weldon they were walking to work from their apartment in River North.

The next day, the gunshot victim died. Weldon was fired from the force and arrested and charged with second-degree murder. The judge released him on his own recognizance.

If not for the fact that the dead man was white, his killing might have blown up into violent George Floyd-type street violence. There were a few peaceful protests, however, against what was deemed by the marchers as the excessive use of police force. Cassell almost wished he could have joined them.

A week after the shooting Weldon disappeared. The Chicago area was plastered with BOLO notices on the fugitive, and a judge issued a bench warrant for his arrest. There were no reported sightings of him. He had no family in Chicago and few friends. No one among those who knew him had seen him since his court appearance after his arrest.

James Weldon was never seen alive again.

2

———————

Seven months later . . . Joe Pye County, Southern Illinois

The problems began when I woke up.

Well, to be precise, the trouble started a few minutes before I lost consciousness in the first place, but it would be a while before I remembered any of that. When I roused, my memory of the Before Time had a big black hole in it. I felt as if I had spent a long interval inside a blissful cocoon of oblivion, unaware of anything going on around me before I was able, with some reluctance, to force myself back into the world.

I should have remained in the cocoon. I recognized soon enough that I had made a serious mistake waking up into the nightmare that would follow.

My head reverberated like a rock band amplifier. My body ached everywhere I focused my attention along my left leg. The sun was warm on my face, and I was stretched out on something comfortable. I considered remaining still and allowing the warmth of the day to leach the pain from my body.

That wasn't going to happen.

"I can tell yer awake, Missy. I can see yer eyes movin' under yer lids."

The male voice was as raspy as a heavy smoker's, the speech pattern definitely not a product of Chicago. I didn't recognize the twang. Not Deep South. But definitely not my hometown. For starters, nobody had ever called me "Missy" before. With luck, it wouldn't happen again.

"Whyn't ya'all open your eyes? Nuthin' scary to see here. It's a purdy day."

I resisted. Something in the man's tone tweaked my apprehension. I felt the chill of fear despite the warmth of the day.

I caught the scent of leaf mold, the earthy aroma given off by years of fallen leaves decaying beneath the trees that bore them. A common and pleasant smell in a woodland. I heard birds chirping and the sound of water gurgling over rocks in a small creek somewhere nearby. All very benign. All soothing. Except for the man, whoever he was. And the alarming situation.

Where was I? What had happened to me?

These weren't the sweet aromas or the sounds of Tahiti. Nor was the man's voice indigenous to Tahiti, where Mark and I were spending a blissful vacation. I must have had too much to drink the night before. That would account for the headache. Had I fallen asleep on one of the woven lounges by the resort pool? Perhaps the man was another guest. If so, why hadn't he called for help? Or perhaps he had, and no one had showed up yet. Or maybe I wasn't in Tahiti at all.

I decided I would lie there for a few minutes until my memory filled in the blanks and then deal with them, whatever they were. I wondered if Mark might show up and help clarify this mess. On the other hand, if she was in serious trouble, his presence might just deposit him in her predicament.

I took a deep breath, which relayed more evidence that wherever I was, it wasn't the South Pacific. The air in Tahiti wasn't so heavily laden with humidity, and Tahiti smelled clean and slightly salty. Where I lay, no ocean breeze cleansed and refreshed the air. I heard no unusual bird calls, no ocean waves crashing gently on the sandy beaches.

A memory returned.

I was standing at the jetway door to a United Air Lines 787 Dreamliner bound from Papeete to San Francisco, the first leg of the trip back to Chicago. Mark was behind me.

Where was he now?

My eyes snapped open. What I saw confirmed that I had not awakened in the last place I recalled being. I closed my eyes against the bright sun and tried to move the memory along, past the airliner door to wherever I was now. But the recording of my recollections was stuck at the bottom of the jetway and wouldn't fast forward.

I felt the first tickle of panic. I had no context for anything.

I knew the man with the raspy voice was on my right. During the few seconds my eyes had been open I caught just a glimpse of the bearded black face with the longish dark hair braided in dreadlocks. I opened my eyes again, slowly. He hadn't moved. He squatted on the ground next to me, a powerfully built man with a long straw of grass lodged in his teeth. I was lying on a brown blanket spread over a bed of leaves. The man was staring at me with unblinking black eyes, his expression impossible to read.

Had I met him before? Had he brought me to this place? What place was it? Did Mark and I board the United flight? What happened to it? What happened to Mark? I fought to remember anything at all. I fought to quell my rising panic.

But beyond that airplane doorway there was only an empty void.

3

———————

I tested my voice. It took two tries to get out one word: "Mark?"

"Nope," the man said, his lips the only part of him that moved. "Name's Drigger. Don't know no Mark. He yer husband? Boyfriend? Son? Dog?"

I started to answer but couldn't get my voice to work again. My mouth and throat were dry. Desert dry despite the humidity in the air. I tried to look at Drigger in a way that I hoped would convey my thirst, running my tongue over my parched lips. It worked.

He rocked forward onto his knees. "Well, I jes' ain't got no manners a'tall," he said. "You need some water?" He reached behind him and held out a canteen that had been lying in the grass. I looked from him to the canteen. He must have seen skepticism on my face.

"No worries," he said. "It's clean. Pristine, in fact. Nobody's used this canteen since I scrubbed it real good, and the water is pure." He reached around again and brought out a second, larger canteen. "This'uns mine." He laid his on the ground beside him and unscrewed the cap from the smaller one. "Lemme hold yer head up, so you don't choke."

He did, and I drank a good bit. The water was cool but had a metallic, artesian aftertaste, as if pumped from a deep-water well. When I finished, he lowered my head and capped the canteen.

Neither of us spoke for a minute. Then Drigger asked, "Who's Mark?"

"My fiancé."

"He a pilot?"

I frowned. "No. Why?"

"That's good for you. And him."

My mind couldn't cope with riddles. I frowned again. Drigger got the message.

"Yer plane crashed 'bout seven miles over yonder." He pointed off toward something I couldn't define. "I was out in my truck and saw it happen. There wasn't no fire, so I hiked off the road to the site and pulled you out. Checked the pilot, but he was dead. Had a metal rod through his neck. I left him for rescuers."

"Good lord, what about all the other passengers?"

"Weren't no others," Drigger said. "Wasn't much room for more. Plane was a small one. Only four seats plus the two up front. There was stuff scattered all over the cabin. You and the pilot was the only ones aboard. The two doors was jammed shut. Had to use tools from my truck to pry the cabin door open so's I could get to you. If you're wonderin,' I found a briefcase and a duffle that I assume belong to you since they was strapped into the seat next to you, and the duffle was full of lady things."

"A small plane?" I was now thoroughly confused. There seemed to be so much I couldn't remember.

Drigger was talking. "Relatively. Beech Baron, I think. Light twin."

I didn't get any of this, but I knew I needed medical attention, and I said so.

I felt for the pocket of my blue jeans where I keep my phone for easy reach. I didn't feel anything, and that heightened my alarm.

I asked, "Do you have my iPhone?"

"I think it fell outta your pocket when I was pullin' you outta the plane," he said. "You crashed in a swampy area that was all water and muck and mud. The phone sank, an' I didn't have the time to go searchin' for it."

"I have to call people to let them know where I am. Except I don't know where I am."

"Call's gonna have to wait 'til you get a new phone," Drigger said. "I saw an iPad in yer bag, but it was low on power and's probly dead by now. Ain't no wifi or phone service out here, anyway. Ain't no real medical help 'round here, neither. I'll do what I can for ya. I was a medic in the Marines in Afghanistan. I don't think you're hurt bad."

A helicopter interrupted him, rotors pounding. It sounded as if it was headed our way. My mood edged up. If we could signal it for help, maybe it would fly me to safety. Drigger dashed that hope.

"Right now," he said, "we gotta get you outta sight. Think you can stand?"

"Maybe, with some help."

"We ain't goin' far," Drigger said, "and your leg ain't broke. Just need to get to the other side-a them trees over there, to my cabin, such as it is."

He helped me sit up. I saw what must have been Drigger's pickup. It was blue and rusted with a hard, flat cover over the bed. It looked maybe thirty years old.

From behind me, he hooked his arms under mine and boosted me to a standing position. He picked up the blanket, gave it a perfunctory shake, and handed it to me. I held it over my right arm. He placed his body on my left and put my arm over his shoulders so he could help keep my weight off the injured left leg.

His clothes were dirty from his trip into the swamp, but he smelled clean. His breath exuded a vague scent of mint, though I didn't take Drigger for an Altoids kind of guy.

"Sorry I cudn't-a driven you to the door," Drigger said. "I been clearin' out underbrush and small trees, but I ain't quite done makin' a car track to the cabin."

He guided me as quickly as I could move through the small grove of pin oak and red maple trees. Most of the understory had been cleared. Drigger tried to stay within those areas, but the short trek was awkward, nonetheless.

The cabin was definitely rustic. I saw the water pump on the right, about sixty feet from the front door, the length of a semi-trailer. It seemed a long way to go for a canteen of water in bad weather. Going off the other side of the house, maybe twenty-five feet, was what appeared to be a covered and walled walkway with a square bulge at the far end. I had no idea what it was.

The front door was bolted with a solid lock. Drigger left me leaning on a tree while he fished a ring of keys out of his pocket and used one key to open the door. Then he helped me inside. Except for light coming in through the door, it was dark.

I started to object and thought better of it. Better to take the chance I had than one I couldn't imagine. When he closed the door behind us we were in pitch dark again.

"Just stand there a sec," Drigger said. I heard the jangle of his keys again, and a beam from a small flashlight cut through the blackness. He relocked the door.

"Is that to keep me in?" I asked, fearing the worst.

"It's to keep them guys in the chopper an' their friends out," he replied.

He used the keychain flashlight to locate a kerosene lamp. A box of kitchen matches rested beside it. He used one to light the lamp, and I could make out the entire interior. It was as rustic as the outside, with rough-hewn beams and unsplit log walls. The floors were wood, too, but appeared to be made of commercial-grade planks. They were clean, as was every other surface I could see. It appeared that the room in which we stood was the only room in the house. It held a cot, a recliner with a side table, a small, propane-fueled kitchen, and a little dining area with a circular table and two Chromecraft kitchen chairs with cracked green faux leather seats. There was a large blue chest in the corner. A cooler.

My bedroom in Chicago was larger than the whole cabin. None-theless, it was better than I expected.

"How long do you expect me to stay here?" I asked.

"No tellin'," he said. He wasn't going to explain further.

Drigger must have come back before I regained consciousness because my briefcase and duffle bag were resting on the floor beside the somewhat dingy recliner. At first I thought there were no windows until my eyes adjusted, and I could make out what appeared to be heavy shutters on three walls. I took the kerosene lamp as an indicator that the shack had no electricity. No running water, either. And very likely no formal bathroom. It had a small wood stove that could be used in a pinch for cooking but most probably was installed to provide heat in the winter, assuming I was someplace that had a winter.

"You should set in the chair," Drigger said. "I'll put up the footrest, which'll keep your leg from swellin'. Got some ice in the box over yonder if we need it." He pointed to a Yeti cooler in a corner. That must have cost a pretty penny.

"Bathroom?" I asked.

"Nope, but there's an outhouse out back. I can help you get to it when you need it. It's only a few steps."

"Is that the closed-in walkway?" I asked, nodding my head in the general direction.

"Yup. There's a door over there to get into the walkway, and another door down at the end to get into the stall house."

"Seems like a lot of trouble to get to a hole in the ground."

"It's on a bench, and it's got a regular seat. So there ain't no need to squat."

"Terrific," I replied. "Why the closed-in walkway?"

"Well, keeps varmints out. An' you don't want-a be gettin' up in the middle of the night with a full bladder an' hafta walk in a cold rain to get out there. Winters here can be a bitch, fer shure."

That alarmed me. "You plan on me being here through winter?" I asked.

"Nope. Hope not."

"You don't have electricity?"

"Nope. Lines don't come out this far."

"This far from where?" I asked. "Where are we?"

"Let's get you settled and the boys outside headed away. Then we can chat."

Drigger pulled a dozen boxes of prepared foods and bottled water out from under the cot. The cartons were labeled with the logo, "Patriot's Supply," which I assumed meant they were developed as emergency rations for survivalists. That did nothing to calm my nerves. He replaced the food and water with my duffle and briefcase, pushing them back all the way back to the wall. Then he shoved the cases of provisions back under the cot. The supplies effectively hid my stuff from anyone taking a casual glance under the bed. He flipped back an area rug exposing a trap door in the floor.

"If the folks outside start to close in, you'll need to go down there," he said. "It'll be awkward, but your leg's only bruised, so you should be able to manage. Ladder's short. Just six rungs. I'll help you."

I nodded toward the chair, and Drigger helped me to it. He pushed the seat back a little and raised the footrest. It was comfortable enough. Then he began what I recognized as a concussion protocol. Apparently, I passed.

"Nothin' serious," he said. "Looks like you got knocked around some, but nothing that won't be better by tomorrow. How're you feelin'?"

I saw no reason to lie. "Confused. Scared. Miserable. I don't know where I am or how or why I got here. I can't bring up any recent memories. And I hurt."

He stepped back and draped the blanket over me. "Don't push it," he said. "Yer memory will come back, but if you try to force it you'll just get more scared and confused. Your head jes needs some Tylenol, which I got. And yer leg jes needs a couple-a days' rest." He pointed to the blanket. "Got a few more if you need 'em tonight. I'll take the cot. It's military issue. Not real comfortable."

"Tonight?" I asked. "So, there's no chance I can leave today?"

"Don't think so. But there's no tellin'. They might not even come here lookin' fer ya, but in case they do we gotta be prepared to hunker down 'til they leave. Don't worry. With the food and water I got stashed we're good here for more'n a couple-a months, if necessary. Maybe longer. We'll be okay."

I wasn't sure I believed that. But one thing I knew for a certainty. It was time for Drigger to tell me what was going on.

I was about to demand that when the chopper flew directly over the cabin. I don't know why, but I knew in that moment that Drigger had been telling the truth. The chopper was hunting for me.

4

———

"Sorry, Missy, gotta move," Drigger said with urgency in his voice.

He opened the trap door and helped me out of the chair. He dropped down onto the dirt floor of the cellar ahead of me and jockeyed me down with strong, sure hands. Then he climbed out and handed down the kerosene lamp.

"There's a wood chair down there," Drigger said. "Sit there and be quiet. I'll pull you out soon as we're clear."

I nodded toward the kerosene lamp. "How're you going to see where you're going?" I asked. "This is your only lamp."

"I got another one. An' I can open the shutters. If you hear me stomp twice on the cellar door, blow out the lantern and take cover as best you can. Over behind them boxes."

Two walls were stacked with large cartons, each stack about six feet high and four feet long. There was just enough room between the boxes and the dirt walls that I could squeeze back there. I'd have to bend down some to make sure my hair couldn't be seen over the top of the cartons. At six feet tall, I'm not the easiest person to hide.

The door closed, and I heard the area rug slap over it. Then quiet for several minutes until someone started banging on the front door.

I heard a gruff voice: "Drigger, you in there? Open up. We ain't got all day."

Drigger's voice sounded muffled and dry, like a man awakened from a sound sleep. "Who is it?"

"Sheriff Sparks," a deep voice replied. "Come on now, Drigger, open up."

I heard a shuffling across the floor and two heavy stomps on the cellar door. "Sorry, Sheriff," my host said. "You caught me takin' a nap."

"We need to have a look around, Drigger," the voice said. "Let us in."

"Whacha lookin' fer?"

"Not your business."

"It's my property," Drigger replied. "And you ain't said nothin' 'bout havin' no search warrant. So, I'm within my rights to tell you to fuck off."

"Let's do this friendly-like," the Sheriff replied, "or somebody's gonna get hurt. There's three-a-us an' one of you. And we're armed."

"I got guns," Drigger replied. "Everybody 'round here's got guns."

"By the time you get to one-a yours, one-a us will-a dropped you like a hot rock."

Apparently, Drigger relented. I heard his keys jingle as he opened the door.

"Not many places to look, Sheriff," I heard him say. "You been here before. What are you tryin' to find?"

There was no response, but I heard footfalls. Somebody was having a look around.

"How 'bout the cellar?" The sheriff's voice again. "We need to have a look there, too."

"If you're goin' down, be careful of them top two rungs," Drigger said. "They's cracked and won't bear much weight. When I go down there, I jump to the third rung."

I didn't recall anything wrong with the top rungs, but I didn't have time to dwell on it. I needed to get behind those boxes, which appeared to be extra stores of food and water. I hobbled behind the higher stack, pressed my body against the wall, and blew out the lantern. I heard somebody drag the rug away from the door. It creaked open, and lantern light from above stabbed through dust motes.

The sheriff apparently decided against risking the ladder.

I heard him give orders to somebody, a deputy.

"Randy, git on the floor and shine your flash around, see if anybody's down there."

Randy's light probed the cellar, finding the chair, cobweb-filled corners, and the box stacks. I pressed into the wall and ducked my head. The beam passed a few inches in front of me and might have found the toe of my boot. Then it moved on to probe other corners.

The flash clicked off, and I was in the dark again, never happier to be so.

"Nuthin', Sheriff," a youngish voice said.

"Go check the outhouse."

"Aw, Sheriff, do we have to?"

"That's an order, son."

Then Drigger's voice. "You'll need a key to get the door open," he said.

There was a moment's silence before the sheriff found his voice again.

"You lock the outhouse? What the hell's in there worth stealin'? You sellin' turds?"

"Helps keep varmints out," Drigger said. "Maybe not those with a key, though. Here, use mine. Shouldn't take ya long." I heard a laugh in his voice.

The Sheriff spoke again. "Found your truck out yonder beyond them trees, Drigger," he said. "The hood's still warm. Where'd you drive it?"

"It's sitting out in the sun," Drigger replied. "A-course the hood's warm."

"Not now, Drigger. That big hackberry tree has the truck in full shade. Probably has been for an hour. The heat I felt was comin' off the engine block, not the sheet metal."

"Tell you the truth, Sheriff," Drigger said, "I can't stay in this cabin twenty-four hours a day. So, I go out driving around most every day, fish or hunt a little for dinner, gather some berries and wild vegetables. Without no 'lectricity I can't have a refrigerator, so I have to hunt and forage and pick up other stuff I need in town. That's what I was doin' earlier. Nothing unusual."

"You didn't see a twin-engine plane crash?"

"No, but I think I mighta heared it," Drigger said, his tone feigning indifference. "I heard a plane flyin' low and a loud noise, like it cudda been a crash, but I didn't see it."

"You didn't go lookin' for it?"

"No, sir. Firs' place, I wouldn't-a known where to look. Weren't no smoke to mark the place where the plane went down, if that's what happened. An' I couldn't jes go sightseein' through there. That's rugged country. Lotsa swamps. Copperheads and cottonmouths, a few rattlers, and quicksand. I knew if it was a plane crash I couldn't drive to it, and hikin' woulda been too dangerous. I'd druther face a mountain lion than one-a them poisonous snakes. Cain't even see the devils 'til they got their fangs buried in your leg. 'Sides, it weren't none-a my bidness. What cud I have done?"

I was still hiding behind the boxes when I heard the subtle rumble of thunder. It was faint, but it was muffled by the wood floor and the fact that I was underground.

"So," the Sheriff said, "if we could find any boot tracks around the wreckage, we wouldn't be able to match them up to yours?"

"I'd be very surprised, cuz I wasn't out there."

"And while you were huntin' and foraging, you didn't see a woman wanderin' around—pretty, white, real tall, mid-thirties, auburn hair, green eyes? Name's Deuce Mora."

"Nope," Drigger replied. "But iffen I had, sounds like a lady I might have invited home with me, Sheriff." I heard Drigger laugh. He sounded convincing.

"You see her, stay away and call me right off," the law officer said. "She's probably armed, and she's big trouble. A stone-cold killer."

My head snapped up with such force that I narrowly missed bashing my head against the wall.

Me? A killer?

If the sheriff was telling the truth, I needed desperately to remember what had happened to me between Tahiti and here, wherever "here" was. If I'd killed someone, I must have been in extreme danger. But armed? I didn't even own a gun. At least not that I could recall. Damn my memory. How was I supposed to understand anything while I still had amnesia?

I felt as if I'd just stepped through the Looking Glass into the movie, "Deliverance."

All I lacked was a canoe and a banjo.

5

———

I opened my eyes to the sound of a sizzle and the mouth-watering aroma of bacon frying in a large cast iron skillet on one of the burners of the propane camp stove in what passed for Drigger's kitchen. Coffee percolated on the second burner. I was lying back in the recliner, my legs elevated, my body covered by two blankets. I was ravenous.

"Is it morning?" I asked. The shutters were still closed, and the only light came from the kerosene lanterns. "I heard a big storm last night. Even the lightning and thunder didn't keep me awake. The rain on your roof was soothing."

"Yep," Drigger said. "I was going to fix you some supper after I got you back up outta the cellar, but you laid down in the chair and went out like a light. Slept right through the night. You gotta use the bathroom?"

"Bathroom?" I said with a raised eyebrow.

"Easier to take if you don't think of it as an outhouse," he said.

He helped me down the walkway and back again. Then he poured some water into a basin and showed me how to use it to wash up.

"It's not very luxurious, but I got no tub. It'll work for the time bein.' I drug your bag out from under the cot, so you'll be able to get at anything you need."

I cleaned up in front of Drigger, but assuming the role of a country gentleman he kept his back to me and his eyes on the bacon he was frying. My leg felt better, and my headache was gone. I sat in one of the Chromecraft chairs at the table set with paper plates, plastic utensils, and cardboard coffee cups. I guessed the throwaways were required because there was no place to wash real dishes.

"Lemme just pile up some eggs, pour some juice, and we'll have ourselves a feast," Drigger told me. "Only thing I can't do is make toast, but I got plenty of bread."

He put an entire package of bacon—likely a full pound—into a cast iron skillet, fried it a while, and transferred it all to paper towels. He poured what was left of the bacon grease into an old coffee can where he could use it for future cooking, then cracked eight eggs into the skillet with the remaining bacon fat. He served it all up with a stack of whole wheat bread. I tried not to make grunting pig sounds as I ate. Given where bacon comes from, it would have been insulting to pigs.

I used two slices of bread to sop up left-over egg yolk and bacon grease on my plate and felt much better.

We finished clearing the table. Drigger dumped the disposable trash into a plastic bag, which he locked in a metal box on top of the cooler. He said he would dispose of it next time he was in town. Drigger scoured out the cast iron skillet with a wad of paper towels, leaving a thin sheen of grease.

"Don't wanna wash these things with soap or it'll destroy the seasoning," Drigger said. "Don't want to do that to a good iron pan." I already knew that but didn't say so. I didn't want to belittle his knowledge after the breakfast he'd just fixed.

"Where do you get supplies?" I asked. "You obviously don't have a refrigerator."

"There's-a general store in town," he said. "I go there a couple-a times a week an' keep stuff that'll spoil in the cooler with a few-a them big frozen shippin' packs. Got two sets-a them. The general store keeps one set froze while I use the other set. Swap 'em out every few days. But mostly I hunt and forage. You need anythin'?"

Something I heard the sheriff say the evening before kept poking at me. What I wanted from Drigger was information.

"What's Sheriff Sparks going to find when he hikes out to the plane?" I asked. "Is he going to be able to match your boots to tracks?"

Drigger smiled. "After that storm we had overnight, ain't gonna be anything left of boot tracks. I knew what was gonna happen before he did. I was hearin' thunder far off even when you was still down in the cellar. And the air smelled of incoming rain. Nice, fresh smell. I doubt he and his men was fifteen minutes away from here when the first drops hit."

When Drigger finished cleaning up he said, "Why'n't you get back in the recliner and lemme take a look at that leg."

I did, and Drigger said the swelling was almost gone.

"By tomorrow you'll only have a bruise," he promised.

Then he conducted the concussion protocol again.

"Yer fine," he announced. "Nothin' to fret about."

I asked, "I don't have a concussion?"

"Nope."

"Then why have I lost my memory?"

"Maybe emotional trauma," he said.

"Okay," I said. "Now I have some other questions."

I STARED AT DRIGGER A MOMENT, trying to gauge how great the chance that he would tell me the truth. I had no reason to anticipate lies, except a lot of people lie to journalists, and I was a columnist for a major newspaper in Chicago. I wondered if he knew that. I had no legal authority to force the truth, but I am by nature an optimistic person.

I asked, "Where am I, and how did I get here? And why am I here? Who are you?"

"You're in Joe Pye County in southern Illinois, a good long ways up the back roads from Cairo," he said, as if that would answer my questions. I'd never heard of Joe Pye County, though I knew Cairo as the place where the Ohio and Mississippi Rivers merged. I remembered it from Mark Twain's Tom Sawyer stories.

"How far is Cairo from here?" I asked. I pronounced the city the way the natives do, Kay-row, like the legendary corn syrup, only spelled different.

"Maybe a hunert an' fifty miles. It's a good three-hour drive, maybe more dependin' on traffic, which can git pretty heavy this time-a year what with tourists and all," Drigger said. "If I had an appointment in Cairo today, I'd leave at least four hours to get there, just to be safe. It ain't like we can get on a interstate or nuthin'."

"Interstate 57 runs to Cairo."

"Wouldn't be no faster. We're deep in the Shawnee National Forest right here. No quick or easy way out. The easiest access to the interstate would take us well outta the way. Easier and just as quick to use back roads. But too dangerous."

Something didn't ring true about this whole situation. "What gives a county sheriff jurisdiction to hassle you here, on national forest land?"

"Sparks got jurisdiction 'bout anywhere he decides to take it," Drigger said. "I think the feds find it easier and safer just to leave him be. He can raise an army here if he needs to fight to keep this place for hisself."

"If we're on national forest land, how'd you get permission to build this cabin?"

"There's plenty-a cabins up here 'round the lakes. They're private tourist bidnesses, but they're licensed by the feds. This here cabin was built back in the thirties, 'fore the forest became federal land. Ownership passed through a couple-a generations to me. That makes me an in-holder, a property owner whose title dates back to before the forest was anything but a bunch-a unnamed trees. But it'll end with me. I got nobody to inherit it, and I cain't legally sell it. So, after I die it'll either git tore down or be taken over by the feds for some forest service use."

Drigger was lying. The cabin couldn't have been in his family for years. As soon as the area around it became a national forest, the cabin couldn't legally be transferred from one family member to another and eventually to Drigger. Its "private property" status would have ended with the departure of the last person to inhabit the cabin before it was designated as federal property.

The other thing that cast suspicion on Drigger's story was the cabin flooring. I had noticed it was commercial-grade planking. Nobody built a cabin like this with commercial-grade flooring, especially not back in the thirties, some ninety years ago. Back in those days the flooring of a shack like this likely would have been dirt.

As certain as I was that Drigger was lying, I didn't want him to know I knew. I still had no idea who he was or how dangerous it might be to me if he knew I doubted his story. So, I changed the subject.

"Is there a city of any size closer than Cairo?"

"Nope. Paducah's almost as close, across the Ohio River in Kentucky. But if I know the sheriff, he'll have cronies over there watching the airport. You'd be kinda hard to disguise, and Sparks owns some tough Kentucky state troopers who'll arrest you the minute they lay eyes on you. They git paid good for their observational skills. Nobody don't ask no questions. They do what they're told."

"So basically, there's no safe way out of here if Sparks is looking for you?"

"That 'bout right," Drigger said with a slow nod. "Cain't even hike out. Nothin' round here but cypress swamps and poisonous snakes. You take a wrong step you'll be dead."

"Cypress swamps? In Illinois?"

"Southern Illinois," he said. "I heared tell once this was the farthest north cypress trees could grow, and they been growin' here more'n 1,000 years. Some of them trees is forty feet around at the base. They tower over the blackwater swamps and provide a home for all manner of critters, including vicious mosquitoes."

"Sounds delightful," I said. "While I appreciate your hospitality, I have to get out of here soon."

"Got no clue yet how yer gonna manage that. But we'll figger it out."

"You could drive me down to Cairo," I suggested. "Then I could either fly home from there or rent a car. I'd pay you for the lift."

"I ain't drivin' you nowhere," he said. "Sparks an' his cronies gonna be keepin' a close eye on the roads outta here, such as they are. Iffen we got caught, they'd kill us both just cuz I lied to him about knowin' where you are. We wouldn't be the first ones to cross him. People who do git disappeared real quick."

"Why?" I asked. "I haven't done anything to upset the locals. Not that I remember. What did Sparks mean when he said I was a killer?"

"No idea," Drigger said with a shrug. "Cuz he said it don't make it so."

I was exasperated and still very frightened. Truth be told, I was scared half to death.

"What the fuck is this place?" I demanded.

"I ain't goin' into that right now," Drigger said. "When you git your memory back, you'll figger it out. But people round here knows you're here, assumin' you survived the accident. They don't want you here. No way. Not for any reason."

"How do you know that?"

"Well, most know who you are cuz a newspaper, the *Paducah Sun,* over in Kentucky, said so in its story about the crash, that Deuce Mora from the Chicago *Journal* was on the plane. I pick up a copy now and then when I'm in town. I know people 'round here wouldn't want you. They don't make no secret of it. They discourage all strangers. They don't even like it when outsiders come in to canoe or kayak or fish the lakes. Most outsiders know that or learn it the hard way and stay to theirselves."

"Friendly place." My sarcasm was sincere.

"Not 'specially. If I cudda talked to you before you left Chicago, I'da tole you to stay home. Whatever you was comin' here to do, it 'tain't worth your life. Or mine."

6

———

I paced the small cabin on a leg still a bit gimpy, but the discomfort took second place to my impatience. Drigger insisted on sidestepping my questions no matter how hard I pressed him. And I couldn't put together anything that would give me leverage to force to talk straight with me. I'd had enough.

"Drigger you know way more than you're telling me," I said with a sharp edge in my voice. "If you don't start being honest with me, I'm going to walk out of this place and try hitching a ride to Cairo. If I disappear, it'll be on you."

"Sit down, Deuce, you're makin' me nervous," Drigger said. "You gotta let that leg rest. Sit down, and I'll answer what I can."

I sat. "I'm listening."

"Derek Sparks runs all the territory in the county, and well beyond, even though it's Forest Service land. Everything he into's either immoral, or illegal, or both."

"What's he doing?"

"I can't confirm anything, but if the gossip is true and not rumor, it should scare the crap outta you."

"It has," I admitted. I shook my head in frustration. "Don't you think, since I seem to be running for my life, that I have a right to know what I'm running from?"

Drigger ballooned his cheeks and exhaled. "Yeah, you probly do. An' iffen I knew fer shure what's goin' on, I'd share with you. All's I hear is he's got his fingers in lots of things where they shouldn't be. The one thing I know fer certain, 'cause I've witnessed it, is poachin' game. Some-a them wild animals, bear, cougar, eagles, feral pigs, what all, people wanna hunt 'em for trophies. There's people who'll pay more'n $100,000 to take down a black bear. A total waste. But Sparks's guys run a smugglin' operation to move the carcasses out of the area, hell, out of the state, where they can be made into trophies by folks that don't ask no questions. He'll do anything fer a couple of bucks and has his own private police force to make sure nothin' goes wrong."

"What does he do, recruit thugs to do his dirty work?"

"Some, yeah." He looked at me with knowing eyes. "An' some bad cops who need someplace to hide out."

That statement touched on a memory I couldn't quite retrieve. I had no idea how long it would take for my memories to reform or, in fact, whether they would. Without knowing how I got here and why, nothing around me had any context.

"Damn," I said. "You'd think the feds, especially the Forest Service and wildlife people would be all over this."

"They've tried. Some agents was never seen alive again, and some was found dead. Hung or strangled or with a bullet hole in the head or a twelve-gauge shotgun blast to the gut. I seen a guy once cut clean in half by a twelve-gauge that caught him in the stomach. It was like being in a war zone."

"Over game poaching? I mean, I hate that it's going on, but it doesn't seem horrible enough to kill people over, especially federal agents. Who around here enforces the law?"

"Sparks makes out, so long as it's *his* enforcement of *his* laws."

I couldn't figure out how one crooked sheriff managed all this activity alone. And what Drigger described, poaching game, might bring in good money, but not in the sums he was alluding to. Once again, I wasn't getting the truthful story. I voiced my doubts.

"He can't control this whole area alone," I said.

"He ain't alone," Drigger replied.

"So, who else's involved?" I asked.

Drigger shook his head. "Cain't say."

"Can't, or won't?"

Drigger just shook his head. Then he leaned forward on his cot and asked, "Why you starin' at me like that?"

"I'm questioning whether I believe a word you're saying. It's such a preposterous story. If it were true, the Fish and Wildlife Service would be in here in a massive show of force to put a stop to it. If they're not doing the job for some reason, why doesn't Governor Latchey mobilize the National Guard to clean this place out?"

Drigger slapped his thighs and pushed himself off the bed.

"You're right," he said. "This whole mess is preposterous. But sometimes the truth is preposterous."

"Am I supposed to believe that Sparks can corrupt a big area of southern Illinois, and nobody will move against him?"

"Joe Pye's got a lotta land but not many people. Population's so small nobody pays us much mind. The Ohio River makes up most of Pye's eastern and southern borders. So's there's plenty of places to cross into Ohio and Kentucky to do the trophy bidness real quiet-like, without stirrin' up problems. I don't know how many folks is aware-a what's goin' on, but it don't really matter. Money talks big. An' fear talks bigger. Besides, most folks here abouts think of poaching as a victimless crime."

"There's nothing victimless about the slaughter of wildlife, especially if some of them are endangered."

"There's lots more to Spark's empire than poachin' wildlife."

"Like what?" I asked.

"Ain't gonna get into that. Might be nuthin' more than rumor."

"So, tell me, anyway," I insisted.

"I've already tole you too much," Drigger said. "I'm holdin' back for your own safety. And mine. I got my own bit-a illegal stuff goin' on down here. Sparks would kill me if he thought I was gonna make a move on him to take over his territory. So I cain't let 'im git suspicious, 'an he leaves me be."

"I don't know about your safety, Drigger, but this whole scene is a threat to mine," I said. "I don't understand any of it. I'm angry and frightened. You refusing to tell me everything is making it worse."

I got up and started to pace.

"Am I supposed to accept that of all the folks living in this part of the state, you alone are the only one who hasn't been corrupted by Sparks?"

"I didn't say I hadn't been corrupted by the sheriff," Drigger protested. "In a way, I s'pose I have been. I'm sure there's folks in Joe Pye who manage to avoid Sparks, but I ain't one of 'em. I jes try to stay outta his crosshairs."

"That would sound more plausible if you'd turned me over to Sparks when he came looking. But in protecting me you've taken sides. That's got to have consequences for you."

"Maybe, eventually. But so far he ain't sure what I know or where I'm comin' from. Right now, he don't know where you might be, but he suspects I do. If he kilt me before he found you, then I take the information he wants to the grave. That's enough for now to protect me. 'Til he knows fur shure, I'm jes' a dumb black hermit who don't know enuf to get hisself a house with a real bathroom."

7

____

Chicago...

Eric Ryland paced impatiently around the outer offices of the U.S. attorney for the Northern District of Illinois. He was angry and frightened. He had arrived a half hour earlier, demanding to see Jerry Alvarez, the Deputy U.S. attorney and the man he held responsible for Deuce's decision to fly to southern Illinois to look for a killer cop hiding from justice.

Alvarez and Deuce were long-time friends, and Alvarez trusted her enough to share tips and information he wouldn't share with other reporters. He knew Deuce wouldn't identify him as a source. It was Alvarez who had tipped her one day to a possible human-interest story about an old Mob associate. It was supposed to be a feature, but it wound up being a story of murderous acts that spanned more than fifty years. It won the paper a Pulitzer Prize.

This time, however, an Alvarez tip might cost Deuce her life.

Ryland knew Alvarez was in a meeting with his boss, but whatever they were discussing could have been set aside for half an hour to talk about Deuce.

Finally, at the forty-three-minute mark, Alvarez appeared. He looked good after dropping nearly sixty pounds, and his clothes finally fit him well.

His parents were from Hermosilla, Mexico, the capital of Sonora. It was prosperous, attractive, and largely isolated from Mexican drug cartels. Alvarez's mother had been a teacher, his father a lawyer. They moved to Chicago along with Jerry's paternal grandmother before Jerry was born so he would be an American citizen. He spoke English flawlessly but had a curious habit of speaking occasionally in Spanish and then immediately translating his words to English. Deuce found it an endearing habit. Because his grandmother refused to learn English, Jerry grew up in a bi-lingual household where using both languages came naturally and out of necessity.

"Hola," he said, walking to Ryland with his hand extended. "Sorry to keep you waiting. We were discussing the subject you came to talk about. Come on in."

Instead of walking toward his own office, he led Ryland into the office of the United States attorney, Alicia Samuelson. Ryland knew her to be a highly regarded public servant, so much so that hardly anyone ever mentioned that she was black, or that her term in office had spanned three presidencies because hardly anyone in sharply divided Washington, D.C. wanted her replaced. She was completely nonpartisan.

Samuelson, a stately woman, moderately tall, slender, and quick to smile, walked around her desk to meet Ryland.

"I apologize for the delay," she said. "We're dealing with a very difficult situation here, and we've been on the phone with my counterpart in the southern district trying to formulate our next move."

She held out a hand toward a conference table in a corner of her office. When they were settled, Samuelson asked if anyone would like something to drink.

"A double Jack Daniels on ice would be nice," Ryland said. "I need that these days."

Samuelson smiled broadly. "I know," she said, "but I was thinking more of coffee or water. My secretary could probably scrounge up a fairly fresh teabag if you'd prefer."

"No, gracias," Alvarez said. Ryland shook his head and spoke what was on his mind.

"Do you have any word on Deuce?" he asked. "I'm quite perturbed that

I'm getting no updates from your office. I don't know if she's alive or dead. And now her fiancé has gone down to look for her. I don't know what's happened to him, either."

"I understand how you feel, Mr. Ryland," Samuelson said. "But you have to understand that the case is in the jurisdiction of the southern district. While we always cooperate on cases that involve something major, this one is sensitive, and information must be held very close. It's the safer course for Deuce and her fiancé, ah . . ." she glanced down at some papers on the table in front of her, "uh, Mark Hearst. The state fire marshal's office is as concerned about him as you are about your star reporter."

"I'm so very glad everyone cares," Ryland said with a hint of sarcasm. "What makes me unhappy is that no one seems to be doing anything about it. What can you tell me?"

"You already know what the NTSB has released," she said. "The pilot was killed in the crash. No trace has been found of the only passenger, either alive or dead."

"Is that true?"

Samuelson tilted her head, a form of a shrug.

"From their point of view, yes. But the NTSB doesn't know everything. It's not their job to account for a passenger, though they would certainly help if they had a clue where she is. They don't. That they haven't found her is better news than if they'd found her dead."

Now Ryland got up and began to pace.

"You're talking in riddles, Ms. Samuelson. Give me something. Is Deuce alive?"

"As of this morning, yes."

"Do you know where she is?"

"As of this morning, yes."

"Is she badly hurt?"

"Not last we heard."

"What about Mark, Deuce's fiancé?"

Samuelson smiled, but there was no mirth in it. "The handsome prince is trying to rescue the princess in distress," she said. "And he's likely to get them both killed."

"Do you know where he is?"

"Not for sure. We're not even positive he's arrived yet."

"Who's your source?"

"I can't tell you that. But he's deep into the crap that's going on in Joe Pye. We've got to find a way to top him."

Ryland stopped pacing and nailed her gaze with his.

"Why," he asked, "do I have a feeling there's more at stake here than a rogue cop hiding out in a national forest?"

"Because there is," she replied. "You have no idea how much more."

8

———————

J oe Pye County ...

The house, which could have been attractive, was a wreck.

From the look of it, its history likely began in the 1930s or 1940s.

It was small, maybe 900 square feet, on one floor. The siding, most likely asbestos, had weathered and peeled in a few dozen places on the exterior walls, and paint trim around the doors and windows was black with mold.

A tin roof deflected heat in the summer. Winter heat was provided, as in Drigger's cabin, by a wood stove. Unlike Drigger's cabin, the old house had an indoor bathroom. Power that flowed from an eighty-watt Generac generator could supply considerably more power than a small structure like this would ever use. The occupants of the house used it to support a large and sophisticated communications system. The generator ran on propane gas from a 250-gallon tank that sat in concrete cradles behind the house.

The wrap-around porch appeared not to have been repaired or replaced since the house was built. It sagged, rippled, and peeled. The porch railing was among the places infested with mold. The house had no landscaping, and the yard was patchy and bug-infested. The hinged door of a root cellar lay nearly flat at the back of the house and was raised six inches above ground level to block rain. The cellar entrance was overgrown with weeds and secured with a heavy-duty padlock that appeared to be impervious, even to an attack with a bolt cutter. A run-down shed squatted beneath some trees in the back yard. The side of the shed facing the house was open but protected with heavy bars.

There was nothing about the house that even rose to the definition of adequate. The propane tank showed large patches of rust, and its concrete cradles had chipped and cracked in several places. A truck came by and topped off the big tank once a month. Several times the driver mentioned to occupants of the house that the tank required maintenance to remain safe. They always nodded and agreed, but they never did anything to fix it. The driver of the truck quit bringing it up.

The entire construct, sitting on three acres of what little private land was left in Joe Pye County, looked like any old home gone to ruin. A visitor with a critical eye might wonder why such a small house needed an eighty-watt generator or a 250-gallon propane tank. In Joe Pye County, some people suspected but didn't talk about it or ask questions.

The interior was quite a different story. It had one bedroom, a small kitchen, and a good-sized living room/dining area. While a bit dingy, the paint was intact, and everything else was clean and in good repair. The furnishings turned what had been a home into an office. There were two desks, each with a computer on it. One desk was much larger than the other. The rest of the space supported an easy chair, a half dozen folding chairs leaning against a wall, and a non-descript wooden table with six old, mismatched wood chairs around it. The bedroom was filled with electronic gear, some of which extended into the main room and sat on a table behind the larger desk. The one bedroom had enough additional space for a queen-sized bed, so in addition to being an electronic hub, it also served as the room it was designed to be.

This day there were four cars parked at odd angles on the dying grass in front of the house. Three of them were Joe Pye County Sheriff's Ford Broncos with bright yellow bodies and black roofs, all-terrain tires, and lifts that raised their chassis well above the ground. The fourth vehicle was a fierce-looking Ford F-series pickup, a 350 Lariat, solid black. It, too, had all-terrain tires and was jacked far enough off the ground to require a step to get into it.

All four vehicles were perfect for the swampy, overgrown obstacles ubiquitous in Joe Pye. The 350 might have been too heavy for some situations—a 250 probably would have sufficed—but the 350 was powerful and imposing and just right for the sheriff's personality. Tricked out as a police vehicle, it probably sold for more than $100,000 new.

The vehicles were clean and undamaged, a handsome fleet that would have been impressive in a small city and were awe-inducing in the second-smallest county in Illinois.

⁓

Sheriff Derek Sparks was talking, his voice raised in anger and frustration. The three deputies arrayed in front of him appeared at once defiant and uneasy.

"You all absolutely certain you ain't seen nothin' suspicious from Drigger Morton or around his shack?" he demanded. "I know he goes out to hunt and fish most every day. Is he still doin' that? Is he always alone? Any sign-a that reporter around his place?"

"No, sir, Sheriff," the oldest and probably most senior deputy replied. His name was Henry Ditmond, a killer cop from Terre Haute, Indiana who moved to Joe Pye County eight years earlier. "We've had eyeballs on him twenty-four/seven since the night after the plane crash. He goes hunting or fishing most every day, like you said. Stops every few days at the general store. When he's got what he needs he goes home. He stopped a few times at the pull-off on Carpenter Road at John's Creek. So far's we can tell, he's just relaxin'—maybe meditating given the hippie he is. He'll sit there for anywheres from fifteen minutes to a half hour, then drive off home. Seems pointless to me."

"I'm betting it ain't," Sparks said. "You all, and the deputies who ain't here right now, all know why that reporter is here and what's at stake for us. I want her, dead or alive, as quick as possible. I ain't askin' politely. Those are orders. If I catch any one of you men coverin' for her, you'll find yourself hanging over Black Marsh."

A second deputy, Tacito Ayala, squirmed uncomfortably in his chair. He said, "Yesterday when I was birdin' him he stripped and took a swim in

Fishy Creek. I didn't think much of it since he ain't got plumbing at the shack, and he has to get clean somewhere. He didn't even dry off. Just sat buck nekkid on a rock in the sun for a bit. Soon's he was done, he drove straight home. Didn't stop nowhere."

Ayala had come to Joe Pye from Oscuro, New Mexico, a nowhere sort of place between the White Sands Missile Range and a Mescalero Indian Reservation.

Sparks sat and listened with his right elbow propped on the arm of his leather chair, his chin resting on his closed fist. He turned back to Ditmond, the deputy from Indiana.

"Anything else that seems out-of-the-ordinary?" Sparks asked the group.

Ditmond frowned and shook his head. "He's got that ongoing project to clear dead trees and understory from his property."

"You've seen him doing this?"

"Once. I stopped and asked what he was doin'" Ditmond said. "It was last summer, when it was so dry an' the fire danger was high. The stuff he was clearing was mostly dead and cudda served as fuel for a wildfire. I still see him come outside after dinner a couple-a times a week to clear under-growth, weeds and tree saplings an' such, but he looks to be mostly done with it. Told me he wanted to be able to drive his truck up closer to the house stead-a leavin' it under the hackberry tree. Maybe he's worried that piece-a rusted junk's gonna get stole from him."

Two deputies laughed. One didn't.

In the time the quiet man had been one of Sparks's deputies, he'd learned to keep his mouth shut when he had nothing serious to offer.

The man's name was James Weldon.

He was from Chicago.

9

---

*M*ark Hearst rolled into Red Twig, the seat of Joe Pye County, just after sunset. He had a plan of action, but the closer he got to his destination the more he began to doubt that his plan would work.

Thoughts he didn't want to deal with snaked through his brain. Anger and worry are a never-ending loop. He was angry that she was chasing another dangerous story and worried that this one might finally be the end of her. He resented that she kept putting herself in so much danger. He resented having to worry what an emotional disaster it would be for him if she died. He allowed himself to consider the odds that he would die with her. They'd both gotten into some fearsome trouble working together on her stories. Even if this one came out okay, he was getting very close to the end of his tolerance.

Hearst had spent most of the drive down from Chicago deciding whether he could, or should, give her an ultimatum: give up this James Bond crap or lose him. The possibility that she would choose the latter course made his heart hurt, but things couldn't continue this way. Not if she still wanted to get married and have children. It was these unresolved issues that had stopped them from getting married on their Tahiti holiday. They *had talked about it once, briefly, and then let the subject drop so it didn't dull the joy of the vacation.*

The uncertainty and anxiety couldn't continue forever. If they both got out of Joe Pye alive, he decided he would have it out with her, no matter the consequences.

His focus shifted to the present when he drove slowly into Red Twig. He had driven his own truck, a black Toyota Tundra, for two reasons. First, he couldn't use his state-owned SUV for private business, and second, the bright red color and state fire investigations logo on the side would draw too much attention.

The town was dark. Almost entirely shut down for the night. The exception was the gas station, which still had lights on over the pumps and inside the convenience store building. He checked his fuel gauge. Under half a tank. He should top it off just in case he needed it.

"Howdy," a local said to him as he stopped in front of a pump. "Need some help?"

"Thanks," Hearst said. "I just need some gas. I can handle it."

"Don't think I've seen you 'round here before," the man said.

"I was here once before," Hearst replied. "I'm a state arson investigator. My partner and I were down here investigating a suspicious fire in a row of tourist cabins. One man died. When we finished we hung out for a few days of R&R. I'm not sure who we offended, but the local attitude didn't exactly encourage me to come back for another try."

"I remember that fire," the local said. "But I don't remember you."

"I'm very forgettable," Hearst said with a smile.

"So, why're you here now?"

Hearst looked away from the clicking fuel pump at the local. "Why the third degree?" he asked. "I only stopped here to top off the tank."

"Jes' askin'," he said. "Don't get many visitors rolling into town after dark. Thought maybe if you was lookin' for something special I might be able to help."

Hearst felt the hair on the back of his neck come to attention. He had a strong feeling this encounter was not going to end well.

"You the owner of this place?" he asked, looking to change the subject.

"Yep. Owner, salesclerk, chef, and janitor. All me. Sometimes I git lone-

some and welcome somebody to talk to." He extended his hand. "Jenkins," he said.

"That's your last name?"

"Yep. But it's what ever'body calls me. Jenkins, or sometimes, Jenkie."

"Well, Jenkins, I need a room for the night, and I didn't see any motels around here."

"That's cuz there ain't none," the station owner replied. "Go back north a bit to around Boardman, and there's a few up there cuz it's on a lake. It's gettin' on to tourist season, though. No guarantee you'll find a room."

"Then I guess I'll have to sleep in the truck," Hearst said. "Wouldn't be the first time."

Hearst paid his bill in cash and pulled away. As his taillights disappeared down the road, a black man stepped out of the door to the convenience store and watched.

"Well, shit," Drigger said.

HEARST WANTED to find the old house that served as the sheriff's headquarters, not because he had any business with Sparks this night, but because he wanted to be able to find his way back to it, if necessary. He remembered passing it the last time he was through. It was a thoroughly dilapidated building then. He didn't expect to find much changed.

After twenty minutes of searching, he found it and drove by slowly. He wanted to stop and look around, but he was certain there must be an alarm system, and he couldn't risk triggering it. Nonetheless, he stopped the truck and left the motor running while he eyeballed the place from the road. From what he could see of the structure, it was still a mess.

There was a loud rap at his window, so sudden he jumped in his seat. He turned and saw a sheriff's deputy standing there holding a truncheon and twirling his finger in a gesture that told Hearst to roll his window down. Hearst hesitated.

"Open the window," the deputy ordered loud enough to be heard through the glass.

"Why? Mark shouted back. "What am I doing wrong?"

The deputy looked furious and grabbed for the door handle. The door swung open before Hearst could stop it.

The deputy was almost snarling. "Git outta the truck, motherfucker."

Hearst thought about his gun. It was in the glove compartment. No help there.

He turned in his seat and put his left foot out on the ground. He wondered if he could overpower the deputy before he had time to use his weapon. Then he realized it was useless. Two more men had walked up to the hood of the Tundra. He recognized one as Sheriff Sparks.

Hearst asked, "What's up, gentleman? I was only driving around on the off chance of finding a motel around here."

"Show me some ID," the sheriff ordered. Hearst pulled out his driver's license and his state-issued ID.

Sparks turned his flashlight on the cards, then looked back up at Hearst.

"I thought I remembered you," he said. "You was around here a couple of years ago."

"Yes, sir," Hearst said, trying to sound relaxed. He had a strong feeling this encounter was not going to end well. "I was investigating an arson fire, then I hung around for a few days to relax and do some fishing."

"Why'd you come back?" Sparks demanded. "More fishin'?"

"Maybe, if I can find a place to stay."

"You can stay right here, can't he, Henry?"

"Yes, sir, he can," the deputy replied as he stood behind Hearst.

Hearst hadn't taken his eyes off Sparks, so he didn't see the deputy raise his truncheon. For a split second he saw red, as though his head had blown open.

Then darkness.

10

Drigger returned to the cabin less than an hour after he left. He had several frozen ice packs and food but no good news.

He had horrible news.

"Your fiancé came down here lookin' for you, a very dumb thing to do but understandable, I guess."

The news took my breath.

"No," I whispered. "Oh, God, no."

Drigger added, "He must love you a lot to step into this hornet's nest."

"Oh, please, no. Is he okay? Did Sparks get him?"

"Yup." Drigger seemed more interested in putting the food away than in talking about what happened to Mark. My heart sank. I was horror-struck for a moment, then realized Drigger was right. It was something Mark would do. I should have expected it. Nonetheless, I was terrified for him.

"Where is he?"

"Sparks's deputies snagged him a couple-a miles outside Red Twig, the town that passes hereabouts for the county seat of Joe Pye. A crossroads, a nothing place that caters to tourists. You know, stuff you might need out on the water with a rod in your hands. Town's so small the sheriff's office ain't even there. Course the reason for that is Sparks don't want nobody lookin' over his shoulder."

I felt frantic.

"I don't give a shit about your crappy little town. Where's Mark? Dammit, Drigger, we've got to find him."

"I think they're keepin' him in a old shed behind the main house."

"What main house?" I demanded.

Drigger told me about the very unusual sheriff's headquarters.

"We've gotta find a way to break him out," I said.

"We gotta get both of you outta here," Drigger said. "Easier said than done, but I'm working on it. I told you that already, a couple of times."

"You keep telling me you're working on it," I recalled. "But you never say what exactly you're doing. You make it very difficult for me to believe you about anything. If Mark's really here, you and I have to do something before they kill him."

"They won't kill 'im, least not until they get their hands on you. My bet would be they'll try to use him to draw you out in the open, figurin' you'll eventually try to come after him. Then they'll kill you both."

I sighed deeply. "I'm really getting sick of you withholding information from me."

"I've noticed."

I said, "When you leave here you always say you're going to find food, but most of the time you come back with nothing but some assorted greens, and we eat those with the rations in the cellar. What are you really doing out there?"

Drigger sat down on the edge of his cot and scrubbed his face with his hands. Then he dropped his head and seemed to be thinking.

Without raising his head he responded, "Don't know how to erase yer doubts," he said, "'Cept sometimes it takes time to find the edible things. Then, like I told you, I got some secret business-a my own to tend to."

"Take me where the sheriff is holding Mark is so I can see for myself."

Drigger turned and stared at me a moment, his black eyes set hard.

"How do you think that ain't dangerous?" he demanded.

"I don't care. I want to see it."

"Okay," he said. "But not yet. Gotta think up a plan first. Meanwhile, I gotta show you what to do iff'en somethin' happen to me."

In the short time I'd been in Joe Pye I'd figured out that I'd gotten myself into something much deeper than the hideout of a rogue cop from Chicago. The prospect of attacking the matter without Drigger was unthinkable.

"I can't deal with all this alone," I told Drigger. "I'm not even sure you and I will be able do it together."

"We'll think on it. Meanwhile, there's somethin' we gotta do first."

"What?"

"Lady, in the next few days you gonna hafta expect the worst and be prepared for it. You cain't hep Mark, iffen you cain't hep yerself. That's the piority tonight."

11

Later that night Drigger showed me how to get out of Joe Pye on foot if I was making the attempt alone or with Mark. He said he would also tell me who I could trust.

The only drawback, aside from the chance of getting killed, was that I had to ride in the bed of Drigger's truck under the hard cover, hidden from outside view, running over roads that could break bones. The cover could be raised or lowered in increments. Drigger told me we would start with the lid at an acute angle of twenty-two degrees, high enough up to give me a good view of where we were going, but not high enough that I could fully sit up. Any way I looked at it, this would be an uncomfortable ride.

Drigger and I would communicate through headphones and microphones that ran off the truck battery through what we used to call the cigarette lighter receptacle. He kept the rig in his cellar, he told me, and got it out only if needed. I was beginning to feel as though Drigger's cellar must have been designed by the people responsible for the children's story, "The Magic Box." If we got into trouble, Drigger said, he would tell me to close the lid and lock it from the inside. I had thought the pickup was an old junker, but obviously it had been retrofitted to more modern capabilities.

Drigger explained what we were going to do, and it sounded like stuff from an old spy novel. Though he hadn't finished clearing underbrush, he found a path that made it possible to drive up to the back of the cabin where the enclosed walkway would shield us from observers. He would raise the lid enough for me to crawl inside. He would show me how to set the cover at the angle we wanted and how to close and lock it if we were pulled over.

"What I want fer you to do is keep a careful watch on where we're going," he told me. "You need to remember it so's you can retrace it if you need to run for your life. The route's pretty easy, and it will take you into Red Twig in a couple-a miles. I'll explain the rest when we git there. Find the owner of the gas station. He's always there when the place is open. If it's night and he ain't around, find a spot to hide 'til he opens up in the mornin'."

I asked, "What am I supposed to tell him to do?"

"You ain't gotta tell him nothin'. He knows."

"Is this what you were setting up when you left the house for a couple of hours?"

"No, I really was foragin' for food, but sometimes, when I go into town for gas or provisions at the general store, it gives us a reason to say hello—and talk a bit. He was gonna help gittin' you outta here safe, but your fiancé showin' up really complicated things. Now I gotta figger out how to free what's-his-name, Mark, and find a way to get you both out. That's a lot more dangerous. This here'll be a last resort for you if need be."

"And what about you?"

"Ain't no call to worry 'bout me. I kin take care-a myself. An' I cain't leave. I got my own unfinished bidness here. For now, try to grab a nap 'fore we hafta leave."

I WAS LYING on the recliner reviewing my situation and anticipating the drive to Red Twig with trepidation. I think I must have dozed off and started dreaming. Things that seemed unrelated flashed through my mind: having coffee with Jerry Alvarez, an argument with Eric Ryland, an argument with Mark. And something about Midway Airport on Chicago's South Side. There were planes taking off overhead. I was standing outside a squat building near a taxiway. I was waiting for someone. It was all gauzy, no details, just images and the whisper of a sensation that I was worried about something. Then, still asleep, I heard gunshots. When Drigger touched my shoulder and woke me up, I could feel myself returning from a deep REM sleep.

"You okay?" he asked.

I nodded. "I think some vague memories returned in my sleep."

"That's the way it happens sometime," he said. "Time to go. Git your wits about you and git dressed."

WE MADE our way down the tunnel to the outhouse and stepped into a pitch black, muggy night. The pickup had been backed up to the door. An old fishing rod rested on the passenger side, its tip sticking out through the window. The truck bed stood open, and I climbed in. He showed me how to operate the lid on the truck bed, whispering so he wouldn't be heard if anyone was listening. Once inside the truck we tested our makeshift communications. Then, with the truck lid open at a 22-degree angle, we set off.

To say the ride was uncomfortable would have been an enormous understatement. Drigger had laid out a sleeping bag to minimize the bumps and bruises, and it helped. A little. A very little. I had firm instructions to memorize the route we would take. "It's purty simple," Drigger had told me. And it was. We bumped over his yard and its remaining understory. My knees begged for mercy. So, I lay down on the sleeping bag on my stomach and peered through the open lid, which made my neck ache. I figured that compared to the danger I faced ahead, bouncing around in the truck was the least of my worries.

Maybe 100 yards out we hit what passed for a main road. I began making mental notes of features along the route. A fallen dead tree, a small bridge with a creek below, a pile of rocks. I was reasonably certain I could remember.

In another mile or so we reached what passed for a town.

The route was as easy as Drigger promised. Problems might occur if deputies were patrolling, and I had to duck deep into the forest to escape. My thoughts ran through a litany of the creatures I might find out there in the dark, or more to the point, those that might find me. I'd have to face those things if the need arose.

I pushed the thoughts away. With any luck, I wouldn't have to make a run for it.

We rolled slowly through the small town, the place Drigger referred to as Red Twig. I felt a tightness in my chest, but I managed to stay focused on what lay beyond the bed of the old pickup. I spotted the ancient gas station with rusting metal poles holding up the roof over two generic pumps. A single security light struggled to illuminate the pumps. One dispensed three grades of gasoline, the other diesel. A circular sign out by the road advertised Clark, a gasoline brand I'd never heard of. The sign was so old I thought perhaps the brand no longer existed. The convenience store section of the station, squatting behind the pumps, looked like it had been around for 100 years. The windows were veiled in smokey dirt. Neon signs for auto products, like Penzoil, Mobil, and Castrol, hung from the outside walls but were turned off for the night. Or perhaps they no longer worked. The front door, bathed in a low-wattage yellow light, held a sign put up with tape. "Bait, fishing stuff inside."

If the place had a bathroom, it was probably around back with doors that locked from both sides. I didn't know what it might look like, but anything would be better than Drigger's outhouse.

An auto parts and repair service crouched hard by the gas station and might have had the same owner. I saw no evidence that the facility had the capacity to do body or mechanical work. I suspected it didn't do much more than sell a few tires and change oil.

We passed a diner that shared space with what looked to be a post office. The building had only one front door above two rotting steps. The diner was to the left, the post office to the right. I saw another dilapidated building with a sign in front that said, "Clinic." I hoped not to have to avail myself of its services. It looked anything but sterile. An identical building in the same condition sat beside it. A sign identified it as a law office. Was it possible the doctor also served as a lawyer? That would be convenient. If somebody wanted to sue the doctor for malpractice, he only had to go next door.

I mentioned the coincidence to Drigger over our jury-rigged communications system. He told me that, so far as he knew, Red Twig never had a doctor or a lawyer practicing there. "I think them places was built for cover," he said, "so when outsiders come in to hike or fish they'll get the impression this is a real town and not some construct to convey normalcy in a place there ain't no such thing."

We also passed a general store, a place probably holding more real food than the snacks at the convenience store attached to the service station. I knew what it was because the sign above the door read, "General Store." I couldn't see anything inside.

The only decent-looking place in town was a one-story brick structure with a sign out front that identified it as the "County Building."

And that was it. No visitors' welcoming facility, no firehouse, no police station. Anyone visiting for the first time in the middle of the night might have mistaken Red Twig for a movie set, or a sad place that had been abandoned and left to rot.

Our communications system crackled in my ear.

"You think you could find the way back here?" Drigger asked.

"I think so," I responded. "You said it was simple, and it is."

"You spotted the gas station?"

"Yep. It looks abandoned. The whole town looks abandoned."

"It ain't. But folks here don't wanna spend a lotta money to fix things up 'cause they don't wanna attract visitors. Also, most of em's in with the sheriff. They don't wanna spend on improvements in case the feds ever show up askin' where their cash is comin' from."

"But you said the owner of the gas . . ."

"He's the exception."

"And his neighbors don't rat him out to Sparks?"

"Not yet. They might not even know, but they probly suspect somethin'. People here don't interact much. They're either part of the problem or scairt of the problem coming to them. We're gonna head back now. You can leave the lid cracked if you want to see the route from another direction. If you think you got it, you can close the lid, git comfortable, and enjoy the ride back home."

Drigger's home. Not mine. I wondered if I would live to see Chicago again.

Or Mark.

12

I chose to leave the cover up and watch the last-ditch escape route in reverse to better fix it in my memory. We were just coming up on the little creek when I saw several vehicles approaching from the rear at a speeds too high for this rutted trail called a road. Their headlights didn't quite reach the truck, but they would within seconds. Drigger had seen them, too.

"Put the lid down an' lock it, quick," he told me. "Don't make a sound."

As I was doing as Drigger asked, I caught a brief glimpse of roof lights begin rotating on four vehicles. A posse. Drigger pulled over. Better to be cooperative than dead.

Minutes passed in silence until I heard Drigger say, "Evenin' Sheriff. What brings you out this time-a night?"

I heard Sparks reply, "I ask the questions, Drigger."

"Yes, suh," Drigger said.

"What are *you* doin' out here at this hour?"

"Thought I'd try my hand at some nighttime bass fishin'. The big 'uns strike at night, and I haven't caught a big bass in quite some time."

"Any luck?"

"Does the one that got away count?" Drigger asked with a laugh in his tone.

"Doesn't look like it broke your rod, though," Sparks said.

"Not fer lack-a trying, Sheriff. At one point he had 'most bent it double. Then he done broke the line over a log in the water and took off. That's when I decided I might as well be in bed getting' my beauty rest."

"If you were fishin', what were you doin' in town?"

"Jenkins ordered a new fishing reel for me. The line I got's getting' old and weak. I wanted to see if it'd come in. I thought he might still be open, but I guess he left early."

The sheriff replied, his tone dripping sarcasm, "If we ever catch you fishin' without a license we'll arrest you and hang you by your thumbs until your hands get so bad you'll never hold a pole again. I've been lettin' it go, but tonight ends it. You understand?"

"Yes, suh. I think I can scrape up enough coin to send off to Springfield to git me legal. Do I need a license from the feds, too, seein' as how this is national forest land?"

"How the hell would I know?" the sheriff snapped. "I ain't the game warden."

"I hope I don't need two," Drigger said. "Not sure I could afford two. Fish is where I git most-a my protein. Cain't afford to be buyin' steaks."

"Speakin' of which, Drigger, where do you get money to live on? You ain't got no job I know of."

"I got my military pension. I put in twenty-two years, so the check I get every month's pretty good. Enough to support me out here, anyways."

Sparks seemed to think about that for a moment. I guess he chose not to press the point. He changed the subject.

"Am I to assume you haven't caught any glimpse of that reporter from Chicago?"

"No, suh. I ain't seen nobody to speak of, and them I have seen been mostly your crew. But if I spot her, you'll be the first to know. If she ain't been found alive by now, though, she's probably lyin' dead in the swamp."

"Yeah," Sparks said. "We can only hope."

I HAD some serious trouble getting back to sleep, and then it didn't last long. I guess it might have been an hour, maybe ninety minutes when I heard a thundering scream from someone who sounded both horrified and in full panic mode. The scream was muffled by the cabin walls and sounded as if it had come from maybe a quarter mile away. Still, the intensity and tone of the screaming made me seriously sick to my stomach. Whoever was making the noise was terrified by some horror in the night. Or in tremendous pain. Or both.

I sat up straight in the recliner. "Drigger?" I said in a trembling voice.

"Yeah, I heared it," he replied.

"Was that an animal or a human?"

"Human, I'm purdy sure. I've heared it before, but not often, thank goodness."

"What happened?"

"I cain't be sure, but I think it was comin' from the Black Marsh."

"That doesn't tell me anything. What's going on?"

"You don't wanna know."

"Maybe I don't want to know, but I need to know about the night-mares stalking people around here. I need to know 'cause if I have to get back to that rusty little town up the road, I need to know what I could encounter."

"Probably not what that poor bastard encountered. But you should see it so you realize all the way to your gut what kinda monsters we're up against out here. Git dressed and bring yer jacket."

WE RETRACED our route toward the town, on foot this time. Drigger said we couldn't risk taking the truck because it was too visible, and it would be hard to explain to the sheriff why he was out twice in one night. We stayed off the road, identifying ways to hide as we slogged through the trees. Drigger had sprayed us with a mosquito repellant called Bullfrog. He warned me I might still get bitten, but less frequently. "Depends on how thick they are out there tonight."

After a half hour outside, I concluded he got it about right.

If anyone was out with us, they were running silent. We didn't see a police unit, or an animal for that matter. It occurred to me that if our destination was so obscene and repugnant that it chased away even wild animals, maybe I'd made a mistake insisting we take a look.

We walked about a quarter mile when Drigger veered off to the left, deeper into the trees. I looked around to see if we had company, saw no one, and put my hand on his arm, a signal to stop.

"Why'd we change direction?" I asked in a low whisper. He didn't answer. Just took my arm and continued ahead. The trees thinned a little as we approached something more like a river than a creek. And when I looked out over the water, I knew exactly where the scream had come from.

My breathing stopped. Then I turned around and vomited into the underbrush.

13

Drigger pulled me away from the riverbank to a place that would provide us with more cover if my retching had alerted any living thing. The half-moon was high, and by its light alone I could still see the horror that curdled my stomach. It was something I would never unsee for as long as I lived.

A length of thick four-strand rope had been strung over the water from a stout tree near us to a similar tree on the far bank. The heavy rope was pulled tight. It didn't sag much even under the weight of the body hanging from it by the hands.

To be precise, it was only half a body. Both legs had been ripped off. If shock hadn't killed the victim, blood loss would have made quick work of him. His abdomen and been torn open. Entrails hung from it, close to the water, dripping blood and other bodily fluids. The remains swayed gently in the breath of a breeze, a macabre mockery of the hanging man's death. The bloodless dead face was turned toward us, the mouth distended and frozen in a long, dead howl of terror and agony. I didn't want to see it, but I couldn't look away until I heard splashing in the river.

"Don't look," Drigger advised. It was good advice I should have followed.

The head of a huge alligator lifted out of the water. It leaped (I didn't know gators could do that), fastened its jaws around the body's chest, and tore. A moment later nothing was left of the hanging man but two arms and his head on a perilous connection of shoulders and the top of the spine.

"The rest of him will be gone by morning," Drigger said, as if he'd seen this before. "Gators take living prey, even though this one came back for seconds. Birds and other creatures will strip what's left to bone in short order."

"Dear God," I whispered again, "does this happen often?"

"When some poor bastard crosses the sheriff, this is usually how it all goes down," he said. "It's meant to deter anybody else thinkin' 'bout goin' off the reservation, Sparks's warnin' to those who work for him that it would be best for them to stay loyal and focused."

"Is this where the sheriff and his deputies were coming when they pulled you over earlier? To do this?"

"Yep, probly so. He likes to bring his deputies along, 'specially the newer ones, to see what happens to traitors. It purdy much deters disloyalty."

"And this is what he'd do to Mark and me?"

"Probly not," he said. "He probly just shoot you in the heads and dump you in the river. Fish are opportunistic feeders, great garbage collectors. They'll eat what's there to find. No offense, but once you dead you really ain't nuthin' but garbage."

"Why won't somebody come in here and stop this?" I asked. "There must be some blood evidence on that rope."

"Tole you before. Nobody wants any part of this hellhole. An' Sparks could mobilize a small army of locals to fend off any assault by the state or the feds. They figure all the sheriff's victims are bad actors to begin with and not worth riskin' the lives of good people."

I glanced back at the human remnants still hanging from the rope and tasted bile rising in my throat again. I turned away from Drigger and spit out what I could.

I asked, "Can we get out of here now?"

Drigger just nodded and turned to start the trek back to his cabin.

It took me a few seconds to convince my brain to tell my feet to follow. I was stumbling, in part because I couldn't see well. There were tears in my eyes. I wasn't crying. I was in shock, an overload of fear and disgust. At that moment I would have killed Sheriff Sparks myself if I could have found a weapon and a plan to get close to him.

Back in the cabin with the door securely locked, sleep was elusive but thoughts of Mark were not. Where was he? How was he being treated? What was going to happen to us?

I felt perspiration pop on my face as anger and guilt consumed me. He wouldn't be here if it weren't for me. I thought about the argument we'd had about me coming down to Joe Pye. He was adamantly opposed. That was the argument that came back to me in my dream earlier, during my nap.

I didn't want to die in this godforsaken place. I didn't want Mark to die here, either. The burning question was how to avoid it. I had no answer.

14

The scream had roused Mark Hearst, too. To say it was blood-curdling would be a cliché, but there was no other way to describe it. He'd been slowly regaining his senses after being knocked down by a deputy's truncheon earlier, but the horrific scream punched him back to full consciousness. The scream cut off so abruptly that he couldn't be certain whether it was real or just a bad dream. He hoped it was a dream, but his gut said otherwise.

Mark decided to check out his surroundings before trying to get back to sleep. The half-moon provided some light. He saw that he was lying on a sleeping bag on a dirt floor in a box with a roof, three walls, and a fourth wall with bars along the entire length. He didn't even try to find the lock and determine whether he could open it. There was zero chance of that, and he didn't want to move any more than necessary. His head felt like it contained two wolverines trying to fight their way out.

Still lying quietly on his back, he considered trying to dig out under the cell wall, but the ground was too hard to do it by hand. His boots had steel aglets at the end of the laces, but they were small, and there were only four of them. Even if they worked, they wouldn't last long enough to make any significant headway. He felt gingerly for the left pocket in his jeans. It was *empty, as he feared it would be. He had hoped to find his go-to knife, a Buck 110 camping model. It was as tough as folding knives came. Digging a hole in the hard pack of the forest floor might ruin the blade, but killing the knife was a more acceptable outcome than getting killed himself. Unfortunately, when two of Derek Sparks's psychopathic deputies took him into custody they apparently confiscated everything he had that might have improved his predicament. That included the knife, his phone, and very probably his gun if they found it in the glove compartment of his truck. He wasn't even sure what had become of the truck.*

To make matters worse, he found only a small bottle of water beside him and the bucket in the corner of his cell likely meant to act as a toilet. He would learn in a few hours that the bucket was drained by gravity into the sheriff's septic system but was never cleaned. The stench was seriously bad. He forced himself to drink the water.

*W*HEN A DEPUTY SHOWED *up the next morning with his breakfast—Spam, toast, and another bottle of water—the sheriff came with him.*

"So, how're you doin', Mr. Hearst?" Sparks asked.

Mark just stared at him.

"Ya know, if you began cooperating with us, we could make your life a lot easier. Just tell us how to find your girlfriend."

"I don't know," Mark said. "I came down here to try to find her, but your thugs caught up with me a few minutes after I got to town. I didn't even have time to start looking."

Sparks heaved a deep breath. "So, you think she's dead?"

Mark screamed at him. "How the fuck am I supposed to know, you piece of shit? I don't even know where to look. Maybe at the site of the plane crash first, but the NTSB's already out there, and they only found the pilot."

"Yeah, and they're fixin' to leave and haul the wrecked plane out with them."

Mark felt his eyes sting. "Then I don't know. I just don't know. That's the truth."

Sparks made a snorting sound.

"If you're gonna stick to that story, then there's nothing I can do to help you. You'll probably wind up like that fella who was screamin' last night."

15

———

It came to me in flashes.

At some point early in the morning, before dawn, I had been able to doze. That's when the flashes began. In the first one I was aboard a large plane, nested in a seat next to Mark. The plane was climbing and banking to the left. I felt happy and safe. In the second one I was boarding a small airplane, climbing over the wing to get to the cabin door. In my flashback, nothing about the moment seemed familiar. Then the sound of gunshots again before the train of memories ended.

I opened my eyes slowly. I was fully reclined in the chair that had become my bed. I could feel that my t-shirt was damp with sweat, as was the hair at the nape of my neck. I could make out only what was illuminated by an oil lamp, turned down low, sitting on a chair near the door to the outhouse walkway. I turned my head to the right, my eyes on the bed where Drigger lay asleep, snoring lightly.

I tried to box up the flashbacks in my brain for safe keeping. They were, perhaps, a key to that part of my past I hadn't been able to remember. The larger plane might have been one of the two that carried us home from Tahiti to Chicago. I figured the second one was the smaller plane that crashed in the swamps of Joe Pye County.

There was no visual with the last part of the flashback. Just sound. Gunshots.

I willed there to be more, but no more came to me. I desperately wanted to know what the gunshots meant.

There was something else new in my head, too. I couldn't define it, but I sensed its importance. I didn't understand why I should try to remember it, but I tried all the same.

I lay there until I could see the first dull light of dawn between the shutters and their frames. I had tried not to doze off again for fear I would lose the substance of my flashbacks. If I stayed awake and told Drigger about them, maybe it would help cement them in my consciousness. Except I wasn't certain how far I could trust Drigger. After all, he had confessed to me that he was involved in something of dubious legality, something he desperately didn't want Sparks to know.

I thought about what I had seen earlier at the Black Swamp. I didn't care how rotten the victim had been; nobody deserved to die like that. Whatever was going on in Joe Pye County had to be the worst shade of grim.

Drigger roused himself in good time and sat up, scrubbing his face with his hands.

"How long you been up?" he asked me.

"I don't think I ever really went to sleep. There are nightmares waiting to strike behind closed eyes, you know."

He smiled and nodded.

"But there's something else," I told him, and then I described my flashbacks. "They felt real, like memories of things that actually happened. I'm worried that they were just vivid dreams and not memories. I tried to bring back more, but that's all there was."

He stood and stretched. "Lemme visit the facilities, then we'll talk about it."

"Two birds with one stone," he said on his return.

"Too much information," I replied. "The dreams?"

"Lemme axt you sumpthin'. This is the second time you tole me about dreams like this. How well you still 'member the first time?"

"Very well," I said.

"Uh-huh. How long ago did them new flashbacks wake you up?"

I shook my head. "I don't know exactly. Maybe a couple of hours before you woke up. I can't be sure because I don't have a watch."

"So that's maybe two hours," Drigger said. "How vivid are them flashbacks now? They beginnin' to slip away?"

"No," I said. "They're as vivid as they were when they happened."

"Well, then, I think it's prolly memories. Dreams, even them that's vivid and you want to hold onto, they begin to fade away pretty quick. If your visions ain't fadin', chances are they're real memories."

"If they were memories, what caused them to come back now?"

"No tellin'. Cudda been time. Your brain stashes away stuff it thinks you cain't deal with. After a spell, sometimes long, sometimes short, it lets those memories start to leak back out. If you cope with 'em okay, it'll probly set more memories free."

I frowned at him. "For a man who lives and talks like hermit-slash-hillbilly, you know an awful lot."

"Learned a lot in Afghanistan. When I was servin' over there we had quite a few guys go down with head trauma, and a number of 'em lost their short-term memories. We were in a real remote place, high in the Hindu Kush, where evac wasn't possible. We was getting' beat up real bad with all sorts-a light weapons and auto rifles. Some small artillery, even. All's I could do for the injured guys was use what medical supplies we had, keep 'em comfortable, and wait it out. One night we were getting' hit particularly hard. The gunfire and explosions was intense. Two of the guys lying there listening to the siege unfold were shakin' with fear, but they began to regain their memories. Trauma caused the amnesia, and trauma broke through the blocks. Eventually, we were able to sneak away and get to a place where a chopper cud come git us."

"That's interesting, Drigger, but what's it got to do with me?"

"That's why I took you to the swamp last night. I hoped the horror of what happened there might work for you. There's no way I'd-a taken you to see that if I hadn't thought it might help you remember things. Otherwise, it wudda just been voyeuristic and cruel. It seems to be working, an' I wanted to explain why I put you through it."

"Am I going to have to see something else that gruesome to remember more?"

"Dunno. I hope not, but everbody's different. I think chances are good the rest'll come back by itself. Jes' don't know how long it'll take."

16

Drigger and I chatted a while longer about the vagaries of the human brain. The conversation, and the surprising extent of Drigger's medical knowledge, reinforced my belief that this man was not who he claimed to be. But I couldn't worry the question to death because he seemed to have my best interests at heart, for now, anyway. And without him I couldn't face the more critical matters of finding Mark and a way out of Joe Pye County without getting shot, knifed, or fed to alligators.

"Drigger, do you have any idea where Sparks is holding Mark?"

"We think it's in a small buildin' that passes for a jail out back-a the sheriff's house," he said. "But I ain't seen him with my own eyes."

"Who's 'we'? Is there more than one of you, whoever you are?"

"Sorry. Jes' a slip-a the tongue. It's jes' me."

"Is there a way I could get close to that house, take a look at the lay of the land, and get out again with my life?"

Drigger squinted. "You axed me 'bout that before, an' I been thinkin' on it. It would be awful dangerous. They got cameras and alarms all over."

"You have a better idea?"

Drigger pondered that for several long moments. "It would be a long way to walk to git there, 'specially since you're still gimpy. An' I can't jes drive in there without no reason an' have a casual look around. Lemme fix some breakfast and think on it."

He didn't mention it again until we were through eating.

"Here's what I'm thinkin'," he said after a long silence. "'Spose I put you in the back of the pickup again late tonight. You'll be able to see the front of the sheriff's place when I drive in, and I'll park 'round back so's you can have a gander if you git a chance. We gonna set off the security system, but I think they'll shut it down when I give 'em my cover story. When we're in the dark again, you can have a quick look around for where Mark might be. Then we'll come back an' talk it over."

"How am I supposed to see anything in the middle of the night in the middle of a forest with only a partial moon to offer light?"

Drigger excused himself and climbed down into the cellar. When he returned he was carrying a small package wrapped in plastic secured with strapping tape. He cleared the remains of our breakfast and set his package on the bare table between us.

He explained. "People think I got a cellar full of emergency rations. Some of them boxes, specially the ones up top, is filled with nothin' but MREs, soldier food. Some with bottled water. But some of 'em, which I got buried in the pile, has more interestin' stuff. Unless you tore open every box down there, you'd never find my toys. Even if you picked the right boxes, you'd hafta dig under the pouches to find 'em."

I nodded toward the small package on the table. "So, what's that?"

He pulled out a pocketknife and began to cut the package open. What fell out was a black leather case with a pair of binoculars inside. He handed them to me.

"These be helpful," he said. "They see inna dark."

"Night vision?" I asked.

"Yep."

I thought about it for a moment, trying to recall the meager amount of information I had on night vision equipment. It wasn't much, mostly news footage of soldiers using it to pinpoint targets in a war zone.

I said, "I thought night vision worked by picking up heat signatures from living things or hot machinery, like battle tanks."

"Thas one kind," Drigger said. "It uses passive illumination, collectin' heat and producing images. But what you got in your hands uses active illumination for when you want to see at night everythin' your eyeballs could see in daylight. Works like a flashlight, only it throws infrared light. Even better than night vision which only sees if there are heat signatures around."

"What if somebody's looking out a window and sees the light?"

"Cain't. It works on a wavelength just below what the human eye can see."

My mind flashed back to a cursed place called Ransom Camp where Mark and I were led through the woods in an epic storm by retired FBI agent Carl Cribben. We were chasing a murderer. Carl was using a flashlight that had something to do with infrared light, but I didn't have any idea what it was.

"So, I'll be able to see everything, steps, porches, outbuildings?"

"Yep."

"I'll also be able to see somebody who might be coming to look at the truck?"

"Yep. You'll definitely have an advantage. You kin see a regular flashlight, but the bad guys cain't see that infrared job."

"Where'd you get these?"

"They sorta followed me home from the Marine Corps."

I didn't believe him. "Then why aren't they painted camouflage colors?"

"Prolly not necessary since they're black and cain't be seen in the dark. Which reminds me, until they turn the alarm system off, leave the truck lid down and locked. When the lights and sirens stop, you can open the lid a little bit, not much, just so's you can see out with the glasses. Don't stick your head or your hand out. Sparks has state-of-the-art security, which almost surely has heat-detection components."

"Sensitive enough to pick up a human hand?"

"Yep. An if som'body happens to be watchin' a monitor, they'll likely see it. I figure there won't be too many deputies around at two in the mornin', and I plan to keep 'em distracted with the news I'll be carryin'. But don't take any chances."

NEITHER OF US saw any reason to wait, so sometime after midnight, we headed out in the pickup, Drigger driving, me under the lid in the back.

Drigger told me he'd be driving a roundabout route, so if anyone was tracking them, what they learned would support the misdirection he planned to give Sparks.

At one point he pulled off the road and stopped. I heard him open his door and the truck rocked a bit as he got out. He started to yell: "You there. Hey, you there near the water. You need some he'p? You hurt? Come on over here. Ain't nuthin' to be scared of." There was silence for a few moments, then Drigger started yelling again. "Hey, don't run off. It's dangerous out there. Please come over here. You'll be safe." More silence. Then Drigger said, "Shit," and climbed back in the truck. I was going to ask him what that was all about, but I figured it was part of his plan.

We drove a while longer, then pulled off the dirt road onto a blessed stretch of smooth blacktop. I knew we had arrived at the sheriff's office. With clouds over the moon it likely was dark as pitch when we drove in. The next moment it looked like Wrigley Field for a Cubs night game. The security lights were so bright they actually shone through the small openings in the truck bed. The wailing sirens screamed so loud it took my ears a minute to adjust. The infrared binoculars might not work in that much light. I wondered if my brain could function in that much noise. I hoped Drigger could get both of them shut off.

We pulled around to the rear. Drigger backed the truck in so I'd have a fuller view of the back yard. I chanced opening the lid just a slit right then, while the occupants of the old house were preoccu-pied with Drigger. As he got out, Sparks banged through the back door wearing only a pair of briefs that had seen better days and a t-shirt with holes in one shoulder and under the armpit. I squinted to see the writing on the shirtfront. As I expected, it was insulting. It showed a rendering of a vacuum sweeper with the words above it, "Women's sports."

Sparks was standing on a small landing seven steps up from ground, rising above Drigger's head so Drigger had to look up at him. It was a position of dominance. I'd seen photos and old newsreel film of Hitler doing the same thing to throngs of followers who adored him. Hitler's stage was much bigger and higher than the sheriff's, but it's always good to have goals.

Sparks's tone projected his irritation at being awakened in the middle of the night.

"Drigger, what the fuck you doin' here at this hour, or any hour for that matter?"

As Drigger began to answer a deputy drove his unit onto the site and, fortunately for me, parked nose-to-nose with Drigger's truck leaving my field of view wide open.

Drigger asked, "Cud you shut down the alarm? It's blindin' me, an' I don't want to keep shoutin' over it."

Sparks turned someone standing on the landing with him and nodded. The man disappeared inside. A moment later both the lights and siren shut down. The headlights from Drigger's truck and the deputy's gave off enough light to see pretty well.

"Now what're you doin' here," Sparks asked Drigger.

Drigger leaned back against his truck. "I was jes' out drivin' around, Sheriff, when I think I spotted that woman you're huntin' for. I couldn't right tell in the dark, but the person I saw seemed about six feet tall. Couldn't tell the hair color. Couldn't even tell for sure if it was a woman or a man. But the way the person moved, I'd judge it was a woman. I called out to see if she needed help and asked her to come over to my truck, but she turned around and ducked into the marsh. I listened to see if'fen I could hear what direction she was goin', but she either hunkered down to hide, or she's pretty good at creepin' quiet through the woods. I tole you I'd keep an eye out, so I thought I should come over and let ya'all know right away."

The sheriff turned to the deputy who'd driven after us. "You see anything, Weldon?"

Weldon? I knew that name.

"Yes, sir," he said. "I saw him stop his truck and get out, and I heard him callin' to somebody. I didn't see no woman creeping through the trees. But I had a different angle on things, and it's dark out there tonight."

"But what you witnessed is pretty much what he just told me?"

"Yes, sir."

Sparks turned back to Drigger. "What were you doin' out at this hour?"

"There's many a night I have a lotta trouble sleepin'" he replied. "I find it settles my mind some if I go out for a drive, maybe pull off the road for a few minutes and meditate, smell the night air. Tha's what I was plannin' tonight before the girl turned up."

"Where was your sighting?" Sparks asked.

"Over by the Clovis Road turnoff."

Sparks turned to his deputy. "Git on over there and keep an eye out. Patrol a bit, see what you can see. An' it wouldn't hurt my feelings none if you had to shoot her and tell me later she attacked you. I'll get dressed and come over to help. Drigger, you best get on home now. You done good."

"Kin I axt you a question, Sheriff? You ever git out to look at that plane wreck?"

The question must have nettled Sparks because he didn't answer for a few seconds. I was sure the poking and the response were exactly what Drigger intended.

"No, I didn't," Sparks replied, irritation clear in his voice. "It rained hard that night. The area flooded and hadn't even begun to dry out the next day. Then the National Transportation Safety Board took control of the site, and nobody was allowed to get close."

Sparks turned and walked back into the house. The door slammed shut. The sheriff was acting out.

WHILE DRIGGER HAD BEEN LYING to the sheriff, doing a pretty fair job of it I thought, I was peering out at whatever I could find at the back of the house. The binoculars had good magnification capability, so when my eyes fell on something interesting, I could zoom in.

The first place I looked at was the outbuilding, which had to be the place Sparks was holding Mark. Drigger called it a jail. It was under a canopy of trees, which at least would keep the sun off it, preventing the occupant from dying of heat stroke or dehydration. I had to fight the urge to jump out and run to the box, but under the circumstances that would have been suicide for Mark and me, and likely condemn Drigger to the Black Swamp.

Because of the angle at which Drigger parked the truck, I didn't have a straight-on view to the inside of the cell. I could see about half of it. The rest was blocked by an exterior wall. As good as the infrared system was, it wouldn't be able to "see" through walls. If Mark was in there, he might have been in a back corner, farthest away from the bars. My disappointment was assuaged when I saw brief motion. An arm, perhaps? A shoulder? Something was, indeed, inside. I kept the glasses trained on the cell, hoping for more, but nothing more revealed itself.

A large exhaust fan built into the rear wall of the house's lower level kicked on, creating something of a din. I spotted the fan with the glasses, but I couldn't tell its purpose.

The whisper of a breeze carried the acrid scent of ammonia. I couldn't imagine its source. Even a dozen dirty cat litter boxes couldn't create that stench. The moving air should have taken the odor away.

The yard was dominated by a large propane tank that looked like it could have fueled an entire Chicago city block for a month. As I moved the glasses, I saw a big square of heavy wood on the ground against the house. It was angled a few inches, the higher edge against the house, the lower edge at ground level, away from the house. It looked like a cold cellar door, defended by a lock that would have been a match for any bolt cutter.

I turned my focus back to the propane tank, trying to imagine why this small, run-down house needed a tank that large. There was no epiphany in my immediate future.

I scanned the glasses over it. It was almost as worn as the house it served. It had rusted in a dozen places, which wasn't a big deal. I'd seen big commercial tanks in the same condition, and nobody seemed afraid for their lives.

The tank rested on two massive concrete cradles. I couldn't see the one at the back, but the cradle nearest me was damaged. A spider web of cracks wove through one leg. Weather and time had gouged out a piece I judged to be about the size of a softball.

I heard Drigger open the truck door. I took one wistful look back at the "jail" and hunkered down for the dark ride back to the cabin.

17

"Want some coffee?" Drigger asked when we returned to the cabin. I declined. I still held out hope that I would get some sleep that night. He fixed coffee for himself on his propane-fueled camp stove. Watching him took my mind back to the propane tank in Sheriff Sparks's back yard. It was tickling my brain with the germ of an idea I couldn't yet put into any usable context.

"So'd you see anything useful?" he asked after he sat down at the table with his cup in front of him. "Any sign of Mark?"

"I'm pretty sure I saw something move inside the cell, maybe an arm or a shoulder. I didn't have a full view of the inside, so I can't be sure."

"I was thinkin' that if I parked directly acrost from the cell it would be too obvious," Drigger said. "But what you saw makes me think it's more'n likely Mark's in there, and we shud move along on that assumption. You see anythin' else?"

I nodded. "A framed door lying flat on the ground. It looked like a door to a cold cellar. But what could anybody have in a cold cellar to protect? Potatoes? Onions?"

"You gotta think about what Sparks has got goin' on. A cellar like that cud grow bumper crops of weed. Or be a whole meth lab. Did you smell anything hinky?"

"Wait a minute," I said. "You didn't tell me Sparks was into drugs."

"Yeah. Big time."

"I knew it had to be more than game poaching. That explains his attitude."

"He don't want no one messing in his bidness."

"Is that what you're doing here? Trying to mess in his business?"

Drigger ignored the question and asked one of his own.

"So, didja smell anything unusual?"

"I did," I said nodding. "The place smelled like old cat litter. I started smelling it when that big fan came on."

"The ammonia odor is a chemical stench that comes from a workin' meth lab," he said. "The exhaust fan draws off the flammable gases that could blow the place apart. It smells like overused cat litter. Or an outhouse." He smiled.

"Why take that risk?' I asked. "Is the payoff worth it?"

"The cookers think so or they wuddn't do it."

I thought about that for a moment. I asked, "But doesn't Sparks live in that house? If the meth lab went up, it would take him with it."

"Apparently he thinks it's worth the risk, too."

"Huh. Well marijuana wouldn't make anybody rich these days," I said. "It's legal in Illinois now. That might have forced him to branch out."

"Yep, it's possible, but weed ain't legal in any way in Indiana or Kentucky, where he could scoot it over the state line an' sell at a huge profit. He's probably got weed and meth both down in that cellar."

"So are the Joe Pye deputies his mules?"

"Most likely."

I felt perplexed. "I don't know how you know this stuff, Drigger."

"I know nuthin'," he replied. "We jes sittin' here speculatin', pie in the sky."

I didn't like that answer, but Drigger was adamant about withholding anything else he knew. I started to move on but a thought stopped me.

"Are you part of the operation?" I asked.

Drigger snorted. "Does Sparks's attitude toward me leave you thinkin' I'm part of his ring? Really?"

"Could be an act to fool me."

"Could be. But it ain't."

Then Drigger added, "I got a thing-a my own goin' on down here. I tole you that."

For some reason I wasn't surprised. I never did believe Drigger was the person he claimed to be.

"I guess you won't tell me what it is," I said. "Your *thing*?"

Drigger just shook his head. I had just about come around to thinking he was a good guy. Now I had to reassess. I returned to the issue of Sparks.

"If Sparks is transporting across state lines, weed and meth, those would be federal crimes, right?"

"I 'spect so. But I ain't a lawyer."

That was the final lie I was willing to tolerate.

"Quit trying to gaslight me, Drigger. You *know* so. I might have amnesia, but I haven't forgotten how to tell the difference between the truth and an alternate reality."

He took a final swig of his coffee, got up, and threw the cup in the trash.

"Let's go to sleep," he said. "We'll talk more after the sun comes up."

He told me no more. When I asked questions, he just shook his head.

So, I stretched out on the recliner and thought it through.

Even for a world-wise veteran, Drigger knew too much about the workings of this particular cartel for a poor country boy living in a one-room shack. The details he dropped like a trail of bread crumbs went beyond gossip he might have heard at the gas station or the diner or the general store.

Now that I had verified that Drigger wasn't who he claimed to be, I had to figure out who he was. Maybe he was working for another drug operation, spying on Sparks with an eye to moving in on him and his territory. Or maybe he was working solo to take over the territory. Either of those would explain why he was trying to help Mark and me. Our deaths might be the final straw that drew the state or the feds or both down to Joe Pye to clean it up. The sooner Drigger got us out of the county alive and healthy, the sooner he could get back to his own aspirations, whatever they were.

I considered briefly that Drigger might be working under cover for some government agency. But I dismissed the thought. If he were, he would have called in his troops and stomped Sparks back to the Stone Age. There certainly was enough evidence to warrant such a move.

I fell asleep trying to figure it out and woke up the next morning with no idea. But I had concluded that I needed to watch Drigger as closely as he watched Sparks.

18

———————

The night's conversation resumed over breakfast the next morning. I felt sleep-deprived and cranky. Drigger, on the other hand, seemed fine on three hours sleep. The lines on his face seemed a little deeper, his dark skin looked a bit gray. But I could have been misreading what was going on with him.

I asked him, "Why aren't you exhausted?"

He shrugged. "A little tired, but I'll push through. I learnt how to manage sleep deprivation in Afghanistan. Most military personnel in combat situations eventually git to where they can operate on a couple hours sack time. Their lives depend on it."

"You said you were in the Marines."

"Yep."

"In Afghanistan?"

"Yep."

"Why were the Marines even in Afghanistan? They're an arm of the Navy. Afghanistan's a landlocked country. No coastline at all."

Drigger smiled. "'Cause Marines are superb fighters. In a time of need, it's all hands on deck. Marines or Army don't make no difference. We was all there to do the same thing, beat back the Taliban and kill Bin Laden."

I rolled my coffee cup between my hands, trying to focus my thoughts. I could feel through the cardboard that the coffee had gone cold.

"Were you part of the hunt for Bin Laden?"

Drigger stood up and snatched my coffee cup. If I'd speculated I would have said he was reaching the end of his patience with my ceaseless questions. He emptied the coffee dregs and refilled the cup from the pot on the little stove. When he'd placed it in front of me, he seemed to put the cup down with a little too much force. He remained standing.

"Alla us was in on it," he said. "Marines, Army, Navy, maybe even a couple-a Coast Guard units. Everybody was lookin' for Bin Laden. My mission was classified. Still is. Change the subject."

He moved toward the outhouse tunnel. "I gotta take a dump. Be back in a few."

I decided it would be better if I didn't press it right then.

Besides, I had something more important to tell Drigger when he returned.

"I DON'T KNOW if you heard," I started when Drigger returned, "but last night when the sheriff was talking to the deputy who followed you, he referred to him as Weldon."

"Yeah, I heard. That trigger any more memories for you?"

Drigger smiled a little at his own words. I'm sure I looked surprised, because I was.

"Yeah, it did. Now I remember why I'm here. But how'd you know?" I asked.

Drigger sat down again. "Lucky guess," he said.

"Oh bullshit," I replied, now projecting anger of my own. "You knew from the outset about James Weldon, and about why I'm here. You made a special point of mentioning that some of Sparks's deputies were former cops hiding out from something."

"I've known all along you came here to find Weldon, and instead he found you."

"And you found this out, how?"

"I know lots of stuff," Drigger said. "I din't mention this particular detail to you cuz I thought it'd be a lot better if you figgered it out alone, 'nuther piece of the puzzle comin' back to you. This one musta been close to the surface if the memory came back that easy. Just hearin' his name."

"If you know so much, why don't you fill me in on the rest?"

"Like I said, it'd be better if you recalled stuff on yer own. It could trigger more memories, whereas me jes telling you would be knowl-edge without experience or context. If yer gonna git all your memory back, it has to happen organically."

"Organically? Big concept for a country boy."

"I said I was a country boy," Drigger replied. "Didn't say I was uneducated or stupid."

"You're a conundrum, Drigger."

"Yes'um," he replied. "I know that word, too."

He came back to the table and turned the chair around, so when he sat down again he straddled it.

"I'm thinkin' it's time for me to tell you everything," he said.

His matter-of-fact statement surprised me. I'd been hounding him for days. I wondered if he'd had a change of heart. And why now? More important, was he finally going to tell me the truth, or would it be just another lie?

Drigger looked pensive, his dark eyes blank, as if he were deep in a phase of introspection. "You ever hear of a businessman up near Chicago named Honus Houssmann? He lives outside Evanston."

"Houseman?" I asked.

"Houssmann," Drigger corrected. When he pronounced the name the double esses came out like a hiss.

The name sounded familiar, but I didn't recall why.

Drigger explained. "Owns a string of rehab facilities and nursing homes north of the city and up into Wisconsin. Uses them to launder money."

Though I didn't find any of this amusing, I couldn't help but smile. "Honus?" I asked. "Who names a kid, Honus?"

"Beats me."

"There was a famous baseball player, Honus Wagner. He's the only other Honus I've ever heard of."

"Honus Wagner? Never heard of him," Drigger said. "Who's he play for?"

"Past tense," I said. "He's dead a long time."

I don't know why he was interested in arcane baseball trivia at this particular moment, but I decided to humor him for fear he'd change his mind about giving me the grim truth about Joe Pye County.

"Who'd he play for when he was alive?"

"Pittsburgh, I think. For more than twenty years."

"Twenty years? No way. I'da heard of him. When'd he play, the eighties or nineties?"

I smiled. "Sort of, but not the eighties and nineties you're talking about. He played at the end of the nineteenth century and early into the twentieth." I was frowning at Drigger. "Who names a baby after a baseball player who died a century ago?"

"His parents, I suppose," Drigger said.

That ended the baseball talk, and Drigger went silent again. It was several minutes before he spoke again, and I didn't press him.

"I shouldn't be doing this," he said, "but you need to know what we're dealin' with so if something happens to me, you'll have a place to start figurin' out what all the crap down here's about."

"Truthful answers?" I asked.

"Yeah. Listen carefully, because everything that happens in Joe Pye goes right back to Honus Houssmann's doorstep. First off, there's almost nothing I've told you about myself that's true. Oh, I was a medic with the Marine Corps in Afghanistan. And I guess it's vaguely interesting that my father taught me to love baseball and football, but that's where the truth ends."

Drigger raised his head. His expression was so pained I felt sorry for him.

"So, who are you, really? Let's start with your name."

"Drigger Morton is the name I assumed when I got here. As far as you're concerned, that remains my name. It's protection for both of us."

"Keep going."

"I didn't inherit this place. It's U.S. Forest Service property. It'd been abandoned. Nobody had any use for it. So, I cleaned it up and moved in. I had to upgrade the well, build the walkway to the outhouse, and put in a floor. Otherwise, it was in good shape. Been here ever since."

Drigger had dropped the backwoods idiom and jargon. But I didn't mention it.

"Where did you move here from?"

"Northbrook."

"Northbrook, Illinois? Really?"

I knew of Northbrook, even been there a few times. Nice, solid upper middle-class suburb of the city not too far north of Evanston where this Honus Houssmann character ran his businesses and heaven knew what else. I asked Drigger if he had crossed paths with Houssmann up there. He hadn't, though he knew Houssmann by reputation.

"It was hard to avoid hearing about him," Drigger said. "He has his hand in so many things—even if you don't include what's goin' on down here."

"So why did you give up a comfortable life near Chicago and settle in this, uh, this place?" I wanted to call it a shack, but I didn't want to be rude. "Did you have some financial or legal problems? Family problems you had to get away from?"

"No. There were some family problems while I was in Afghanistan, but they wouldn't have wrecked my marriage."

"Why, then?"

"Well, I should say it's none of your business, but since you're trapped here with me for the time being, and because all this has put your fiancé in danger as well, I will tell you that what I'm doing here is my business and none of yours."

I objected. "We're not even close to tell all." I paused for a beat. "How long have you been here?"

"A little over a year."

"You got any family?"

"No comment."

"What? Why? Don't you think you're taking secrecy too far?"

"No. I got my reasons. Believe me, Missy, if you was me you wouldn't be sayin' nothing that didn't need sayin' right now."

Drigger's speech had slipped back into hillbilly jargon, and I mentioned that.

"Ain't no hillbilly 'bout it," Drigger said. "Jes' who I am right now."

"You mean sometimes you're somebody else?"

"Sometimes, when I need to be. You need to quit yer questions now and move on."

I considered it. I wasn't sure what Drigger's motives were for helping me. If he'd come to Joe Pye because of Houssmann, the reason was ambiguous at best. What was Houssmann's relationship with Sparks? Associates or enemies? Could have been either—or both. Maybe Drigger was trying to bring the whole drug operation down and take over. Or—and this is what I hoped to be the truth—he was who he said he was, and his efforts to help Mark and me were genuine. There were still incongruities I couldn't resolve, but for the moment I chose to go along with him for the ride, wherever it took me.

He began clearing the table. I asked, "Okay, you know so much. What's it take to blow up a propane tank? A gunshot?"

"No ma'am. They ain't built to be blowed up that easy. Fact is, it's purdy hard."

"Propane's flammable, though, right?"

"Yes, and no. When it's put inna tank, it's liquid, an' it stays liquified as long as there's moderate pressure inna tank. In liquid form, it ain't really flammable. There was a movie where James Bond blew a propane tank with a handgun. But that wouldn't work. It ain't that simple. Even if you used incendiary bullets chances are they wouldn't work."

"What's an incendiary bullet?" I asked.

"They got something highly flammable in the nose, like magnesium, that explodes on contact an' burns very hot. But if there's nothing around that's flammable, it won't start no fire. If the round penetrated the top of the tank, where there's a collection of propane in gaseous form, an incendiary round could set that off. Otherwise, no."

"But propane tanks do blow up occasionally."

"Sure, if they're subjected to high heat for a long time, like in a big bomb or a forest fire. Then the liquid will turn to vapor. If the pressure of the vapor buildup overwhelms the tank's release valve, the tank could rupture. If the gas finds fire, it will explode. In the case of the tank in Sparks's yard, the blast would be enormous."

We were both quiet for a few moments before Drigger said, "I know what yer thinking, an' it would be a hugely difficult thing to pull off under them damned security lights and cameras. An' there's one other thing you gotta consider. That little jail house where they're holdin' your boyfriend, it's purdy close to the tank, an' it's made-a lumber. If flyin' shrapnel didn't kill him, the fire would incinerate him."

"I did think of that, Drigger," I said. "Let's take this one step at a time. First, how do we get the tank's interior pressure to climb high enough to break open the release valve? From what you told me, I gather the valve is specifically designed to release the flammable gas and then reset when the pressure falls back to normal levels."

"Right."

"We couldn't just hang out around there with a couple of flamethrowers—assuming we had a couple of flamethrowers—and wait for the process to begin."

"Right again. An' we ain't got no flamethrowers, nohow."

"So, what if we disable the valve, so it doesn't do what it's supposed to do? What would happen then?"

"When the pressure got high enough, the tank would rupture. But if you wanna blow it up, then you have to figure out a way to ignite that gas as it comes barrelin' outta there. You wouldn't have much time, maybe thirty seconds, tops. Soon as the ruptured tank vents all the built-up gas, there won't be nuthin' left to cause an explosion."

We both went quiet, thinking about our improbable plan, both of us seeing its myriad flaws. How could any of these things be done without us being detected? We couldn't just drive into the back yard and say, "Howdy, Sheriff, we're here to blow up your office. Won't be long, and we'll be out of your hair." How would we rescue Mark, a question that would have to be answered no matter what plan we settled on? And how would the three of us all climb into Drigger's truck and clear the blast before we turned into cinders?

So, while we knew how to carry out the plan, there were too many points at which it could go very wrong and get us all killed. Not to mention problems arising that we hadn't thought of. Blowing the propane tank simply wouldn't work.

"It's too much exposure for too long," I told Drigger, who nodded.

"But there might be another option," he said. "That exhaust fan under the porch works on a sensor, too, turning itself on when the gas level in the meth lab gets too high. We'd have to figger a way to disable the blades while the motor still worked so nobody inside would get suspicious. If we cud think of a way to add fire, we could explode the trapped gas and blow everything to kingdom come."

I shook my head slowly. "I noticed the fan is covered by a heavy screen bolted into the house. You'd have to get the screen off, somehow disable the blades, and light a match. There'd be no time for you to get away. The place would blow before you could take two steps. There has to be a way to do this that all three of us can survive."

I had another thought. "Maybe we can mitigate the danger," I said. "You got a rifle?"

"A couple of 'em, sure."

"Do any of them fire incendiary bullets?"

Drigger frowned, "Yeah."

"Next question, do you have any incendiary bullets?"

"Actually, I do. I see where yer goin'."

"Does the basement have a window? I don't remember."

"Yeah, just to the right of the fan."

I said, "Put a couple of incendiary bullets through the basement window, and you've got yourself a fire. You could do that without getting close at all."

"The window's covered by heavy screening, too," Drigger said. "An' it's probly made of bullet-proof glass. Incendiary bullets might not be heavy enough to penetrate the screen and the window glass. There is one thing could work. A rifle-launched grenade."

I laughed. It wasn't a laugh of amusement.

"Okay," I said, "where would we get those?"

Drigger looked at me and grinned. His dark eyes sparkled.

"Would it surprise you to know I already got 'em?"

Now I laughed in amusement.

"No," I said. "Not really."

19

───────

"**S**o, let's run through the plan," I said. "Spell out who does what and when, including how any of us gets out of this alive."

Drigger did. It was chancy, with far too much that could go wrong. That some part of the plan would fail seemed to me to be a given, a dread that, once again, kept me awake for most of the rest of the night.

It felt as though I would never be able to make up for lost sleep.

We decided we'd do it the following night about three a.m., when most of the people in the house would be dozing or asleep. Our time window for success was critically limited.

THE NEXT AFTERNOON Drigger said he was going out to fish and forage, so anybody watching would see him going about his daily routine. I took the opportunity to try to get a nap. I must have fallen asleep at some point because it startled me when I heard Drigger key open the heavy lock on the front door. I remained stretched out in the recliner, reluctant to let go of my short period of sleep.

Drigger was carrying his mesh grocery bag loaded with greens. From his previous foraging trips I recognized watercress, mustard greens, wild grapevine, and dandelion from young springtime growth. The leaves in Drigger's bag looked good and fresh.

"Some vinegar and olive oil an' we got ourselves a real healthy salad," Drigger told me. "I think maybe I still got some grated Parmesan cheese in the cooler, which will top it off real nice." His other hand held a stringer with a fairly large bass hanging from it. The wild greens and the fish would sustain us through our rescue operation that night.

Drigger suggested we eat and then lie down and rest until it was time to attack the meth lab. He had a reliable inner clock, he said, that would wake him at 2 a.m., which would give them plenty of time to get to the sheriff's office by three.

DRIGGER CHOSE a round-about way to the sheriff's office so he could watch for a tail. I was stuffed into the passenger side well of the cab where I couldn't see or be seen. Just in case someone peeked in the window, Drigger had thrown the sleeping bag from the truck bed over me. He said there was no way to tell that someone was beneath it.

The .45 automatic Drigger had given me pressed uncomfortably into my ribs. I hadn't been able to practice with it, only dry fire it at the coffee pot on the stove. I would only use it if threatened. And then, if I did fire, I was likely to miss. Drigger told me not to take time aiming. Just point the gun as I would point my finger and pull the trigger. The gun had seven rounds in the magazine and one in the chamber, so I would have eight chances to protect myself if the need arose.

"Remember to release the safety," he said, "or the gun won't be of no more use to you than slingin' a paperweight."

Drigger thought maybe we were being followed by a sheriff's deputy running without lights. So, he started tapping the gas. It made the pickup jump a little each time, as though it was having mechanical problems. He pulled off the road. We turned on the earpieces that would allow us to communicate at a distance of a mile or so.

He put his compact night-vision binoculars in his pocket and grabbed a regular flashlight. He walked around to the front of the truck, lifted the hood and moved the light around as if looking for an engine problem.

He walked around to the tailgate, opened it, and pulled out a massive bag of tools. He walked back to the front and pretended to tinker with something, then lowered the hood, slamming it shut with more force than necessary.

"Well, shit," he said, loud enough to be heard by anyone on our tail.

He locked the truck and set off toward his cabin on foot, still carrying his tool bag. He left the truck's engine idling. If anyone asked why, he would say he wasn't sure he could get it started again. His plan was to get out of sight then circle back toward the sheriff's office, less than a quarter mile away.

The timing from here had to be perfect.

I had never felt so vulnerable and alone.

Drigger walked with his head lowered, his eyes on the ground, using the standard flashlight to light his way. He wasn't concerned about being seen. If deputies were tailing him, they would have witnessed his "trouble" with the truck and understood why he was walking home. The only curious thing about his trek was why he was carrying his tools with him.

Drigger lifted his eyes every once in a while to check for observers but saw none. They wouldn't be able to drive off the road to observe him from a hiding spot along this stretch because the trees and understory were too dense. When he was certain he was in the clear he ducked into the trees and doubled back, switching from the flashlight to the night-vision binoculars. He knew this stretch of trees well, so he felt confident that the glasses and the compass in his head would guide him accurately back to the sheriff's office.

He could barely see his truck through the trees when he hiked past it, but all was quiet, so he had no choice but to assume that everything was going as planned.

Ten minutes later, Drigger caught sight of the shed where he believed the sheriff had imprisoned Mark Hearst. He dropped to the ground onto his chest, paused to catch his breath and slow his heart, and spoke to Deuce using their makeshift radio system.

"You okay?"

"So far," Deuce replied.

"I'm comin' up behind the cell. I gotta set up the rifle and the grenade then crawl up there and alert Mark. When I say, "go" you put pedal to the metal but not before I say. Gotta wait 'til the fan starts up."

"As long as I've got time to crawl over to the driver's side."

"You will. Like we planned, I won't fire 'til you ram the shed. And don't forget to unlock the truck. Be a shame if, after all the work, we got locked out of our only means of escape."

When the rifle was set up, Drigger started a slow military crawl toward the shed, arm over arm, moving noiselessly over the rough ground and closing on the target. He had to stay almost flat so he could keep the top of the shed between him and the house. If he raised up too much, he would trigger the security, which would not be a good thing.

He was two feet from the shed's back wall when he stopped and pulled the flashlight from his pocket, but he didn't turn it on. Instead, he used it to tap lightly against the wood, but he got no response.

He tapped again and used a stage whisper.

"Mark, you in there? I'm a friend."

Still no response. Either Mark was sleeping soundly—unlikely in this place—or he didn't trust his unexpected visitor. Probably the latter. He scoured his memory to find something that Deuce had told him that only she would know.

"Hey, Deuce told me about that dinner you had on the beach in Tahiti. The Poisson Cru. She said it's a fabulous Tahitian take on ceviche."

There was a moment's pause, then Mark whispered, "Who are you?"

Drigger responded patiently, "A friend."

"Is Deuce okay?"

"She will be when we get the two of you out of here. We're gonna ram this shack with my truck..."

"What?" Mark said in what could only be described as a shouted whisper. "Oh, shit."

"Take it easy," Drigger said. "When you hear the truck coming, get as far as you can from the back wall, drop and cover. You understand? You got anything you can use to cover yourself with?"

A hesitant, "Yes and yes. There's a sleeping bag in here."

"Good. Get inside it. Cover your head. Don't get out 'til you hear a truck roarin' toward you an' then an explosion. It's important you stay covered through the explosion. Then git up an' start tearin' that back wall apart enough for you to get out. I'll be helping from this side. Any questions? If so, make it fast."

"You're sure Deuce is okay?"

"Worried about you. She's the one who's gonna ram the shed."

Drigger turned back to his radio.

"Everything still clear?" he asked Deuce.

"All clear."

He waited until he heard the exhaust fan activate.

He took a deep breath. "Go."

20

———————

Drigger had pinpointed a good spot where he could hide and still have a clear shot at the window. He calculated how long it would take Deuce to get to him. Maybe twenty seconds or less. It seemed like an eternity before he heard the throaty growl of the engine approaching. From the volume of the sound, she must have been driving the old truck hard.

When she came into view she was flying, almost literally, as the truck hit ruts and potholes hard enough to lift it off the ground. She barely slowed as she made the turn. The rear wheels fishtailed on the gravel, but the truck maintained its course.

As Deuce closed in on the shack, the movement triggered the security system. Outdoor floodlights came on, a siren wailed, and lights came on inside the house.

This was going to be close, he knew. He had to get off his shot before anyone had time to leave the building.

Deuce gave him that time, ramming the shed at maybe forty-five miles an hour. The rear quarter of the building disintegrated.

Drigger set his sights on the basement window and fired.

～

I HAD serious second thoughts about this operation.

I saw the cell building as a flimsy construct that wouldn't be able to stand up to the truck's collision. What if I was pointed at the corner where Mark was hiding? What if he had no way to hide from the collision or the power and debris from the explosion that followed? What if he died, and I was the one who killed him?

I felt my breath quicken and my heart accelerate. I was overwhelmed with an urge to stand on the brakes and try to stop the truck before it could carry out its mission. But it was too late. The alarm system came to life, the wailing almost deafening.

What had Drigger told me about launching his grenade? Suddenly I couldn't remember. Now? After I rammed the cell? All I could remember was that I needed to be back in the passenger-side well before the building blew, to keep most of the truck between me and the blast. That would be close. Really close.

All this slashed through my mind in just a few seconds.

There was no turning back now.

The truck bore down on the cell, and I began to pump the brake. I wanted to create an escape window for Mark, not bring down the whole building on top of him. I had managed to slow only a little before the collision. I had aimed for the back corner of the shed closest to me. If I clipped off the corner, perhaps the roof would hold. I would know soon enough.

And then, the collision. I didn't have time to evaluate the outcome. When the truck stopped I dove over the console into the foot well on the passenger side, curled into a ball as tight as my six-foot frame would allow, and waited.

I didn't have to wait long.

The explosion was enormous. Through the windshield I saw debris from the house blowing over the truck. Or maybe it was debris from the cell. Or both. I couldn't tell. I dared sit up and look toward the house. It appeared to have been obliterated. I raised my head and looked at the cell. I was amazed to see that the ramming had done exactly what I hoped. The corner of the building was badly damaged. The roof had held.

I scrambled to get out of the truck just as Drigger arrived with his rifle.

"Damned fine job, Deuce," he said. "Let's get Mark and get out of here."

As we turned toward the cell, I saw somebody clawing the splintered wood and my heart soared. He was alive.

We got to the cell, and I knew we didn't have much time. The explosion had started a small forest fire that was spreading into a ring around the devastation. The fire was already climbing dry tree trunks and would soon begin to crown trees over our heads.

Drigger and I began ripping out splintered pieces of the cell wall. Mark saw where we were working and began working with us to dislodge as much material as we could.

"Watch out for nails," Drigger yelled. We did.

The heat from the fire intensified. I realized there was a chemical stench in the air, probably from the wreckage of the meth lab. I didn't know how it could be, but if there was still gas around, it would feed the fire. And if the fire reached the propane tank, it might explode, too. What had Drigger told me, that a propane tank could explode if exposed to a fire hot enough and long enough to turn the liquid fuel into a gas?

I wanted to climb into Mark's arms, but there wasn't time. Drigger was yelling at us to get into the truck. He lifted the lid over the truck bed.

"Mark, in here. Quick. Here's a headphone. Put it on."

I hung back for a moment not knowing if Drigger wanted me to drive or be his passenger. I glanced at the truck. I had expected the front end to buckle under the force of the impact. It hadn't. I could see that the leading edge of the hood had minor damage, but the engine never missed a beat. The grill guard on the front end had cut though the cell wall like a cleaver through a ripe banana. It protected the engine.

I was about to climb into the cab, and Drigger had jerked open the driver side door when I saw motion off to my left. A man was staggering toward us, badly burned, with an assault rifle held across his body, his index finger inside the trigger guard.

"Drigger, look out," I yelled.

"Down on the ground," he ordered.

As rounds began digging holes in the dirt and smacking holes into the truck, Drigger dropped and rolled. I saw him pull a mean-looking handgun out of his belt. It began burping return fire. He hit the attacker three times in the chest and stomach, once in the head. The guy dropped and lay still. He appeared quite dead.

Drigger jumped behind the wheel.

"Get in Deuce," he commanded. "We need to leave *now.*"

He executed a three-point turn and roared out of the gravel to the road. He turned the truck toward town.

"Behind my seat. A compartment. Open it and hand me the phone inside. Use your headset. Talk to Mark."

I checked and found my headset still on my head. I opened the compartment Drigger had mentioned and searched it. It held a satellite telephone. Drigger took it from me without explanation. I really didn't need one.

I tried to talk to Mark and listen to Drigger's call at the same time. I told Mark we were clear of the mess, unharmed, and racing to get farther away. I told him I'd talk to him again in a few minutes. I turned my attention back to Drigger. I didn't know who he was talking to, but I got this much:

"No casualties on this side. I think everyone inside the house died, but I can't be sure. It was still burning, and there was still gas around. I could smell it. You need to get fire fighters out there stat. There's a forest fire—small last I saw it. But if the flames cook the propane tank, well, you know." He paused to listen and responded, "That's a copy."

He turned to me. "Don't ask. You'll know it all soon enough."

It was only then that I realized Drigger's accent and jargon were gone. Again.

The ruse was over.

I hoped the nightmare would dissipate with it.
It didn't.

21

---

*C*hicago . . .

Eric Ryland, the metro editor of the Chicago Journal, grabbed the phone even before his secretary finished telling him Jerry Alvarez was holding.

When the connection was made, Ryland said, "What?" Less a question; more a demand. He thought he could feel his blood pressure surge.

He listened in silence as Alvarez updated the news.

When the call ended, Ryland put the phone down gently. He swiveled his chair so he could look out his window at the skyline of his city. Dark clouds roiled, and the first spatters of rain hit the glass. The forecast for the afternoon had been for heavy rain and thunderstorms with possible tornadoes in Chicago's western suburbs.

The forecast didn't frighten Ryland. He doubted that anything could ever frighten him again as badly as the last few days.

He bowed his head and watched as a tear that had tracked down his face slid off and left a wet spot on his shirt.

His voice was not much louder than a whisper.

"Thank God," he said. "Thank God."

He dropped his face into his hands, and he wept.

22

Joe Pye County, town of Red Twig . . .

Mark and I sat together on a small sofa in a subterranean chamber. With my claustrophobic tendencies the experience would have terrorized me—if I had any remaining capability of being terrorized by anything. Someday my emotional reserves might regenerate, but it wouldn't be this day. I had no strength left to accommodate any more fear. It had been replaced by a fatalism that if it was my day to die, I would die, and there was nothing I could do to stop it. Where there should have been elation that Mark and I had survived to get to a place of safety, I felt only the numbness of exhaustion.

Several people were staring at me, including Drigger, or whatever his real name was. The woman was the only one who had spoken so far. To me and about me.

"What you're suffering is a letdown from days of adrenaline over-load," she said. "You've used it all up. You need to find a way to relax and recharge. If we were in a larger city we could find you psycholog-ical support, but right here, right now, you only have Mark. He's been traumatized himself, likely with similar fallout. You can be sources of emotional stabilization for each other, but both of you will need professional counseling when we get back to Chicago, or some other metropolis bigger than Red Twig."

The woman was introduced to us as Alexandra Barstow. I guessed she was about five feet, five or six inches. She was slim in a way that looked physically strong. Maybe in her early forties, short brown hair, brown eyes. All this I noticed on my own. Nobody seemed inclined to explain more. No disclosure of who she was or who she worked for. She had kind eyes, though, full of softness and sympathy. And she was dressed informally: blue jeans, t-shirt, and hiking boots. The others called her "Alex."

The man who showed up a few minutes later was introduced as Frank Desartis. If I'd had to guess his occupation, the guess would have been an accountant, though he was dressed as informally as Barstow. He was slim and as solid as she was, maybe an inch or two taller. He had an impassive demeanor, an expressionless face. His hair was a dark blond, his mouth pinched into a straight line of concentration. His unreadable gray eyes were covered with almost square eyeglasses in gunmetal gray frames. He blinked about once a minute, almost disconcertingly slow.

Barstow continued. "I have some training in helping people with psychological trauma—injury, death, loss—but it isn't my specialty. However, for as long as we're together, you both should talk with me, singly and as a couple. And you should talk to one another privately. Right now you look shell-shocked, which doesn't surprise me. Don't let yourselves become controlled by your reactions to what you've been through. Or at least try to avoid it."

"We're in Red Twig, right?" Mark asked.

Barstow replied, "Yes."

"Why the underground hidey-hole? Won't we be leaving soon?"

Now Desartis spoke up.

"We don't know how long you'll have to stay here," he said. "And we won't move anyone anywhere until we're certain it's safe."

I asked, "How do you define 'safe'?"

"Until we determine the extent to which your ambush at the sheriff's office depleted his crew. I suspect most of those still alive are running for the hills. But I can't be sure. As long as there are any so-called deputies left, we can't guarantee your safety. Even beyond them Sparks has allies around here who made a lot of coin acting as his minions. After what ya'all did, there's probably some of them that wouldn't mind feeding you to the alligators."

I tensed, remembering what Drigger and I had witnessed at Black Marsh. Mark was holding my hand and felt my reaction.

"What?" he asked.

"I'll tell you later," I said. Right then I wanted to change the subject. "Are you two the owners of this place?"

I knew we were in a space below the gas station. Drigger had driven us there after we raced away from the fire and the carnage at the sheriff's office. Drigger had told me days earlier that the owner of the station had created an underground railroad of sorts. Its purpose was to help people who incurred Sheriff Sparks's wrath escape to safety. I presumed that's where we were headed.

Drigger spoke up. "No, they're not," he said. "The owner's the guy who took the truck and drove it off to hide it somewhere where it won't be found. Since he's still exposed, I can't tell you his name. Wouldn't mean anything to you, anyhow."

"Speaking of trucks," Mark said, "anyone happen to know what happened to mine?"

"Probably in a chop shop in St. Louis by now," Drigger said.

I stared at Drigger. "And who are you, really? You've dropped the accent and any pretense that you're some hillbilly hermit hiding in the trees from the rest of the world."

"I'm not," Drigger said. "This is true. I told you I'd tell you all about me when the time came. It isn't quite here yet."

Now Mark got caught up in the intrigue.

"What the hell's going on here?" he asked. "And why can't we know the rest of the story? Seems to me you've brought down the guts of this operation, whatever this operation is—or was—so why not explain it?"

Desartis took over. "Drigger, along with the two of you, hacked up the body of the snake, but its head survived with a whole lot of hunger for vengeance and motivation to rebuild this operation."

I was surprised. "You mean Sparks didn't die in the house?"

"We don't think so. There's still some searching to be done."

"We're not going to say any more," Barstow offered. "I think right now the two of you need some food and rest. There's a bedroom down that way." She nodded toward an opening behind Desartis. "If you're shy, we can give you separate bedrooms."

Drigger smiled at me and added, "Believe it or not, the larger room has a shower, and both bedrooms have real, honest-to-God toilets. Now go clean up and try to unwind. We'll bring you some breakfast in an hour."

23

To say I slept well for more than six hours would be an overstatement. Now, freshly showered, lying in a comfortable bed with Mark's arms around me, I felt my muscles begin to unlock. As I mulled over the events of the night, I trembled a bit, realizing how close the three of us had come to ugly deaths. As the events unfolded I had concentrated my focus on my part of the operation and how I could pull it off without killing Mark. Now that I had time to think about it, it was more like reliving a nightmare.

Drigger let us sleep until shortly after 10 a.m. We only knew what time it was because he told us. There were no windows on this underground railway.

The three of us had one of Drigger's cholesterol loading breakfasts, and after eating I felt in need of a nap. But Mark wanted to ask more questions of our hosts, and I needed to hear their answers, assuming there were any. So, I struggled to keep my eyes open. I could understand Mark's curiosity. For most of his stay in Joe Pye County he was locked in that barren cell with no chance of learning what was going on around him He didn't know if I was dead or alive, no inkling of if, or how, he would make it home alive.

I yawned.

"Why don't you go lie down?" Drigger suggested. "Mark probably has lots of questions I've already answered for you. If you miss anything, we'll brief you later."

He didn't have to ask twice.

I woke up fifty minutes later, still far from rested, but wanting to get back to Mark and Drigger and their conversation. Alex Barstow was sitting at the small conference table with Drigger and Mark. She had a shopping bag on the table next to her. I wondered what it was, and Barstow apparently saw the curiosity in my face.

"Oatmeal, whole grain bread, fruit, and veggies," she said. "I figured after you ate a week's worth of Drigger's breakfasts your heart could use some relief."

I was curious to know where the food came from. Red Twig was woefully short on supermarket choices. Though, I recalled, there was a general store.

Drigger looked annoyed at the criticism of his breakfasts, and I smiled at him.

"Feeling better?" Barstow asked me.

I took a deep breath and shrugged. "I don't know if I'll ever feel rested again," I admitted. "What did I miss?"

Mark replied. "Not much you didn't know according to Drigger. I don't know who Alex and Frank are or their purpose here. I don't know who Drigger is, except that he's not who he's been telling you he is. I don't know if there's anything newsworthy from the sheriff's office or how long we can expect to be here. Drigger did fill me in on what you saw at Black Marsh, though. That must have been horrible."

I nodded, thankful I didn't have to relive the story. I turned to Drigger. "Your truck. Why is your friend hiding it? Why not destroy it, even on the slim chance that somebody will find it and all the gear you have stashed in it?"

"We got all the sensitive gear out before the truck was moved," Drigger said. "Besides, it's too valuable to simply discard."

"It's a piece of junk," I replied, "no offense intended. Seats are worn and frayed. When I was driving it sounded as though the engine would break apart at any minute. It must be thirty years old."

Drigger and Barstow both smiled and laughed lightly.

"Yeah," Drigger said, "it looks and sounds that way. And to be honest, there are parts of it that are maybe twenty-five years old, but none of them critical. It's been almost fully rebuilt and more resembles a tank than a truck. You hit Mark's jail cell at a pretty high rate of speed. Given the way the impact looked, it should have rammed the engine off its mounts and pushed it through the firewall into the cab. It would have driven the steering wheel into your chest and crushed you."

"I didn't see much damage," I replied. "I looked. Just a quick glance. All I saw was one dent in the hood, and some bullet holes in the sheet metal. But none of the windows broke, and none of the shots from the assault rifle got through to the cab or the bed."

"The whole thing is reinforced and armored," he said. "The glass is the same as in the presidential limo, the one the Secret Service calls The Beast. The gas tank is made like that propane tank, pretty much impenetrable. Even the floor is reinforced against IEDs. The tires are solid rubber. No chance of a blowout, even if they're hit by gunfire. But no chance of a smooth ride, either." He smiled. "The sheet metal, on the other hand, is a collection of fenders and doors and bumpers from a dozen junk yards. The rust is real."

"No wonder it drove like a loaded garbage truck on square wheels."

Everything Drigger told us made sense, assuming he was a government agent with access to the design skills and technology to produce a vehicle like that. If Drigger knew how the presidential limo was built, then perhaps he was an agent with the Secret Service.

I was about to ask when Desartis entered the room. He was dressed in a hazmat suit, except for the hood, and he looked grim. He poured himself a cup of coffee and slouched into the chair next to Barstow.

"We've been collecting bodies all morning," he explained. "We found four inside and one outside. The one on the outside was carrying an automatic rifle, just as you described it, Drigger. I don't know how he managed to use it, though. He was horribly burned."

Something didn't ring true.

I asked, "Presuming he's not one of the dead, why is Sparks letting you do all this?"

"Good question," Desartis said. "Alex and I are FBI. We trump a county sheriff. We have jurisdiction on federal land. That aside, Sparks's crimes trump everything else. We sent word to him that if he fucked with us, we'd arrest him on the spot. Then we'd hit him with drug, murder, and kidnapping charges."

I interrupted. "How'd you get word to Sparks when you don't know where he is?"

"He's got a girlfriend who owns a restaurant up in the lake country. We touched base with her to make sure she wasn't giving cover to Sparks. She denied it, so we just sent the message through her. We didn't hear a word from him. On the other hand, we haven't seen him since. He's making himself scarce."

"Or he's dead," I said, "and nobody's found the body yet. Are you sure he wasn't in the house we blew up? It was his home, and at that hour he should have been asleep."

Drigger nodded. "He might have been staying someplace else, just because of a contingency like this." He turned to Desartis. "How long will it take to ID the bodies?"

"We've got some medical examiners on the way. The bodies haven't been moved yet, but we did get blood samples from all of them—unless there was someone in the basement we haven't found yet. If someone was down there, we'll probably have to extricate him in pieces and smears. Our tests so far are preliminary. Just quick DNA field tests. The more thorough tests will take a week, ten days. But we were able to make tentative IDs on all five. Since they were all law enforcement, their data is on file."

I asked, "All cops running from somewhere else?"

"Yep," Desartis said, "from all over the country. Your man from Chicago wasn't among them. If he'd been in that house, we'da found at least pieces of him."

"Why," I asked, "does it feel like there's another shoe to drop?"

"There might be," Desartis said. "The sheriff has disappeared. We think he's gone underground. If what I know about him is accurate, I'd guess he's out there somewhere plotting his next move."

Mark suggested, "Maybe he took his stash of cash and headed straight to Mexico. Start a new life, maybe in cooperation with the cartels down there."

Desartis replied, "We think we've got that covered. We've sent BOLO alerts to every border crossing and police precinct in Mexico and Canada, at every fixed-base operator in Illinois, Wisconsin, Indiana, Kentucky, Tennessee, Iowa, Missouri, and any other states he could reach in a day's drive if he wanted to rent a private plane and a pilot. We're also circulating a photo of him and asking TSA to post it at every checkpoint at every airport, every bus depot, and every train station everywhere in the United States."

"Can they do that quick enough?" I asked.

Desartis grinned. "It's already done. Ain't technology wonderful?"

"What if he has hideaways around here?" Mark asked. "You all tell me he has loyal supporters in several states. Maybe they'd give him cover somewhere." He waved his hand around our underground encampment. "At least until the furor dies down."

"If he's hiding, it will be a good long while till he can poke his head above ground, Desartis said. "This hunt won't wind down any time soon. We'll find him."

"And we have to live here the whole time?" I asked.

Now Barstow jumped in. "No," she said. "Just until it's safe. You're one of the top reporters in Chicago, Deuce. I'm sure Sparks understands that if something happens to you, he'll never find a safe place to hide. Killing a reporter is like killing a cop. Nobody ever drops the hunt."

I didn't find that terribly comforting and said so.

Barstow smiled. "He's also got no reason to come after you again. You came down here to expose him and locate that cop from Chicago, Weldon. That's already happened. He'd gain nothing by killing you or Mark."

"Revenge," I suggested.

"Don't think so. He's in this for the money. So are his associates. If Sparks can't produce money, and if there's a substantial reward for information leading to him, somebody will turn him in."

24

The phone in Desartis's pocket chirped. It was a satellite phone and appeared identical to Drigger's. Desartis excused himself to take the call privately.

When he returned, he looked glum.

"Looks like you're gonna need a new place to live, Drigger," he said. "That was the Forest Service. The cabin you've been calling home is in the process of burning to the ground. They're trying to confine the fire to the main level on the assumption that you've got more explosives in the cellar. That was the reason for the call. They were trying to assess how much danger their guys might be in."

Drigger shook his head.

"Only surprise is that it didn't happen earlier. Tell your guys to keep a safe distance. There are a couple grenades in the boxes in the basement and some high-octane ammo."

"That's what I figured," Desartis said. "I told 'em to stay well away. But it's their property. Their call."

"It looks like you're going to need some new clothes and a new iPad," Drigger said to me. "I presume your computer and maybe a backup hard drive are some place safe."

"Back at the office in Chicago," I said and then turned to Desartis. "Does anybody know what started the fire?"

"Arson. From the look of it lots and lots of gasoline. The fire guys could still smell it when they arrived on the scene. Given the fuel loading and the age of the structure, it went up pretty fast. Sorry about your stuff."

"They're gonna need explosives experts in there after the site cools down," said Mark, who had some expertise on the matter.

"You volunteering?" Desartis asked.

"Not my area of expertise, and you don't want a novice on this," Mark said. "But I know the weapons and ammo will be unstable. Might be better to blow up what's left rather than risk lives. From what Deuce told me about the place, it wouldn't be a great loss, especially if most of it's already charcoal."

I stared hard at Drigger. "When are you going to start telling me the whole truth? About everything. What are you doing there, who you work for, and what the hell's your name? I gather Drigger Morton is a construct all your own."

Now Drigger laughed. "You gather that, huh?" He turned to Desartis. "What do you think? Can we tell them?"

"You can tell 'em your real name. But not the rest. Not yet."

Drigger turned back to me. "Charles Gerard. Honest. If you want, you can still call me Drigger. Lotsa folks do."

"I'll try to remember to call you Charles, but chances are I'll call you Drigger a lot. Force of habit."

"So," I asked, "what do we do while we wait in the dark, literally and figuratively?"

Barstow, who had been sitting and listening to the conversation, probably looking for clues as to what was going on in Mark's head and mine, spoke up.

"Well," she said, "we could start the process of getting your emotions in check, your nightmares toned down, and everything else that would help get your heads on straight. Talking about your experience will help, believe me."

"I won't get over this with just a couple of sessions with a shrink," I told her.

"Yeah," Mark said, "especially because she's got plane crash memories to get past, in addition to all the rest."

Barstow looked sharply at me. "The memories of the crash have come back?"

I shook my head. "Not yet. I remember boarding the plane, but nothing else. You'd think a plane crash would be something I'd want to forget. But until I remember it all I won't feel whole."

"Understood," Barstow. "So let me practice my shrinkery. Who's first?"

25

I spent seventy minutes alone with Barstow. I didn't love it, but I didn't hate it, either. Speaking gently and projecting compassion she took me through the totality of my experience, from my decision to travel to Joe Pye County to the assault on the sheriff's office. She said we would talk again the next day. When I left her makeshift office, she followed me back to the conference room and invited Mark to come back. He looked at me with the raised eyebrows of skepticism.

I smiled at him. "She doesn't bite, at least not so far," I told him.

When they left I sat down on the sofa again and was trying to figure out how to pass my time when Desartis walked in.

"Oh, good," he said when he saw me. "How did it go?"

"It was okay," I replied. "I think at some point it will begin to help."

"Well, I got a phone call for you."

I was startled. Nobody was supposed to know where I was. I said as much.

"He doesn't know where you are," Desartis assured me. "His call was a relay, and I'll return his call on your behalf through the same relay using my sat phone. Sat phones can be hacked, contrary to popular belief. But it's more difficult and complex than a cell phone."

"To quote you, 'Ain't technology wonderful?'"

"Until it isn't, yes."

I wondered if that was a caution.

I dismissed the thought. I knew who was calling. It had to be Eric Ryland, my editor. Or perhaps my brother, Gary, a lawyer in Denver. The first guess was the right one.

When I said, "Hello," there was a moment of dead air, and then I heard Eric's voice.

"You know the last time I cried?" he asked. "I don't mean shedding a tear at a wedding or a funeral or when you won the Pulitzer Prize or a concert by the Mormon Tabernacle Choir. I mean sobbing."

"Hi to you, too, Eric. To answer your question, no."

"When my daughter was born. I was in the delivery room watching this miracle happening. Well, technically, that was the last time before yesterday, when Jerry Alvarez called to tell me you'd been found alive and mostly well. I sat staring out at the skyline, and I couldn't stop the tears."

I didn't know how to respond. While I was touched, I fully expected there would be a stern lecture to follow.

"Tears of joy or disappointment?"

"Dammit, Deuce, could you stifle your love affair with sarcasm for a few minutes?"

"Yeah, sorry."

"Will you tell me how you're doing?"

I did, even as I watched Desartis scribbling a note, which he slid across the table to me. It read, "Say nothing about location." I nodded.

Eric and I talked for maybe five minutes as I tried to ease his concerns. When he pressed me for where I was so he could send a plane to fly Mark and me back to Chicago, I told him I couldn't disclose that, and that Jerry Alvarez could probably explain why.

Then Desartis gave me the flat hand-across-the-throat gesture that meant it was time to end the call. I made a final request, for Eric to call my brother and assure him I was well. He said he would.

I leaned my head back against the sofa.

"Do you suppose you could have somebody bring me a new iPad?" I asked. "My insurance will pay for it, or maybe the *Journal* since I lost it in the course of my work. I'm going stir crazy down here. With the iPad I could at least download my Kindle library and have something to read."

"You can't download without wifi or data service. There's a big bookcase full of things to read in the bedroom across from yours. Help yourself."

"I already looked at them. They're a bit heavy on drama. I don't need Stephen King right now. I need David Sedaris."

26

Three days passed—at least I guessed it at three—and nobody had heard anything about Sheriff Derek Sparks or any of his associates who might have survived. No sightings at airports, train or bus stations, no unusual inquiries to FBOs about renting private planes, not even so much as a hitchhiker who resembled Sparks.

Two more bodies, or what was left of them, had been found in the blasted-out wreckage of the sheriff's meth lab. Forensics had managed tentative IDs on all of them. Neither Sparks nor Weldon was among them.

Mark and I stayed locked up in what could pass for a two-bedroom underground condo beneath the old gas station in Red Twig. We could only imagine life drifting on overhead as it had drifted through this part of the state for decades.

Drigger spent more and more time away from us, and we never knew where he was. He had replaced his dreadlocks with a close-cut style, cleaned up, shaved, and acquired a new, upscale wardrobe. Combined, they changed his entire "look." I'm not sure anyone in Red Twig would have recognized him. I didn't recognize him the first time I saw the transformation, though I did think I saw something vaguely familiar about him.

Mark and I had gotten a bit snappish with each other after three days of such close confinement without even a glimpse of the sky. If Drigger spent more than a day underground with us, he got a bit churlish, too.

Fresh air was piped in somehow from above, but it was filtered so it didn't produce as much as a single allergy sneeze from any one of us. I would have given a week's pay for just one hour in the sun. As close as I got was the smell of rain and the scent of lightning-generated ozone as a storm raged above us. I loved the smell. I read somewhere that some loony chemist had tried to duplicate the scent in a perfume.

Eau d' Ozone? I wondered what the market for it would be.

I had just finished re-reading an early Carl Hiaasen novel called "Tourist Season" and would have thoroughly enjoyed it the second time except for the alligator parts. I'd never been squeamish about 'gators until the experience at Black Marsh.

I was debating whether to start another book or take a nap when Frank Desartis and Alexandra Barstow returned. Drigger was with them. I had developed a deep curiosity about how they could come and go without arousing suspicion among area residents. They could feign car problems for a while, but not this long. With Drigger I could accept that the change of appearance provided cover. With Desartis and Barstow I had no clue. They were strangers in Red Twig, posing as tourists. Maybe they were going out to fish, to reinforce the visitor ruse. But how long would that charade last? I finally asked about it. If anybody was finding safety at the surface after Sparks's disappearance, I wanted to find it, too.

"We weren't here long enough to be noticed as a problem," Desartis said. "Since the sheriff's office was demolished, nobody seems to care."

"Don't even think about making a break for the surface," Barstow said. "You'd never make it. You'd have to take an old freight elevator up thirty feet or so, assuming you could get it running. That takes a special key, fingerprint ID, and a retinal scan. Three pathways to escape, and neither of you has found even one of them."

"So," Mark observed, "we might as well be in prison."

"In some regards," Desartis replied. "But the food's better here. The company, too."

Barstow sat with Desartis at the little conference table. Drigger sat alone in an easy chair in the corner, saying nothing. Barstow looked from me to Mark and back again. She guessed correctly that Desartis's attempt to take my question lightly wouldn't be appreciated. She elected to change the subject.

"How are you two doing?" she asked.

"I can't speak for Mark," I said, "but I think I'm okay. I still get panicky at night when I hear a sound I can't identify. You'd think I'd be used to it. I live in an old house in Chicago. It's very sturdy, but it sometimes makes creaking sounds. I guess all houses do. It doesn't freak me out, so I don't know why it bothers me here."

Barstow explained. "Because in Chicago you're living in a place subject to the vagaries of wind and weather, heat and cold, and you expect creaking. You don't expect it when you're thirty feet underground with little but solid rock around you."

"She's not telling you everything," Mark said. "Deuce tends to be claustrophobic. She wakes up some nights in a sweat. Not every night, but between the dark and being so far underground, it's unsettling. I don't like it much, either."

While we'd been talking, Desartis got a phone call. When the call ended he looked deeply concerned.

"What?" I asked.

"Don't worry about it," he said.

"How can we not worry about it," I replied, sounding cranky. "If there's something going on that affects us, we have a right to know."

"Yeah, I guess you do."

"So? What?"

"We've confirmed that Sparks survived the blast at his office. He wasn't on the property because he and the Chicago cop, Weldon, were over at Drigger's shack spreading the gasoline that burned the place to the ground."

Drigger finally spoke up. "Well, we knew somebody was responsible, and Sparks seemed to be the logical candidate. Deuce and I might have missed him at the office, but being away from the shack probably saved our lives. If Sparks had succeeded in burning us to death, he would have had no remaining reason to keep Mark alive. I'm certain killing all three of us was his final solution."

I said, "But he had no knowledge that I was ever in the shack with you."

"He had a powerful suspicion," Drigger replied. "He was coming up on a week with no word on you. No clothes, no sightings except my fake one, and no body. So, he figured he'd burn us out. Derek Sparks operates by his own rules. He considers the law to be merely a suggestion."

Desartis said, "He's been telling people he figured you and Deuce had to be inside the shack, and he was determined that both of you would die in the fire. He took special care that the fire would be high and hot at both doors, at the front and at the outhouse."

"Great," Mark said.

"And he's put a bounty on all three of you. Twenty-five-thousand dollars each. Dead or alive. If I was you, I'd prefer dead, I think. If he caught you alive he'd kill you anyway, and it wouldn't be quick."

27

The time passed without sightings of Derek Sparks or James Weldon in Joe Pye County. During what I had come to call his "daily briefings," Frank Desartis said all transportation and border crossings alerted initially to watch for and detain Sparks had received an update. If he resisted arrest, endangering the lives of the officers who tried to pick him up, it was likely he would be shot to death. Same for Weldon.

Alexandra Barstow's visits with Mark and me had dwindled to every other day. I never asked Mark what he talked about with her, and he never asked me. But she had told each of us separately that she had gone about as far as she could, given her more limited mental health training, in helping us deal with our experiences. She would recommend a couple of shrinks in Chicago when we returned home, she said.

On the evening of the fourth day Drigger hung around to have dinner with Mark and me. The three of us were alone. Something about his demeanor and attitude signaled to me, at least, that he would be leaving the area soon, and this would be the last meal we shared. The prospect of never seeing him again prompted me to seek his permission to ask some personal questions.

"I'll answer what I can," he said. "But there are still things I can't disclose."

"Like what?" Mark asked. There was no challenge, just curiosity, in his tone.

"Like who I am, what I do, and why I'm here. Some of that I'll never be able to disclose because it could jeopardize future cases."

I said, "But you already told us who you really are. Charles Gerard."

"Yeah, that's my real name, but it's not necessarily who I am."

"You're talking in circles," Mark said.

"You're probably right," Drigger said.

I asked, "What do you do when you're not doing life-threatening shit like this?"

Drigger chuckled. "I'm always doing life-threatening shit like this. I have been since I was discharged from the Marines and came back to the States. Actually, my time in the Marines was life-threatening shit. It never stops."

"Don't you have a personal life?"

Now Drigger turned pensive. I thought he looked a little sad.

"Yeah, I do, but unfortunately not enough of one. Being away so often cost my marriage, and even worse, I don't see nearly enough of the kids growing up."

"How many kids do you have?" I asked.

"Two. They live with their aunt and uncle while I'm gone, and thank God they all love one another. It doesn't lessen my guilt, but it eases my mind."

Mark said, "That's terrible, Drigger. Couldn't you find another line of work? If you keep taking risks like this, you might miss your kids' entire childhood."

Drigger took a shaky breath.

"I know that's true, Mark," he said. "When I get back home I'm going to try to work out a change in assignments. At this time in my life I'd like to do something that isn't life-threatening shit. I'm tired of getting up every morning thinking it might be my last day on earth. The kids know what I do is secret, and intuitively they know it's dangerous because I never talk about it. They've learned not to ask. It creates a lot of stress for them, and sometimes that stress comes out in ways that make me heartsick." He looked from Mark to me and held my eyes for several seconds. "That's all I have to say on the subject."

He looked thoughtful. "There is one other thing I'd like to tell you, though."

I said, "Okay."

"I haven't told you everything about Houssmann."

"I figured."

"He's into something else, something you're very familiar with, something so despicable it's painful even to discuss."

I waited. Drigger would tell us in his own time.

Which was now.

"You remember asking me why Governor Latchey didn't mobilize the National Guard and send them down to clean up Joe Pye? Well, only a state's governor can mobilize the National Guard. Not even the president of the United States unless he has the governor's approval for it."

I had been leaning forward in my chair, hanging on Drigger's every word. Now I fell back against the cushions and asked, "Are you suggesting William Latchey is protecting Houssmann or Sparks by letting them run things any way they want?"

"Yeah. There might even be money changing hands."

"He wouldn't be the first politician to get mixed up in something dirty," Mark said.

"This goes way beyond dirty," Drigger said. "Deuce, you know that child trafficking ring you helped break up? You thought you dismantled it. But you didn't. You helped get rid of a lot of the bad actors, but not all."

I was stunned almost beyond words. "Houssmann?"

"It's his operation. Was then. Still is."

28

───────

I was stunned silent.

Six months earlier, at the height of a Chicago winter, there was a brief break in the grey and the cold. Mark and I took his Irish setter for a run in a nice park on the city's South Side. Murphy found a human bone. Forensics determined it was the femur of a child. Eventually a police investigation uncovered an entire burial ground for kidnapped children who died while being held and abused as part of a child trafficking ring. A club of wealthy Saudis were primary customers of the ring, and they were killed after being put on a plane back to their country. Their deaths were as brutal and terrifying as those they meted out to the kidnapped children. I found and rescued one of the boys myself. The poor child would have died of dehydration and malnutrition in another day or two. And now I learned that the ring was still in operation and belonged to Honus Houssmann. I had trouble accepting that this was still going on.

Before I could ask for details on Houssmann's role, Frank Desartis yanked open the door from the outside and spoke the words we'd been waiting to hear:

"Get out of here, right now. *Move!*"

We did, not even stopping for personal belongings, though I

noticed Drigger had his gun secured in front, under his belt. I suspected his wasn't the only gun in this crowd. We moved down the corridor away from the conference room, past doors to three bedrooms and the bathroom. Drigger was leading because he'd made the trip before.

"Where are Desartis and Barstow?" I asked. They had not come with us.

"They'll meet us up top," Drigger said. "Now let's go."

From there the corridor got dark, the way the world looks when the sun has gone down, but the light hasn't totally drained from the sky. I figure we walked about a quarter mile when the tunnel ended in what looked like a solid stone wall.

Drigger turned to us. "Don't worry," he said. "This isn't a dead end."

He began to scan a section of the wall using his pocket flashlight until he found what looked to me like a loose piece of rock about the size of a softball. He pulled it out, handed it to Mark, put his hand through the hole and pushed.

The door swiveled on a heavy metal rod embedded in the ceiling and the floor. The door swung easily around it, sort of like the cliched bookcase in an old murder mystery. When closed, it hid a secret room. Removing or tilting a particular book caused the bookcase to swivel open. It became an overused visual gimmick in old mystery movies. Here, and now, it made me smile.

"How was that built into solid rock?" Mark asked.

Drigger replied, "No clue, but I think it used to take brute strength to move it. At some point it was modernized to be less physically demanding."

"How old is this facility?" I asked.

Drigger turned to me. "Remember when I told you about this place? I called it an underground railroad. It actually was part of the system to help runaway slaves make their way north to freedom before and during the Civil War. So, I'd have to say it goes back a bit. About two centuries."

We walked through the opening, and I watched as Drigger

pushed the door closed again. Both sides were identical. Nothing but granite. The hand hole ran all the way through it. When Drigger replaced the rock he'd removed on the other side, the door became invisible again. Now we were confronted by a tunnel that might have been long or short. It was too dark to tell.

"In case you're wondering," Drigger said, "the next leg is a little over two miles. You both up to it?"

Mark replied, "If it's our way to freedom and safety, I don't think any tunnel would be too long."

It was a tiring trip. The floor of the tunnel was slippery with water seepage, and strewn with rocks, most of them small. The perfect size to cause a fall. Mark and I both struggled for balance a couple of times. It felt as if we had gone two miles when, in fact, it had been only about half a mile. Drigger pointed his flashlight to a deep cleft in the tunnel wall that served as a mile marker. But you had to be looking for it.

I have no idea how long we walked. Too far for my liking. I'd lost some muscle tone in the enforced, exercise-free stay in Drigger's cabin, and my legs were getting tired. I focused on each step. "Another one down," I kept repeating in my head. But I was ready for the trek to end.

Which is why the next part of the trip didn't appeal to me at all.

The tunnel finally stopped at a solid wall. I couldn't tell at first if it was another camouflage or real. Then I noticed a long flight of steps to our left. They were stone steps, just as damp and treacherous as the floor of the tunnel.

Drigger asked if we were up to a three-story climb. Both of us agreed to it. He knew the territory and its dangers, so he led. Mark and I followed.

"Watch your step," Drigger said. "These stairs were chiseled out of solid bedrock. They weren't even to begin with. Time and wear have made them more precarious."

Except for the dim glow from the small flashlight, we were operating in total darkness. How was it that workmen skilled enough to make the revolving door below us couldn't even up these old steps and add handholds, like grab bars in the shower. I moved one step at a time. One foot at a time. Put one foot on a step, then drag the toe of the other up beside it. Don't try to use my eyes. Don't look down. Feel for stability rather than looking for it. The effort was nerve-wracking.

When we reached the top I realized I was sweating heavily despite the cold of being underground. We were standing in front of another door that pretty much mimicked the one below. I wondered what this one looked like from the outside.

I never had a chance to notice.

When we stepped through into daylight I only had a chance to breathe the fresh air once before we were surrounded by four men armed with heavy shotguns pointed at our heads. I recognized one of them as James Weldon, the fugitive from Chicago I came here to find. The man at the front was Sheriff Derek Sparks.

He was laughing.

29

"Did you dumb shits think I didn't know about this passageway?" he said. "I've known about it for years. I know what it's used for now and historically. Usually, I don't give a damn who comes and goes through. This time I did. I knew y'all'd try it sooner or later. So, I've had deputies staking out the gas station on three shifts a day. Soon as they saw strangers goin' into the gas station at all times of day and night an' staying for hours they alerted me. We just been hanging out waiting for y'all to walk right into our arms. It took y'all long enough. What's it been? Three days? I know it's killin' my overtime budget. But now we're together at last."

The air was cool and fragrant, but I could also smell the sour wetness of my own sweat. My mind flashed back to the night at Black Marsh, much as I tried to shut down the memory. Mark stepped forward and put his arm around my shoulders. Then he pulled me slightly behind him. I knew what he was doing. He'd done it once before when he planned to push me to the ground and shield me when the bullets started flying. In that instance there was no shooting. In this instance I would rather die by gunfire than by alligator.

I remembered that Drigger had that nasty handgun in his belt. He could drop and roll and pull it out of his pants, maybe even take out one or two of the deputies. But there was no way he could get four of them before the shotguns erupted on all three of us.

I tried to formulate a plan where Mark and I could help Drigger, but I couldn't come up with anything. If I could get close enough to Sparks, I might be able to use some of my martial arts training to take him out. But I doubted he would let me get anywhere near him.

Sparks turned to Drigger.

"I'm really gonna enjoy takin' you out to Black Marsh," the sheriff said. "You out there, dangling over the water. Waiting. If the gator's not hungry, you might have to hang there for a couple-a hours, thinking about what's coming. Will you be able to handle that, boy, or you gonna stroke out on me?"

I saw Drigger stiffen at the racial slur, but he never took his eyes from Sparks.

Then Sparks ordered, "Take that gun outta your belt and toss it over my way. Any other weapon you got on you, too."

Drigger made no move to comply.

I began to put a little distance between Mark and me, which meant moving away from Drigger, too. Sparks didn't fail to notice.

He turned his gun on me.

"Where you think you're goin', little lady?"

"I'd like to stand in that patch of sun," I said. "Been living under ground so long I don't think I'll ever get warm."

"You'll be going back underground soon enough. Go ahead. Enjoy it while you can."

What I was trying to do was make it harder for Sparks and his men to loose a barrage of bullets that would take out all of us at once.

Sparks turned his attention back to Mark.

"You got any weapons, cowboy?" the sheriff asked. Mark shook his head, and raised his hands to show they were empty, not at all a conclusive gesture but an effort to mollify Sparks for a few valuable moments. I was pretty sure Mark had a gun like Drigger's. I'd heard Drigger giving him some basic instruction one night after dinner on its operations, and what it could and couldn't do. I just hoped my plan would give both of them a chance to catch our four captors off guard.

Sparks had returned his attention to Drigger.

He was angry. "I told you to throw your gun over here," Sparks repeated. "Do it now, or I kill the woman where she stands."

If I was going to act, it had to be right now.

I took three quick steps toward the sun and pretended to trip over a dead tree branch lying in the leaves. I cried out and fell, and that did the job. All eyes turned toward me except Drigger's and Mark's. Instead, the two men dropped and rolled and had their guns out, blasting at our captors before they had time to react. Almost. Sparks managed to fire his shotgun in Drigger's direction. I couldn't tell if Drigger had been hit, though I doubted that Sparks could miss with a shotgun at close quarters.

Wounded or not, Drigger managed to kill two of the deputies almost immediately, catching both in the chest with multiple shots. Mark fired several shots that missed, then caught James Weldon in the throat. Weldon fell in a geyser of blood and didn't move. Sparks, unhurt and wearing body armor, raised his shotgun at Drigger's head. Before he could fire, Drigger shot him in the gut, below the vest, and Sparks went down, writhing in pain. He had dropped his shotgun, and it lay a few feet away from his outstretched hand.

I heard people crashing through the underbrush behind me and saw Frank Desartis and several of his people racing in our direction, their own guns drawn.

Sparks rolled onto his side, ignoring his intense pain, picked up his shotgun and aimed at Desartis. Drigger saw the move, raised his gun, and shot Sparks in the head, just above his left eye.

Drigger rolled onto his back and winced. The left leg of his blue jeans was soaked with blood. Mark, a trained paramedic, knelt at Drigger's side and yelled for a knife. One of the men who came in with Desartis rushed over, pulling a knife from a sheath on his belt. The knife was terrifying, looking more like a nightmare than a cutting implement. There were deep serrations along the top of the blade. If someone was stabbed with that thing, it would pull out half his guts when it was withdrawn.

Mark took no time to admire it. There was no time. He had to get Drigger's jeans cut open. Sparks's shotgun had torn the bejeezus out of Drigger's leg, and the blood was coming from several puncture wounds from below the knee to the upper thigh.

Mark stripped off his tee-shirt and ripped it from the neck down. He used it as a tourniquet as he yelled at Desartis: "We need to medivac this guy to a trauma hospital."

"Chopper's already on the way," Desartis replied. "Just keep him from bleeding to death until the paramedics get here to carry him out."

Mark put a hand on Drigger's shoulder, a gesture of reassurance.

"Don't worry, Drigger," he said. "The femoral artery wasn't hit. You're not going to bleed out on the flight to the hospital."

"Thanks, Mark," the wounded man said, barely above a whisper.

I heard the chopper coming in, and within five minutes it was hovering over us, its rotor slapping tree branches around. The paramedics lowered a basket, careful that it didn't become entangled in the trees. The medics were lowered in harnesses. They put a saline IV in Drigger's arm, checked the wounds, and lifted him gently into the basket. I saw Drigger's face contort in pain, but he uttered only a soft moan. He'd probably seen a lot worse in Afghanistan, I thought, assuming he'd really been there.

I got up off the ground and joined Mark.

"Is he really going to be okay?"

"Should be," Mark said, "with a couple of surgeries and a lot of rehab."

"He didn't deserve this."

"The good guys rarely do."

And just like that, it was over.

Or so I thought.

30

―――――

Chicago...

Mark and I sat in Eric Ryland's office along with Tomas Messina, deputy director of the Illinois State Fire Marshal's office, the department Mark worked for. Neither executive looked particularly pleased to be there. Both Mark and I expected severe tongue-lashings and even possible suspensions. When we were notified the day before to be in Ryland's office at 10 a.m. sharp, Mark commented, "And we thought we were in deep shit in Red Twig. Here's where it really hits the fan."

When we walked in, I noticed that Ryland and Messina had coffee in large cardboard cups. We weren't offered any, and there were no pastries on the conference table. This wasn't going to be a pleasant social occasion. Because Messina was a visitor, he deferred to Ryland to open things.

"Deputy Messina and I have been discussing your actions down in Joe Pye County," Ryland said. "To say we were concerned about your welfare would be a mammoth understatement. But beyond that, we were furious. I can't speak for Deputy Messina, but there were times during that week or ten days that I would have fired you on the spot had you been here. You made a dangerous trip in a private plane with the company's money and without backup. You needlessly put yourself in mortal danger."

I thought, Leave it to Eric to place company money ahead of a staffer's personal welfare. But I held my tongue, which wasn't at all like me. I might even have smiled a little. Eric was acting out after a reporter under his supervision came very close to an ugly death.

Now Tomas Messina was speaking.

"I came very close to a decision to fire you, too, Mark. Not out of some petulant snit, but because your actions were so ill-conceived and emotion-driven that it raised serious questions about chances you might take on the job. Your judgments and decisions could jeopardize the lives and health of the men and woman under your command. Stupid. Stupid. Stupid." He drew a deep breath and continued "Your sudden appearance in Joe Pye County didn't help Deuce. It exacerbated her jeopardy. She wasn't going to leave without you, so she and Drigger had to come up with some cockamamy scheme to break you out of that prison and then run for your lives. It's a surprise any one of you made it as far as the tunnel. If you thought for a minute that Sparks somehow didn't know about that tunnel, then you're not only a dimwit, you are hopelessly naïve."

Mark had his elbows on his chair and his head bowed. He knew that Messina was right, and his actions helped shove the three of us in front of a firing squad. Knowing Mark as well as I did, I knew he was feeling remorse at the tenuous position in which his actions put Drigger and me. But I was willing to bet, even knowing what he knew now, he would do the same again. I knew I would if our situations had been reversed.

The lambasting went on a while longer, the two of us being slapped around like ping-pong balls. We were offered no opportunity to defend our actions, not that we deserved one. Our best course was to sit mute, not argue, and let the men's frustration run its course. Then it was Ryland's turn again.

"Deuce, I'm suspending you with pay for a month. It's not gratuitous punishment. You need that long to rest up, clear your head and see a psychiatrist to deal with your nightmares and night sweats. This is not a suggestion. It's an order. Failure to comply will result in your termination."

Messina meted out essentially the same punishment to Mark.

Finally, I felt as if we'd taken enough of the beatdown.

I asked if I could respond.

"No," Eric said. "Get what you need from your desk and go home."

Messina agreed. "The department can get along without you for a few weeks, Mark," he said. "Just go home and don't argue. I'll see you back at work next month."

As Mark and I walked out of the conference room, I knew Ryland and Messina thought they had put everything to rest.

I knew they hadn't. Sparks might be dead, but Honus Houssmann was still out there.

31

———

I t took me exactly two days to get bored to tears. I might as well have been back in the bunker in Red Twig.

Or maybe not.

When I left Ryland's office I picked up my cats, Caesar and Claudius, from the lady across the street who always kept them when I was gone. She lavished them with love and treats, and they made me feel they'd be a lot happier living with her full time. I vowed I'd play with them more in the future—at least for the next month. When they arrived back in my living room they began the ritual race around the whole house to make sure I hadn't replaced them. Satisfied that the house still belonged to them, they curled up with me on the sofa, where I was stretched out, reading in my favorite angle of repose.

I had called Rush Memorial Hospital to find out how Drigger was and when he could have visitors. He had been airlifted to Rush because Rush had one of the finest orthopedic departments in the country. Drigger was going to need serious surgery on his torn-up leg. I was told that the hospital wouldn't give out any information about a patient unless it was to a designated family member or acquaintance. I was neither. But unless specifically requested not to, they could disclose a patient's condition. The trouble was, they had no patient named Charles Gerard or Drigger Morton.

I wanted to argue, but the woman knew her job, and if the patient wasn't on the roster, then the patient wasn't at the hospital. Unless he's been checked in under an alias. Another alias.

Jerry Alvarez would know. The deputy U.S. attorney for the northern district of Illinois had called me the night before, almost as soon as I got home, to find how I was and to apologize for giving me information that nearly caused my death. But it wasn't Alvarez's fault. He had merely told me where his office thought ex-patrolman James Weldon had been hiding out. It was my own decision to fly to Joe Pye County to have a look around. Even Eric Ryland didn't really blame Alvarez. He put the blame squarely on me, and I couldn't argue the point.

When Alvarez returned my call, he said Drigger was exactly where I thought he was, but under an assumed name. There still were bad guys out there actively looking for him. The assumed name was for his protection. He would be moved to a more secure facility in the next few days.

"He has more aliases than a murderer on the FBI's "Ten Most-Wanted List," I said. Alvarez didn't think it was funny. But it did prompt him to tell me that Drigger was in serious but stable condition and wouldn't be allowed visitors until this case was closed and all those on the wrong side of the law were in prison cells.

I said, "That doesn't explain why I can't visit him."

"Seguro que lo hace," Alvarez said. "Sure it does. If somebody's watching you, which is sufficiently reasonable as to be likely, they'll tail you to the hospital, see what room you walk into, and next thing you know, Drigger's dead. Besides, he's not in sufficiently good condition to be strained by visitations."

"But you get regular reports on him?"

"I do."

"Will you give me reports as they come in?"

"I will."

"Shit. After the chances he took for Mark and me, I'd hate to think he might conclude we don't care enough about him to visit."

"I'll see that he gets that message."

"Thanks. There's something else I need to talk to you about," I told Alvarez. "Can I come to your office? It's really important."

"I'm pretty jammed up these days," he replied. "Maybe early next week."

"You're not putting me off?"

"Maybe a little bit, to let this whole mess cool down some. But I know better than to try to avoid you forever. That you will get what you want is an indisputable law of physics."

"I'm glad you understand that," I said.

Nine days passed during which I called Alvarez every two or three days. His secretary always told me she would give him my message, but that his days were jammed with court actions and meetings, and he might not be able to get back with me for a while. I countered with —threat would be too strong a word—but notice that I wouldn't stop calling until he returned my calls. When he finally did, his voice had an impatient edge to it.

"I won't apologize for delaying so long, Deuce," he said, "but I do have other matters to attend to beside your curiosity."

"Just wanted to be sure you didn't forget," I said. "I also want an update on Drigger."

"He's doing better and has been moved to a more secure facility. If someone tries to break in or force their way past security, they'll be shot. Other than that, there's not much more I'm going to be able to tell you. After I disclosed where we thought Weldon was holed up, you went down to Joe Pye alone and almost got yourself killed several times. Now you come back panting for more. I won't be a party to more."

"You never told me not to go," I reminded him. "You never said the tip was off-the-record, either."

"I remember using the word, 'confidentially.' A difference that makes no difference is no difference, to quote the philosopher, William James, more than 150 years ago. And Mr. Spock more recently."

"*Star Trek,* Jerry? Really?"

Alvarez didn't respond, so I repeated my request. "I'd still like to talk to you, and if you want it off-the-record, just say so. Don't mince words."

I heard him sigh. I almost heard him rubbing his hand over his eyes.

"My office at seven o'clock this evening," he said. "Most everyone will be gone by then, but I'll leave word with security to send you up. Use a fake name, Emma Stevens. How's that? Wear a baseball cap and sunglasses and whatever else you can to disguise your identity. Eyes in this building are always attached to ears on the outside. And those ears are sometimes attached to hands holding guns."

"Point taken, Jerry. I'll see you at seven. Thanks."

THERE WAS STILL a lot of daylight left when I walked into the Dirksen Federal Building on South Dearborn Street in the Loop. After I'd been waved through security and camouflaged as requested, I passed several people in the halls I didn't recognize, but they sized me up anyway. They weren't used to seeing strangers in their midst at this time of the day. Alvarez's secretary had left for the day, but the door to his office was standing open, an invitation for me to enter.

He came around his desk and gave me a brotherly hug, then held me at arms' length.

"You don't look terribly beat up, thank God," he said.

"I'm not. Just minor bumps and scrapes."

Alvarez motioned me to his small conference table. Before he sat down he detoured to his office door. He closed and locked it.

"We don't need eavesdroppers," he said returning to the table.

Alvarez had lost a lot of weight a year earlier in preparation for becoming a husband, and it looked as if married life suited him. I said so.

No cambiaria nada," he said. "I wouldn't change anything. I wish I'd done it years ago, but then I would have married somebody other than Cynthia, and it wouldn't have been nearly as pleasant." He leaned back in his chair with his hands flat on the table. "So, what are you turning over in that hyper-active brain of yours these days? I heard Eric Ryland suspended you for a month. He let you off pretty easy considering what could have happened to you in Joe Pye. It's a hell hole, though less so than before you and Drigger blasted through the territory."

I looked away from him. I didn't want to meet his eyes. What the hell was I doing here? A series of flashbacks to Joe Pye County crawled through my head, things I could never unsee, things I never wanted to experience again.

But I couldn't back off. Not with so much unresolved.

Alvarez broke into my thoughts. "Deuce? You okay?"

I raised my head. "Yeah, Jerry, I am. As much as I would like to put the Joe Pye experience behind me, there's something Drigger told me just before we escaped that I can't let go. He said this businessman named Houssmann might be behind the crimes in Joe Pye and beyond. His name's Honus Houssmann. It's pronounced . . ."

"Yeah," Alvarez said. "I know how it's pronounced."

"He owns rehab and nursing facilities that stretch from Skokie into Wisconsin."

"I know that, too. *Oh, mierda.* Shit." Alvarez's reaction was vehement. I didn't think I'd ever heard him swear before.

I let the other shoe drop. "He thinks Governor Latchey might have been protecting Houssmann and Sparks. I told him when we were still back at the cabin that I couldn't understand why no state or federal agency had stormed Joe Pye and cleaned out Sparks's operation. Why hadn't Governor Latchey mobilized the National Guard? He didn't deny it when I suggested Latchey might be on Sparks's pad. Now I think, if there were payoffs, they probably came from Houssmann. Drigger pretty much stonewalled me, and the matter never came up again. Until we were in that cave."

Alvarez had a pretty good tan, but I saw him go a little pale as I was speaking.

He was silent for nearly five minutes. He swiveled his chair and stared out his big glass window looking east past the Chicago skyline and out to Lake Michigan. After the long, awkward silence, he turned back to me.

"Deuce, you've just survived one of the most harrowing experiences I've ever heard of. You should not have taken your quixotic trip, though the world is a better place because you did. But in this case the windmills are far more lethal than those Don Quixote tried to fight. These windmills fight back. If you promise me you'll stay out of it, and I mean totally turning your back on the whole thing, I promise to give you a heads-up on the story before it's released, if it's ever released. Deal?"

I said, "I don't know yet. I won't know until I hear the whole story. Until I do, I can't make any promises either way."

32

"We thought we had her covered, but she gave us the slip," the man told his employer. "We saw her leave her house at 10:30. She Ubered to downtown and spent about an hour in the Apple Store. Don't know what she did in there, but she came out with one-a those white Apple bags with the drawstring. From there she grabbed a cab to the Phoenix on Archer in Chinatown. It's a big place."

"I know it," the older man said. "Good crab Rangoon and Beijing duck. Then what?"

"We saw her go in. Never saw her come out. Siggy went inside after maybe forty-five minutes just to check and couldn't find her."

"How can you lose a woman who's six feet tall with auburn hair, for chrissake? She shudda stuck out like a giraffe at a cat show."

"Maybe she changed into a disguise or went out a service entrance. I don't know. We parked almost dead in front of the place and never lost sight of the front door."

"Fuck the front door," the older man said. "I know where the fuckin' front door is. What I need to know is, where's Deuce Mora? Get out there and find her. Capiche? Sparks might be gone, but his pet alligator's still around, and probably gettin' hungry."

"Aw, man, don't go there. We're doin' the best we can."

"It obviously ain't good enough. Now get outta here and find the bitch."

I HAD ENTERED the restaurant a little after noon and took the stairs to the second-floor dining room. There was an elevator, but I was still trying to regain the muscle tone I had before the enforced inactivity in Joe Pye County, and the elevator wouldn't help.

The aromas that surrounded me made me hungry and wishing I could stay for lunch. But there was no time, and there were a dozen people waiting for tables to open up, making the notion of staying even more difficult. I was on a strict timetable. So, I asked the hostess if I could order a small takeout hot and sour soup and paid her for it. While she put in the order, I told her I had to use the ladies' room and would be right back.

I went into a stall, away from curious onlookers that might remember seeing me put on the clothes I had stuffed into the Apple bag. I used the same getup I wore into the federal building for the meeting with Jerry Alvarez: medium-length black wig, baseball cap, and sunglasses. Then I stood in front of a mirror and applied some makeup that looked remarkably like the result of two hours outside in the sun.

I didn't go back for the soup, and I hated abandoning it since it was paid for. Instead, I found the back stairs and pushed through the service door. Alvarez was sitting outside in a bland white Ford sedan that no one could mistake for anything but a U.S. government vehicle. If anyone was watching, it would be a dead giveaway. I glanced around to check. There were no vehicles around and nobody on foot. So, I slipped into the passenger seat.

"You always do undercover work in a bland sedan with government plates?" I asked. It was a rhetorical question since I was pretty sure Alvarez didn't do undercover work.

"It doesn't have government plates," he said, sounding a bit miffed that I would even suggest such a thing. "The garage switched them out for plates that went into a junkyard last week on a totaled car. If anyone calls the DMV and runs the name attached to these plates, they'll come back to a man killed in a one-car DUI accident on the Eisenhower."

"Why not just bring your own car?"

"Because if anyone calls the DMV to run the name attached to those plates, it would come up with me. Now *that* would be a dead giveaway."

"Touché," I said. "Sorry. I guess you didn't become deputy U.S. attorney because you were an idiot. So where are we going?"

"Cicero. A safe house we keep there."

Cicero. That brought back memories. The story I'd broken, for which the *Journal* won the Public Service Pulitzer Prize, began at a bar in Cicero at the cost of a man's life. While most thought of Cicero as a suburb of Chicago, and many who lived there worked and shopped in Chicago, it was actually a city unto itself, a working-class area with historic ties to the Mafia or the Mob or The Organization, whatever those guys were being called these days. Al Capone hid out in Cicero when the feds were hot on his trail. So, thinking of it now as a place where the feds kept a safe house for witnesses who don't want to be found, well, "irony" would be a good descriptive.

"Are we being followed?" I asked.

Alvarez chuffed. "What do you think we're doing, making a Netflix cop show?"

"No, but it's possible somebody got suspicious, or recognized you, and followed us."

"*No te preocupes,*" he said. "Don't worry about it. Worrying is my job. That's why I'm taking side streets and back alleys. Easier to spot a tail. So far, no sign of anyone."

"So, this is where Drigger is?"

"We'll talk about it when we get there."

"THERE" turned out to be a standard two-story yellow brick house like so many others in the area of Cicero that lay in the shadow of

Midway International Airport. The structure seemed to be somewhat larger than similar homes that surrounded it, but I couldn't tell for sure. It had a driveway and garage, which most of the other homes did not, and the standard window boxes of red geraniums. I wondered if red geraniums were the official city flower of Cicero. They were ubiquitous.

Alvarez didn't park in the driveway. Instead, he parked expertly at a curb three blocks away on a different street.

"If you don't mind the walk, we'll put a little distance between us and the house so we don't inadvertently draw attention to the car," he said. "You up for a stroll?"

It was a gorgeous late spring day with a slight breeze and lots of old shade trees lining the sidewalks. A walk, even if just three blocks, sounded great. When we got close to our destination, Alvarez turned up an alley of chopped-up asphalt. The alley took us to the back of the house. We had to push through some high hedges that shielded the house, but we were none the worse for it. Jerry rang a buzzer. I could barely hear it through the door, which was protected by a heavy steel gate. If someone had asked why the house needed fortification, they were told it was because the door was too secluded to be safe from intruders, Alvarez said.

"They get many intruders in the 'hood?" I asked.

"No," Alvarez said. "And they don't want any. Mostly burglars stay away from this area. You never know whose house you're breaking into, and your intrusion might be met with a lot worse consequences than a 9-1-1 call."

A disembodied voice came from a tiny speaker above the door.

"Look at the camera with your eyes open," it said.

We did that, one at a time.

"We register you, Mr. Alvarez. We have no record of the woman."

"She's with me," Alvarez replied. "I called ahead. Deuce Mora."

There was nothing for a few seconds, then I heard a loud click. Jerry pulled on the gate, and it came open. Somebody else opened the inner door. We were invited inside.

Jerry had to show his ID, and it was accepted. I had to acquiesce to a body scan and a pat down from a female agent to find any weapons I might have.

"The most lethal weapon I have is a nail file," I said, trying to be helpful. The female agent didn't so much as crack a smile. But she found the nail file and confiscated it, doing a good impression of a TSA airport security officer. She said I would get it back when I left. So much for breaking the tension.

"Your party is in Suite Two," the male agent said. "Do you need an escort?"

"I think I can manage," Alvarez replied. "I helped design this place."

Now it was the male agent's turn not to smile. He motioned us through a metal detector and didn't even turn around as we headed up the short hallway to a large elevator of the kind you might find in a hospital. Large enough to hold a surgical gurney and a half dozen other people.

"We could have taken the stairs," I said.

Alvarez replied, "No we couldn't. There's always suspicion about the stairs. I don't know why, but if we'd walked into the stairwell we'd have been met almost immediately by heavily armed men with no senses of humor."

"They'd fit right in here," I said. More people who didn't smile. I began to develop an inferiority complex. I could usually elicit a chuckle. I put it on my list of things to work on.

WHEN WE GOT off the elevator I saw an armed guard down the hall sitting in front of a closed door. He looked up sharply when he heard us, and I might have seen his hand move slightly toward the Glock on his hip. He relaxed only when he saw Alvarez.

"Afternoon, Sir," he said.

"How're you doing, Gino?"

"Good, Sir. How's married life treating you?"

"Couldn't be much better. God knows I waited long enough to pull the trigger—no double entendre intended."

Alvarez turned to me. "Gino, this is Deuce Mora from the *Journal*. She's with me."

"Yes, Sir. I was notified." He turned to me. "You don't look anything like your picture in the paper."

"Camouflage," I said.

"Figured," Gino said. "I see you and Fred"—he cocked his head toward the door behind him— "had a pretty bad time of it recently."

I smiled at him. "We did," I said. "Fred?"

"I'm told that's his name," Gino said.

I glanced at Alvarez. This really was feeling like a bad James Bond flick.

"How many names does he have?" I asked.

Alvarez shrugged. "Who knows?"

The door behind Gino opened abruptly disclosing a man who might have been a doctor. He was middle-aged, his light brown hair beginning to show gray at the temples. His blue eyes were clear, and his smile genuine, a nice change of pace. I say he might have been a doctor because he was wearing a white medical jacket with "Rush Memorial Hospital" sewn into it over the left breast but without the man's name. He had a stethoscope hung around his neck. Not that those accoutrements define who is and who isn't a doctor, but my suspicions were confirmed when he pulled off a pair of blue surgical gloves and casually deposited them in a medical waste bin hung just inside the door.

"How is he?" Alvarez asked.

"He's been through two surgeries and is doing okay. I'd stay he's in serious condition. In some pain, which we're managing. And he's got another surgery in a couple of days. I can't tell you any more than that. HIPAA privacy rules. I can tell you he's bored. You're the first visitors he's had. He perked up when he heard you were coming."

"Then let's get in there," I said.

Lying in bed as he was, Drigger looked like a contortionist. His head was raised to a reclining position, his left leg splinted and heavily bandaged from the ankle to mid-thigh and held in traction at about a forty-five-degree angle. His right leg elevated, too but not as much. It probably was more comfortable that way. The TV was tuned to CNN. Drigger looked tired, but he gave us a big smile, which let me know his sense of humor was intact. But his dark brown skin had an ashy look about it, a sign he wasn't well.

"How are you feeling?" I asked.

His smile faded. "I might lose the leg," he said. I heard myself gasp.

"Why?"

"A lot of vascular damage, blood vessels an' all. Maybe too much to fix."

"Your femoral artery wasn't hit," I said.

"But a lot of other blood vessels were. A lot."

I wanted to convey deep sympathy without sounding maudlin. "I'm so sorry, Drigger. I really will hope for the best. There isn't a day goes by I don't think about you."

We passed maybe ten minutes in small talk. We knew we didn't have much time with him, so Alvarez got to the point.

"We're building the case against the man up north, Drigger. Can you give me any details about his involvement in Joe Pye that we don't already know?"

Drigger shook his head weakly. He seemed to be tiring.

"Not much," he replied. "There was a time before Deuce arrived that I was chatting with Sparks and let Houssmann's name drop, just to see what the reaction would be. The sheriff got a look on his face that was part concern and part anger. He asked what I knew about Houssmann. I said I didn't know him, wouldn't recognize him if he walked in the door, that I'd only heard his name mentioned once. Sparks demanded to know how Houssmann's name came up, and I said I didn't recall the circumstances. I remember Sparks got really upset, maybe even a little scared. I don't think he believed me then. I don't think he ever believed me. And I think that was the reason he immediately suspected me of harboring Deuce after the plane crash. My cabin was probably the first place he wanted to search. He told me I was never to mention Houssmann's name again or I would wind up in Black Marsh. I don't think there's anyone in Joe Pye wouldn't have understood the meaning of that warning."

I said, "And then there's Governor Latchey. If he's on the take, he wouldn't be a first dirty governor in Illinois, This a state has sent five of its last eleven governors to prison."

"Five?" Drigger asked.

"I looked it up. Two others were charged but acquitted at trial. That's sixty-four percent convicted or indicted for criminal activity. Not a record to envy." I glanced at Alvarez. "Don't blame Drigger. All he told me was there wasn't yet enough evidence to make a move against the Joe Pye organization. When I asked if Latchey might be on Houssmann's pad, he asked me what that meant. The conversation didn't go any farther than that. When I was trying to get to sleep that night, I was tossing the situation around in my head and jumped to the conclusion that Latchey might be culpable."

Drigger smiled at me then at Alvarez. "You know, the way this lady thinks, maybe she should be working for you."

"Some days," Alvarez replied, "I think she is."

33

W e chatted for a few more minutes until the doctor stuck his head in the door and said his patient needed rest. I told Drigger I'd be back to see him again if I was permitted, and I felt bad about letting my first visit wait so long.

"Not to worry," he said. "I'll see you when I see you."

I stopped at the door and looked back at him. "Thank you for all you did. I'd most certainly have died down there without you."

"Just payin' back a debt," he said.

I showed my confusion. "You told me that once before. I don't understand."

"You will," he replied.

When we were back in Alvarez's car headed back to Chicago I asked Alvarez straight out, "Does Drigger report to you?"

"No."

"Who, then? FBI, CIA? NSA?"

"I don't think so."

"You mean you don't know?"

"*No exactamente, no.*"

"Oh, come on, Jerry."

"As God is my witness, Deuce. I don't."

"Well, who does?"

"I suspect he does."

I sighed deeply. "That's no help at all."

"It's the truth."

"Then can you tell me what that comment meant as we were leaving the room, about a debt he owed to me? Do you know what he was talking about?"

"I think I know, but I can't and won't discuss it."

"Even off-the-record?"

"Yep, even."

I replied, "You know I love you like a brother, Jerry. But sometimes you can really piss me off."

"I hope so," he said.

ALVAREZ TOOK South Cicero Avenue down to West Ogden, better known perhaps as the historic Route 66, turned east on Cermak and through Little Village to my home in Pilsen. I told him I had to stop by my house to pick up some clothes and stuff for the cats. I would let Mark know where I was, and he could pick me up to return to the condo.

"That's not a good idea," he said. "I'll stay with you until he gets there."

"You don't have to do that, Jerry. You should go home."

When we were stopped for a traffic light, Alvarez got a text. He read it and replied before the light changed. I admit I was a bit nervous, too, about being at my house by myself for too long. I assured Alvarez I would go directly inside, lock the door, and wait for Mark. It wasn't until I climbed my front steps that I allowed myself a sigh of relief.

I felt my heart rate jump when I saw a man waiting for me in a glider on the front porch. I only began breathing easy when I realized it was Mark.

"Hey, Roy Rogers, what are you doing here?" I asked.

Mark smiled. "Jerry texted me from the car that he was bringing you here. I didn't think you should be alone. I was close by, up at Costco getting gas. And I was bored."

"Bored? Haven't you just had all the excitement you need for a while?"

"Need? Yeah, probably. Maybe it's an adrenaline letdown, like Barstow suggested."

I sat down on the swing beside him. "Well, it's nice that I'm useful for something, if only in the field of boredom alleviation. On one hand, you have Murphy to frolic with you. I, on the other hand, have two cats who spend most of every day sleeping or sitting in the sun and chattering at birds that fly by. When they're at the condo they usually sleep on the dining room table or at the foot of my bed, the two sunniest places in the unit. They may still be on the bed, hoping for more sun any minute."

He asked, "Are you okay with the enforced tranquility in your life?"

"Well, I'm relieved that Derek Sparks is no longer around and threatening to feed me to the Black Marsh alligators. Still, I have this nagging certainty that the episode isn't over."

"How do you mean?"

"Honus Houssmann, nursing home king of the Upper Midwest, is still out there trying to reorganize and probably planning to come at us. And we don't know what William Latchey is up to."

"The governor?"

"He could-a sent the National Guard into Joe Pye to clean up that nest of killer hornets, but he didn't. He didn't even mention the problem publicly so far as I can tell from a long search online."

Mark began rocking us in the glider, a nervous response to learning I was still working on this story.

I asked, "Don't you have any concerns?"

"It crossed my mind. Drigger said he gave you some shooting instructions. I'd like to continue them and even help you pick out a gun you feel comfortable with. And stop shaking your head."

"I didn't feel comfortable with the gun Drigger gave me, including the lessons. I was so nervous holding it and scared I might my foot off."

"Drigger said you practiced with a Glock with a specially designed silencer so that the noise wouldn't bother you. We can do that again."

"Mark, what Drigger did at the meth lab, and what you and he did at the Bat Cave require shooting skills I couldn't develop in a year. If I'm gonna waste good bullets shooting and missing with a handgun while the bad guys have AR-15s, they're going to have everything sprayed down before I can even get my weapon unholstered."

"You'd be willing to just give without a fight? That's not like you."

I sighed. I knew Mark had pragmatism on his side, but I wasn't ready.

"I'd rather spend my month off doing research that might expose Houssmann and his cronies—maybe even the governor."

"Good luck with that," he answered with a tone bent under the weight of sarcasm. "You brought down one governor last year. Isn't that enough?"

"Depends on whether Latchey deserves it."

IT WAS FIVE O'CLOCK, a little early for dinner, but we decided to walk the three blocks up to Bacchanalia and have a couple of drinks at the bar before we ate.

Danny and Paula, co-owners of the restaurant as well as brother and sister, were both behind the bar, an uncommon occurrence. Paula, an effusive Italian of middle age who looked like a college homecoming princess, rushed around the bar to hug each of us. I heard her voice crack a bit when she said, "I was sobbing when I read how close we came to losing both of you." She pushed back, and I saw that her eyes were full. Mark wanted to change the subject.

"Is there a special occasion?" he asked as I watched delivery people setting up vases of varied white hydrangeas, peonies and roses as centerpieces on each table in the main dining room in back.

"Rehearsal dinner," Danny replied. "I got the bar. Paula's gonna handle the kitchen."

"A fair division of responsibility," Mark told Danny. "We gonna be out of your way sitting at the bar?"

"No problem, 'specially not for you two. You're welcome any time. If half-a what I'm readin' in the papers is true, you need some vino."

"You've only read half of it," I said as Mark frowned at me. If Danny noticed Mark's irritation, he didn't comment. Instead, he set the glasses on the bar in front of us and said, "First round's on the house. *Buon Appetito.*"

Paula set a plate of focaccia between us. "Also on the house," she said. The flatbread with tomatoes, mozzarella, and basil was an Italian staple that offered a tantalizing blend of aroma and flavor. It also served as a way to get something on our stomachs, so the alcohol didn't go straight to our heads.

Paula and Danny turned their attentions to the pre-wedding crowd that had begun to fill the restaurant, and no one was giving us a second look. It seemed a good time for Mark and me to talk amid the din.

Mark asked, "You still gonna carry on with this project?"

"To the extent that I can," I said. "I don't plan to take to the streets with a banner that accuses Latchey and Houssmann of heinous federal crimes and murder, but I want to research their connections and see where, if anywhere, their paths crossed."

"It would be surprising if they didn't," Mark said. "Two men with similar political views, money, and influence. It's a natural case of mutual interests. But it doesn't even suggest, let alone prove, that they've been partners in crime."

"You're right," I said. "I concluded there might be a link given Latchey's apparent reluctance to mobilize the National Guard to bring down the Joe Pye bunch. At the very least, I think Latchey needs to answer some tough questions. Houssmann, too. All that entails right now is me scouring public records for anything suspicious."

Mark shook his head in a give-up gesture.

"Are you going to give Eric a head's up? He is your supervisor, after all."

"And he suspended me. Technically I don't work for him for the duration of the thirty days. I'm working as a freelancer."

"That's a real stretch, Honey," he said.

The wedding celebration had reached a cacophony of conversation and laughter that precluded much more serious discussion with Mark.

"Let's have another glass of wine and order dinner," I said. "It's getting hard to hear."

An hour or so later we paid our bill and got up to leave. We tried to find Danny and Paula to thank them for their hospitality. But the restaurant owners were too busy at that point to talk.

When we turned to leave we had to push through a small group standing behind us, swapping out members now and again as the evening wore on. Except for one man. He had been standing close behind Mark and me since shortly after we sat down. He was young, perhaps in his early twenties. He was as tall as Mark with dark hair and brown eyes. His beard looked to be a three-day growth of stubble carefully manicured to look neat and scruffy at the same time. He wore an expensive suit that appeared tailored just for him and had an aura of foreign design and stitching. His serious expression said he was not among those celebrating anyone's pending nuptials. I noticed him when he came in because he was wearing a light application of a Clive Christian cologne for men. It was my favorite, but I didn't often get a whiff of it since a small bottle sold from $400 to $500. Most men wouldn't pay that, even if they could. I wanted to know who was wearing it and sized him up by his reflection in the mirror behind the bar.

Curiosity satisfied, I didn't give him a second thought. I would wish later that I had.

34

I lay in bed for a long time later that night, unable to sleep through the clutter of scenarios in my brain. I was trying to figure out ways Latchey and Houssmann could have become partners in crime. If they were linked, what was the connection? It seemed logical that Houssmann or his nursing home empire or both would have made political donations to Latchey's gubernatorial campaigns. There might also have been secret personal payoffs made in return for the governor's cooperation in letting the drug business continue unchecked. Latchey won his first campaign in 2018 by the very narrow margin of 16,000 votes statewide. He had been trailing in the polls until a massive, last-minute statewide advertising campaign carried him over the top. Those ads would have cost a small fortune. Did Latchey have that depth of political support? Would his personal wealth have allowed him to pay for those ads out of pocket? He ran for reelection again in 2022 and found himself once again in a very close race which again he narrowly won.

Each election involved two races, one to win the nomination and one to win the general election. I couldn't even imagine how much money changed hands. I would go online in the morning and check contributions on the state board of elections website.

But another possibility nagged at me. If the two men were joined at the hip by the crimes of Joe Pye County but wanted to bury those links deep underground, wouldn't they avoid anything as obvious as political contributions? Out-and-out payoffs would have been much harder to trace. On the other hand, if they avoided political contributions altogether, wouldn't that be suspicious? The possibilities made my brain hurt.

If Latchey and Houssmann were linked by something beyond politics, I would abide by the axiom of political journalism, "Follow the money."

I greeted the new day with profound sensations of anticipation and dread. And a headache. If I were able to put the two men together, it could be tantalizing. A big if.

Mark and his gun had spent the night on the sofa again, but he left before breakfast to get Murphy and the cats and bring them back to my house. The poor animals probably thought they no longer had a regular home.

I needed to talk to Drigger again as soon as he felt up to another visit. It was my conversation with him in his shack that first caused me to consider the possibility of a Latchey role in the criminality. I needed to find out if he knew anymore and would share the information, or new leads I could follow. I had only Drigger's one mention of Houssmann to tie him to crimes. I was a long way from proof of complicity by either man. I needed help. But Alvarez had been explicit in saying he wouldn't be a part of my windmill tilting any longer, and Drigger was so secretive I wasn't sure he could or would help.

I brewed a pot of much-needed coffee and blended a fruit-and-veggie smoothie for myself. I put the smoothie in the refrigerator for later and carried a large mug of the coffee up to my office.

Negotiating the state board of elections records wasn't difficult if you knew what you were doing, but I had no clue. I hadn't even looked at the site for years. So, it was mid-afternoon before I was able to determine that Latchey's 2018 general election campaign had reported $127 million in contributions. Less than ten percent of that money—$11 million—came from the candidate himself. He had mortgaged his home to the limit to get some of those funds. And I'm sure he had the wherewithal to leverage more. There also were a lot of contributions from the executives in Latchey's companies and members of Latchey's family. Latchey's opponent, Richard Russo, spent $181 million, more than half of which came out of his own pocket.

Costs for his 2022 campaign were higher, but it didn't appear from filings thus far that Latchey contributed more of his own money than he had four years earlier. He was facing Russo again, who seemed to have contributed as much personal cash to his second run as the first. Perhaps more. I couldn't tell for sure since final campaign reports weren't filed yet from either campaign.

The only knowledge I could take away from all those numbers was that Latchey's opponent was willing and able to raise and donate a lot more than Latchey, though Latchey kept winning. There was nothing wrong with that. But in the age of big-money politics I couldn't help but find it curious. That was my only takeaway from a full day's work. If I was going to figure this out before the next election in 2026, I would have to pick up the pace.

35

"**D**euce, honey, I couldn't make time to see you this week even if I was so inclined, which I'm not. *Imposible,*" Alvarez told me when I got him on the phone the next day on the sixth attempt. "You can't keep calling me. It could leave the wrong impression. I know what you want to talk about, and I can't do it. *Imposible.*"

"Let me ask you one more thing, Jerry," I said and heard him sigh in exasperation. I didn't give him a chance to say no. "I'd like to visit Drigger again. I won't lie to you and promise not to bring up the topic of Joe Pye. But the man saved my life. And the least I can do is visit him in the hospital now and then, to let him know I'm thinking about him and wishing him well."

There was a full thirty seconds of silence before Alvarez replied. "I can't say yes on my own authority. Drigger doesn't work for DoJ. The United States attorney general himself couldn't give you that permission. But I'll reach out to someone who can get in touch with people. Though I think it's a waste of time. They'll likely say no, and if they give Drigger an option, he'll likely say no, too."

"Can't hurt to try."

"You do understand, Deuce, that I don't work for you."

"Actually, Jerry, you do."

I NEVER KNEW who Alvarez talked to, but two days later he called.

"Sorry, Deuce, the answer was a resounding no. But I did convince the contact to relay a message to Drigger that you had asked to see him to check how he was getting along, and I was promised that your concern will be relayed."

"Do you think it will be?"

"*Quien sabe?* I wouldn't even hazard a guess. My guess is that your good wishes will be relayed. Another visit, well, it seems reasonable to suspect he'll be pressured by his supervisors to turn you down."

"At least he'll know I'm thinking about him."

So, I was dead in the water without an oar.

I was tempted to make the Board of Elections my new home-away-from-home and camp out there every day from opening to closing, going through the election records for both Latchey and his opponent. I also wanted to check Latchey's personal finance disclosures to see if anything popped out at me, or even squeaked at me. I didn't care how loud the alert was if only I could find one.

I took a chance and called Josh Fujita, the *Journal's* election finance specialist, to get some tips, if he had any, on what to look for and how.

"I thought you had the month off," Fujita said.

"I do. This is something I'm doing off the books."

"Could I get in trouble by helping you?"

"Maybe. I'm not sure. I won't be upset if you say no."

"If I do it on my days off it will give me some cover."

"I don't want to slice into your down time."

Fujita thought about it for a few seconds. "Tell you what. Let's have lunch tomorrow, some place well away from the office, and you can tell me what you're up to and what it is you think I can do to help."

WE MET the next afternoon at two o'clock at The Crepe Shop on North Broadway in the Lakeview neighborhood, far enough north of downtown that Fujita and I agreed it would take a coincidence of monumental proportions for anyone we knew to see us. In case someone recognized me from the mug shot that ran with my column —when there was a column—I put my hair up under a Cubs baseball cap and wore very casual clothes and sunglasses. I thought it would be best if we took an outside table so the ambient Chicago noise would cover our conversation, but it looked like rain, and the forecast suggested a high probability. The inside tables were spaced sufficiently wide to cover us.

We stood in a short line at the counter to place our orders.

"You buyin'?" Fujita asked, "or is this month putting a hit on your wallet?"

"I can afford it," I said.

"Good, I'll have one of everything."

I ordered the roasted turkey crepe with spinach, sauteed onions, and mushroom gruyere sauce. Fujita ordered the ham and cheese crepe and the wildberry cheesecake crepe for dessert. When we were settled with our food and very good pour-over coffee, he asked me *sotto voce* to give him an idea what I needed from him.

"I'm looking for a toxic needle in a very large haystack," I said and filled him in on everything I knew. "I've run through as much as I know how to do in the election reports, and I'm not coming up with anything. But I'm not an expert."

"Well," he said, "as you might expect I run through those reports thoroughly every time a reporting period ends, and I haven't found anything that would set off bells and whistles for me, except the extraordinary amounts of money the two men spent."

"That's pretty much the way it is with all campaigns," I said.

"Were you looking for anything that would explain the discrepancies?"

"Between what the Latchey and Russo campaigns spent and the

unexpected results? Yeah, I looked, but I didn't find anything out of the ordinary. Russo wasn't exactly popular in the state, but there wasn't a lot of love lost on Latchey, either. It was almost as if voters chose the guy they hated least."

"That's not unusual at any campaign level," I said.

We'd been almost whispering, and I dropped my voice even more.

"What about dark money?" I asked. "It's legal in Illinois, right?"

"That's complicated."

"Is there a book called, 'Election Law for Dummies'?"

Fujita smiled. "No, but I can keep it simple. Dark money is the name for funds that can't be traced by donor or amount. Dark money is associated with big, national super PACs that fund candidates for federal offices, like the U.S. House and Senate and the White House. Two big super PACs are Citizens United, Republican, and Blue Tent, Democrats. The super PACs have to register with the Federal Elections Commission and have a formal treasurer. But donors' names and contribution amounts are anonymous. There's no way to trace who gave how much or where the money went. Their spending is out of sight. With me so far?"

"I think so."

"Super PACS cannot contribute directly to the candidate or the candidate's political committee. The PACs can spend on behalf of a candidate, but without consultation with the candidate or his campaign. There's supposed to be a legal wall between them."

"That's insane," I said. "Who's going to stop a campaign official from having a private lunch with a guy from a super PAC, and together they formulate a giant, state-wide media buy that the super PAC pays for? Who's around to tell them it's illegal?"

"I'm telling you how this is supposed to work. Nobody said anything about reality."

"I thought there were limits on contributions."

"There's an escape clause. It stipulates that if a candidate donates more than $250,000 of his own money to his own campaign, he is considered self-funded. At that point all contribution caps are lifted for everyone. It's called busting the cap."

I shook my head in disbelief. "I knew that, and I always thought it was outrageous. Gubernatorial candidates in this state are all millionaires. Billionaires. They probably pay their teenaged children more than $250,000 a year in allowances. By the time they launch their campaigns they've all assigned millions of their own money to their committee. There might as well not be any state campaign limits at all. They're a charade."

"A lot of people would agree with you," Fujita said. "Once the cap is busted there's no limit for anyone, any organization, any political action committee, nothing."

"I'm trying to identify the biggest donors to Latchey and how much they spent."

"May I ask why?"

"He might be involved in some questionable activities."

"All politicians are involved in some questionable activities," Fujita extended his hand. "But it sounds like fun. Count me in."

I didn't notice the darkly handsome, well-dressed young man standing in front of a bar across the street from us when we left the restaurant. But I might have been able to identify him had we been close enough for me to catch a whiff of his super-expensive Clive Christian cologne.

36

Over the weekend Fujita and I did some research. We found plenty of news stories from Latchey's first campaign that dwelled on how far behind his fundraising was compared to Russo's. For Latchey supporters there seemed to be little on which to hang hopes that he would win. Not only was he well behind in fund-raising and spending but his approval rating among likely voters was in the cellar, drifting between thirty-five and forty percent in the final months.

Duplicating his first campaign, Latchey unleashed a late barrage of TV, radio, and newspaper advertising that touted him and his accomplishments and spewed accusations of cronyism and conflicts of interest at Russo. Some of his ads came uncomfortably close to outright lies about his opponent. His most egregious statements came so frequently and so late in the campaign that Russo's team had no time to refute them effectively. While Latchey's questionable statements about Russo got a lot of newspaper ink and TV commentary, everything seemed to abide by election law, if not good taste.

After the election some media asked where Latchey's late funding came from. Latchey deflected all the questions. He would only say that he wasn't in charge of the money side of the campaign, that he was 'the chairman of good ideas.' It was BS. But that's the law, and Latchey walked a straight line right down the middle of it. Nothing illegal.

I called Fujita. "Did you find anything indicating Latchey skirted elections laws, such as they are? Shouldn't they be fairly easy to spot?"

"Some are, some aren't. There was a national super PAC created out in California maybe ten or eleven years ago called, 'Citizens for Asparagus.' They did huge fund drives and advertising campaigns, mostly to the benefit one state senate candidate."

"Honestly? A super PAC for a vegetable?"

Fujita explained. "California's a big asparagus producer. That's why it never occurred to anyone that something might be shady. I'd have been curious if I'd noticed that most of the ads were on behalf of George Stalk. One of his campaign slogans was 'Stalk for Asparagus.' The Federal Elections Commission got a tip that the bulk of Stalk's money originated with a national super PAC. As we know, it's unusual for a national super PAC to pile money into a state race."

I couldn't help it. I burst out laughing.

I said, "Well, it might have been illegal, but it was imaginative."

"It was serious business but not illegal at that point," Fujita replied. "The national super PAC for asparagus supporters collected millions to back Stalk. They channeled it through the national Republican Party Committee, which in turn paid it to the California Republican Committee, which did a ton of advertising on behalf of Stalk. The scheme stepped over the legal line when Stalk paid off his campaign debts and pocketed the surplus funds without reporting them as income. Most elections end with campaigns deep in debt. In the rare circumstance where there' a surplus, the candidate usually banks it for the next election. As this story played out, the candidate and his wife were going through a vicious divorce. Somehow, she found out about the activities of the asparagus super PAC and ratted out her husband in revenge for years of alleged abuse. Stalk was indicted for elections fraud and tax violations. He paid some very hefty fines. In the end, the wife hurt herself, too, because the fines wiped out a lot of the money she might have gotten in a divorce settlement. When revenge bites you, it hurts."

"So, if the wife hadn't turned on the husband, nobody ever would have found out?"

"Likely not," he said.

37

I needed a break, so Mark and I walked up to Bacchanalia. He would have preferred going back to his condo and maybe going to dinner in Chinatown. But I would be more comfortable working in my own office in my own house, so we stayed closer. Harry, the security man at the front desk of Mark's building, said he would take Murphy for a stroll.

Bacch's was a lot quieter this night than it had been the last time we were there during the wedding rehearsal dinner. It was a beautiful evening, and all the tables outside in the sidewalk café were occupied. So, we took our usual places at the bar. I took an involuntary glance into the mirror behind the bar, but the young man with the expensive cologne wasn't there. Paula was working behind the bar alone this evening. When she came to get our drink order, I asked her if she knew the guy.

"He's young," I said. "Brown hair and eyes, a two- or three-day stubble of beard, neatly trimmed. About Mark's height. His suit looked hand-tailored, maybe in Europe. Shoes likewise. And I could swear he was wearing a light application of Clive Christian cologne. Does that ring any bells with you?"

Paula laughed lightly. "If he was wearing Clive Christian, it would have been a light application," she said. "You know what that stuff costs?"

"I do. My father used to use it on special occasions. For this guy, it sort of went with the elegance of his look. There was a lot of movement around the restaurant that night, socializing. This guy stood behind Mark and me the whole evening, and to my knowledge he never said a word to anyone."

"Doesn't ring any bells," she said. "If he was a regular I'd remember."

She went off to get our drinks. Mark was staring at me.

"What was that all about?" he asked.

I was about to answer him when we were interrupted by a member of the wait staff, Janet Andreas. She smiled and said, "Paula said you wanted to ask me a question."

I told her about the suspicious man at the reception. I had started thinking of him as the Stranger in the Mirror.

"I was working tables in the main dining room that night, but I also had the tables here in the bar," Andreas said. "I didn't smell any cologne, but when I looked around I did see a man who fits your description standing behind you and Mark. It was almost like he was trying to overhear your conversation. He had his head tilted toward you."

I asked, "Had you ever seen him before?"

"No," she replied with a grin. "And I would remember."

I smiled at her. "You're happily married, Janet."

"Nothing in our vows said I couldn't appreciate other male beauty. Hey, I gotta go. One of my orders is up."

Mark leaned in closer to me. "I repeat. What was that all about?"

I took a sip of water. I told him about the evening of the rehearsal dinner.

I replied, "I didn't mention it because I really didn't think much of it. Except that night he seemed anti-social, like he didn't belong. I wouldn't have noticed him except for the cologne."

"Don't keep this sort of thing to yourself," Mark said. "We aren't that many days removed from the Joe Pye nightmare. There are bound to be people we left behind who don't much appreciate how we dismantled their money machine."

"You think they'd come at us in Chicago?"

"Especially in Chicago. We're more exposed here."

I looked at Mark's reflection in the bar mirror.

"Oh shit," I said softly.

38

Mark insisted on spending the night, which was fine with me. But again he insisted on sleeping on the living room sofa, which was not so fine with me. But we made up for the separation with a memorable interlude in my bed upstairs before he went downstairs to intercept trouble, should any arise.

It was quiet all night.

I called Fujita the following morning.

"You know what Clive Christian cologne for men smells like?"

"What? Never heard of it. Why?"

I gave him a description of the Stranger in the Mirror. "If you see anybody who looks like that and he's wearing a light cologne, get away from him as fast as you can and keep watch over your shoulder for him. We think he might be following us, and we have no idea about his motives or intent."

"Why would he care about two people looking at election reports?"

"If I knew the answer to that I might have all the information we've been hunting for. Just stay alert. Please. And be careful."

⁓

I WAS EXHAUSTED, as was Mark, so we decided to take the day off and just chill around the house. Maybe take a nap. We ordered a pizza for dinner from Phil's in Bridgeport, which was delivered a little after six. I was putting leftovers away and cleaning up when Mark's phone rang. I couldn't overhear the conversation and didn't really try, but when he hung up, he swore.

"Dammit."

"What is it?" I asked.

"Three arson fires in Rock Island and Moline," he said. "Sounds like the same arsonist who set some fires I dealt with last year. The captain is pausing my suspension long enough for me to fly over there and brief the crew working the case. I explained why I didn't want to go over there right now, but he said it's too important. It should be a quick trip. I'll take Murphy with me so you won't be going outside to walk him."

"I understand," I said. "I'll stay locked away."

"I'll be back as quick as I can," he said and went to the bedroom to pack for the trip.

I stretched out on the sofa with a delightful book by Walter Satterthwait called *Miss Lizzie.* I was nearly done with it, and this was as good an excuse as any to finish it. So I did.

When I closed the book I had nothing else to turn to. I decided I might as well work. To do that I would have to retrieve the laptop from my SUV in the garage. I wished I'd asked Mark to get it for me before he left. I had promised to remain locked in, but I could get to the garage and back in two minutes, and I couldn't do anything without my laptop.

I opened the garage with a code on a pad by the door and ducked inside. The laptop was on the front passenger seat. I grabbed it, closed the door again, and headed back to the house, walking considerably faster than normal. The tingle on the back of my neck warned me that I should have taken Mark's suggestion to stay behind locked doors.

There was a rustle in the bushes beside me, too heavy for the light breeze on the Chicago evening. I had one of those fight-or-flight moments that froze me while I tried to figure out exactly where the noise was coming from.

"Who's there?" I demanded, trying to sound at once pissed off and unafraid. I didn't think it worked very well. "Come out and show yourself."

The voice that answered was deep, without threat, even mildly reassuring.

"Don't be frightened, Deuce," a man said. "I'm not here to hurt you. I just want to talk about the investigation you're working on. Can I come out and have a conversation with you without you turning your martial arts skills against me?"

"That request works both ways," I replied and thought I heard the man laugh.

"I don't have any martial arts skills," he said, "and in case you're wondering, I have no weapons with me, either."

I debated, but my curiosity got the best of me.

"Move slowly," I instructed, and the man did as I asked.

I suspected who he was, and his identity was confirmed when he came through my spirea hedge. The Man in the Mirror. It was only then that I got a whiff of his cologne again.

"Who are you? What do you want? Why have you been following us?"

He was nodding. "All good questions that deserve answers. Is there somewhere we can go to talk?"

There was no way I was going to let this man into my house, so I suggested we go around to the front and sit out in the open on my porch. I checked my watch. Mark wouldn't be back for another hour or so depending on how long the briefing took. I needed to keep this guy talking and away from me.

"You go ahead, around the side, and I'll follow."

I trailed him into the open front yard, which was illuminated well by a streetlight. I ran up the five steps onto the porch and stood by the swing. I pointed him to sit on the steps on the side away from me. If he made a wrong move, I could vault the porch railing and take off.

He did as I directed. I noted that instead of his European-made clothing he was wearing blue jeans, a golf shirt, and a pair of Saucony running shoes, black and gray with red trim. They looked new.

"First of all," I asked, "who are you and what do you want with me?"

"My name is Grey, spelled with an e. Let's leave it at that for now."

"Why have you been following me?"

"To talk to you about Honus Houssmann. He seems to be the focus of your work right now. I think I can help you."

"How?"

"I know him. And I know he's a violent crook. A madman. I know where he's getting his money, aside from the nursing homes, and I know how he's been spending it. I can help you put two and two together and figure it out."

"I'm listening."

"First let me tell you what a vain, violent, money-grubbing asshole he is."

I raised an eyebrow and asked, "What do you really think of him?"

"Much worse," Grey said. "Let me give you an example. Back in early 2020, when we were just learning the true horror of covid-19, Houssmann ordered as much of the first vaccine as he could for the residents and staff of his twenty-seven nursing homes, and he got them because his residents were among the most seriously threatened by the virus. Even if you add up all the patients and staff at the homes, and families of patients and staff, the number doesn't come close to the 32,000 doses he applied for and got."

"And?" I asked though I knew the answer.

"He sold all he could to the highest bidders. Took in millions. The doses left over went to patients and staff, but by then there weren't nearly enough doses to go around. I'm not sure what algorithm he used to decide who got the leftovers, but the supply was well short of what was needed. He treated the second vaccine the same way. By the time the boosters came along, the supply was plentiful, and nobody had to pay a fortune for them."

"No one had to pay a fortune for them, anyway," I noted. "Medicare paid the bills."

"That's why his take from the first vaccine was so huge. He got the doses for nothing and sold them for a fortune. As for Medicare, that was fine if you were 65 or older. But not everyone who wanted or needed the vaccine was that age. Even the older people wanted doses for younger family members and were prepared to pay. It played right into his criminal conspiracy."

"You know all of this how?" I asked. "Were you—are you—a member of his staff, or did you have relatives in one of his homes who didn't get the vaccine?"

"Neither," Grey said. "My name is Grey Houssmann. I'm the motherfucker's son."

39

I had almost been able to wrap my mind around Grey's extraordinary confession of family cruelty and greed when Mark returned, actually sooner than I expected. He was as surprised as I was to find me sitting on the front porch with a total stranger.

I introduced Mark to Grey, using only Grey's first name as the young man had done with me. I didn't want Mark to form any opinions about the Houssmann family until he heard Grey's story.

Mark asked me, "What happened to your promise to stay inside with the doors locked? And who's this guy? I don't recall ever seeing him before."

"You haven't seen him before," I said. "And I'd only gotten a glimpse. But he's wearing some of his very expensive cologne."

Mark's expression hardened, and he glared at Grey. "So, what the hell is going on with you? You get some kinda kick terrorizing people?"

Grey started to protest, but Mark held up a hand. "Why don't you two bring me up to date? I'll accept CliffsNotes. For now."

We went through it again. Grey's presentation sounded spontaneous rather than a recitation he learned to intrigue us.

Mark didn't interrupt him, but when Houssmann got to the disclosure of his parentage, Mark looked as shocked as I had felt.

He asked, "So why are you ratting out your father?"

"Because his reign of terror has to stop," Grey answered.

"Reign of terror?" I asked. "Why do you describe it that way?"

Grey shook his head. "I can't tell you that."

"Then how are we supposed to evaluate your story?"

"You might try listening to the rest of it," he suggested with a note of sarcasm and what might have passed for a knowing smirk. It was as if he knew the additional information would be even more shocking than what we'd already heard.

"So, your father's a creep," Mark said when Houssmann finished his story again. "The info might get him dragged into a federal court, but that wouldn't help get to the bottom of the issues Deuce is looking at."

Grey nodded. "That's why I've been following you, trying to catch onto what you're looking for. Election stuff, right?"

I asked, "Do you know anything about elections stuff?"

"Yes, some," Grey said. "I was part of what was goin' on. But I don't know all of it."

"How do you know as much as you do?"

"I'm the vice president of my father's company, Houssmann Health. He's grooming me to take over when he retires. Every couple of months he moves me from one assignment to another to learn about all aspects of the business. A few times I heard people talking about donating millions to this one super Pac based in D.C called Future America Fund. I couldn't figure out why they were all donating to the same PAC."

I asked, "Did you find out?"

"Not right then. Oh, I was curious, so I went online and looked it up. It seemed legit, registered with the Federal Elections Commission. But details of the PAC's incoming contributions and outgoing payments aren't disclosed, so I couldn't find out who or where the money came from or where it went. I let it slide until one day I was sitting just outside the company's board room before a meeting. I heard two guys bitching about my father pressuring them to make the donations. They were talking real low so nobody could hear. I guess they didn't notice I was sitting behind a boardroom door."

"Do you know who they were?" I asked.

"One of them. I didn't recognize the other voice." Grey shook his head. "What caught my attention was their claim my father pressured them to donate to that PAC. Something told me that wasn't legal. But my father's into so much illegal shit that it didn't surprise me. One of them was worried about the legality of the contributions. The other one, the one whose voice I didn't recognize, was brushing it off. He said, 'What're you worried about? The contributions aren't public, so they can't come back to you. And the PAC's channeling all the money back to Bill Latchey, which is good for business in Illinois. Besides, it ain't your money. Honus is reimbursing you. So if Latchey loses, you're not out a dime.'"

"As election illegalities go," I said, "that's a twofer."

"Honus pulled the same stunts in both the 2018 and 2022 elections," Grey said.

I asked, "You have any idea how much money changed hands?"

"Maybe a week later I went to the board member whose voice I recognized and talked to him about it. He's a politician, so he'd know what's illegal. He confirmed my suspicions. I took the whole thing to somebody else I knew, and he's the one who practically ordered me to come to you."

"Who was it?" I asked.

"I can't tell you that," the young man said.

"Why?

"I gave my word. Unlike my father, that means something to me."

I thought about all this for a moment, then asked Houssmann the million-dollar question. "There had to be a *quid pro quo*. What did your father expect from Latchey in return for all that money? It had to be some really big favor."

"I can't answer those questions."

"Can't or won't," I asked.

"A little of each," Houssmann replied. "And I don't want to speculate. I've given you enough leads to pursue. Now it's up to you."

40

———————

After Houssmann left, Mark and I moved inside and sat on the sofa, just looking at one another, at a loss to put any perspective on what we'd heard. Each of us was waiting for the other to speak, to offer some reaction to Houssmann's story and some thoughts about acting on his accusations. The information—if indeed it was information and not a string of lies concocted to create trouble for the father he despised—we would have to proceed with care. Neither of us could afford to wind up in a libel suit against a man who can drop millions of dollars on political campaigns without batting an eye.

"I think we've been going at this bassackwards," I said. "We've been chasing our tails looking at campaign records for anything out of the ordinary instead of having a clear objective. We should be looking at money flowing down the pipeline from the national PAC to Latchey's campaign committee."

"That's not public information," Mark reminded me.

"Right. So, what if we started with Latchey's campaign committee and worked our way back? If the committee reported those contributions accurately, there are a lot of large contributions from the state GOP. If the state party accurately reported large sums of money rolling in from the national party, and the national party reported sizeable contributions from the national super PAC, we'd be way ahead of where we are now. We could, for the sake of discussion, know that a national super PAC had contributed large sums to a state race when its normal support would go to candidates for federal offices."

"And how would you do that?"

"First, I need Josh to search all of Latchey's campaign reports for unusually large donations from the Illinois Republican party. Political money flows downstream. If Latchey's campaign committee got millions from the state GOP, which got the same sizeable donations from the national GOP, and the national GOP from the Future America Fund, then there is reason to think the FAF took in enormous amounts earmarked right out of the gate for Latchey. It would be reasonable to assume the funds were passed down the line penny for penny.

"It's still not illegal," Mark said.

"No, not yet. And it's speculation anyway. But if Houssmann was reimbursing people who donated their own money or giving them the funds to donate, that certainly would be unethical. If the donations were coerced then, yes, that is probably illegal, and probably enough to prompt a federal investigation of possible election improprieties. And we still don't have evidence of a *quid pro quo*. What, if anything, did Latchey do for Houssmann? That would be illegal, too."

I added, "Then, of course, there's the child trafficking. It doesn't get any more illegal and inhumane than that."

Mark offered his help, but I told him he should stay out of it from here on.

"If this backfires you should be out of the way so you can testify to what you know, if necessary. Josh and I are covered by the *Journal's* insurance if things go south. You aren't. That should concern you."

"I'm more concerned about your safety."

"I appreciate that, honey, I really do. I'm never going back to Joe Pye County, and I have to think I'll be safe in Chicago."

"Really? What on earth gives you that idea? I'll give you a safer alternative. Come back to the condo until this is over. Or longer. You know the kind of security my condo has. And I can notify the chief of security what to watch for. It will be a lot safer than your house. Look how easily this Grey guy slipped onto your property."

Mark sighed in thought. "You know, I think there's a whole lot more to Drigger than we know about. Do you have any idea why he was living in Joe Pye, I mean why he went there in the first place to live in that squalor? I'm not buying the idea that he was a hermit living on fish and squirrels and whatever plant life he could forage in the forest."

"I didn't, either. So much of the rest that he told me were lies."

"Did you call him out on that?"

"I considered it, but I was injured, and he was taking care of me and protecting me from Sparks. I didn't want to become *persona non grata.*"

"Boy, you weren't Drigger's only secret."

"No, but none of that matters any more. Now the only thing I need to know from him is why he wouldn't tell me the whole story about Spark's criminal activities."

"Ask him."

I sighed and looked out the living room window, staring at nothing in particular. "His handlers, supervisors, whatever you want to call them, won't permit me to get even close. They let me check in with him once to see how he was doing, but they have turned down every one of my requests to visit him again. Jerry Alvarez even intervened on my behalf. Drigger himself sent word that I should stay away. I don't know why. Drigger's a big boy and can make his own decisions. If there's something he shouldn't be discussing with me, he could tell me that, and I'd back off."

"Maybe his supervisors, even Drigger himself, don't buy that. You don't exactly have a reputation as a quitter."

41

———

I wanted to talk to Grey Houssmann again. I needed him to tell me the name of the person he had heard raising doubts about the campaign contributions coerced by his father. In a courtroom the testimony of Houssmann, the younger, would be dismissed as hearsay, something he overheard but couldn't vouch for. The man I wanted had been involved himself. He would be a primary witness.

I checked the internet and found Grey Houssmann listed as a vice president of Houssmann Health, and I found an address for the home office of the corporation, which I already knew was in Evanston. But where in Evanston? I searched for the company, Houssmann Health, and found it quickly on Linden Avenue less than two blocks from the CTA Purple Line. The Purple Line was the Chicago Transit Authority's shortest and northern-most section of the city's train routes, running from Wilmette through Evanston to Skokie, all stops north of the city. During rush hours, the train came all the way south to The Loop. I decided it would be prudent drive to drive and not have to worry about the Purple Line's hours of operation.

Interstate 94 was almost always a massive traffic jam waiting to infuriate commuters. I left Mark's condo at 1 p.m. to get to Evanston before the evening rush northward began to build. Returning would be easier because I'd be going south, against most of the evening traffic.

The headquarters of Houssmann Health was an unimposing three-story building that had an older look about it, as if it had once been some sort of warehouse that had been gutted and turned into office space. There was a lot of that sort of repurposing of old warehouse space in the region. The brick was red, the roof flat, and streaks of white stain ran down the outside walls, caused by rainwater seeping from the mortar between the bricks. An average-looking sign stood out front read, "H.H Health," and in smaller letters, "Parking in Rear."

I drove around to the back, which looked more like it should have been the front. It had been spruced up with nice landscaping, modern automated doors at the entrance, and more windows beside the doors that gave visitors a good view of the lobby. It looked quite nice without being extravagant, a place of business that made a good impression without looking like a company that spent lavishly on its corporate ego.

I parked and got out of my car, took a deep breath and walked toward the entry. This was not going to be easy.

I told the uniformed guard at the front desk I needed to meet with Grey Houssmann. The guard said Houssmann had just returned from an off-site meeting and might not have gotten back to his office yet.

"Do you have an appointment?" he asked. I judged him to be in his fifties, not very tall, a bit out of shape, with rimless spectacles and a graying hairline that seemed to be racing backward. He was slightly tanned.

"No, but he'll know who I am if you tell him it's a woman here to talk about political contributions. We've spoken before."

"Why don't you just tell me your name?"

"Why don't you just ring him up and tell him I'm here."

Apparently he wasn't. I heard his phone ringing, but nobody picked up.

The guard shook his head. "Let me call his secretary," he said.

He pushed a button on his phone console that prevented me from listening in to whatever conversation I might want to hear. Downright unneighborly. I heard a voice at the other end of the phone say, "Yes, Jacob?" And then nothing.

The two of them had a brief conversation, and that was the end of it.

Jacob regarded me with suspicion.

"Mr. Houssmann has just returned to his office. His secretary will ask if he wants to see you and let me know. Why don't you have a seat, meanwhile."

I figured they planned to wait me out until I got tired of sitting and left. I was wrong. The receptionist's console buzzed lightly, and Jacob picked up. There was a silence of a few seconds. Then Jacob nodded.

"She's quite tall, at least six feet, reddish brown hair, green eyes, about thirty or so," he said. Apparently the secretary asked what I looked like. I liked that Jacob thought I might be thirty. It was the "or so" that would lead me to a long look in a mirror when I got home.

Jacob put the phone down and looked at me with curious eyes. He said, "Mr. Houssmann says he hasn't time to talk to you now, but he will meet you later where the two of you met the first time." Jacob's look and tone of voice made me think he believed Grey and I were in a relationship.

I agreed, despite the fact that the first time we talked was on the front porch of my house, and now I was bunking with Mark. I didn't see any reason why I couldn't return to my house for just one evening and rock on the front porch until Houssmann showed up. Mark would insist on being there.

I called Fujita and told him, too. It would be nice to have him there to cover the campaign contribution discussions, if there were any. Josh said he would bring copies of what he'd been working on so I could review them.

"Be careful when you pull into my street, Josh," I told him. "City's doing some work at the corner of South Oakley, and it's pretty muddy and slippery." Fujita assured me he would proceed with caution.

The three of us assembled on the porch at six. I didn't know when to expect Houssmann, or whether he might change his mind. If he wanted to wait for the cover of darkness, it might be nine-thirty or ten before he arrived.

When we were assembled on the porch Fujita handed me a thick manila envelope with copies of everything he'd found about donations made to Latchey's four campaigns, two primaries and two generals. I took them in order and scanned the names of contributors. Some names were familiar: a few city officials, business people, professionals like doctors and lawyers, and Republican activists. Nothing that struck me as unusual.

"Anything jump out at you, Josh?" I asked.

Fujita ran his hands through his lush head of hair. "Honus Houssmann contributed $50,000 directly to the Latchey campaigns. Same amount each time. Grey Houssmann gave $25,000 each cycle. I recognized other names, but none that jumped out as suspicious. A lot of Republican political operatives you'd expect to find. That doesn't mean they all couldn't have made much larger contributions under cover of the Future America Fund. There are quite a few names I don't know. I thought maybe you would."

I started with the 2018 campaign and got through all of them in less than an hour. A lot of money passed hands, especially after the contribution cap was busted. The only thing that piqued my interest was the father's donation. Given his financial stature in the region, I would have expected him to have dropped even more money in the pot.

Of course, he might have given a whole lot more through the Future America Fund, the campaigns' anonymous back door.

Then one name caught my attention. Aidan Coughlin. Coughlin had been the regional administrator in Cook County for the Illinois Department of Children and Family Services. He had committed suicide by overdosing on Xanax and vodka after being exposed as the facilitator for a horrendous sex ring. It was too gentle an ending, I thought, for someone who trafficked in young boys kidnapped in the Chicago area and rented out to people who liked to abuse kids mentally and physically. The abuse included whipping and using bamboo canes to thrash boys. Coughlin grew the bamboo in a garden in his yard.

There was nothing illegal about Coughlin's contribution. It was only $5,000. But just the memory of the man made me want to stand up and scream at a world that looked the other way while helpless children were being abused.

"Josh," I said, "check the records for the 2022 campaigns and see if Aidan Coughlin's name shows up while I finish looking through the 2018 group."

My discovery didn't get past Mark.

"Aiden Coughlin?" he asked. "Wasn't he . . .?"

"Yes," I replied a bit curtly.

"Here he is," Josh said. "He gave $5,000 in the primary and $20,000 in the general. Why do you ask about him?"

"Because when he made those two donations he was dead and buried."

42

———————

"This is all so fucking illegal," Fujita said as if he'd just discovered a bag of counterfeit twenty-dollar bills in the passenger seat of his car.

"All of it?" Mark asked.

Fujita explained. "Chicago has an unenviable reputation for allowing dead people to vote. It seems to come up every time Republicans think they can derail a Dem candidate by accusing their campaigns of raiding cemeteries. But while I've heard of the city's voting dead, I've never seen evidence to support the allegations. Until now."

"So, what do you conclude from this?"

Fujita had just started to answer when a voice came up from the sidewalk. "That you're beginning to crack open this egg of conspiracy."

It was Grey Houssmann.

I introduced Houssmann and Fujita and asked Houssmann, "Does the name Aidan Coughlin mean anything to you?"

Houssmann snorted and sat down on the front steps.

"I met him a few times."

"Did your father know him?"

"My father knew him very well."

I put a hand over my eyes. I was entering a world I had hoped never to see again. Without taking my hand away, I asked Houssmann, "How? How did he and your father know each other?"

"I don't know how they met, but when I first met Coughlin, he and my father had become fishing buddies. One of their trips was down to Joe Pye County with Coughlin's fishing boat to spend a few days on the water. While they were there, they met Derek Sparks, the sheriff. Well, at least that's when my father met him. Coughlin had known Sparks for years. From the way my father described Sparks, he was a sadistic, ruthless man. I think there were a lot of people in southern Illinois scared to death of him."

"I can attest to that," I said.

"Since my father already knew Coughlin, he knew that anyone Coughlin associated with was probably unsavory. My father, also unsavory, pressed Coughlin until Coughlin told him how Sparks was trying to grow a drug business in the basement of the house that served as the sheriff's headquarters. Weed at first. When it was legalized, he branched out into meth. But he was having trouble getting his hands on enough money for construction, maintenance, and hiring staff to run the operation without blowing up the whole forest."

I said, "And your father, already a wealthy man, offered to finance the operation for a healthy return on his investment?"

"That's about right."

Mark asked, "I'm not sure I know how Coughlin fit in to the operation?"

"Distribution," Grey said. "Before he killed himself he was the regional administrator of Cook County for the state Department of Children and Family Services. You know that, Deuce. And he knew where the biggest drug markets were and who was eager to make a pile of money, legal or not. He had broad access to street gangs that would buy as much junk as they could lay their hands on for resale to addicts all over the city."

I said, "But there was more, wasn't there?"

"Lots more," Grey responded.

I ventured a guess. "Sparks needed money, more than your father had committed, to set up his operation to take fullest advantage of his new careers in agriculture and chemistry. He envisioned himself flooding the region with product. But he needed mules to make the drops and reliable street people to handles sales and distribution and cash."

"Right again," Grey acknowledged.

"And that's where your father came in again?"

"Correct. Coughlin suggested to my father that he might want a bigger piece of the action in return for a larger percentage of the take."

"And your father did. For how much?"

"To start, $100,000. To dear old dad that was pocket change. I think the financing kept going up, but so did my father's share of the profits. He made back his initial investment in two months. The business flourished. Eventually Sparks began a new production line outside the village of East Cape Girardeau, a tiny town of strip clubs, gas stations, and a population of fewer than three hundred. The per capita income was under $18,000 a year and a third of the residents fell under the poverty line. There were lots of people who needed a way to earn good, tax-free money in return for their silence. The village is on the Illinois side of the Mississippi River, just a bridge away from Missouri and its considerable appetite for drugs. Anybody with a pickup truck could cross the bridge delivering the goods and bringing back the cash."

"Indiana?" I asked. "Kentucky?"

"Both easily accessible from southern Illinois," Grey said. "There were plans to build another facility near Riverville, another economically depressed little town down on the Ohio River at the southern tip of the state. It had easy access to Kentucky and Indiana. But last summer's river flooding got real close to the site they were looking at, so they put that facility on hold. Instead, they planned to enlarge the Joe Pye operation to serve a three-state distribution system, leaving East Cape Girardeau to take care of Missouri."

Grey stood up and stretched. The steps weren't the most comfortable seats on the porch. "Since you and Drigger and Mark wiped out the Joe Pye facility, my father has continued running East Cape Girardeau while he figures out what to do with it. He's already made so much money in the six years of funding Joe Pye that he has to assess whether continuing the remaining site is too risky to justify the profits. A lot of people suspected Joe Pye was a drug factory, and now that it's been leveled they know it for sure. My father was never implicated, but if he rebuilt Joe Pye he would get some serious scrutiny. He might just leave well enough alone and close down the rest of it, too."

"By the rest of it," I asked, "do you mean the drugs *and* the trafficking?"

"I don't know for sure how big the trafficking part still is," Grey said. "When you and Mark wiped out the Saudis, you probably thought you were done with the whole damned mess. You weren't. The locations changed, but the trafficking continues."

"Who's running it?" I asked in a voice barely above a whisper.

"My father tried to run it for a while. But it was too much and too dangerous. I honestly don't know who his accomplices are now."

"Did Sparks ever handle it?"

"No. Sparks wasn't involved with the trafficking and didn't want to be, but he knew about it. My father was planning to kill him for fear he'd rat everybody out."

I asked, "So where did the Saudis fit in?"

Grey sighed deeply. "They were in it as clients with a ton of cash. My father always owned and ran the ring."

We fell silent as a group, each trying to think through the ramifications of what we'd heard. I found it nearly impossible to fathom.

"How old are you, Grey?" I finally asked.

"Twenty-three."

"So, when all this was going down, you were barely out of college, right?"

"I never went to college. I hope to someday."

"You were never a part of the trafficking?"

"Oh, yeah. I was, but not the way you're thinking."

"So, your father told you?

"No." Grey let his head fall and scrubbed his hands through his thick hair. I thought I heard his voice crack. "My father didn't tell me anything. He showed me. On my eleventh birthday he turned me over to the ring. I was passed around and sold to the highest bidder for the next seven years. I wasn't an accomplice. I was a victim."

43

———

The three of us sat silent for what seemed a very long time, stunned into silence. Grey was trying without success to control his emotions. He moved his hands down to cover his face and sobbed gently while the three of us tried to get our heads around a father who could so cruelly treat his own innocent child as chattel. It was a moment of shared grief for this man whose innocence and trust had been so grossly abused. Out of respect for Grey, we mourned silently with him. It was one of the saddest most gut-wrenching moments I could recall ever experiencing.

For maybe ten minutes we remained still in a tableau of tragedy. Then Grey spoke softly, his voice shaky, his head congested.

"I'm sorry," he said. "I've been out of that life for five years. I've been in therapy I paid for myself. You'd think I'd be past it all by now."

"Damn, dude," Mark said as he moved to set on the steps with Grey. Mark sat down beside the young man on the steps. He made no effort to touch him in any way, but they sat close, and their arms brushed. Houssmann flinched. Mark would say later it felt like his skin was burning. He handed Grey a handkerchief.

"You must have been told this before," Mark said. "Friends. Your therapist. They must have tried to assure you that none of this was your fault. I know that's easier said than accepted, but your acknowledgment that you were victimized by your own father should be a step toward reconciliation for yourself. As for getting over it, I'm not sure that's ever possible. Not for you or for anyone who's gone through this. It's a problem to take up with your therapist."

"I have," Grey said, "though without implicating my father." He didn't elaborate, and none of us pressed him.

I asked, "Do you want some water, Grey?" He shook his head.

So, I asked, "How did you escape from the horror?"

"On my eighteenth birthday I told my father I wanted out of the ring. He told me I might as well leave since nobody wanted a relationship—that's what he called it, a relationship—with an adult." The young man sighed. "He called his lapdog banker while I was sitting right there in his office and opened a trust account for me with the banker as the trustee. It was for $250 million."

"Million?" Fujita asked.

"Yeah. It was a bribe to keep quiet. Any transgression would result in the immediate and permanent revocation of the trust. My father told me it would help me put together a worthwhile life as I got older if I invested the money wisely. If I learned the business, going from office to office, changing every couple of months, I would be prepared to take over the company when the old man retired, or died. He has no one else to leave it to. I guess he could sell it, but he certainly doesn't need the money, and he wants the Houssmann name to continue. The lesson I learned during seven years of abuse was not to argue with my father when he wanted something. It was just easier and safer to go along."

I said, "It might be an easier sell if he ended the trafficking activity."

"He's scaled it back. Not that the market's dying, but when Aidan Coughlin offed himself, my father lost his shoehorn into that world. He didn't have anybody left with access to children as a sexual commodity. I think he got scared that the law was going to close in on him. My father had no idea what evidence or documents or confessions Coughlin had stashed away to use as blackmail or for his own protection if the need arose. My father told me just recently that he's only begun to breathe easy now that nothing has happened to implicate him, and Coughlin's estate has been settled."

We all fell silent again for a few moments while Grey used Mark's handkerchief and did some deep breathing to calm himself. I asked him the question I had wanted ask since I first met the young man.

"What can you tell me about the governor? Latchey?"

"Nothing, because I don't know anything."

"Was your father bribing him? Or blackmailing him?"

"Why would he?"

"To keep him from sending in the National Guard to bust up Joe Pye or asking the feds to come in and handle it."

Grey heaved a deep sign and shook his head. "If that was a loop, I wasn't in it. They knew one another. My father contributed a ton of money to Latchey's campaigns. So did I, for that matter. But the rest of the story, if there is any more, is a mystery to me."

I stood up and began to pace little circles around the porch.

"Is this why you sought me out? Do you think I'm a resource for you, someone who can expose your father's sins and see that he pays for them—in full?"

He turned and looked me straight in the eyes. "Yes, it is. I might have let it go—old history and all that—but lately my father's been talking about rebuilding the trafficking business. He feels enough time has elapsed to give him confidence that no one is onto him. He's found somebody new, somebody he trusts to run that end of things for him. So why not grow it again?"

I thought I knew the answer, but I had to ask. "Who's the new guy?"

Without hesitation Grey replied, "Me."

~

We talked for another twenty minutes or so about Grey's situation and why the young man had turned to me for help.

"Why not just go to the authorities?" I asked.

"My father is the authorities," he said. "He owns most everybody with the power to do something, and those he doesn't own know what a rat bastard he is and would just as soon not cross his path. If you guys hadn't-a killed Sparks, my father would have. Like I told you, he was planning Sparks's exit, anyway. I think he was disappointed that you got to him first. I'm sure Sparks would-a much rather died in a hail of gunfire than by whatever method my father had planned for him."

My thoughts went back to Black Marsh, and I pushed them away.

Mark asked, "If your father knows you're talking to us, would he take his vengeance out on you? And maybe on us, if he really wanted to bury what we know?"

"He might want to," Houssmann said. "But I don't know that he'd take the chance. Too many people are aware that you were being hunted in Joe Pye. My father said he was worried that Sparks would murder you and bring down the wrath of God on everyone in the operation. He said criminals never get away with two things: killing a cop or a reporter. He really worried about it. So, his fear might keep you safe."

"How about you?" I asked.

"I should be okay. The old man needs me, and he knows that during the seven years I was out on his slavery circuit I learned to take care of myself. I haven't forgotten."

He stood. "I gotta go. I'm supposed to have a phone conference with my father at ten. If I'm late, it could raise his suspicions."

We watched Grey walk east, toward Oakley Avenue.

Fujita, sounding as shaky as we all felt, asked me, "So you go back to the newsroom on Monday? You feel good about it?"

I nodded. I'd been thinking about it a lot. I felt certain my editor had heard about what I'd been doing during suspension. My return wouldn't be pleasant.

Grey had almost made the intersection when we heard the roar of a big engine, squealing tires, a scream cut short, then a loud thump. The tires squealed again, and the big engine roared away.

None of us doubted what happened.

44

The three of us raced off the porch, nearly knocking each other to the ground, and ran the half block to the intersection. People had come out of homes and restaurants to see what happened. I slipped in the mud left from the day's construction work but caught myself on Mark's arm. He stopped short, staring straight ahead.

"Oh, no," he said.

I looked where he was looking. Grey Houssmann's body lay in the street a few feet off the curb. It looked like someone had taken a tire iron to the right side of his head, and his back was caved in with muddy tire tracks running across his clothes.

I pulled out my phone and started taking close-up photographs.

"What are you doing?" Fujita asked. He still sounded shell-shocked.

I kept working and replied," The police are going to need images of these tire tracks to figure out what make and model of vehicle ran over him. The tracks are wet mud. When they dry they won't be as definitive."

"This is sick," Fujita said. Then he turned and walked back a few steps and retched.

Mark had walked closer to the body and felt for a pulse in the neck. He backed away, shaking his head.

"There's very little blood considering the head wound," he said.

"So, he died immediately?"

Mark nodded.

"What kind of psychopath does this to his own son?"

Mark answered as if I'd annoyed him. "Before you jump to that conclusion, Deuce, you might want to wait for some evidence. The father's a legitimate suspect, but that's all."

"I know that," I said, and I thought I sounded snappish.

Mark didn't answer. He looked angry.

The police and paramedics arrived at almost the same time. The lead EMT knew Mark from the job. Both had worked out of the same station before Mark became an arson investigator for the state.

"You a witness?" the EMT asked.

"Only peripherally," Mark replied. "The three of us were sitting on a porch about half a block down and heard the accident."

"Well, we'll wait here for the cops. When they're done and the ME has pronounced, we'll load up the vic, and he'll be off to the morgue. The only question, I guess, is whether the blow to the head killed him or the big set of tires that ran over him."

The EMT looked back to Grey Houssmann's body and asked over his shoulder, "You know him? His name?"

"Grey Houssmann," I replied and spelled it for him.

"Well, that's a start. The detectives will have lots of questions, so don't go far. They're having a busy night. I don't know when they'll get here. Shouldn't be too long."

When the EMT returned to Grey's body, two beat cops replaced him on the street in front of us.

"We need to get preliminary statements from all youz," one of them said with an accent I couldn't place as Chicago or New York. "How 'bout ladies first?"

I said, "I thought we were waiting for detectives."

"They'll be along," the cop said. "We're just doing the preliminaries. We need your names and some form of ID."

We all reached for our wallets and handed over drivers' licenses. The second cop jotted down the information and returned the plastic cards.

"What was the three-a youz doin' here?" he asked.

"As you can see from my license, I live here," I said. "I own that house with the porch light on. Mr. Houssmann came here to talk to me. Josh was there for a beer I owed him to cover a lost bet. Mark just happened to be here. He's my fiancé. He's here a lot. They had nothing to do with Mr. Houssmann being at my house. The man had come to speak to me."

"About what?"

"I'm a columnist for the *Chicago Journal* and wanted to talk to him about a story I'm going to be working on next week."

"The story involve him?"

"That's one of the things I wanted to find out."

"And did you?"

"That's not something I can discuss unless my editor and the paper's lawyer are present. I'll take it up with them when I go back to work next week."

"Do you have any idea who might have wanted him dead?"

"No, again. For all I know this was just a tragic accident. And why are you asking? Isn't that a job for the detectives?"

"They'll ask you the same questions, and more," the cop said.

"Can we go back to the house now?" I asked.

"Are you going to be there tonight?"

Mark jumped in. "I'm taking Deuce back to my condo tonight. You've got our phone numbers if the detectives need more."

"And I've got to get home," Fujita added. He glanced down at Grey's body. "I need a few more beers. I won't be getting much sleep tonight."

Fujita walked straight to his car, a police officer following. He was allowed to leave after his tire treads had been photographed. Mark's big, red, arson investigations truck was more interesting to the authorities. Big vehicle. Big tires. But there was no physical damage to it and no blood on it that anyone could find. Still, the vehicle was impounded for testing.

"That's a state vehicle," Mark said in protest.

"Yeah, but we still need to take it for a day or so," the cop said. "If it's clean, you'll get it back. Where's your car, Ms. Mora?"

"In my garage. It's been there since this afternoon."

The police insisted on seeing it. The engine block was cold, evidence the vehicle hadn't been driven for several hours. They left it alone.

When we got back to the accident, Dr. Anthony Donato was there. He was the Cook County medical examiner and was just finishing up with Grey Houssmann's body. It had been bagged and loaded for transport to Donato's morgue.

Donato wandered over.

"You involved in this?" he asked.

"Only as witnesses," I said.

He nodded. "Trouble seems to follow you, kiddo."

"Can you tell me anything about this? I took photos of the muddy tire tracks on his back, if you want them. If they'll be any help."

"I took some myself. Yours are probably fresher. Hold onto them for the detectives."

The drive to Mark's condo wasn't long, but it was particularly difficult. Mark didn't say two words, just sat in the passenger seat staring straight ahead. I tried to make conversation and was met by silence.

Finally, I asked, "You angry with me about something?"

"It'll wait until we get home."

And that was it. As hard as I tried to pull details from him, I got nothing.

When we walked through his front door I remarked, "I could use a drink."

"Wine or Scotch?" he asked.

"Scotch. Not too many rocks."

When we had our drinks we sat down in the living room. Mark didn't sit next to me on the sofa, as he usually did when we were having a pleasant moment overlooking the vast beauty of the Chicago skyline and Lake Michigan. I had the big sofa to myself while he sat in a nearby swivel chair.

I waited for him to start.

"How the hell much longer is this going to continue?" he asked. "You gonna keep pokin' around in stuff like this until one or both of us is dead?"

"Excuse me?" I snapped, suddenly angry.

"How many dead bodies have there been since we met while you were working on the Vinnie Colangelo story? A dozen? Two dozen? If you count the Saudis who got tossed out of an airplane, maybe three dozen. How many times have you wound up in a hospital? How many concussions have you had?"

"What's your point, Mark?"

"I don't think I can continue this way, Deuce. I love you, and that's part of the problem. What should be a really happy time in our lives we spend too much time running for our lives. Unless we're together with my gun close at hand, I can't sleep at night. I lie awake wondering who's breaking into your house, who's creeping up on you when you're out, who's planning to firebomb your house with you inside, who's targeting you with a sniper's rifle. I don't know how much longer I can do this."

I couldn't deny that he was right, but I wasn't ready to admit it.

"So, what are you asking me to do? Quit the news business?"

"That's up to you," he said. "But if you still want to get married and have a child or two, it's not going to happen unless you make some changes. What those changes should be is your choice. Stay at the paper and change jobs. Leave the *Journal* and teach. You'd have lots of choices of schools. The University of Chicago, DePaul, Northwestern. You've got your master's degree. If you work on your Ph.D while you're teaching, you should get tenure pretty quickly. Given your accomplishments and your Pulitzer Prize, you could have schools fighting to bring you aboard. But I can't stand looking at any more dead bodies, especially if one of them is likely to be yours."

"I'm not cut out to be a teacher."

"How do you know until you try?"

"Kids aren't dedicated like they used to be. They're in college to get through it and go off and get rich. They don't take studying seriously. I couldn't deal with that."

"You could learn to. Give it a chance."

I didn't want to get angrier or emotional, so I took a big sip of my drink, coughed once, and continued staring out the big glass windows toward the giant, fully lighted Ferris wheel turning slowly up at the Navy Pier. I wasn't sanguine about the dangers I'd endured in the last few years, the threats, the actual physical attacks. I didn't want to go through any more of that, either. But changing jobs at the paper or becoming a college professor didn't appeal to me. The only things that did were marrying Mark and having a child.

"Is this an ultimatum?" I asked.

"It's not a decision you have to make tonight. But you need to start thinking about it. You're not getting any younger, Deuce. But I desperately want us, you and me, to grow old together. For that to happen requires that both of us stay alive."

"This is an ultimatum then. Right? My work or you and a family?"

"I've been thinking about this for a long time," he said bitterly. "I don't want to call it an ultimatum, but yeah. It probably is."

45

———————

Once again Mark and I spent the night under the same roof but not in the same bed. He told me to take the bedroom, and he would sleep on the sofa. I objected.

"You should have your own room, Mark," I said. "The sofa is big and comfortable, and I'll be perfectly happy there except that it won't be with you."

"There's a reason I want the sofa," he said. "My gun will be closer to the front door, just in case."

As it turned out, it was a quiet night, but I slept very little, and Mark said the next morning he hadn't slept at all. Fending off intruders didn't keep him awake, he said. The possible end of our relationship did.

Both of us were grumpy at breakfast.

"Let's not do this," he asked me. "What we're dealing with right now in terms of our relationship is difficult enough. We don't need to add snappish conversation and make it harder. I want you to know I'll respect whatever choice you make, and I won't ever stop loving you."

As hard as it was dealing with Mark's ultimatum, I had little doubt I was going to go through a similar confrontation with Eric Ryland when I met with him this morning. It would be my first day back at work. In fact, it wouldn't shock me if he fired me—Lord knows he had sufficient reason. But if he did, at least it would make the choice for me. I couldn't say that a life as a college professor with Mark as my husband and a couple of kids running around was totally unappealing. At least Mark wasn't insisting on a decision right away. I hoped Ryland would allow me to wrap up the Houssmann story before I started going door-to-door looking for work. That wouldn't extricate me from danger, but it wouldn't be as painful as my week in Joe Pye County. And I wouldn't want it to be. That sort of danger is exhilarating, but it ain't fun.

RYLAND WAS WAITING in his office when I re-entered the newsroom for the first time in four weeks. I didn't even drop off my stuff at my desk. That way I wouldn't have to go by my desk to get them if I got canned.

I stopped at his secretary's desk but said nothing. She said very little, but her face told me of her disapproval.

"Go on in," she said. "He's waiting for you."

I'll bet, I thought.

"Welcome back, Deuce," he said in a neutral tone. "Close the door and sit down."

We were starting out on more pleasant terms than I had anticipated. My gut told me it would heat up pretty quickly. And it did.

Ryland began, "It probably wouldn't come as a great surprise if I fired you right now for a whole litany of transgressions. You got yourself into a highly dangerous situation without fully disclosing your intentions to me, without ever checking in. Then there are the matters of insubordination, exposing yourself and the newspaper to all manner of lawsuits, dereliction of duty. Should I go on? Or should I show you the door now?"

I held Ryland's gaze for a few beats, then took a deep breath to steady myself.

"Let's address your issues one at a time. How am I guilty of insubordination?"

"You flew down to Joe Pye after I expressly asked you to wait until someone could go with you. But you went anyway, by yourself."

"It never occurred to me that it would be a problem."

"Why didn't you ever check in? We didn't even know if you survived the crash."

"I was unconscious when a fellow called Drigger reached the plane. The pilot was dead. My leg was banged up, but it wasn't serious. He pulled me out and put me in his pickup truck. He said my phone slipped out of my pocket and fell into the muck of the swamp. There was very little reason to search for it. The prospect of success was near zero, and the phone had probably been ruined. Drigger knew I was in danger. The sheriff of Joe Pye and his merry band of misfits and outlaws would be looking for me, or my body. Getting the phone back didn't seem as important to him as getting me out of sight."

"Then why didn't he drive you to the nearest hospital in another county?"

I went through it all with Ryland. It took most of an hour to relate all of Joe Pye's grim details. When he heard about the punishment meted out at the Black Swamp he went pale. I thought for a moment he would be sick. There was a lot of that going around.

For every point he tried to make, I had an answer. The only place where he scored points was my disregard for my promise to him several months earlier to quit going off alone into dangerous situations.

"Your brother's a lawyer," he said. "It's conceivable he would file a lawsuit charging the *Journal* with reckless endangerment and who knows what else. A legal judgment could cost the paper a fortune we don't have."

"I'll accept that, but I seriously doubt Gary would do it. It's not like him. He's the least litigious lawyer I've ever known. Besides, that's why the paper has insurance."

He leaned back in his chair and began to waggle his pen between the index and middle fingers of his right hand. I'd seen him do that before when he was considering something but wasn't ready yet to put it to words.

I filled the void of silence. "You can fire me. That's your call, not mine. But I do need to tell you that Mark has already given me an ultimatum. He wants me to change assignments at the paper or leave on my own to find another line of work. It's come down to the job or him. He's serious."

"I don't blame him," Ryland said. "That's not a decision I have any right to make for the two of you."

"If I give you my word, a solemn oath, not to get into one of these messes again without your full agreement with the objectives, will you let me finish this story?"

"I thought it finished with the shootout in Joe Pye."

"No, it didn't," I said. "Let me bring you up to date with what I know and what I suspect. Then you can give me an answer."

46

———————

Ryland had just extended his open hand in a signal I could proceed when there was a light knock on his door and the sound of the door opening behind me. I turned and saw Jonathan Bruckner, the *Journal's* top attorney, enter the room with a grim smile on his face. He stopped beside Ryland's desk, peered at me, and asked, "Why is it, Eric, that every time you call me about trouble it involves Deuce?"

"Hello to you, too, Jonathan," I replied before Ryland could answer. "Hard to believe I'm the only problem lurking around here."

Ryland suggested, "Why don't you sit down, Jonathan. Deuce has just answered some questions and was about to go into why the killings in Joe Pye County weren't the end of the story."

Brucker's eyebrows shot up. "There's more?" He turned to me. "Why don't you start at the beginning?

I did, much to Ryland's chagrin. He kept waggling his pen, a signal demanding that I get on with the story as quickly as possible. Brucker paid no attention to my editor's impatience. He wanted every detail. That's what lawyers do.

When I finished, he asked, "What did Grey Houssmann have to

do with any of this? The police report said he was in Pilsen to see you and Josh Fujita, and Mark happened to be there. He was killed walking to his car, presumably to go home. I understand his father was tearing the police department apart last night demanding answers."

"Well," I said, "his father might already know the answers and was putting on the rage act for show. In fact, it's possible Honus Houssmann ordered a hit on his son himself."

Ryland was interested again.

Jonathan spoke first. "So, it's your theory that Houssmann, the elder, conspired with the governor to pour money into his campaigns, more than enough to get Latchey elected against the odds, in return for something. What?"

"I only have a theory, but it includes the possibility that Houssmann was bribing Latchey into giving his drug operation in Joe Pye some cover by not mobilizing the National Guard to go down there and clean it out. Bribery of a government official is a heavy crime. It's also possible that Houssmann strongarmed a lot of people he knows, and more who worked for him, into pouring huge sums into Latchey's campaigns. It's even possible that Houssmann gave large sums to some of those donors, who then turned around and donated the money for Latchey. That's a very serious infraction in election law. I suspect that Houssmann took the proceeds from Joe Pye and laundered them through the nursing home empire, which allowed him to pay no taxes. What I was about to do was try to prove it all, and Grey Houssmann was willing to lend a hand. He absolutely hated his father."

"Did he tell you why?" Bruckner asked.

"Yeah, and you're not gonna believe it. You remember the Saudis and the child trafficking ring? Well, it seems dear old dad was actually the head of that operation. It was all his idea, the Saudis heard about it somehow, and a lucrative friendship was born."

"Good Lord," Ryland said. "But that doesn't explain Grey's hatred for his father. Was it just a family thing?"

I looked him straight in the eye for impact. "When Grey was

eleven years old, his father turned him over to the ring. He was sold, raped, beaten, and sodomized for more seven years, until he was eighteen and aged out of the program."

I saw Bruckner's face go slack, and Ryland's mouth dropped open.

"There's more," I said. "Daddy gave Grey a $250 million dollar trust fund and made him vice president of Houssmann Health—basically set him up for life—to keep him quiet. He also wanted to train Grey so he could keep the nursing home empire running, along with the other sordid businesses, when Grey inherited the whole mess."

"This isn't going to sound very lawyerly," Bruckner said, "but aw fuck. I can't begin to wrap my head around this crap."

I looked back to Ryland. "You still want me to drop this?"

The editor shook his head and closed his eyes.

"No," he said. "But you will continue under my supervision. I will want to know everywhere you go, everything you do, everything you want to do, everything you find out, everybody you talk to, and everybody you plan to talk to. Dates, times, and locations. I want a briefing three times a day. And you don't make a single move without my approval. When it's over, one way or another, then we'll have a conversation about your future and whether any of it will continue to be at this newspaper. *Capiche*?"

"Thank you," I said as a wave of relief rolled over me.

WE WRAPPED up the discussion quickly. Both men had questions and asked them, but my recitation seemed to have satisfied their curiosity.

Bruckner explained the legal ramifications of what I was walking into, like lawsuits: libel, defamation, willful disregard, and a list that seemed to go on forever. I was familiar with all the terms but uncertain how some of them related to my project. I didn't ask. I just resolved to clear everything with Ryland before I got into uncharted territory. If he felt the need to discuss any of it with Bruckner, he wouldn't need my approval.

I had promised Mark I would call him after my conversation with

Ryland was done. I didn't relish listening to his response to Ryland's decision to let me continue with the Houssmann story. I would try to explain to him how this last part of the story would be less dangerous than the events in Joe Pye, even if I was uncertain it was true.

If Honus Houssmann was evil and brutal enough to give his own son over to a child-trafficking ring and then murder him on the streets of Chicago, he surely wouldn't hesitate to put me out of business permanently if I got too close to the truth. I wouldn't be able to hide that reality from Mark. So, I didn't try.

"Sounds like Eric intends to keep you on a very tight leash," he said after I brought him up to date.

"In a way," I said, "it's sort of a relief. I'll know his feelings about everything so I can proceed with his approval . . ."

Mark interrupted. "What if something comes up on the spur of the moment, and you don't have time to call ahead for approval?"

"I'll cross that stream before it gets to flood stage," I said. "Nothing's a given."

I heard Mark's exasperation. The sigh was hard to miss.

"Jesus, Deuce, this scares me to death," he said.

"Me, too, a little bit," I told him honestly. "Until our conversation Saturday night I think I was trying to ignore the risks I was taking, and also the dangers to you. You're much more important to me than the job, so once this story is wrapped up, we'll discuss it all again. Settle on a future, maybe for both of us."

"I'd like that. But I have one caveat. For the duration of the Houssmann investigation, you have to stay with me. And when you drive into the condo garage at the end of a day, you have to call me so I can come down with my gun and escort you upstairs. If I'm not available, I'll arrange with the building security people to do it. They're always looking for ways to earn extra money."

"Okay," I said. "But I feel like I'm leaving a lot of freedom behind."

"You are. But think of all the protection you're gaining."

I thought back to the Vinnie Colangelo case, when Ryland hired armed security teams to watch over me twenty-four hours a day. I thought having them so visible might have stopped some trouble. But Mark wasn't armed security, and I didn't think his big, red state SUV would intimidate a professional killer. But I was sick of talking about it, so I thanked him, and we ended the conversation.

47

―――――

When I got back to my cubicle I found a young intern sitting at my desk. She seemed surprised to see me and embarrassed that she was occupying my space.

"Hi," I said. "Shania, isn't it?"

"Yes, ma'am," she answered. "Are you back? They told me to take any desk in the newsroom, and I figured yours might provide some good karma. Besides, nobody knew for sure that you were coming back."

"You're over-explaining, Shania," I said, feeling almost sorry for her discomfort. "I won't rush you. There's someone I need to go talk to right now, anyway. Why don't you take that desk," I said pointing to a cubicle across the aisle. "Maybe the air handlers will push some vibes over to you."

While Shania gathered up her things, which oddly enough contained a collection of Chicago Cubs bobblehead dolls, I walked across the newsroom to see if Josh Fujita was in yet. He was.

He looked up with apprehension. Was the whole world nervous around me today?

"I saw you in Eric's office when I came in," he said. "Do you still have a job?"

"At least for the near term," I replied. "I'm going to finish out the Houssmann story, then Eric and I will talk again. He's pissed at me right now, so I'm glad he put off a decision."

"I'm happy you're still here. Did he mention whether I'm still on or off the Honus Houssmann trail?"

"He said he would talk to you, but I imagine you'll still be on as necessary, subject to the same terms as me. But without the threat of losing your job when the story's finished."

"What's your next move?"

"I'm going back to what I planned originally. Checking for Houssmann executives and other employees who donated to his campaign by name, not through the Future America Fund. I figure some of them came back later with big donations that went in the back door. Frankly, if this needle exists, it might be buried too deep in Houssmann's haystack to be found, but it won't be for lack of trying."

Fujita said, "If you find likely suspects, shoot their names over to me, and I can earmark them for special attention. It would be easier to wait for all the names in one big list, but I don't think we have that kind of time. We have to stay ahead of Houssmann."

We split up, and I began to miss the availability of Grey Houssmann to help sort out his father's crimes. He died before I could ask him about the identity of the Houssmann board member he overheard complaining about being coerced for big contributions to the Latchey campaigns. Without Grey I would have to find someone within the Houssmann organization who would talk to me.

Good luck to me.

I WAS WELL into Tuesday afternoon and hadn't found anything promising. I had finished the stultifying chore of compiling all the names of the executives in the Houssmann Health parent company and of each of the twenty-seven facilities the company owned. Of the roughly 100 names on my list, there was only one I recognized, a member of the board of directors I had met a couple of years earlier at a fundraiser for the National Museum of Mexican Art. His name was Emilio Martinez. He was a neighbor. His home was just a few blocks from mine. Martinez was a frequent patron of Bacchanalia restaurant, perhaps even more frequent than me. We had a nodding acquaintance and had engaged in some bar small talk occasionally. But we weren't friends.

Though we had planned to eat Thai that night, we changed plans and went to Bacchanalia—again. I was happy to see Paula working the bar. Nothing happened in the Pilsen neighborhood she didn't know about. We took our regular seats, and I asked if Martinez had been in lately.

"I haven't seen Emilio for a while," she said. "I've got a fresh bottle of Don Julio on the shelf waiting for him."

I wasn't a tequila drinker, but I bought a bottle once to have in the house for a party. The variety that Martinez drank was the least expensive, but even so it retailed for something between twenty-five and thirty dollars for a 375ml bottle, what used to be known as a fifth. Higher qualities in larger bottles could cost more than $400.

Paula called me on Saturday evening. When we got to the restaurant, Martinez and a friend were sitting at the end of the bar deep in conversation with tequila shots in front of them. Some things never change. Paula smiled at us and cocked her head at Martinez, as though we hadn't noticed him.

She leaned over the bar and whispered, "I think the guy with him's leaving soon. He didn't order dinner. Said he had someplace to be."

Paula started to walk away, then turned back.

"We've got lamb chops on the menu tonight," she said, knowing how I loved the way the restaurant prepared them. "Want me to save some for you?"

I ordered a Caprese salad. Mark ordered calamari. It was a hard choice. The place made the best calamari in the city. But I hadn't been able to eat octopus, squid, crabs, and lobsters since British scientists determined, and the UK government accepted their findings, that these are sentient beings, capable of feeling fear, harm, and pain. I could no longer eat them with a clear conscience.

At one point I saw Martinez look over his friend's shoulder and spot me. He smiled. A moment later his companion threw back the rest of his tequila and stood. The two men shook hands, and the companion turned for the front door. When he passed us he said, "Hi. How're you all doing tonight?" He didn't wait for an answer, just walked out.

I picked up my drink and moved down to the chair just vacated. "Haven't seen you in a while, Emilio," I said. "Are you going to be here for a while?"

"I should be," he said. "My driver's pickin' me up at eleven. You wanna talk about something specific?"

"I do," I said. "Give me half an hour or so."

"I'll be here."

When Mark and I finished eating, he ordered a Peroni, and I ambled down the bar to sit with Martinez. Except for Paula, who was making herself scarce in the kitchen, the two of us were alone.

"How've you been, Senator?" I asked.

"Well, thank you," he said. "But not a state senator anymore. Thinking about running for city council. This city needs a lot of new ideas and a lot of help."

"Not the legislature again?"

"Oh, no. That's why I didn't run for re-election last time. The governor drives me crazy. There's no way he's qualified to run Illinois. The legislature's a bunch of shills for him. I don't want anything more to do with Springfield. I want to stay right here, go home to my house and family every night, and do what I can for Chicago. I hope you'll support me."

"Not publicly," I said. "Conflict of interest. But I will vote for you."

"Thank you. Now what can I do for you?"

I told him.

48

―――――――

When I started talking I wasn't sure how productive the conversation would be. Martinez's eyes were slightly glassy, a testament to his intake of tequila in the previous ninety minutes. But the more he listened the deeper the furrows between his eyes grew, and the clearer his eyes became. I started the story with my quest to find James Weldon, the Chicago cop who murdered one Northwestern medical intern and injured another.

I went through all of the events in Joe Pye County, including some general details about Drigger. Not knowing who Drigger really was, who he worked for, or why he was in southern Illinois made me cautious about how much I revealed. When I finished Martinez looked completely sober and hadn't touched the shot glass on the bar beside his elbow.

Instead, he crossed himself and whispered, "Oh, my God." He thought about what he'd heard, then lifted his head and locked eyes with me. "Who in hell would do something like that?"

"It gets worse," I said. Without naming names, I told him how we thought the *Journal* and I had pretty much eviscerated the child trafficking operation, but now I wasn't so sure.

"You mean it's still going on?" he asked. He sounded genuinely shocked and angry. A number of the children involved in the ring when I was dealing with it had been Hispanic. I knew that disturbed him to his core. It was time for me to stop avoiding the truth and tell him the whole shocking story.

"I've always heard that you're a good guy, Emilio," I said, switching to his first name to generate some intimacy with a man who might know more than he thought. "I voted for you for state senate every time you ran. I will vote for you for city council. But before you think seriously about running for public office again, there are some things you need to know."

"What's this got to do with me?" he asked.

I told him what I knew or suspected about Honus Houssmann. He listened intently but didn't interrupt. I updated him on the child trafficking, possible election frauds, and more serious criminal activity but left Gov. Latchey completely out of it. There was no solid evidence at all yet that he was involved, though his lack of action against the operations in Joe Pye made me think he was, wittingly or not.

"The founder and boss of the trafficking operation is the owner of Houssmann Health, where you serve on the board of directors. Grey Houssmann told me that before one meeting he had heard two board members discussing the forced contributions to Latchey's campaigns. One wasn't worried about it. The other shared concerns about its propriety, even its legality."

I expected Martinez to be shocked, disbelieving, angry at me for even suggesting such a thing. But I was totally unprepared for his reaction. His face creased like an unironed shirt, and his hands closed into tight fists, which he slowly pounded on the bar.

"I was the one Grey heard arguing that the contributions might be criminal," he said. "I still think so."

He picked up the shot glass and threw the tequila back in one swallow.

"That fucking son of a bitch," he said. "I've been thinking about leaving his board because something about the operation seemed all wrong. He came to me asking for contributions to some super PAC in D.C. Said he'd reimburse me or give me the money in advance. I told him that was unethical and possibly illegal. He brushed me off. Every time I asked about it he insisted that nothing was amiss, and he wouldn't answer direct and specific questions. He got mad."

"Can you expand on that?"

"Well, lemme think. The first time was back in 2016, I want to say. Latchey was making his first run to be the Republican candidate for governor. He was okay. Had a good head for business, and the state is, after all, a very large business. But the Democratic candidate, Richard Russo, was a good friend of mine and, I thought, more qualified than Latchey. So, I wanted my money and my vote to go to Russo."

"He's the CEO of Great Lakes Shipping, right?"

"Right. Anyhow, Houssmann asked me to hang around for a few minutes after a board meeting. He had something he wanted to talk to me about. That was when he raised the possibility a of donation from me to Latchey's campaign. I explained that Russo was my choice, and that's where my money and vote would go. He said there was no reason I couldn't donate to Latchey, too. You know, hedge my bets. I told him I didn't have that kind of money. He offered to give me a million bucks to donate to Latchey through a national super PAC called the Future America Fund, or something like that. He was quite insistent. He reminded me that contributions to national super PACs were anonymous, and nobody would ever find out it wasn't my money. I refused."

"What did he say?"

"He let me know my refusal could have dire consequences for me and my family. I didn't doubt what he meant. So, I changed my mind. When Latchey won the primary, I was sure Houssmann would come back and demand I do the same thing for the general. But he didn't. He just went ahead and did it behind my back. Now that's fraud. Misrepresentation. Maybe additional crimes. I found out what had been done behind my back last year when a man I'm not going to identify came to me and told me the truth. He said Houssmann gave him a million dollars each election, which he donated in my name. The guy said he couldn't live with it and wanted to apologize."

"You think he was telling you the truth?"

"I was skeptical at the time, and I told him so. He gave me four receipts for cashier's checks made out to the Future America Fund. A million each time. Four fucking million dollars total. In my name."

"Why didn't you go to the FBI and the Federal Elections Commission?"

"He threatened my family. The guy's morally reprehensible. I figured if the donations were going to remain anonymous, it wasn't worth the risk to turn him in."

"Did you keep those cashier's check receipts?"

"Damned right," Martinez said. "I knew they might come in handy someday."

"I think, Emilio, that day has arrived."

49

We talked for another ten minutes about Houssmann and how Martinez might salvage his political career if he testified against the nursing home king.

"I don't mind testifying to what I know, which involves the questionable campaign contributions," he said. "But I don't know anything about the child trafficking or drugs. Would anybody believe me if I said that under oath? The cops, the prosecutors, the judge and jury—the voters?"

"You'd have to sell it, for sure, but you've been good all your political life at convincing people of your honesty," I said. "You should be able to do it again.

"What about my family? Would they be safe?"

"If you let the U.S. Marshals take care of that, I'd say yes."

"Witness protection? That's not infallible, as you know. But I'll think about it. Can I ask you something? What happened with Houssmann's son the other night?"

"Hit-and-run driver, from what I've heard," I said.

"I heard it was a setup. Deliberate."

"You mean murder? Where'd you hear that?"

"I was having dinner at Il Vicinato, and some people at the bar were talking—speculating, actually—based on what they heard the cops saying at the scene."

"And that was?"

"That if it was a simple accident, say a truck lost traction in all the construction mud and hit the kid, why would the driver take the time to back up and come at him again to roll right over the body?"

"I don't know. I don't know for sure that's what happened. Maybe the impact threw the kid forward, and the vehicle ran over him getting away."

"Maybe, but that's not what the cops were saying, at least that's what I heard at the bar. I got no first-hand information. I can't figure out what Grey was doing down here. He lives, lived, up in Lincoln Park. That's a pretty good hike from Pilsen."

I took my time responding. I was conflicted about telling Martinez the truth.

"He was down here to see me," I answered, finally. "He was turning on his father. He hated the man and wanted to give him up. I think he wanted to know I had his back."

Martinez shook his head slowly. "I don't know if I'd take everything he said at face value. The kid had some anger problems. For all I know he and his father had a bad argument, and Grey decided to take revenge for a real or perceived insult."

I told him what Grey had said about the seven years of his life he spent being used by his father's trafficking ring. I said, "If it's true, I could understand his anger issues."

"Oh, Christ," Martinez said dropping his head into his hand with his elbow propped on the bar. "How could anybody do that to a kid? Honus thought enough of Grey to set him up with a $250 million trust fund when he was about nineteen and insert him into the company as a vice president when he was twenty-one. He made no secret that he was grooming Grey to take over. Honus is so goddamned egotistical that he'd want somebody with the family name to carry on when he retires or dies. Grey was his only heir."

"Grey isn't here to tell his story. That's why I came to you. Even if you can't attest to the trafficking and drugs, maybe you'll think of someone who might. Meanwhile we could start on the election crimes. I'm tugging on a thread and hoping it unravels a sweater."

"Let me think about it, Deuce. I have a law degree, even though I was only in practice a couple of years. I want to think this through and see if I can find a way to make this work without ruining my own life or jeopardizing my family."

I noticed that Mark switched from beer to a cup of coffee. It was probably time to go back to his condo.

I asked Martinez for his card so I could contact him again. He wrote his private cell phone number on it. I thanked him and encouraged him to do the right thing.

"That remains to be seen," he said. "Meanwhile, while I'm pondering this, could you have somebody talk to the U.S. Marshal's Service about protection for me and my family?"

"I know just the guy," I said.

50

Martinez had said "nights," plural. I hoped it wouldn't be too many.

On the drive back to his condo I brought Mark up to speed. I was wondering where to go next and whether I had enough journalistic ammunition in hand to approach two very key people I hadn't interviewed yet. One was Honus Houssmann, of course, and I hoped that when I approached him I would be accompanied by five or six FBI agents with guns and arrest warrants. The other was Gov. William Latchey, around whom all the events of Joe Pye seemed to coalesce, like the funnel of a massive tornado. Trying to talk to Latchey was tricky. If I asked him tough questions, and he reported the details of our conversation back to Houssmann, the rest home king would then know everything I knew or suspected. I had no doubt that would put a target on my back. Somehow I would have to convey that the Justice Department knew what I knew and supported me. That could raise the stakes.

"I don't like anything about that plan," Mark said. "But if you're going to bring this story to a close, you can't do it without talking to them, or making the strongest possible case for them to talk to you. If you go to press with this, it won't do to have two principals saying nothing but 'no comment.' Though I suppose if you ask maybe half a dozen times each and still don't get anywhere, you wouldn't have any other choice."

"I'm going to call Jerry Alvarez first thing. If I'm going to invoke the Justice Department's support of my activities I have to have at least one DoJ official agree to back my play." I paused and then expressed a private thought out loud. "I sure wish I had Drigger to talk to about this."

"So, ask Jerry tomorrow if he'll take another shot at interceding with Drigger's handlers and let you sit down with him. Even if they agree, there's no certainty that Drigger will. Didn't he turn you down last time?"

"Yeah, Drigger and his supervisors said no. But time has passed, and shit has happened, so maybe, if they're really serious about bringing down this operation, they'll have a change of heart. It's worth asking. I'm sure the news of Grey Houssmann's murder has reached all of them by now."

When I got to Jerry Alvarez's office the next morning a little after 10, he was waiting with a freshly brewed pot of coffee.

"*El nuevo yo*," he said. "The new me." He pointed to a table. Sitting on top of it was what appeared to be a brand new Zojirushi coffee maker with an Oxo coffee bean grinder next to it. A half dozen gallons of spring water were arranged under the table.

"I got tired of hearing everybody bitch about my coffee," he said. "When a friend introduced me to this setup, I finally understood what the bitching was about. It's like drinking two completely different beverages. I'm hooked now. When people in the other offices hear me grinding fresh beans, they show up at the door with cups in hand."

"So, you're making coffee for the whole floor?"

"No. I close the door."

We both laughed.

"Why don't you get the door now," he suggested. "My colleagues know the signal. The guy next door got so tired of seeing my door closed at coffee time that he created his own setup. It's an epidemic of good taste."

"What's next for you, Jerry? I'm overwhelmed. First you lost a ton of weight, then you get married, and now the coffee. I don't know where you can go from here."

"Parenting," he answered. "We're pregnant."

At first I thought he was joking, but no such thing. "Due in mid-November," he said. "We're almost through the first trimester. Every minute I have to myself I'm doing baby things. I think it will be easier to have a baby than to prepare for one."

"Well, congratulations. You need to keep taking care of yourself and saving money. You're going to be close to seventy when you send the kid off to college."

We sat at the conference table in the corner of Alvarez's office, excellent coffee at hand, and he got right to the point.

"You were there when Grey Houssmann died, right?" he asked.

"On my front porch, less than half a block away. It's all in the police report."

"Want to tell me what happened?"

"I can repeat what I told the police," I said. "I didn't actually see the accident, but I heard it. Well, I think accident's the wrong word. Can we keep this between us?"

"As always," he replied.

I stifled my curiosity for the moment and took Alvarez through the whole story, from the night I found Houssmann in my back yard to the conversation on my porch and his subsequent death. I covered his disclosures about his father, his teenage experience on the auction block, and then, newly wealthy, going into training to take over the family business from his father when the time came.

"Good lord," Alvarez said, not much above a whisper. The color seemed to have drained from his face. "I'll be honest with you. The feds have suspected some election improprieties for a while, though nothing on the order you're talking about. Are you really staying on the story? What do you think you can uncover that the FBI can't? And how can you keep working on this and keep your job? I hear Ryland wanted to fire you when you went off on that outrageous foray into Joe Pye Country. I could have told you before you left that was a place you should steer clear of under all circumstances."

"Eric and I have reached an agreement on that," I said without going into details. "I have my job for now. When the story's written, if it ever is, then we'll talk about my future, assuming I have one, which is not a sure thing."

"Let me guess," Alvarez said. "You want to talk to Drigger again?"

"I'm dead in the water at the moment, yes, and if he'll do it, I need some guidance on stuff he mentioned when we were holed up together in Joe Pye."

"I'm not sure he'd be allowed to talk to you, even if he was willing."

I slammed my hand on the table, making the coffee cups jump a little.

"Dammit, Jerry, I'm out of options here and so are the spooks—or whatever they are—who supervise Drigger. Before he was killed, Grey Houssmann give me some clues I can follow, but I need some help from the people who've been chasing this a lot longer than I have. Why the resistance? Why can't we work this together?"

"They don't think they need you," Alvarez said. "You don't know who you're dealing with here, Deuce."

"Who cares?" I snapped. "FBI, NSA, CIA, DIA, I've run into all of them at one time or another, and the outcomes were always fine. What's different this time?"

"Because you've never worked with, dealt with, or even learned the existence of the agency running Drigger. They live in a different universe."

Alvarez pressed a button on his office phone. "Shana, could you ask her to come in?"

I looked at the door then back to Alvarez. "Who?"

"You'll find out what she wants you to know. Nothing more."

51

———

I was somewhat taken aback by the woman who walked through the door. Everything about her both surprised and impressed me. She looked to be in her forties, maybe a youngish 50. Her dark skin was smooth and clear, and her attractive hairdo looked to be its natural color, or close to it. Everything about her was firm. Her neck, her upper arms, her breasts, her legs, all perfectly shaped and conditioned. Nothing jiggled, especially I would learn later, her tongue. I stood up. For some reason I thought it the right thing to do. She reached out to shake my hand.

Her eyes captured my attention. They were dark and deep, focused on me and very intelligent. I was deeply impressed, and she hadn't opened her mouth yet.

"Deuce," she said. "It's nice to meet you. I'm an admirer of your work, if not your penchant for inserting your nose into situations you aren't equipped to handle."

"It's nice to meet you, too, uh . . ."

"Why don't you call me Sally?"

"Is there a reason you can't tell me your real name?"

"Yes. What can I do for you?"

"I have no idea," I said. "I don't know who you are, who you work for, what your objectives are, and why you won't let me talk to Drigger. Until I know those things, I have no idea what we have to discuss."

Alvarez brought her a cup of coffee. He didn't ask her if she wanted cream or sugar. I guessed Sally had been here drinking coffee before.

She smiled at him as she took the mug and turned back to me.

"You ever hear of black ops?"

"Yes," I said. "If you're talking about U.S. security matters, I would know exactly what's involved. Clandestine missions so secret that only a handful of people know they exist. Like hunting down Bin Laden and escorting him off this world. Is that what we're dealing with here?"

"Most black ops missions are overseas. I can't discuss what they involve, even after they're over. What makes this one so much more sensitive is the domestic angle . . ."

I didn't mean to interrupt Sally, but the question was out of my mouth before my brain could stop it. That happened to me a lot. I had no mental regulators. What came up in my brain came out my mouth. "What about the Saudis? They played a big role in the child trafficking ring. They weren't domestic."

"No, they didn't, and no, they weren't. But you're getting ahead of the narrative."

"Sorry."

"Let's leave the Saudis out of this. Your investigation took them out of the picture. From what we know, their government hasn't even attempted to find and retrieve whatever is left of them."

"Okay. What are we talking about, then? Just election crimes? Why does that require black ops intervention?"

Alvarez intervened. "Deuce, let Sally talk. Then you can ask questions."

I nodded. Sally continued.

"There are three threads to this investigation, separate but intertwined. All three have international implications, which I'm not at liberty to explain. You understand me to this point? It's okay to ask a question or two, just to be sure we're on the same page. But I reserve the right not to answer them."

I replied, "Well, I would repeat one of my previous questions. Why does a purely domestic mission involve black ops?"

"It's not purely domestic. You took the Saudis out, but there are other international players that aren't exactly our allies. That's all I can say about that now. Maybe ever. This involves a large and very lucrative interstate and international drug trade and murder. Then there is the continuation of the child trafficking matter. Here's the bottom line. This matter, taken as a whole, has the potential to shatter entire segments of American life and do irreparable damage to our constitutional governance."

I sat back in my chair and stared at Sally for a few long moments.

"And Drigger is involved in this? On which side?"

"There are several sides, but it's safe to say he's on ours."

"That's a relief."

52

Sally agreed to allow me to see Drigger again, but only at the secure hospital facility where I saw him the first time. Alvarez would go with me.

Any discussion of the Houssmann case or events in Joe Pye would be strictly off-the-record. She would be there to monitor and record the conversation, so if it got into forbidden territory it could be steered back to more banal topics. A government driver would pick us up here, at the Federal Building, at 10 a.m. two days from now.

That settled, Sally stood, gave Alvarez a curt nod, and left. She left a half mug of coffee behind on the conference table.

"Happy now?" Alvarez asked.

"I think apprehensive is more like it," I said. "I don't want to face Houssmann yet. I don't know enough. I think my next move has to be to the governor."

"And this would be about the election fraud, right?"

"Yeah. I don't have enough information about the other stuff to come up with productive questions."

Alvarez got up and cleared Sally's coffee mug from the table and put it on a table by the coffee maker for washing later. He picked up the coffee carafe.

"Want a refill?" he asked. I accepted.

"What are the horses you need to corral?" he asked.

I told him about Emilio Martinez and his experience with Houssmann's clandestine election plans. Also about the threats against his family.

"I don't think he'll help us unless we can protect him and his family."

"Witness protection?" he asked.

"Unless you have a better idea."

"I'll set it up."

"Thanks," I said. I gave him Martinez's cell phone number. "If I can turn the governor, a lot of other things could fall into place."

"Oh, there's a way to turn him," Alvarez said. "Secrecy about almost anything, including lawyer-client privilege, can be negated if courts believe the secrecy was invoked to hide the commission of a crime. If this PAC was formed for illegal purposes, or was hijacked for an illegal activity, the right to secrecy vanishes. It's a ruling the courts must make, and with the possibly long appeals process it could take time. But we would get a ruling eventually."

I felt buoyed by this possibility. I was on a roll and tried to sustain my luck. "If my inquiries are going to have any clout, I need to be able to say that the feds are interested in the same matters. I don't have to use your name, but I could use your support so he can't claim later that I lied to him."

"Sally told you I'd be there if you get another shot at Drigger. Same for the governor and anyone else you contact on this matter," Alvarez said. "If you get an interview with the governor, I'll go with you. My presence should give you the clout you're looking for."

Since he was the Chief Deputy U.S. attorney for the northern district of Illinois, and since white collar crime was his area of responsibility, I figured he wasn't exaggerating.

ALVAREZ CALLED me at home the following evening. I feared he was delivering bad news, that Sally had changed her mind, or Drigger wanted nothing more to do with me. But he was calling to let me know we had another appointment to see Drigger, and both she and I would be there with me.

"That's some heavy support," I said.

He chuckled. "You don't know the half of it. They wanted to blindfold both of us for the trip to ensure security They neglected to do it the first time, and there were reprimands over that. I explained that I helped design the safe house and had known the location for years. They relented, but not graciously."

"Blindfolded?" I was appalled and amused at the same time. "What is this, an Alfred Hitchcock spy movie? You can't be serious."

"Did Hitchcock make spy movies?"

"What?"

"I don't see many movies," he said.

"No kidding. 'North by Northwest?' 'Notorious?' 'The 39 Steps?'"

"I heard-a the first one."

"Jerry, you are impossible."

"*Entiendo.* I know. My wife tells me all the time."

WE ARRIVED AT THE HOSPITAL/SAFEHOUSE at least half an hour before our appointment.

When we walked into Drigger's room I was happily surprised to see him in street clothes, in an easy chair by a window. The only image that bothered me was seeing Drigger's blue jeans leg cut off to mid-thigh and wrapped in thick dressings. An IV dripped into his arm, carrying antibiotics no doubt. His leg was propped up on a footstool. Other than that, his color was good, and his eyes were bright. I introduced him to Alvarez, who disclosed that he and Drigger already knew one another. Alvarez shouldered past me to shake Drigger's hand.

I offered a wide smile and asked to be brought up to date on Drigger's condition and prognosis. "I want to know everything," I said.

"I'm doing well, Deuce," he told me. "The docs think I'll need one more surgery, then a lot of rehab, but I'm not going to lose the leg. The knee, the ankle, and the Achilles tendon got pretty messed up. So did the tibia and the femur. The tendon still needs work, but the consensus is that the next surgery will be the last."

"How many've you had?"

"Four up to this point."

"Holy crap. How do you deal with that?"

"I'd say one step at a time, but I'm not doing a lot of stepping yet. You get the idea."

"But you're feeling okay?"

"Like I was kicked in the leg by a horse, but that's okay. I like horses."

"I'm being serious, Drigger."

"So am I," he replied. "I could have lost the leg or bled to death in the chopper. The EMTs were very good, and I got lucky. So here I am."

"Do you plan on going back to work?"

"To work, yes. To be doing the same sort of work you saw me doing, no. I'll probably walk with a limp the rest of my life. I won't be quick enough on my feet to keep going with the undercover assignments. So, I'll fly a desk until I retire."

I leaned back in my chair. "Do you know Pete Rizzo?"

Drigger nodded. "The police spokesman? I know who he is, but I don't think we've ever met."

Rizzo had been hit by a car, likely on purpose, after he stopped a gang banger on a city bridge and began writing a citation for speeding. A second car, driven by another gangbanger, came out of nowhere, also speeding. It hit Rizzo with enough force that he should have died. As it was, he spent months in the hospital and in rehab and had been driving a desk ever since. I had learned in dealing with him that he drove a desk quite ably. I told Drigger the story.

He said, "I know a lotta guys who came home from Iraq and

Afghanistan in the same circumstances. Most of them wanted to retire from the military and go into another line of work. A few wanted to stay in the service and work at anything that would help."

The door to the room hissed open and Sally walked in. She nodded to everyone and took a position in a corner, resting against a wall.

"There's a chair over here," Drigger said to her. "You want it?"

Sally shook her head. "I'm fine, thanks. I'm just here to prevent a food fight."

I caught her eyes. "We were just discussing surgeries. Is that okay?"

"Yes."

Drigger spoke up. "Hey, Deuce, she's just doing her job. Lighten up. She's not going to interfere unless we drift toward subjects that are totally off-limits. Our biggest concerns are for the integrity of the investigation and limiting the exposure for the organization we work for. I hope that makes sense."

"It does. I'm just frustrated."

Sally said, "I understand that, Deuce. If it's any comfort, you're the only reporter I can think of that I would trust to have in this room at all. You are extremely good at what you do, you're fearless, and most important, your integrity is unquestionable. So instead of scrapping, let's be civil and see where our interests overlap."

I felt my blood pressure begin to recede as Sally talked. I found it reassuring that she seemed to take me seriously and would allow Drigger to speak somewhat freely. At least I might leave the room with more information than I had when I walked in.

But until the final moments, I got nothing but a rehash of what I already knew.

I asked another question. "If Houssmann was dumping all this money into the PAC, conditioned on it going to Latchey's campaigns and crediting the donations to a slew of other people, how did he get the people who run the Future America Fund to go along? They had to know they were breaking a dozen federal laws. How did Houssmann get them to agree? Bribes? Threats?"

Sally smiled. "He didn't have to do any of that. The PAC belongs to Houssmann. He set it up. He runs it. It does what he wants with its money."

I closed my eyes and bent my head back. "How on earth did we miss that?" I asked. It was a rhetorical question.

"More feints and aliases," Sally said. "Don't beat yourself up about it."

Jerry Alvarez spoke up. "You said you trust Deuce's integrity. So far, the only person I've heard speaking about this crime ring is Deuce. She's given you everything you wanted to hear, and you've given her nothing. That hardly seems to be a gesture of trust."

Sally glared at Alvarez. He glared right back.

Without taking her eyes off of Jerry, Sally said, "Deuce, if you go after Latchey you should have protection standing by. Armed protection. Latchey will report your meeting back to Houssmann, and Houssmann will freak. Remember, he's sort of man who would kill anyone to keep his secrets, including his own son."

That statement surprised me. "Do you have evidence that he ordered his son's murder?" I asked.

Sally looked at me again, appearing to debate with herself on how much more to say. When she made up her mind she pushed away from the wall and walked over to stand directly in front of me.

She said, "He didn't order anything. He did it himself."

53

———————

As we walked out of the safe house my new phone chirped. The ID said it was Pete Rizzo, the principal spokesman for the Chicago Police Department.

"Hey, Pete," I said. "We've just been talking about you."

"Why?"

"Just talking to a guy who got his leg torn up pretty bad. He's going to have to ride a desk for the rest of his career. I told him maybe the two of you should meet. Whatcha got?"

"Nothing as exciting as you," he said. "But I have some news, and I wanted you to hear it before it went public."

"Sounds ominous," I said.

"We've put out an arrest warrant for Honus Houssmann for the premeditated murder of his son, Grey Houssmann."

"I just heard that he's a suspect. But not that an arrest is imminent. I don't know what the evidence is."

"Video," Rizzo replied. "From your old condo. They've mounted security cameras all around the building. Most are aimed at access doors, the outdoor parking lot, and the alley. A few point out at the street, including the intersection where Grey Houssmann died."

"And?"

"The guy driving the truck that hit the kid is an idiot. After he ran him down, he thumbed down the driver's side window to look at what he'd done. It was only open for a few seconds before the driver realized his mistake. Then he backed up and rolled over the body before squealing away. The ID is irrefutable. We've issued a warrant for Houssmann's arrest on first degree murder charges. We're going to try to pick him up later today. He'll be going away for a long time. Keep this to yourself until we're ready to make the announcement. If he hears about it he might squirrel away from us."

54

Mark had left that morning for Urbana-Champaign to investigate a dormitory fire on the University of Illinois campus. Two people had died, and two more were injured in what the campus police described as the culmination of a series of racial incidents in a residence hall. He called me when he and his team quit for the night, about 8 p.m. I was just headed out the door.

"Where you off to?" he asked.

"Bacchanalia," I said.

"Haven't you had enough of it for a while? We've practically been living there."

"I could use a great cassoulet," I said. "Maybe we can find a good French bistro when you get home from college."

"Do you have to go out?" Mark asked.

"I do. I'm hoping to meet up again with the guy I talked to the other night. Unless the place is empty I won't talk serious business with him there. I'll suggest we meet up at a very public place somewhere tomorrow. I don't want to be recognized or overheard."

"Will you have backup?"

"Do you really think I need it?"

"I don't like this, Deuce. You have his cell number. Just call him."

"This is a little too sensitive for a phone conversation," I said.

"Crap. Will you call me when you get home? If you don't I'll be up pacing all night."

I FOUND a parking spot directly across Oakley Avenue from Bacch's. As I crossed the street I saw a man sitting in a car on the opposite curb wave at me from behind the steering wheel of a late model black Chevy sedan. He startled me for a moment until I recognized him as Martinez's personal bodyguard. Martinez had been a cop before he was elected to the state senate, and he always had a driver who doubled as a bodyguard, though why Martinez needed a bodyguard I never understood. Jimmy was an active-duty cop. I never saw him without a gun on his belt. Being a retired cop qualified Martinez to carry a concealed weapon, too, though I wasn't sure he did. I never saw a weapon in his possession. Jimmy always sat with Martinez at the bar. I wasn't sure why he wasn't inside this night.

I walked in the front door to find Danny, Paula's brother and co-owner of the restaurant, behind the bar.

"Deuce," he said with a grin. "Haven't seen yuz in a while. Where ya been?"

"Well," I said, "if you'd work the dinner shift instead of lunch most of the time, we'd see each other more often. We've been here almost constantly. Mark was just complaining earlier that you might start charging us rent on the stools."

"We do," Danny said. "You don't notice 'cause it's folded into your bill."

At the far end of the bar Martinez was watching and listening to us. I walked down and took the seat beside him, the one Jimmy usually occupied.

"Can we talk?" I asked him.

"Yeah, but not at the bar," he said. "Let's go inna back. It's practically empty tonight."

The back was the main dining room. It wasn't crowded, so it was easy to find a table out of hearing range of other diners.

"Yuz guys never sit in the dining room," Danny said when I told him we were changing seats. "You wanna eat back there?"

I wasn't sure I was going to eat anything. Martinez might, though when I saw him in the bar he was generally throwing back shots of Don Julio, not lasagna.

When we found a good table a waitress, who must have been new because I didn't recognize her, brought Martinez a fresh drink and poured water. She asked if I wanted anything from the bar. I did and ordered a glass of the house red.

When she left, Martinez and I looked at one another, each waiting for the other to open the conversation. Finally, I did it, just to fill the void.

"You give any thought to our conversation the other night?" I asked.

"Yeah, I did," he said. "And I don't like the idea any better tonight than I did when you first brought it up."

"Emilio, I'm going to be honest. I don't care whether you like it. We're both at risk here, but we're facing a problem that has to be fixed. Before any more kids are trafficked, before any more drug manufacturing spots can be set up. And using the scope of your personal knowledge, to bring people involved in the election scam to justice."

"Including me?" he asked. "You put me in a damned-if-I-do and a damned-if-I-don't situation. If I do what you're asking, I could face a double tap to the back of the head, or tire tread marks all over my chest. If I don't, I become an accomplice who would very likely land in prison for aiding and abetting a long list of felonies. Houssmann's undoubtedly got arms long enough to reach into any prison. It wouldn't be a shock if somebody inside with me snuffed me in the recreation yard. I'm inclined to take my chances. I think I might come out better in the end. The good guys ain't usually near as efficient as the bad guys."

"You used to flash a shield and count yourself among the good guys."

"I did, yes. And that's where I learned a life lesson, which is 'don't count on the good guys.' For one thing, the actions of those on the side of law and order are often hamstrung by the very laws they're charged with enforcing. Bad guys couldn't care less."

I couldn't argue with Martinez's conclusions. But I had to argue with his position.

"If you get called before a grand jury, that could become public knowledge," I said. "And what the grand jury is investigation could become public knowledge, too. You can't wade in that swamp without getting muck all over you. Do you really think that will help your political future?"

"It could help save my life, or someone in my family."

"Not really," I said. "How long do you think you'd be allowed to live if certain parties have no idea what you might have told a grand jury. Your testimony there is not public. Their interest would be in seeing that you never testify at a public trial."

Martinez fell silent. I saw a man in turmoil and torment. He ran his hands through his thick, dark hair and shook his head.

I tried again. "Look, Emilio, I got a commitment from the feds to give you and your family protection at least until all this is really and truly over. All of you will be safe."

"That's a guarantee nobody can make."

"True, but there are no guarantees in life, no matter what you're doing. You could be on your way to work tomorrow, and Jimmy's car gets run over by a semi. That's the end of you. And you haven't made any move that would set you up for that. I speak from experience. It happened to me. I don't know how or why I survived. Both the people in the car with me were killed."

"I remember that," he said. A thin sheen of perspiration hung on his upper lip as he struggled with his conscience and his fear.

He nodded. "Who's offering us protection? I know there are no guarantees, but I want to know where the effort is coming from."

"U.S. Marshals Service. They're very good at this."

"Yeah, they're about as good as it gets. But I want to talk to them and to your source at DoJ before I make a final decision."

I asked, "Which way are you leaning?"

"I don't know yet. I need to be sure my family will be safe, and I need to know whether this protection is a lifetime commitment for all of us, or just for me until this crap is under control. If I have to spend the rest of my life looking over my shoulder, with no idea who or what I'm looking for, it doesn't sound like much of a life. And it will end my political career if I just disappear."

I had no idea what Martinez would decide, but at least he hadn't said no. I allowed myself to enjoy the first tingle of elation. His decision could make all the difference.

55

While I waited to hear Martinez's decision, I debated where we could hold a meeting involving a former state senator, a deputy U.S. attorney, an official of the U.S. Marshal's Service, and me. My first choice was Alvarez's office, but that would mean everybody would have to go through the Federal Building where lots of eyes could see and recognize them. I called Alvarez's office first thing the next morning. I told him the witness with whom I was dealing was Emilio Martinez.

"I think we have a real shot at turning Martinez," I said. "I think the promise of federal marshals support to hide and protect him and his family swayed him toward us."

Alvarez interrupted. "I haven't approached the Marshal's Service yet," he said. "You might have promised to deliver more than you can."

"He wants a meeting," I continued, "with you, me, and somebody from the marshal's office who is empowered to decide. I was thinking about it last night. We can't go somewhere we might be recognized. How about the nature walk at the North Pond in Lincoln Park? Not the restaurant. It will be too crowded. The boardwalk itself. Casual clothes would be the order of the day. Blue jeans, sunglasses, baseball caps. Disguises."

"*Si, probablemente.* I think so," Alvarez said. "I'll call Johnny Crawford. He's a senior inspector with USMS. If he can't make the decision by himself, he'll know how to get it done. And he'll understand immediately why it's so important."

"And why time is so essential."

"I'll find out how soon this week he or someone else could be available."

When we hung up I called Martinez and told him what was happening. I wanted to get him committed to the meeting he had requested before he had time to change his mind. He told me he could arrange to be at the North Pond whenever we wanted him there.

It was a start.

THE MEETING WAS SET for 10 a.m. the next day. I got to the boardwalk fifteen minutes early and hoped the three men would recognize me. I had stopped at one of the benches that ringed the North Pond. It was the area that provided access to the acreage devoted to the camel and zebra exhibit and to the center for African apes. While normally I didn't approve of zoos, the Lincoln Park facility provided open air habitats that resembled what the animals would find in the wild. I was reasonably okay with that. The bench afforded me an exhilarating view of the Chicago skyline to the south. The pond itself was teeming with ducks and Canada geese. Despite the crowd gathered for a late breakfast at Brauer's Café just to the north of the pond, the boardwalk itself was fairly quiet.

Martinez arrived five minutes before the appointed time. Alvarez showed up a few minutes later in the company of a large African American man I'd never seen before. He had to be three inches taller than six feet, had a middle linebacker's shoulders, and looked as though he could take out a regiment of Marines without breaking a sweat. We quietly introduced ourselves. The U.S. marshal was Johnny Crawford.

"Hope we're not late," Alvarez said. "We got caught in some construction traffic. Let's do this fast and get out of here. He turned to Martinez. "Tell us what you know, Senator."

Martinez looked over the railing at the pond. His facial expression said he wasn't enjoying himself and might have been having second thoughts. He was watching a group of mallards diving to find food, their feathered tails pointing toward the sky.

"Any of you carrying or wearing a wire?" he said.

We all answered in the negative.

I don't think he quite believed us, but he started his story anyway, basically covering the same ground he'd covered with me.

Nobody interrupted him, but when he finished Alvarez asked, "You actually made illegal campaign contributions from Houssmann on behalf of Latchey despite knowing they were in violation of federal elections law?"

"Under serious duress, yes. One time."

Alvarez asked, "What duress?"

"I was told if I didn't do it my entire family and I would disappear, never to be found. The threat of death is powerful persuasion."

"And it wasn't your money?" Alvarez asked.

Martinez smiled, but there was no mirth in it. "I've never seen a million in cash in my life," he said. "At least not until then."

Crawford jumped in. "How was the money delivered to you?"

"By a courier sent by Houssmann."

"Not by Houssmann himself?"

"Might as well have been Houssmann himself," Martinez said. "The money was packed into a cheap briefcase delivered by Houssmann's son, Grey, the kid who was killed by a hit-and-run driver a couple nights ago."

"Did he look angry or upset in any way?" Crawford asked.

"He looked mean," Alvarez replied. "Or as mean as any kid his age can look. He gave me instructions on how to transfer the funds. He wanted them deposited in four equal payments of $250,000 each, and each at different banks in different parts of the city several days apart. That way no bank official would recognize me making those large deposits multiple times."

"They'd still show up in your account," I said.

Alvarez said, "Only if someone is looking for them. Something we'll have to do at some point. We can get a court order to open your checking account."

Martinez shrugged. "I figured."

"You told me you kept all the receipts," I said. "You must have been planning to do something with them someday."

"Yep. I wasn't sure what, though. Still not."

Alvarez asked, "What about the drugs and the child trafficking? What do you know about all that?"

I thought I saw tears in Martinez's eyes.

"I didn't get a chance to think," he said. "But last night I remembered the day Houssmann had asked me to stay for a few minutes after the company's board meeting ended. At this point I wanted nothing to do with Houssmann's election scheme. When he asked me if I'd thought any more about it, I told him my attitude hadn't changed. He opened a desk drawer and pulled out a photo of my son in a Little League uniform. I demanded to know how he got it. He told me, "It doesn't matter. You'll get it back when I'm done with it." Then he looked at the photo and smiled. He added, "Good looking, boy. Athletic. I could make a lot of money with a kid like this."

"Oh, shit," Crawford said. "Did the photo ever come up again?"

"No, probably because I caved in and did what he wanted."

Martinez had never mentioned this to me, and I didn't understand why.

"How long ago was this?" I asked.

"Maybe eight or nine years ago. The boy was five when the photo was taken."

Alvarez looked surprised. "Playing Little League at five?"

"There're different divisions," Martinez said. "The kids can start as young as four."

"You didn't tell me Houssmann threatened your son," I said.

"No. I forgot about it."

I found that hard to believe. "This jerkoff threatens your baby, probably thinking of selling him into child slavery, and you *forgot about it*? How in hell does that happen?"

Martinez looked up at me. The tears were now leaking out of his eyes onto his face. He said, "You can forget anything if you want to bad enough."

56

———————

The meeting lasted a little more than half an hour and broke up when Johnny Crawford said he would recommend conditional protection for Martinez and his family, the condition being that he cooperate with the federal investigation of Houssmann's operations and Latchey's involvement.

"Does that mean you cut us loose if at any point it becomes too difficult or too dangerous for me to continue?" Martinez asked.

"Any contingency like that would be measured by the extent of your previous cooperation, the circumstances of your withdrawal, and whether the lives of you and family members were seriously endangered by your continued cooperation with investigators. In other words, you can't just say you're bored and want out and expect us to continue protection services."

"Let me talk to my wife about it again tonight, and I'll let you know in the morning."

"Fair enough," Crawford said. "Meanwhile, before we leave here I'll call my office and have a couple of agents detailed to you today, overnight, and until we hear from you tomorrow. If you opt out, the detail will be withdrawn, and you'll all be on your own. If you decide to proceed we will keep temporary details on you until a more permanent arrangement can be made. Where will you be going from here?"

"Home, probably. Lock myself in and wait for my wife to get off work so we can talk. I mentioned it when Deuce first proposed this. She was half scared to death."

"I'm sorry about that, Emilio," I said. "No bar hopping tonight. Understand?"

"Okay."

Crawford volunteered to follow Martinez home and keep surveillance on him until the first detail arrived. Martinez gave Crawford his address and phone number, and our little party broke up.

Alvarez called me as he was driving Crawford back to his own car.

"You think the senator's good with this?"

"Hope so," I replied. "We'll know in the morning."

He was.

He called Crawford at nine the next morning and agreed to the plan. Crawford called Alvarez, who called me. Martinez would have a regular detail within the hour, and his family would be on the way to an undisclosed location by afternoon.

Now I had to figure out what I should do next.

As I PULLED into the parking garage at the *Journal* office building I made up my mind. to tackle the governor today, if Eric Ryland agreed to it. I chose Latchey over Houssmann because I thought he would be an easier conquest. I wouldn't get very far with Houssmann now that there was a warrant for his arrest. He undoubtedly knew about it. If I could flip Latchey, Houssmann would be crushed under the weight that suddenly dropped on him.

Latchey, on the other hand, came across as accommodating, a man who would rather negotiate than fight, a strong proponent for the safety and happiness of children and animals, both wild and domestic. If he learned that Houssmann was behind the child trafficking travesty, he'd go ballistic. While his fight for child and animal welfare gained Latchey some voter respect, it likely wouldn't provide him enough public relations cover to get him past a scandal spinning around his deep-money ties to a billionaire committing election fraud while he's also running a ring involved in the manufacture and sale of illegal drugs and child sex-trafficking. Houssmann might have been the more despicable, but Latchey was no slouch in the underworld of evil.

All this I explained to Ryland and described my plan to him. He seemed displeased, but then my editor spent most of his life displeased with me.

"You were supposed to get my approval before you launched anything like this," he scolded. "And don't tell me you forgot."

"No," I said. "I didn't forget. But if Senator Martinez hadn't agreed to go along with the plan, there would've been nothing to get approval for. As it is, we didn't hear from him until ninety minutes ago, and I spent much of that time on the nature boardwalk at North Pond in the Lincoln Park Zoo. I wasn't there to count fish."

Ryland shook his head in exasperation. "You planning to go alone?"

"No. Jerry wants to go with me to lend the imprimatur of the Justice Department."

"Be careful and let me know your progress."

It took me a while to get anything worth reporting.

I called Latchey's office in the state capital in Springfield and asked for Harry Conaway, the governor's press secretary. It's always more successful to go up the chain of command. But I wasn't successful. Conaway's deputy—I thought I remembered that his name was Brett—asked me what I wished to discuss with his boss.

"Isn't that for him to ask?" I inquired. "After all, he's the governor's press secretary. It's his job to ask questions and find out stuff."

"I have to tell him what you wish to speak about, you know, so he can be ready to respond more quickly to your questions."

I was thinking he had it wrong, that telling Conaway what I wanted to talk about before we actually were talking would give him more time to construct an evasive or misleading response. I really wanted to say this out loud. But out of respect for the *Journal* reporters who dealt with the governor's office every day and given that their success at their jobs depended on good relationships with the press secretary, I held my tongue.

So, I just said, "Campaign finance reform."

The response from the assistant was momentary silence. I got impatient.

"Brett, you still there?" I hoped I remembered the assistant's name correctly. Otherwise, this would be a very brief and embarrassing conversation.

"I'm still here. I wasn't aware that campaign finance reform was under scrutiny."

"Isn't it always?"

"I guess. I'll relay your message, Ms. Mora."

I waited all afternoon and didn't get a callback. Perhaps I had offended poor Brett, and he was trying to return the insult.

I tried again the next morning. And during the afternoon. And still nothing. Brett returned the morning call and promised he would tell Conaway I had called again. Nobody even bothered answering the afternoon call.

The next day Latchey was scheduled to be in Chicago to meet with the mayor about a public schools improvement project. They were meeting in the mayor's office.

I figured I'd go with Alvarez, if he was available. We could hang out and make thorough pests of ourselves.

57

———

When I got to the office in the morning I called Jerry Alvarez to see if he was available for this adventure.

"I'm supposed to be in a conference for a couple of hours," he said. "But the boss knows what's up. He'll take over for me if I'm needed somewhere else."

There was a great sushi restaurant between the office and City Hall, so we decided to stop there on our way to the mayor's digs and discuss our plan of attack. We knew if we didn't come up with a decent approach all would be for nothing, and we might not get another shot. Belligerence would get us nowhere.

"We gotta make nice, at least in the beginning," Alvarez said. "Play to his responsibility to voters."

"I don't want it to sound like a prelude to a lecture, either," I replied. "We should start out solicitous and get tougher as the situation requires."

"Okay," Alvarez said. "But I want to play the fly on the wall, let Latchey know the DoJ is also interested but not butt heads with him. So, you take the lead."

I chuckled. "So, you want me to do the head-butting?"

"Yeah," he said. "You got the harder head."

OUR VARIOUS CREDENTIALS got us through security at City Hall and into the outer office of the top of city government, Mayor Benjamin Locke. The receptionist offered to help us.

We introduced ourselves. "We're not actually here to see the mayor," I said. "We have a couple of quick questions to ask the governor when he finishes up his meeting. We're happy to sit quietly in a corner of the outer office until we get a chance to chat with Harry Conaway."

She looked somewhat baffled. "And he is?"

"Governor Latchey's press secretary."

Her answer took me aback. "He's not on the visitors' list I was given."

"The governor doesn't get dressed in the morning without Conaway," I told her. "If the governor is here, Conaway will be walking right behind him."

"You can have a seat over there while I check with the mayor's secretary," she said, nodding toward a bank of chairs against a window wall.

"Can't we wait in the anteroom?"

"Not until I check with the mayor's secretary about who is cleared to attend this meeting. I'll let you know."

I nodded and looked at Alvarez, who gave me a raised eyebrow suggesting his doubts about our chances. We waited about ten minutes. The mayor himself came in.

"Hey, Deuce," Locke said. "What's up?"

I stood up. Alvarez did the same. We all shook hands. "Jerry and I are old friends," Locke said. "How're you doing these days, Deuce? Sounds as if you went through quite an ordeal down south. That's Joe Pye County, I hear. So, what can I do for you?"

"Well, I'm not actually here to see you, Sir, and I mean no insult. I'm actually hoping to get a few minutes with the governor when your meeting is over, assuming I can get a hall pass from Harry Conaway, who's been ducking my calls."

"So, you're using my office as a jumping off point for an ambush?"

"Um, that's too strong. I just think I'll get farther with Conaway if we can talk face-to-face. He seems to be squirrelly about giving me access to Governor Latchey."

"Jerry's presence should put the fear of God into them," he said. "The governor's a coward. I don't know a lot about Conaway. I do get the impression that neither of them thinks the mayor of Chicago has the same stature as the governor of Illinois. Anyhow, as soon as they arrive and we're in my conference room getting our business under way, I'll have my secretary show you both into my office so you won't miss Latchey when the meeting's over. If he decides to talk to you, you can use the same conference room. I presume you don't need me or my staff there."

"Thanks," I said, "but we'll be good. I don't want to unnerve Latchey."

The mayor smiled and turned to leave.

"You probably will, anyway," he said. "The governor has always struck me as a man who's easily unnerved."

58

I was checking my phone for email when I heard some conversation that seemed to have begun in the mayor's office. Then I heard a door close, and the talk stopped, or at least my ability to hear it was blocked. Mayor Locke's secretary appeared a few minutes later.

"The mayor suggested you wait in his office instead of here," she said. "The governor and a member of his staff came in the back way, but Mayor Locke said he would direct them out the front door, so the governor couldn't get out without going by you."

"That's great," I said. I was thinking that in Illinois political officials of one party will go to almost any lengths to embarrass an official of the other party. Locke was going all out to put Latchey in an awkward place.

The conference room door opened 35 minutes later, and I saw Locke move smoothly to assure that Latchey and Conaway left through the main office.

"Unless you're serving coffee and scones to us, there's no reason to use the back door," Locke said to Latchey with a broad smile. I didn't know if Locke was enjoying getting one up on Latchey or being polite.

Latchey walked into the mayor's office, his eyes picking through the details as if he'd never seen the place before. It was Conaway who spotted me first.

"Uh, hey," he said, quite obviously surprised and flustered. He turned to Locke. "What're they doing here?"

"Why don't you ask them?" Locke said. "Here, you can use my conference room." He held the door open with an attitude that gave Latchey and Conaway no choice. When the door closed Latchey looked from Conaway to me and back.

"Can anyone tell me what's going on?" he asked.

No one answered. Latchey knew who I was. I introduced Alvarez. I gestured to the chair at the head of the table and said, "Governor, make yourself comfortable." I issued no invitation to Conaway. Payback is hell.

"Should I get a lawyer in here?" Latchey asked. "Talking to a United States attorney without advice would be very ill-advised."

"Why?" Alvarez asked. "I'm here only as an observer."

I said, "Governor, we're here because I need to get your take on campaign finance reform. I explained that to Mr. Conaway, but he didn't share my interest."

The press secretary showed no sign of emotion but quietly sat down near his boss.

"Why would you want to discuss that?" the governor asked.

"There are a number of people who think reform is in order."

Latchey shook his head. I knew he was in his mid-fifties, but he seemed less animated at this point than he did in public. Behind his wire-rimmed glasses his brown eyes never wavered from me. His comb-over was slightly windblown, mussed a bit by Chicago's constant breeze off Lake Michigan. Latchey's tie was properly knotted under his collar, and I couldn't see any wrinkles in his summer-weight wool suit. But his face was almost ashen. I could do that to people.

"Well, I don't know who those people are," he said. "And I have a busy schedule today, Ms. Mora. Let's get this over quickly."

"A colleague and I have been going through campaign records

from your two primaries and two general elections. There are some very large, late-game contributions to your campaign committee that are identified only as coming from the state GOP. No donor identifications or contribution amounts as the law requires. Can you tell us why?"

Latchey looked annoyed. "How the hell should I know? If they weren't identified when we reported them, then they weren't identified when they came in. You'd have to ask the state party. Or Harry here." He nodded toward Conaway. "He serves as my campaign treasurer. I'm certain he knows the laws and abides by them."

"What we're wrestling with, Sir, is the fact that we've traced the money back all the way to a national super PAC called Future America Fund in Washington. The Future America Fund channeled several hundred million dollars to your four campaigns over the years. Because it's a federally registered super PAC, it doesn't make its donors or their contributions public. The question is why a national fund-raising organization like that would focus so many of its assets on a state election."

Conaway joined the conversation. "Seems to me you should be asking them."

"We intend to," I said, "unless you can satisfy our curiosity first."

"I can't," Conaway said. "I don't have any more access to federally registered super PACs than you do. I suppose they judged that an Illinois governor's race was important."

"I'm sure they did, as we all do," I said. "But Illinois election law offers no anonymity to election donors or their contributions. Violations are crimes." I paused then spoke again before anyone could usurp the floor. "Oh, by the way, the Future American Fund was created by a friend of yours, Honus Houssmann. He also runs it. I'm sure the PAC's donations go where Houssmann wants them to go. What I'm looking for is the *quid pro quo*—what did Houssmann get from you in return for all that campaign help?"

Conaway was losing his cool. He slammed his hand on the table. "We know what the laws are, but we can't report information we don't have. What are you accusing us of?"

I turned to Latchey. "Governor, do you have any knowledge or information that might help us clear this up?"

"No," he replied. "I have no knowledge of any of this. That's why I hired Harry. He's the expert. He handles all the money. All I know is what he tells me our campaign can afford to spend and on what."

Conaway looked like a man who realized he was about to be thrown under a bus.

"I'm not a lawyer," I said. "But I see something suspicious in all of this."

"Suspicious of what?" Latchey asked.

"Without making any accusations, Governor, I'd say this looks like a very sophisticated money-laundering scheme. I'm not saying you're behind it, or even that you knew about it. But I could be wrong."

Conaway jumped up, pushing his chair back so violently he nearly tipped it over.

"Governor," he said, "we have an appointment." He turned to me. "And, Deuce, you and your newspaper can go to hell."

59

———————

Alvarez and I sat in silence and stared at the governor and his press secretary as they left by the back way. We didn't try to keep them. There was no reason. We had thrown down the gauntlet, and it was theirs to pick up if they chose. Conaway looked furious. It would be difficult to be specific about Latchey's demeanor. If I'd had to guess, I would have said that, if not frightened, he looked apprehensive and agitated.

I suspected his first call when he was back in his official car would be to Honus Houssmann, and that spooked me.

I kept my eyes on the open door from the conference room to the back hallway. "It's time to start being very careful, Jerry," I cautioned. "If either one of them reports this conversation to Houssmann, he could very well come gunning for us. I'm staying with Mark, so I feel fairly secure. I'll talk to Eric about getting a place where Josh Fujita will be safe for the duration of this, whatever 'this' turns out to be."

I turned to Alvarez. "I shouldn't have exposed you," I said.

Alvarez smiled at me. "And miss this? Not for the world. Makes me believe more than ever that something is very wrong. Those two, their attitudes when they left, were not the looks you get from innocent men."

~

THE TWO OF us shared a cab back to the *Journal* building. Alvarez wanted to sit with me when I filled in Eric Ryland. Alvarez thought, and we agreed, that hearing about our meeting from both of us would lend credence to the conclusion on which we seemed to agree. We had unsettled Latchey and infuriated Conaway, and both blew out of the mayor's conference room at the earliest possible moment.

"So, what's next?" the *Journal*'s metro editor asked when we finished. "I can see how the mention of possible money laundering might have upset both the governor and his press secretary, but I don't know what you gained by it."

Alvarez jumped in. "Eric, if you could have seen the looks on their faces when Deuce laid out the case, you'd have your answer. She definitely struck a nerve. Conaway was furious. Latchey looked like he was about to soil his britches."

Ryland shook his head subtly. "Any politician and his mouthpiece would feel some degree of anger and panic at speculation about possible money laundering over two election cycles. Conaway especially, since he also served as Latchey's campaign treasurer, the scandal would land him square in the middle of any investigation of how funds were handled. And ultimately, whatever Conaway might have done lands equally on his boss."

Alvarez jumped in. "If one or both of them is sufficiently worried," he said, "they would feel obligated to report the meeting to Houssmann. A man who would murder his own son on a city street wouldn't think twice about ridding the world of two nosey reporters —Deuce and Josh—threatening his empire."

"Not to mention a deputy U.S. attorney empowered to convene a grand jury and bring charges if necessary," Ryland added. "As I understand it, you and your wife have a baby on the way. Don't risk missing that."

"This isn't about me," Alvarez said. "Besides, DoJ is already putting a protection plan in place for me and my family. I appreciate the concern, though."

Ryland turned to me. "You were okay with Lasher Security, the company we used back during the Vinnie Colangelo case, weren't you?"

"Very," I said. "They always seemed to be where I was or following me where I was going. They wouldn't even let me unlock my condo door without going in first and clearing the place. It was annoying but comforting. I think they should cover Josh, too, for a while. And Mark. They could try to kidnap him, again, and use him as leverage against me, again."

Ryland's eyes hit me with rockets of exasperation. "Deuce, you do know that the paper's in dire financial straits. Expenses like these don't help. But I'll cover Mark, too. But I draw the line at your collective pets."

"No worries," I said. "My cats are with a neighbor they like more than they like me, and Murphy went out on the arson investigation with Mark."

"Good," Ryland said.

While we all still sat there, Ryland placed a call to the owner of the security operation. The editor described succinctly what he needed.

When the call ended Ryland turned to me and said, "I don't want either you or Josh leaving the newsroom until you've got a detail on you. I don't care if you have to sleep under your desks, you don't leave this building without armed escorts."

"Yuck," I said. "I don't even want to look under my desk, let alone sleep there."

Ryland told me Josh would be taken to a secure hotel with agents on him there. He wanted me to continue living with Mark with Lasher agents at the condo.

"But they don't want you going there until they clear the building and the condo."

I left Ryland's office somewhat relieved about our prospects for staying alive.

What was one of the first rules of journalism?

Never assume anything.

60

———

The ramifications of the Latchey investigation began to reveal themselves two days later. First, the *Journal* building was evacuated at 3:30 when the newsroom was as full of people as it ever got in these days of staff cutbacks. Eric Ryland passed my desk on his way to the stairwell. "Walk with me," he said.

On the way down the four flights he told me about my Subaru Outback.

"The security company sent a team to move it to the second spot in Mark's condo garage," he said. "I gather the space belongs to Mark, and he lets you use it."

"Yeah," I said.

"Before anybody touched the Outback they used one of those under-vehicle inspection systems like Customs agents use at border crossings to look for drugs or bombs or both. They didn't find any drugs, but . . ."

"No," I whispered. "A bomb?"

"Two, actually. One under the gas tank and one under the hood near the firewall between the engine block and the passenger compartment. Setting off either one would have set off the other.

Anyone inside would have been incinerated before they could even think about getting out alive."

"Jesus," I swore. "How did the bombers access the garage? I thought it was guarded."

"Don't know yet. It will be thoroughly investigated by the city and probably the FBI, and the ATF. Right now, they're evacuating the building because the bomb squad's on the way to defuse and remove both devices."

"And they want everybody out in case the removal backfires."

"So to speak."

"We're going to get you and Josh out of the area," Ryland said. "Your detail is waiting downstairs to drive you to Mark's condo. They don't want you standing around in the street. At six feet tall you'd be an easy target for a sniper."

I asked, "Do you know how insane this is?"

He looked at me and smiled, trying to be reassuring.

"At the risk of pissing you off," he said, "I have to point out that you started it."

THE WORD that an attempt had been made on Josh Fujita's life hit the newsroom a little after 7 p.m. the same evening.

"What the hell happened now?" I demanded of Eric Ryland when he brought me the news. "Is Josh hurt?"

Ryland attempted to quell my anxiety. He put his hands up, palms out from his chest. "He's fine. Shaken but undamaged. The attacker rushed Josh with a hunting knife as his detail was taking him into the hotel. Nobody got a good look at the attacker, and he ran off before anyone could tackle him. One agent got cut on the arm, but the hospital's right there. He got a tetanus shot and stitches in the ER. He'll be back on duty in the morning."

"How could anyone have known where Josh was staying?" I asked.

"I don't know," Ryland said. "If someone was trying to identify a place where Josh could hole up, I seriously doubt they would think the EMC2 hotel would be among the top ten possibilities. Most people haven't even heard of it. They must have been followed."

"How do you arrange for an attack like that so fast?" I was bewildered.

"Assuming this is on Houssmann and not a random street attack, I'd say that when you've got his kind of money you can arrange anything you want as quick as you need it."

"Now that they know where Josh is staying, is he going to be safe?"

Ryland nodded. "The security company thinks once he's in his room he'll be battened down. Knowing where Josh is, and knowing the bad guys know, too, they think security will actually be easier. Josh will work from him room, eat in his room, and probably go stir crazy in his room. But he'll be safe."

"Incredible coincidence," I said, barely above a whisper.

"What?" Ryland asked.

"The EMC's on East Ontario, as I recall, just a couple blocks south of the Northwestern Chicago campus."

"Yeah. That's the hospital where they took the agent to get stitched up."

"You get the irony? That's just a few steps from where the rogue cop, James Weldon, fatally shot the medical resident. Weldon's the whole reason I went down to Joe Pye. It's where this whole mess started."

As soon as my detail cleared and secured Mark's condo, I went inside, locked the door, and with some trepidation, called Mark in Moline. I told him about the attempts on Josh and my Subaru. I heard him pound out a string of f-bombs. He didn't ask for details at that point. He simply said the arson investigation that sent him to western Illinois could be turned over to others, and he was on his way home.

He walked in the door a little before 10 p.m. Murphy leaped onto the sofa beside me and went to sleep with his head on my thigh. He was getting older, and the trips with Mark were tiring him more than they used to.

Marked leaned down, planted a kiss on my forehead, then stepped back.

"You okay?" he asked. He sat beside me, put his arm around my shoulders and asked to hear all the details of the twin attacks.

When I finished, he made drinks and brought up our No. 1 topic: When was I going to stop getting my butt in a wringer? The conversation was brief and inconclusive but very serious. And again, I began to wonder if our relationship could survive.

Adrenaline is addictive. I couldn't be an editor or a feature writer or a food critic. I could only be me and try to stay out of trouble. Mark didn't see it that way. He remained unhappy that I was still on the story after our return from Joe Pye.

I said, "I think the only way I can make you happy is to leave the newspaper." My tone made it clear that, for me, it wasn't an option. Unless, of course, Eric Ryland fired me at the conclusion of the current investigation. It might be prudent for me to assume I'd be fired and begin planning a future in some other job. How about a customer service agent for Amazon? Oh no, wait. Amazon doesn't offer customer service. How about a produce supervisor at Whole Foods, the one who makes sure all the carrots are stacked in the same direction, pointy tips out.

I slumped a little in my chair. I wouldn't be able to consider a new career unless and until I lost the old one. I saw no way that leaving the newsroom was an option. But if I didn't find an alternative, I would lose Mark. That wasn't an option, either.

Mark recognized my anxiety. He'd seen it before.

"Look at it this way," he said. "Suppose you keep your job, and we get married. Have a baby or two. And then something horrible happens to you. If the loss only devastated me, I could eventually deal with it. But given my job, how could I raise kids alone?"

"Then we don't have children," I suggested.

"That's not an option for me, either," he said.

I didn't like where the conversation was going. But I should have let well enough alone, let him vent until he got all his frustrations out. We could plan a new future another time. But I can't keep my mouth shut. I don't have a filter.

"Don't you think maybe you're being selfish, making this all about you? Your loss. Your responsibilities."

He threw his napkin on the table and got up.

"Where're you going?" I asked.

"I'll be back later," he said. "Don't go anywhere."

"Mark, wait."

He would have none of it. He grabbed his keys.

"Get some sleep," he said and went out the door, slamming it, then locking it.

The most important relationship in my life was crumbling.

I didn't know how to save it.

61

It was almost 1 a.m. when I gave up.

Mark hadn't come back. He hadn't called or texted or emailed. I had no idea where he was or what he planned. So, I padded into the next room and stretched out on his big bed with an afghan over me. Murphy curled up in his crate and was snoring within thirty seconds. I was tired, but it was an emotional exhaustion, and I didn't know if I'd be able to doze until Mark returned. In retrospect I must have fallen into a deep sleep because I didn't stir until I heard someone shuffling around on the bamboo floor in the living room. I fully expected that it was Mark, and I got up to go greet him.

It wasn't Mark.

There were three men standing in the living room. Two of them were very big and looked very mean. The third man was Honus Houssmann.

"How the hell did you get in here?" I demanded.

"Max is very talented," Houssmann said. I wasn't sure which of the goons was Max until the man standing on Houssmann's right held up a formidable set of lock picks to answer my question.

"These locks are supposed to be pick-proof," I said in honest amazement.

"They ain't," Max observed unnecessarily.

I started sniffling as if allergies or dust was playing havoc with my sinuses.

"Excuse me a second," I said. "I need a tissue."

I looked around for my bag, a cordovan leather combination purse and briefcase. I spotted it on a chair in the dining room. If I wanted to get something out of it, my back would be turned on Houssmann. Just under the zipper I had a small, voice-activated digital recorder. I hadn't used it in a while. I hoped the charge was still adequate. If I was about to have a problem, at least the cops would be able to hear what happened.

In one quick motion I unclipped the recorder and switched it on. The power light came on, burning steady green. The charge was good. I reattached the recorder in its pocket, power light hidden, and pulled out a sleeve of tissues to use for cover. I used one to blow my nose.

When I turned back I saw that Max had drawn an enormous weapon. It wasn't an AK-47, but it looked just as lethal. The barrel alone was eight to ten inches long. I figured Max had unholstered it in case I had grabbed a weapon from my bag. It would have given him an excuse to shoot me. Max looked like a man who would enjoy that.

I looked Max's gun again. I said, "Well, Dirty Harry, it's nice to meet you."

As I turned back to Houssmann I saw the Lasher Security guard assigned to Mark's condo lying on the carpet just outside the door. I couldn't tell if he was alive or dead.

Honus Houssmann watched me in silence. He didn't look evil. In fact, he was smiling.

〜

WE STOOD STILL, saying nothing, taking stock of one another. Houssmann was a slight man with thinning hair he made no attempt to disguise. He had a pallor to his face, a grayness to his eyes, a droop of loose skin to his chin and neck, and hands that hung loosely and relaxed at his sides. I could see a paunch just visible beneath his vest. The suit had narrow white pinstripes against the medium gray of a summer-weight wool. Houssmann stood several inches below my six feet, maybe at five-eight or five-nine. When I stood close to him, he had to look up slightly to catch and hold my eyes. Some men were intimidated by that. Houssmann appeared not even to have noticed.

He looked like an aging Chicago mobster from the 1930s who wore dark suits with white chalk stripes and exuded an aura of authority, power, control, and bravado. They accessorized with machine guns. I didn't see any among the three of them, but that didn't give me a lot of comfort. There was still Max's cannon.

"Thanks for coming in the middle of the night," I said. "Like I wasn't having enough trouble sleeping already." My flippancy was intended to throw Houssmann off guard, to affect a demeanor that said he didn't frighten me. It didn't work.

Instead, Houssmann cocked his head toward Max and said, "Think what a gun like that could do to you."

"Is that your plan? Blow my head off with a single shot? It'd make a hell of a mess."

Houssmann seemed to be growing weary of my schtick. He shook his head slightly and drew a deep breath.

"I'm not here to kill you," he said. "If I wanted to do that I'd have ordered it already and been long gone. I simply want to talk to you."

"If that's the case, why did you plant two bombs in my car? Why did you send somebody with a hunting knife after the other reporter? That doesn't exactly support your contention that all you want to do is talk."

He shrugged. "Killing the two of you would have been the faster solution. And just so you know, I had your boyfriend targeted for extinction, as well, but I called that off. I know your protection company, Lasher Security. They have an excellent reputation. The fact that they found the bombs and stopped the knife attack impressed me. After being stymied twice I knew we shouldn't try that plan again. So, I am here to talk about alternatives that are physically harmless and lucrative for everyone."

"So talk," I said.

"Okay then. I came with an offer to make you a very wealthy woman."

"Really?" I said, allowing sarcasm to leak into my tone.

"Yes, really. You drop this investigation of yours for good. No more about election donations, drugs, or children, and I pay you $25,000 a month, cash. That's $300,000 a year. For life. Hide it offshore—I can advise you how to do that—and you will soon be very rich."

"Is that how you control Governor Latchey?"

"The arrangement between the governor and me is private, just as my arrangement with you would be private."

"Do you really expect me to believe you?" I asked. "What happens if and when you get tired of lining my bank account? How can I believe my life is secure if that promise comes from a man who killed his own son?"

Now Houssmann bristled. "He was my son in name only," he said, his voice rising slightly. "He belonged to my second wife. I adopted him because she wanted me to. I saw potential in him. I thought I could toughen him up and make him a suitable heir for my business. Unfortunately, that didn't work out."

"By toughening him up, you mean sending him off into seven years of emotional and sexual bondage?"

Houssmann didn't even blink. "I was willing to do what it took. When it became clear he was not up to the task and, even more egregious, that he was turning on me, I had no choice but to strike him down. I do not and will not ever find disloyalty acceptable. Traitors must be annihilated. That includes you, if necessary."

"I haven't accepted or rejected your offer yet," Mr. Houssmann. "Aren't your threats a bit premature?"

He had broken beads of sweat on his upper lip. I saw fire and hatred in his eyes.

"It all depends on you," he said.

I waited for him to calm down and then suggested, "You know, you might be able to find a twelve-step program to help you with that."

62

Houssmann and his two sidekicks had pushed out through the front doors of the condo building and disappeared into the night six minutes before Mark re-entered from the steet. He walked around to the security desk, which was staffed twenty-four/seven. He was surprised to find it vacant. Harry was supposed to be working the overnight shift. Perhaps he had just gone to the bathroom.

Mark began to feel uneasy and started calling Harry's name. On his first try he heard nothing. The second time he got a response, a muffled yelling and pounding on the door to the storage room. He went to the door and opened it slightly, standing away from the crack in case an ambush awaited.

When nothing happened, he looked inside and found Harry, bound and gagged, lying on the floor. Mark knelt and began to free him.

"You hurt, Harry?" he asked. "Who did this to you?"

When Mark pulled the duct tape from his mouth, Harry was breathing hard.

"Three men," he said. "Caught me by surprise. Two of 'em were mean-looking motherfuckers, I gotta tell you. The third one was older, dressed in a very expensive suit. They said they wouldn't hurt me as long as I stayed *quiet, so I stayed quiet. I think I mighta heard 'em leave about five minutes before you came in. Deuce . . ."*

Mark was certain he knew who Harry was describing. Where was Deuce, and in what condition? He made a quick call to her phone. No answer.

When he helped Harry to his feet, Mark asked, "Do you need an ambulance?"

"No, I'm not hurt."

"Then call the cops. And the EMTs. Get the two Lasher guys in the garage to go up to my unit, stat."

Harry nodded, and Mark ran to the elevators. As he turned the corner of the hallway to his unit, he saw one of the Lasher Security men lying on the carpet outside his door, beginning to stir. Mark bent over him.

"You okay?"

The man nodded. "Dizzy. Headache. Not hurt."

"Cops are on their way with medics. And two of your buddies are on their way up from the garage. I'll be inside if you need me. Just rest."

When he got to the condo, the door was closed but unlocked. He knew he had locked it when he left. He dreaded what he might find inside. He called for Deuce and got no response. His heart raced. He inched the door open and called for Deuce again.

"IN HERE," I replied. I could hear that my voice sounded strange but felt enormous relief that I was able to speak at all.

Mark found me on the sofa with a bloody compress of wet paper towels pressed to my lower lip. He sat down gently beside me and put his arm around my shoulders. I was shivering, the deep, hard trembling that can't easily be stopped. I didn't look up at him. My eyes were focused on the floor and stayed there.

Mark pulled the bloody paper towels away from my lip and checked the damage.

"Deuce?" he said softly. "Honey. What happened? Was it Houssmann?"

I nodded. "And two very large helpers. The whole thing should be on the digital recorder in my bag." I moved away from Mark so I could stretch out on the sofa. "I just need to lie down for a minute," I said.

He got up and found the bag. He removed the recorder, powered it down, and returned to the sofa at my feet.

"Who hit you?"

"Max."

"One of Houssmann's pals? What'd he hit you with? Your lip's split pretty good."

"His fist," I said. "To show me they meant business."

"About what?"

"Killing me if I didn't accept $25,000 a month from Houssmann to forget about him."

"That's a lot of money," Mark said.

I knew I looked surprised. "Are you suggesting I consider it?"

"Not at all," he said. "I am so sorry about this."

"For what?" I asked. "For leaving? You not being here might have saved us both."

"How?"

"You've got a gun, and you're keeping it close by these days. If you'd been here and they had spotted the gun, they might have killed us both. That's not why Houssmann was here. Not what he wanted. At least not this time. "How's the agent outside?"

"He'll be fine. The two from the garage came up to stay with him until the police and EMTs get here. When the Three Horsemen got here, they overpowered Harry in the lobby and locked him in a supply closet. He'll be fine, too. So will you. I'll get some ice for that lip."

"Why'd you decide to come home?"

He came back with a cotton kitchen towel wrapped around a plastic bag with a pile of ice cubes and water inside and exchanged it for my paper compress.

"I was on a low burn and needed to cool off. No better way to do that than to walk down to The Club and drink a couple of beers with the neighborhood characters. I have tomorrow—well, I guess it's today—off, so I drank until I sloshed the anger away."

The Club was a nameless hole-in-the-wall on South Michigan Avenue.

"You walked? Are you nuts? Houssmann could have killed you on the street."

The Club was two long blocks west on Roosevelt Boulevard then two more blocks south on Michigan. It was such a dive that nobody had ever given it a proper name. To regulars, it was just The Club. The thought of Mark making that trek without security made me furious. I wanted tell Mark how irresponsible he'd been, but I didn't want to criticize him for exactly the same reason he was pissed at me.

"Can I listen to the recording later?" Mark asked.

"Sure, but don't mention it to anyone. I need to talk to Eric so he can get an opinion from the lawyers on how to handle it. Especially don't tell the cops about it."

Someone knocked at the door frame and walked into the room. Startled, Mark and I both whirled to see who it was. We found Eric Ryland walking toward us.

"Where is she?" Ryland asked. Then he spotted me on the sofa with ice pressed against my face. "Jesus, what the hell happened here?"

"How did you know anything happened?" Mark asked.

"I called him as soon as Houssmann left," I mumbled.

"I was still in town, so I got here quick," Ryland said.

Mark looked at him in surprise. "You were still in the city at this hour?"

"Yeah, I have a social life, too. It was a small college reunion."

Before Mark could remark on that, Ryland sat down on the sofa with me.

"Are you okay?" he asked. He turned to Mark. "Did you call an ambulance?"

I said I didn't need an ambulance, trying to talk around the cut lip and very sore jaw.

More people showed up. There were four medics, two police officers, two detectives, and Sgt. Pete Rizzo, the Chicago Police Department's liaison with the city's media. Pete, who'd been a friend for several years, squinted at my bloody face.

"Somebody did quite a number on you," he said. "You need one of the medics?"

I shook my head.

"What're you doing here?" I asked.

Pete smiled. "Might as well be here as anywhere," he said. "I was only sleeping."

The detectives broke up the social and introduced themselves. The older one was Yeager and the younger one Quadrelli. They started in with their standard questions. I kept shaking my head and remained silent.

Ryland stepped in to explain.

"Deuce can't talk to you until she and I speak with the newspaper's lawyers," he said. "You'll have to get in line."

The two detectives obviously didn't approve. Yeager's face hardened, and Quadrelli's eyes stormed.

"She was assaulted and threatened," Yeager said. "Several others were assaulted. You can't just let that slide while the lawyers do their thing. Every minute we waste the bad guys go deeper underground."

"I can't speak for the agent from Lasher Security or the man who was on the desk in the lobby downstairs," Ryland said. "They can do what they want, or what their employers tell them. But Deuce waits for guidance from the *Journal*'s lawyers."

The second detective stepped in, Quadrelli. "The guy down in the lobby says he was overpowered, tied up and gagged, and locked in a storage room. They threatened to kill him if he made any noise. The security guy in the hall said something stunned him before he could get a look at the intruders."

"I'm sure they're telling the truth," Mark said.

"What they're telling us isn't worth squat," Yeager said with growing irritation.

Mark said, "Look, Deuce knows who the bad guys were. So, they're not gonna get away unless they have very deep and secluded hidey holes somewhere. In that case, they evaporated before you even showed up."

Ryland interrupted. "Look, the senior partner in the firm that represents the newspaper is Jonathan Bruckner. He's on his way from Lincoln Park. He should be here soon. Maybe we can tell you more after he makes some sense of all this. Be a little patient."

"Patience isn't what the taxpayers expect from us," Quadrelli said.

Bruckner came through the door in time to hear that. He introduced himself. He asked Mark if there was a place he, Ryland, and I could talk in private. Mark told them to use his office.

I stood a bit shakily, supported by Pete Rizzo.

"That reminds me, Murphy needs to go out," I said. "He's in the office. Take a couple of the Lasher people with you and stay close to the building."

"Yes, ma'am," Mark said with a grin. He reached for the leash and told the detectives, "Don't feel like you need to leave. You can wait for Deuce's meeting to end."

He got two glares in reply.

63

When Ryland, Bruckner, and I returned to the living room, the parameters had been set. I agreed to submit to interviews. Some material would be withheld for the time being, like the digital recording. Bruckner said he wanted to listen to it again before he decided on its disposition.

I would not tell the detectives I could conclusively identify Houssmann, but I could say I'd seen photographs of him, and the man at the door looked like Houssmann. He was the one who did all the talking and didn't make much of an issue of it when I refused him permission to come in. He promised me they hadn't come to kill me. But Houssmann added that he would be back to retaliate if I reported his visit to the police.

I could, Bruckner told me, decline for now to say why I was having anything to do with the man who looked like Houssmann. Not the sex trafficking, not the drugs, not the killings. Governor Latchey hadn't come up at all, so Bruckner said I should leave him out of it. And definitely not mention Houssmann's proffered bribes. That could lead them to questions I didn't need to address at this point.

Bruckner said he should take possession of the Houssmann

recording, just as he'd done with recordings I'd had made while reporting other stories. I walked out and saw that Mark had returned safely with the dog. I waved him over to the office door, asked him to grab my bag, get the digital recorder, and give it to Bruckner. Don't tell the detectives about the recorder, I said, and don't let them see it.

He understood.

"Jesus," Pete Rizzo said when I wrapped up the brief interviews with the detectives. "You must have been terrified."

I nodded. "A little, yeah. But I confess to being a bit of a smartass to cover how I was really feeling."

"You can be a smartass when you're not scared half to death."

I cocked my head. "Why are you here, Pete? Word about this couldn't have gotten around town yet."

"But it will," he said. "And when I talk to your media colleagues I have to know what and how much I can say."

I replied, "What you always say. That the matter is under investigation."

Rizzo smiled. "You can also be a smartass when you're bleeding on Mark's sofa."

"It's a gift."

It was after 5 a.m. when Mark and I finally got to bed. When the sun came streaming in the bedroom windows, I wasn't sure I'd ever gone to sleep.

When my phone rang at 8:46 a.m. I figured it probably was my editor. But it was Saturday, and Ryland didn't generally work on Saturdays. Unless it was a news emergency. I didn't need another one of those. I didn't want to talk to anyone. While the bleeding had stopped, my lip and jaw had stiffened overnight. Talking would hurt. The screen on my phone confirmed Ryland as the caller so I knew I had to answer. I picked up and said quietly, "Hold on a sec."

I climbed out of bed and walked into the bathroom, hoping I

wouldn't wake Mark, who was sleeping soundly. Not surprising. We'd gone to bed less than four hours earlier.

"Hey," I said when I closed the door. "What's up?"

"You sitting down?" Ryland asked.

"No," I said and asked again, "What's up?"

"Latchey's dead."

I put the lid on the toilet down and sat. The news took a minute to process.

"What's the rest?"

"Not much detail yet. His wife found him hanged this morning from a rafter in the garage of their Naperville home. She was going out to pick up dry cleaning."

"Oh, God. Oh, God," I said barely above a whisper. "Did anybody try to stop it? Was his security around?"

"Apparently not."

"You know what I'm thinking, right?"

"Same thing I'm thinking, I imagine."

"Why would Houssmann do that? Latchey was protecting him."

"Maybe the tide was turning."

I felt sick. "I did this, didn't I? I accused Latchey and Conaway of election law violations, and Houssmann found out. Maybe Latchey wanted the charade to end. So Houssmann had him killed."

I heard Ryland sigh. "First his son. Now the governor. That's tragic. And ballsy."

"And who knows how many before them," I said. "Cronies, opponents, people who were on his pad down in Joe Pye County. And who knows how many children."

"This isn't your fault, Deuce, and don't think for a moment that it is. Whether the governor killed himself or died on Houssmann's orders, it's all on him. He got himself into this mess. He wanted to be elected and allowed his baser self to justify his actions and decisions. If he thought the roof was about to fall in, or if Houssmann thought Latchey might turn on him, either choice would have provided motive."

"What about Harry Conaway, Latchey's press secretary? Where's he?"

"Fielding media calls, I imagine. If he was a party to all this and remains loyal to Houssmann they'll probably leave him alone. Having Latchey and Conaway both die would be way too big a coincidence for the cops to accept as a suicides."

64

———

Ryland agreed that I should work my sources on the Latchey story. I needed to talk to Emilio Martinez again, and in a location the Federal Marshals chose as safe. If Latchey's death was murder, Martinez might be able to expand on what I already knew or suspected about the relationship between the dead governor and the retirement home kingpin. He also might know of other present or past members of Houssmann's inner circle who might be sufficiently horrified by events to agree to help bring Houssmann down.

I didn't like interviewing sources on controversial subjects without seeing them face-to-face. But Ryland was emphatic that he wanted me working from the well-guarded condo and not setting foot outside. If I absolutely had to see someone in person, they could be escorted to the condo. I could talk to them in Mark's office with an abundance of federal cops and Lasher Security agents all around us. This would be the second time in a month I'd been locked away for my own safety. At least this place had a kitchen and a couple of bathrooms. And windows. Lovely windows.

When we ended the call, I found Mark sitting on the edge of the bed.

"I'm sorry," I said. "You need the bathroom?"

"I did," Mark replied. "Good thing the condo has two. What's happening?"

I filled him in. He listened without interruption, his face expressionless.

"Sounds like the whole conspiracy is shattering," he observed when I finished.

"Something's shattering," I said. "Whether it's the conspiracy or my brain, I'm not sure. I'm going to call Jerry. Maybe he'll be able to add something of value."

When Alvarez answered he sounded distracted. I apologized for waking him up.

"No apology necessary," he said. "When you're getting ready to have a baby in the house you're almost always distracted. How're you feeling this morning?"

"Okay," I said. "Have you seen the news?"

"I haven't even seen coffee yet."

I brought him up to date. If he had any reaction, he didn't voice it.

"I need to talk to Emilio Martinez, stat," I said. "Can you get your federal marshals to make that happen. They'd have to bring him to me. I'm confined to quarters."

"And well you should be. And so should he. From my experience putting witnesses in protective custody, the marshals won't expose him to anyone for any reason. I'll ask, but don't get your hopes up. What else?"

"If it's possible I'd like to talk to Harry Conaway."

"State cops and maybe FBI probably have him squirreled away by now. I don't think it will do any good, but I'll see what I can do. I'm gonna be tied to you at the hip from here out. We're all pretty sure pieces of this puzzle will be landing on my desk sooner or later."

I felt guilty about not keeping Josh Fujita in the loop, but he was as much a prisoner in his hotel as I was in Mark's condo. I called him and filled him. He'd already been briefed.

"I wanted to call you last night to see how you were, but Eric told me to leave you alone, that you were hurting."

"I was kind of tied up with cops and lawyers and editors. I'm fine. Thanks."

"Suicide's a stretch," Fujita said. "Latchey seemed too soft to have the guts for it."

"Sometimes shaky people are more afraid of consequences than death."

"Lemme know if you need a hand with the money stuff," Fujita said.

I called Tony Donato, the Cook County medical examiner. We'd worked together before on sensitive cases. The last time I'd seen him was at the scene of Grey Houssmann's murder. But Latchey died in DuPage County, so it wouldn't be Donato's case. However, MEs gossip, like those in almost any profession. Maybe Donato could get some information from his DuPage counterpart on whether Latchey's death was suicide or murder.

When I reached Donato he put the hammer to my hopes.

"The DuPage guy's an old codger and old-school," he said. "I've had more arguments with him than civil conversations. He doesn't like me, and I don't like him. We don't gossip. But if I do hear anything, I'll let you know if I can."

A few minutes after the call ended somebody knocked hard at the door. I glanced at Mark. He held up his hand and nodded, a gesture that said it was okay.

"A Lasher agent called up from the lobby," he said. "I told him to bring the guy up. It's Harry Conaway. I figured you'd want to talk to him." Mark flashed the gun on his belt. "Just in case," he added.

Two Lasher security people escorted Conaway. One was a woman, and she looked every bit as capable as her male counterpart of taking care of business.

Conaway looked shell-shocked.

"You hear?" he asked while still standing in the hall.

"I did," I said. "Why don't you come in?"

"We'll come, too," the female Lasher employee said. "He's not armed, but after what happened this morning, we're not takin' any chances."

Conaway and I sat in Mark's office. Mark made a full pot of coffee. Conaway accepted a mug and seemed grateful for it. One of the male Lasher agents waited just outside. We had barely started talking when Jerry Alvarez showed up.

"You two remember each other?" I asked. "From the meeting in the mayor's office?"

Both nodded, but they made no move to shake hands. The tension was palpable.

"Why's he here?" Conaway asked me.

"Why don't you ask him?" I suggested.

"*Es mi trabajo,*" Alvarez said. "It's my job."

"What happened in Naperville?" I asked Conaway.

"I don't know," he said. "I honestly don't know. I was in Evanston most of the day and spent last night at the Hilton Garden Inn down here. I needed a good steak after the day I had, and Morton's is right across the street. I have the receipts if you need proof. I hadn't seen the governor since early yesterday morning."

"What was his mood like?" I asked.

"Subdued," Conaway said. "Your accusations shook him up bad."

Alvarez said, "We're going to ask you some questions that you'll also get from the police, the FBI, I don't know who all else. But you need to answer them now, if for nothing than your own safety. Do you think you might be in danger?"

"I know I am," Conaway replied. "Honus Houssmann spelled that out for me in no uncertain terms. That's why I was in Evanston yesterday."

He had been summoned by Houssmann the day before, Conaway said. No summons from Houssmann could be ignored, but he was given no reason for the meeting.

"I met him in the parking lot of his building, and his driver took us over to the Northwestern campus. We parked out on Industrial Road, under the water tower, and talked in the car. Houssmann put the windows down. It totally creeped me out. It was like a Mafia movie where you go someplace alone or with someone you don't quite trust, and some gunman walks up and caps you with a silenced gun. I felt like I should be looking over my shoulder every other minute."

I suggested, "He probably wouldn't have wanted your blood all over his car."

"What did he want?" Alvarez asked.

Conaway rubbed a hand over his eyes. He looked exhausted.

"It was a warning," he said. "Houssmann told me that if anything happened to the governor, the best thing I could do to preserve my health—that's the way he said it, 'preserve my health'—was to profess complete ignorance and then shut my mouth."

I jumped in. "Ignorance about what? The election money laundering?"

Conaway nodded. "That and everything else. The drugs, the kids. Everything."

Alvarez asked, "Was there an implicit threat?"

"No, it was quite explicit," Conaway said, his voice trembling. "He said his people would come to my house and kill my family in front of me then kill me. He said I would die slowly. I didn't know what he meant and didn't want to know."

Houssmann was the man who condoned hanging turncoats over Black Marsh to be eaten by alligators. I thought it might be best for Conaway's sanity not to mention it."

I glanced at Alvarez. I hoped we had similar thoughts. He nodded at me.

"I'll make the call," he said. Then he turned back to Conaway. "We're going to get you and your family some protection, but since it's the weekend I don't know how fast it can be set up. Do you have someplace safe to hole up?"

"If I know Houssmann, he's having me followed. I can send my wife and the kids to her mother in Indianapolis. But I need to stay visible and loyal."

"You think you were followed here?" I asked.

Conaway shook his head. "I don't, but I can't be positive. I went through some pretty elaborate steps to get here. I arranged with your security to get inside." He cocked his head toward two Lasher agents standing behind him.

I asked, "Your car's still at the Hilton?"

He nodded.

I said to Alvarez, "We need to get someone to pick it up. If people are watching the car they'll get suspicious when Harry doesn't claim it."

"Give me the parking ticket," Alvarez told Conaway.

Conaway dug into his wallet and pulled it out.

"What are you gonna do?" he asked Alvarez.

"We'll tell you later. Meanwhile, you're going to have to sign an agreement to turn over the evidence and testimony under oath to help bring Houssmann down."

"Okay," Conaway said. He looked and sounded like a beaten and terrified man.

Alvarez continued. "Call your wife on her cell—not a land line—and tell her to pack up herself and the kids and leave the state. You have a garage?"

"Three-car," Conaway said.

"Tell your wife to keep the garage doors down while she packs for the trip so no one can see her with luggage. When they leave, put the kids down on the back floor where they won't be seen. By the time Houssmann's goons realize she hasn't come home, they'll be safe, and you'll be under protection."

"You do this a lot?" Conaway asked.

Alvarez sucked down a deep breath. "A whole lot more than you want to know."

When we walked out of Mark's office one of the Lasher agents had a message. "Our boss just got a call from the Federal Marshal's office. They said to keep Mr. Conaway secure in the condo. Two marshals are on their way to get him and take him somewhere temporarily until a permanent setup can be arranged."

Alvarez called the marshals' office to confirm. He was told that an agent who was Conaway's age and build would go to the Cubs' afternoon game dressed in a lot of Cubs gear. The marshals would take Conaway to the stadium dressed normally. He and the Cubs "fan" would exchange clothes, and the newly redressed marshal would leave. When Conaway left, no one would recognize him, and marshals could drive him to pick up his car at the Hilton. At least that's what they hoped for.

As they sat and drank coffee, Alvarez asked Conaway, "Hey, do you happen to be a Cubs fan?"

Conaway looked stunned. "What? The baseball team? No. White Sox. Why do you ask me that now?"

"Well, you're gonna have to suck it up for the day. For the time being, your new favorite sports venue in Chicago is Wrigley Field."

65

———————

Ryland and Bruckner showed up at the same time as the two Chicago police detectives who'd been so frustrated the day before. They had more questions for me. I had no more answers, so I ignored them. I took Ryland and Bruckner into Mark's office and filled them in on the visit from Conaway. Bruckner wasn't representing Conaway, but it was a development he needed to know about. He had a few things to tell me.

"You know there's a BOLO and an arrest warrant out for Houssmann for the hit-and-run murder of his son?" Bruckner asked.

I nodded. "His adoptive son, yes."

"Okay. In the aftermath of the governor's death, the cops are going to try to badger you into giving up more information. Do what you did last night. Give them a limited version of the truth. But don't tell them everything."

"Still not mention the recording?"

"No, I think we're legally obligated to give it to them. We can ask them to make a copy and return the original to me."

"Are they going to demand to know why I didn't it turn it over the same night?"

"Maybe. I'll tell that until I had a chance to listen to it, I wanted to hold it close."

"Got it," I said. "What about Conaway? Should I tell them about his visit?"

"Again, I think you have to. Tell them Conaway was shaken and concerned about his future. He said he didn't personally know if the governor's death was suicide or murder. He had an alibi for yesterday, last night, and this morning. Don't be specific about the conversation Conaway had with Houssmann up in Evanston. Coming from you, it's only hearsay and might not even be true. I don't really doubt that it's true, but it's still hearsay. Don't mention the smart aleck remarks you made about anything."

"Why do you think I made smart aleck remarks?"

"Because you can't draw a breath without doing that."

Bruckner reviewed a few more instructions then said, "Let's do this in the living room where everyone can hear your story. That might stop the cops from harassing you. And remember, answer their questions but don't elaborate. If it's a yes-or-no question, give them a yes-or-no answer. Nothing else. Understood?"

I confirmed that I did.

We went out to my waiting audience.

The detectives were Yeager and Quadrelli, the same two who'd come the night before. To say they were waiting patiently for me would be a gross exaggeration. Following my lawyer's instructions, I gave them the most abridged version possible of my discussion with Conaway. They sensed they weren't getting the whole story about Conaway just as they hadn't gotten the who story about Houssmann. They pressed me several times to elaborate. I did, but very judiciously.

Quadrelli asked, "Where's Conaway now?"

"I have no idea," I said. "Not here." In fact, the marshals had picked him up ten minutes before the detectives arrived.

"You're not telling us everything, Ms. Mora," Yeager said. "This Houssmann is a bad guy. Do you want us to get him or not? If you do, we need your cooperation."

Bruckner held the digital recording out to Yeager. He explained, "Deuce had this turned on while Houssmann and his goons were here. I didn't want to turn it over until I had a chance to review the contents. Evidence gathered by a journalist is a bit like a lawyer/client work product. It's private. In this case there is a confession to a murder, and that belongs in police custody. What I'm offering you now is a full copy of the original. You leave the original with me."

"We don't take orders from you," Yeager said. "Especially when it's about relevant evidence you've been withholding."

Brucker closed his hand around the recording. "Then you don't get it."

"Okay," Yeager said. "I'll ask the Loo if this is okay and let you know. Could we at least listen to it and make some notes before we go?"

Bruckner looked like he was thinking about it. Finally, he said, "Okay. But you listen at the dining room table with Deuce and me sitting right there with you. And I hold the recorder while it's on playback."

"You know we could charge you both with obstruction of justice," Yeager said.

"You wouldn't have a prayer. We're giving you a copy of the recording of my client's free will." Then he smiled.

"You know one of the tenets of the law? It came out of British jurisprudence: 'You can charge the Bishop of Birmingham for bastardy. But can you convict?'"

66

———————

The rest of the day and early evening were quiet. I tried to get a nap in the bedroom while Mark and two Lasher agents watched baseball on television and drank iced tea. I thought later that I had dozed. That evening Mark ordered six large pizzas and a half dozen two-liter bottles of Coke from Phil's, a great pizza joint in the Bridgeport neighborhood. It would be delivered to the front desk by Grubhub. Harry, who was back at work, would parcel them out to the Lasher agents, Mark and me, and keep one for himself. They were all the same: sausage, pepperoni, green pepper, onion, and mushrooms. Mark put our two bottles of Coke in the refrigerator for another time and replaced them with two bottles of Matilda, a wheat ale from Chicago's Goose Island brewery.

My phone rang a little after eight, just as I was thinking about going to bed early. The ID on the screen said, "CALLER UNKNOWN." Great, I thought, some robocaller wants to discuss renewing my car warranty or a non-existent debt to a company I never heard of and probably doesn't exist.

It wasn't a robocall, but I wished it had been.

The caller didn't identify himself and didn't need to.

"I warned you," the familiar male voice said, "that if you went to the cops you would be forfeiting your life."

"I didn't go to the cops, Mr. Houssmann. They came to me. I wasn't the only person who was assaulted. The desk attendant in the lobby, a member of the Lasher Security detail. Either of them could have placed the call and probably did. I emphatically did not."

"Have the police questioned you?"

"Yes," I said. "Twice. On the advice of my editor and my newspaper's lawyer, I gave them nothing of any importance. Your name never came up. Neither did Governor Latchey's. Last time the detectives left here one of them told me they would come back if I remembered anything useful."

"Why would your editor and lawyer tell you not to talk?"

"As far as I know that's the way all news organizations do business. They don't want reporters saying anything that could generate a lawsuit or turn out not to be true."

There was silence for a moment, then Houssmann asked, "Have you given any thought to my offer?"

"I have, though not a lot. It's been very hectic around here in the wake of your visit."

"We've noticed. I'll be in touch." He hung up.

Mark was gawking. "Houssmann?" he asked in surprise. "Man, he's got a set of brass ones, doesn't he?"

"I think he wants me to know he's watching me."

"We should ask Eric if there's a way to increase your security."

"I don't know how he could," I replied. "Lasher has people in the garage, people at your door. They just added a detail in the lobby. I guess they could put people on the roof with anti-missile weapons in case Houssmann gets his hands on a cruise missile and tries to put it through your window."

"This really isn't funny, Deuce."

"I'm not laughing. But I think I will go to bed. I was tired before, but the beer and the pizza have knocked the stuffing out of me."

"I'll be in shortly," Mark said. "I want to think about things for a while, then take Murphy out. And yes, yes, yes, I'll take security and stay close to the building, but Murphy needs stretch his legs. So do I."

"Stay close to the building and take security with you," I cautioned. Mark grinned at me. "Okay, Mother," he replied.

When I got to bed I sank into a deep sleep quickly. Once again I had a nightmare that included gunfire. And this time there was an additional detail. I was falling. I assumed the new element had something to do with the plane crash. I still didn't understand the recurring dreams about gunfire, though heaven knew there had been enough of it when Drigger blew up the meth lab and again when we had to shoot our way past Sparks and his posse to escape Red Twig.

JERRY ALVAREZ CALLED the next morning while Mark and I were on our second cups of coffee talking about what we were going to have for breakfast. His choice was cold leftover pizza. Mine was brown sugar and cinnamon oatmeal. That decided, neither of us could get our bodies into motion. The emotional drag of recent events was taking its toll.

When the phone rang, though, I had no choice but to pick it, hoping with all the strength I had that it wasn't Houssmann again. I smiled when I saw Alvarez's ID.

"You on baby duty?" I asked.

"No, I'm in the office," he said. "What's going on at your end?"

I told him about the Houssmann call the night before.

He thought about that for a moment.

"Listen, Deuce," he finally said, "we've been tailing Houssmann since the night he showed up at Mark's condo. We decided to keep him on a long leash instead of arresting him right away on the murder charge. We want to try to wipe out his whole sordid life at once and put an end to the trafficking once and for all this time. We had hopes he would lead us to the site where he has the kids imprisoned. We were doing fine—until we weren't. We didn't see him leave his house in Lake Forest yesterday, and he never showed up at his

Evanston office. The FBI swung by his office in Milwaukee. They were told he hadn't been there in several days and wasn't expected. Two offices, same story: Not in. Not expected."

"You've lost him?" I asked.

"Not necessarily. He might be holed up inside his house. The place is huge. I think Lake Forest could be the most expensive suburb Chicago's got. His place must be worth millions. Lots of places to hide inside, I'm guessing."

"Maybe a secret office behind a revolving bookcase," I suggested, only half serious.

"We're going to keep watching the house and the Evanston and Milwaukee offices. We'll take him into custody on a murder charge as soon as we find him, just to make sure we've got him on something. That would take some of the heat off you. Unless a judge releases him on his own recognizance. I definitely don't want that to happen."

"I didn't think that was ever done on a first-degree murder charge," I said.

"When you're Honus Houssmann all things are possible," Alvarez replied.

"How can you stop it?"

"We'd need to convince a judge that he's too dangerous. To that end, we'll have Conaway's interviews, and we're going to do one with Emilio Martinez. I wanted to let you know because if we have to explain all this in open court, it will blow your story. We'll ask to do it in the judge's chambers, but I'm sure Houssmann's lawyers will object."

"Better I lose the story than we lose any more lives," I said.

"Well, we have to find Houssmann first. We do have the option of trying to get a search warrant for his house, but we won't have the paperwork to present our case to a judge until tomorrow. We have to interview Martinez first. Evidence from both a dead governor's press secretary and a former state senator will have credibility. At least that presentation won't be public."

I sensed a heavier tension than usual in Jerry's voice. "Is something else bothering you?" I asked.

"Yeah. With his money and his resources he could get away from here in a heartbeat. Fly to a country that doesn't have an extradition treaty with the United States—maybe Morocco or Cambodia—and live the rest of his life sitting under a tree sipping pink cocktails with fruit and small, colorful paper umbrellas stuck in them."

An escape would at least get Houssmann out of the country and unable to run his disgusting business enterprises, but as soon as the notion occurred to me, I realized it wasn't true. And Alvarez confirmed it.

"In this age of high-powered and encrypted computers and almost untraceable satellite phones, there probably wouldn't be so much as a hiccup in his enterprises, assuming there's someone he can trust to run them."

"We've got to stop him, Jerry," I said. "Why doesn't an FBI sniper just kill him?"

"Even if that were in the cards, Deuce, we couldn't consider it until we know where to find him.

"Then would you consider it?"

"No."

67

At the same moment Houssmann was pacing his study, his mood swinging between nervous and furious. The furious part could be described more as murderous. He'd concluded that he should have killed Deuce when he had the chance at her boyfriend's condo. They could have killed the guy from the front desk on their way out. Except that would have intensified the manhunt. He would have killed a journalist, and he'd have three newspapers and a city full of cranky cops and FBI agents on his ass. On the other hand, they were already on his trail for the Joe Pye business and Grey's murder. If he continued running the businesses, the manhunt would remain a threat. So, as usual, he decided what was in his own best interests.

That seemed to be getting himself and his cash out of the country. He would have to give up his retirement home business, which would be a shame. But he had more than enough liquidity to live like a king for the rest of his life without coming close to running through his money. He would be able to enjoy himself for a change instead of worrying and wondering when the legal rug would be pulled from under him.

He already had upwards of $27 billion stashed in banks in Luxem-bourg, a country with deadly serious banking secrecy laws. In one case where banking officials were found guilty of sharing private information *with outsiders, they all went to jail. Houssmann figured he had at least one billion dollars more in liquidity in the United States between his investments and the cash stashed in the vault in his home. He had acquired an island paradise two years earlier in The Maldives, a string of tropical islands in the Indian Ocean west of India and Sri Lanka. It was an all-cash deal under an assumed name. There would be no way for Interpol or other police agencies to learn the real identity of the owner. In the intervening months he paid a local company to maintain and improve the property, including construction of a vault with security specifications so tough a freight train couldn't breach them. All the work had been completed, and the seven-acre property was ready for him to assume as his new residence as soon as he could clean up his business and leave the United States forever. The Maldives had no extradition treaties with the United States, so he would be untouchable.*

Houssmann had set up a meeting in his study with Conrad Mobley, a trusted member of his board and the enormously wealthy owner of a retail conglomerate spread over four states. Mobley should show up any minute, totally unaware that he was about to "inherit" one of the most lucrative corporations in the country. He had more inside information on Houssmann operations than all the other board members combined. It had been his suggestion that Houssmann Health order as many of the earliest covid vaccine doses as it could, ostensibly for the patients and staff at all the Houssmann Health facilities. But the idea was to sell doses off to the highest bidders and only then to distribute what was left to patients and staff. That maneuver had earned the company just under $10 million, not a fortune by Houssmann standards, but a nice secondary haul. Ten million here, ten million there; pretty soon it adds up to real money. Mobley had a thief's mentality, which made him a good choice to succeed Houssmann.

Six minutes later the chosen successor arrived. He had never been in Houssmann's home, and especially not in the secret, hidden places. He was quite obviously impressed.

The two men shook hands and sat down at a conference table that took up maybe eight hundred square feet of Houssmann's home office.

"Impressive, Honus," he said as he sat down. "But where the hell am I?

On your property, I know, but where? It actually took an elevator to get here."

"Two levels underground," Houssmann replied. "My secret hideaway and a place I wish to remain secret, if you get my drift."

"Understood," Mobley said. "Nice touch, hiding the elevator behind the back of your bar. Who would ever guess that a wall with all those liquor bottles on it could be balanced so perfectly that it could be swiveled with one hand?"

"It also requires a key," Houssmann said. "A special key. One of a kind. Can't be duplicated. And I'm the only one who has it."

"Smart," Mobley said. "So what can I do for you?"

"It's what we can do for each other," Houssmann said. "First I need to disclose to you the full extent of the activities of the business."

Houssmann took nearly an hour to lay it out, along with the events of the last two months. He didn't pull any punches. Mobley nodded at the explanation of drug dealings, as though he already knew at least part of that story. Houssmann thought he saw Mobley flinch at the details of the child trafficking ring. He appeared not to be surprised at all when he learned of Houssmann's relationship to the late governor of Illinois, William Latchey. And he might have smiled when his boss described how he'd killed Grey, his own son.

"After all," Houssmann said, "you were the one who told me Grey was a danger, that he was going to turn on us."

Now Mobley spoke. "You needed to know, Honus. I knew you weren't fond of the boy and needed to take some remedial action. I did not, however, think you would do the deed yourself. But I guess if you want something done right . . ." His voice trailed off as Houssmann nodded. Houssmann needed to add some details, and he didn't pull punches or lie.

He recounted all of the events in Joe Pye County, including the destruction of the principal meth lab, the deaths of Derek Sparks and more than half his deputies, the events surrounding the Journal *reporter, Deuce Mora, and the strange black vagrant known to the rest of the world only as Drigger.*

"Well," Mobley said, "we know Deuce Mora's still alive. What became of Drigger?"

"Nobody knows," Houssmann said. "He was badly wounded in the final shootout. So, he might have died. Or he might have fled Joe Pye with Mora. Nobody I know has seen or heard of him since he was airlifted away from the tunnel."

They stared at one another for a long moment. Then Houssmann asked his guest, "You want a drink?"

"No," Mobley said, "but I need one. Double Scotch, neat."

"You have a brand preference?"

Mobley mustered a small laugh. "You got Johnny Walker Blue?"

Without answering, Houssmann punched a button on his desk phone. Someone answered, "Yes, Sir?"

"Double Johnny Walker Blue, neat, and a large iced coffee with a double pour of Bailey's. Bring 'em down as soon as you can."

"So, what do you want from me?" Mobley asked.

"I want you to buy me out."

Now Mobley was more animated than previously in the entire meeting.

"You can't be serious," he said, his eyes wide and his eyebrows arched.

"Completely," Houssmann said.

"Even if I wanted to do that, I don't have that kind of money."

"I'll sell you everything for a dollar, including all the money in all the accounts in both states. The company will be yours. You will be insanely wealthy for the rest of your life, and you will be assuming control of Houssmann Health to do with as you want. Sell it. Shut it down. Keep all or part of it. Whatever."

"And I'll be sitting out front to take all the blame when the roof falls in."

"It won't fall on you," Houssmann promised. "Once I'm gone, I want you to give it all up to the state and the feds. Clean out the bank accounts first and put the money in your own offshore account in a country with heavy banking security and secrecy. If nobody finds out about it, you won't even pay taxes. Leave enough in the accounts for the feds to seize, and they'll think they got it all. Say, a million dollars."

"Just leave a million on the table?"

"And walk away with twenty million or so. That sounds like a good deal to me."

Mobley smiled. "It is. What about the drugs, the trafficking, and the elections fraud?"

"Also on me," Houssmann said. "You didn't know about any of it until you bought the company. You didn't make any of the decisions or take any of the illegal actions. You seemed a bit shaken when I told you about the trafficking. So shut it down immediately and turn the remaining kids over to the cops. A sign of your horror. You have no culpability for anything."

"I'll probably be facing a couple dozen lawsuits that will settle for a fortune."

"The company's got insurance against that sort of thing. Any company that takes responsibility for the lives of others incurs a huge liability. So, the insurance won't look suspicious. Whatever suits arise, just tell the insurer and the company's lawyers to handle it."

"Wow," Mobley said. "Can I think about it overnight?"

"No."

"No? This is a gigantic undertaking. I can't make a knee-jerk decision."

Say 'yes' and my next call will be to my lawyer to draft the bill of sale and everything that goes along with it. We'll both sign, I'll leave, and the rest will be up to you. Decide now."

Mobley agreed, albeit with some obvious reservations that would never be resolved. But twenty million tax-free dollars couldn't be ignored.

*M*OBLEY WAS ESCORTED BACK *to his car in the driveway and watched by Houssmann's security team until he disappeared through the front gate and gate closed behind him.*

Back in the study, Houssmann placed a call to his chief attorney and told him about the plan. He said he wanted the sales agreement ready to sign within three days. The attorney wasn't surprised. Nothing Houssmann did or requested surprised him anymore. He asked some questions. Houssmann declined to answer most of them. The "why" of the deal, what would happen to the money, where Houssmann planned to go—all left without answers because Houssmann knew he would be more secure that way.

When the call ended, the nursing home king called his personal banker and ordered that all his liquid financial assets—CDs, stocks and bonds, T-bills, everything—be cashed out and the money wired to the usual places in Luxembourg.

"We can't wire it all at once," the banker said. "It would be reported, and the FBI and IRS would be all over you."

"Then get an armored truck and deliver the cash to the house. Three days."

"It isn't possible to complete all those transactions in three days," the banker replied.

"Then deliver what you can," Houssmann said, his voice rising in irritation, "and wire the rest to Luxembourg as the funds come in."

"How will I get in touch with you if there are any glitches?"

"You won't. Until all the transfers are complete I'll call you once a week for an update on an appointed day at a predetermined hour. There will be a nice bonus for you when all the transactions are done."

Houssmann had one more call to make. He didn't ID himself; it wasn't necessary. The two men on the call each knew the other was using a throwaway phone. Houssmann was the only person who had the pilot's throwaway number, the only one who used it.

Houssmann told the pilot what he needed and when. The pilot said he understood and would make it happen as Houssmann outlined.

"A week from tomorrow at 10 p.m.," Houssmann said. "Bring a van. I need something that can carry about ten tons in payload. Is that a problem?"

"No, Sir," the pilot said. "That's plenty of time, and I have the plane you need."

And so, it was done.

68

———

I was making painfully little progress.

No one involved in the hunt for Houssmann had seen him. Jerry Alvarez presumed he was holed up in his mansion. Alvarez was working with Maeve MacAuliffe, the head of the FBI's Chicago division, to get a warrant to search the entire place. Houssmann's lawyers argued that the warrant request was too broad. It would, they said, have to be narrowed to specific locations within the house where there might be a reasonable expectation of finding evidence of illegal business dealings.

"His home office, for starters," MacAuliffe had told the judge.

"He doesn't have a home office," Houssmann's lawyer shot back.

"Then bedrooms, safes, closets, storage rooms, wherever business documents might be stashed," MacAuliffe shot back. "And Mr. Houssmann's business offices in Evanston and Milwaukee. Any storage facilities. Any auxiliary offices and properties."

The argument went on for an hour in the judge's chambers, and the judge took the whole matter under advisement. Given the seriousness of the allegations against Houssmann, search warrants were reasonable, she said, but had to be focused more narrowly until evidence was found dictating that the search be expanded. She promised a decision within a week.

I was appalled by the delay and said so to Alvarez. I wished we could discuss all this face-to-face, but he didn't have time to come to me, and I wasn't allowed out of the condo to go to his office.

"It gets worse," Alvarez said. "I just got a call from a source in the Secretary of State's Office. Apparently there's some interesting filings coming in on Houssmann Health."

"Like what?" I asked.

"I don't know specifics," he said. "But my source tells me they are the types of filings they see when a company is in the process of being sold."

"It's starting," I said. "Any indication who he's going to sell to?"

"Not yet, but I've assigned an FBI specialist, who's also a CPA, to keep an eye on the moves and report back on what he sees. In your poking around Houssmann's dealings did you identify anyone who might be a potential buyer?"

"No," I said. "Who'd have the kind of money that would take?"

Alvarez chuffed. "In Chicago? Maybe fifty. But I don't know why any of them would take the risk. I wonder if it would do any good to try to talk to Harriet Latchey, the governor's widow. Maybe she has some insight that would help."

"We've tried," Alvarez said. "She says she is too grief-stricken to talk to the authorities now. She also says she really has no idea why anyone would want to murder her husband, or why he would want to commit suicide."

I frowned in thought for a moment. "Sometimes people going through emotional trauma don't remember what they know, or they stuff it away in a vault in their brain where they don't have to think about it or deal with it."

"Possibly," Alvarez said. "Or maybe she's lying."

"You remember when Carl Cribben was murdered?" I asked. Cribben was a retired FBI agent who sometimes used his former sources to help me gather information on investigative stories. "You and I went to the wake at his house."

"I remember," Alvarez said. "It still makes me sad."

"His wife, Nancy, was so distraught I don't think she even recognized us, and she had met me a half dozen times. She was in a stupor, almost unable to function. That might be what Harriet Latchey is going through. I understand she's the one who found his body. There's not much that could be more traumatic than that."

"Well, we'll keep trying to talk to her without pressing so hard that we become a part of the trauma," Alvarez said.

I stood up and started to pace Mark's living room. I was thinking out loud.

"You know if Houssmann is selling his business, then he's probably planning on leaving the area. Maybe leaving the country if he feels a legal net closing around him. I don't understand why the judge needs a week to decide on the scope of the search warrants for his home and offices. He's a flight risk. By the time she makes up her mind, he could have run off to Mongolia by this time next week."

"Hmmmm," Alvarez responded. "I don't think we have an extradition treaty with Mongolia. I should check."

"This isn't funny, Jerry," I said. "You interviewed Conaway and Martinez yesterday. Did you ask them if they had any notion of what Houssmann might do or where he might go if a major case was being built around him?"

"I did ask," Alvarez said. "Neither remembered the subject ever coming up. There'd be no reason for him to discuss the matter with Conaway. With Martinez, maybe. But both said independently they never really had a social occasion with Houssmann when he might have loosened up. It was always business with him."

"Shit," I said. "I feel like this thing is getting away from us."

Then I had an idea. "You think we could talk to Drigger about this? He seems to know more about Houssmann than anyone."

"I already asked," Alvarez said. "He is reported to be on assignment and unavailable for at least a month."

"He's out of the hospital?" I asked, completely surprised. "That's great. Damn, the least he could have done was let me know."

I dropped my butt onto the sofa again.

I had no idea what to do.

I WAS in a morbid mood over dinner. I had told Mark everything I knew and everything I didn't know. He had no bright ideas to open things up for me.

It was around 8:30 p.m. when the phone rang. It was Eric Ryland.

"How're you doing?" he asked.

"Getting nowhere with time running out," I said.

"Have you gotten any of your memory back?"

The question surprised me.

"Some of it," I said. "A lot of it came back while I was still in Joe Pye. But there are empty spots where I've been told what happened after Mark and I left Tahiti. But I have no independent recollections. Why?"

"I just got a call from the NTSB," he said. The National Transportation Safety Board is the federal agency that investigates accidents involving planes, trains, and commercial trucks, among others. "They're ready to release the final report on the crash in Joe Pye County, and they wanted to give me a courtesy heads-up before they make it public."

"And?"

"Your plane was shot down."

I felt my mouth drop. "What? Are you serious?"

"They calculate the gunfire came from high-powered rifles on the ground. The rounds hit both engines, the horizontal stabilizer and the cabin. There was no way to keep the thing in the air."

Gunfire. I'd had at least three flashbacks that involved gunfire.

I was silent, thinking, remembering. As with a curtain opening slowly, I saw slivers of things that began to solidify into solid scenarios. I realized I was sometimes hearing gunfire in my dreams because my brain was trying to wake up memories. It had been terrifying. I wasn't sure I wanted to remember.

"Deuce," Ryland said, "you okay?"

"Yeah," I replied. "Is that it? I need to process this."

"Call me if you need help," he said.

I told Mark, and he held me well into the night.

69

———

A week passed. Still no sign of Houssmann. I feared that he'd gotten away, flown overseas and was hunkered down with forged papers and passport in a country with no extradition treaty with the United States. Much like Julian Assange, he would be waiting for whatever imbroglio developed over Houssmann Health to flame up and then die away. Eventually the hunt would wind down if all went as expected, and he wouldn't have to be so cautious about being recognized.

I was following the paper trail which led to a change of ownership for Houssmann's holdings. The buyer was a member of the Houssmann Health board of directors, a wealthy man in his own right. He wouldn't have to dip into his investments to acquire the company. Houssmann sold it to him for a dollar. Lawyers and bankers worked day and night to close the deal in so short a time. Other sales with so many moving parts took a year or more.

Then the other shoe dropped.

Conrad Mobley, the new owner, called Maeve MacAuliffe, the head of the FBI in Chicago, and asked for a meeting. He said it was urgent. MacAuliffe invited Jerry Alvarez to come but wouldn't allow any media, including me. Alvarez said he would brief me after the meeting, assuming he could do so legally. It probably would be off-the-record.

I sat in Mark's home office for nearly three hours after the appointed hour for the meeting. For the commander of a big-city FBI division and a deputy U.S. Attorney to give any case so much time seemed either improbable or a bombshell.

It was the latter.

Mobley had laid it all out, even as he claimed he knew nothing about any of it until he got into the company's books after the sale. I couldn't imagine anyone postponing a look at a company's books before buying it, but these are strange times.

Alvarez finally called. After securing my pledge of silence, he began.

"Mobley was forthcoming," he said. "He talked about the drugs, the smuggling, about hiring disgraced law enforcement officers to fill out the Joe Pye operations. Then came the trafficking. Houssmann had twenty-three boys ranging in age from nine to seventeen imprisoned in a windowless warehouse. When a client came along and described what he wanted and what he wanted to do, Houssmann picked out a candidate and sent him on his way to serve the buyer. Mobley claimed to have been appalled and reduced to tears when he found the children in a remote South Side warehouse, brutalized, under-nourished, and terrified. It's not the same warehouse where you found that little boy the last time."

"Have you found the twenty-three kids?"

"Mobley gave us the address. Cops, FBI, and a slew of psychologists trained to deal with abused children are on their way, if not already there. They'll be taken to hospitals and checked out immediately. As soon as they've been debriefed, they'll be reunited with their families. The care will continue as long as necessary, no charge."

His intercom beeped. Alvarez answered. I heard her say, "Maeve MacAuliffe on two."

Alvarez punched the appropriate button. "Hey, Maeve."

I couldn't overhear both ends of the conversation, but it was apparent quickly that the news was both shocking and ugly.

"Okay," he said. Thanks for letting me know. Who's going to tell his mother? You?"

I gathered the answer was in the affirmative because Alvarez said, "Good. You'll do fine. This explains a whole lot. Let me know how it goes."

He hung up and came back to me.

"Absolutely off the record?" he asked.

"I already promised that," I said.

"One of the boys rescued from the warehouse is Bobby Latchey, the fourteen-year-old son of the late governor. There's an excellent chance that's the way Houssmann kept Latchey on a short leash. The threat that your child will be sexually abused, tortured, and killed would bend most fathers into submission."

"Will he be okay?" I asked.

"The boy? No telling," Alvarez said. "He told the medics he hadn't been raped or beaten. But who knows if there's any truth to that. We can only hope."

"So is the trafficking business buried for good this time?"

"It should be. Mobley said there were no more. The kids you helped recover from the big house on the North Side last year undercut a big piece of the operation, and they were never replaced, according to Mobley. Now we've freed the rest."

I asked, "Does Mobley have any culpability?"

"To be determined," Alvarez said. "He reported the trafficking deal just two days after he took over as owner of Houssmann Health. He also owned up to the company's involvement in illegal political funding, meth manufacturing, and illegally smuggling shit across state lines for sale. That's a federal felony. A whole list of federal felonies."

"And he can't be held responsible for any of it?"

"Only if we find out he was involved. Or if he wasn't personally involved but knew of the criminal activity and failed to report it. He won't get rich from his new company, either. It's likely the IRS will seize all of the Houssmann Health assets to pay off the back taxes and a slew of federal and state fines."

"What's going to happen to all the patients?"

Alvarez groaned. "Shit, Deuce, I don't know. Mobley said he's going to try to buy the operation from the government and keep it going as the legit enterprise Houssmann claimed it to be. That remains to be seen. I wouldn't bet on it."

"So, what happens next?"

"When this whole package is straightened out, Mobley wants to disclose everything himself. In an interview with you. Exclusively. Can you do that?"

"I think I'll be able to find the time," I said.

70

____

I received another call from Alvarez late the next morning.

"He's gone," Alvarez said. He sounded dejected.

"What happened?"

"We finally got the search warrant and went into the house late yesterday. Except for two members of the staff, it was empty. But the house is huge, so it took all night to get through it. We found two offices there, one on the second floor, which I gather he used for everyday business, and one two stories underground with a big vault attached. The door was standing open. There were some incriminating business papers inside. I don't know why he didn't take them or burn them. There might have been a lot of money there at one time, but it's gone now."

"Did either of the staff members know where he went?"

"One of them knew nothing. The other one said Houssmann sometimes disappeared without telling anyone where he was going or when he'd be back. And no one saw him leave or return."

"If this didn't sound like a bad movie I'd venture a guess that he had a secret way in and out of the house."

"He did," Alvarez confirmed. "It took the FBI all night to find it.

It's a tunnel more than three miles long. It has a concrete floor, stone walls, electricity, and a golf cart."

"That sounds like a lot nicer tunnel than we had to use to get out of Red Twig. And we had to walk it. Where does Houssmann's tunnel come out?"

"In the heavily wooded area of a cemetery. The exit is well-camouflaged. There's an old road maybe fifty yards away. Rarely used, I'm told. He could easily have had a car waiting for him there. Then it's only about a mile to Western Avenue, and from there he could go anywhere he wants, and no one would be the wiser."

I had some idea where he might have gone.

I said, "When I was researching Houssmann, I remember one article made a big deal of the fact that he had a very plush private airplane. An Airbus 320, I think. The article didn't say who it was registered to."

"Did it say where he kept it?"

"Not that I recall."

"The FBI is checking in with the FAA, but so far they haven't found a plane of any kind registered to Houssmann or his company."

"Mind if I try?" I asked.

"What do you think you can accomplish that the FBI can't?"

"I won't know 'til I try."

I CALLED FRANK ZIKAS. Zikas was the chief spokesman for the FAA in Washington. He was a pain to work with: aloof, sarcastic, and eager to tell you how little he cared about your inquiry. I had dealt with him before, and I could only hope he would remember and be experiencing a more magnanimous mood than usual.

"Yeah, I remember ya," he said. "Your weird name makes it hard to forget."

"You mean weird like Zikas?" I asked. I could match him sarcasm for sarcasm.

"Zikas is Greek," he said.

"And Mora is Italian," I said. "So what?"

He fell silent for a moment, then apparently decided the sparring wouldn't take us anywhere useful.

"So, what can I do for you?"

"I'm trying to find a plane, Frank. It's privately owned."

"Must be a million of those," he interrupted.

"Probably not that many Airbus 320s."

"Huh. That would be a much more manageable list to pull together. You got an N-number for it?"

"No," I said. "I wish I did."

"Who's it registered to?"

"I'm not sure what the name is on the registration, but it's owned by a man named Honus Houssmann."

"That name's weirder than yours."

"Frank. The plane?"

"I heard this morning that the FBI had called, trying to track down a jetliner registered to that guy. We found bupkis. Course, they didn't have as much information as you do, so we didn't know what we were looking for."

"Could you run the shorter list?" I asked.

"Doing that right now." He went silent. I could hear him tapping on his keyboard.

"Nope," he said after several minutes. "No plane of any kind registered to that dude. I didn't find an Airbus, so I ran the guy's name. Still nothing."

"Let's go back to the Airbus list," I said. "Anything there that could be Honus Houssmann or his company, Houssmann Health."

He went silent for a moment then said, "I got one registered to HH Enterprises," he said. "But it's got an address in Des Moines, Iowa. Not Chicago."

Everything clicked. Houssmann had escaped from his home, probably to a car waiting for him at the far end of his tunnel. It was only about a five-hour drive to Des Moines. Very doable."

"Do you have an N-number?"

"I wonder if the guy's got vanity plates on his car," Zikas said. "Because the plane's registration number is N89HH."

"I'd bet money that's my man. Any notion where the plane is now?"

"Not this very minute," he said. "But the crew filed a flight plan for it at 3 a.m. yesterday. Destination SMF, Sacramento International Airport. Nothing after that."

"Can you track it?"

"Sure, but . . . hold on a sec," Zikas said. "I got something weird here. Let me check it out, and I'll get right back to you."

And he did. SMF air traffic control had filed a complaint against the plane. Apparently it was only on the ground in California long enough to refuel. Then it took off to the west without a flight plan. When it got offshore about seventy nautical miles, its transponders shut down. It became impossible to track."

"Is there a way to determine where it landed?"

"If it didn't crash, yeah. I can try to find out if international air traffic controllers have a record on where N89HH might have landed. I'm gonna put you on hold."

He didn't wait for my objection. So, I sat there at Mark's desk both excited and apprehensive. None of the information I got so far would help us find the plane. Or Houssmann. I hoped the FAA could provide more.

After a time, Zikas came back online to tell me they were still working on it. Then he went away again. In all, I was on hold for more than forty minutes.

"Colombo," he said when he came back. "The capital of Sri Lanka. Landed at zero-nine-eighteen today, local time. It's currently in a hangar having some work done. I don't know if it's mechanical or aesthetic, but it's gonna be on the ground a while. If it's got a problem that forced a landing, there's no guarantee that Sri Lanka was its final destination."

"Extradition treaty?"

"With Sri Lanka, yes, which makes me wonder if that's where he intended to land. Maybe once the renovations are done he'll be on the move again."

"It's a place to start, Frank. Thanks."

71

I relayed the FAA's information to Alvarez.

"Well, what do you know," he said. "Sometimes you *can* find out more than the FBI. I'll relay the data with the caution that Colombo might not be Houssmann's final destination. That raises an unsettling possibility. What if the plane was a decoy? Houssmann dispatched it to Sri Lanka to throw everyone off and flew somewhere else."

"I suppose that's possible," I said. "But for now I think we need to act on the assumption that the FAA's information is accurate. For one thing, we have the plane's registration ID, and it fits the Airbus that landed in Colombo. Let's see where that takes us."

Switching subjects for a moment, I asked what was going on with Conrad Mobley, the new owner of Houssmann Health. Several federal and state law enforcement and tax agencies were scouring the few documents and records found in Houssmann's Lake Forest estate. More evidence was uncovered in his offices in Evanston and Milwaukee. None of it implicated Mobley in any criminal activity.

Investigators were incredulous at the amount of incriminating material Houssmann left behind. They concluded that he never intended to return to the United States, thought he would never be prosecuted, and didn't give a righteous damn what his countrymen and government thought of him. He had become a ghost who would haunt the region forever.

Mobley told them that he and Emilio Martinez had two dozen discussions about what was really going on with the company. The suspicions focused on the political fundraising, but their speculation wasn't enough to take to the authorities.

Alvarez continued, "Mobley said he only learned the truth when Houssmann told him all about his business as a prelude to the sale. The trafficking, the drugs, the politics. He claimed he knew nothing about any of it until Houssmann told him."

"And he still bought the company?" I asked.

"He saw it as an opportunity to clean up the illegal stuff and enlarge his own fortune by turning the company totally legit."

MARTINEZ AND CONAWAY both were informed of the current situation and told they would be allowed to return home as soon as the federal marshals were convinced it was safe. They suspected that Houssmann had fled the country and would never be seen in the United States again. In the meantime, both would be deposed extensively. When the feds were certain they had everything there was to get, the body of evidence would be presented to a grand jury, with the goal of amassing as many charges against Houssmann as possible. That said, if Houssmann were hiding in a country that had no extradition treaty with the United States, he might never see the inside of a courtroom.

The only thing investigators hadn't found so far were significant amounts of cash. The assets Houssmann left behind amounted to only slightly more than a million dollars. Given the size of the company and its range of enterprises, that didn't sound like enough to cover all contingencies. I thought, and the investigators tended to agree, that Houssmann took anything of true value with him when he fled, including cash.

Some of this had been disclosed to the media in general at a tumultuous press conference held by the FBI, the U.S. attorney, and the IRS two weeks after Houssmann flew off to his hideaway, wherever it was. While the media knew some of the story, Mobley's interview with me produced a prodigious amount of information that hadn't been made public. Since Mobley's lawyers came with him, I was concerned that a lot of my questions would be blocked by one side or the other. Since everyone had agreed to the interview, I hoped I was wrong.

The interview went off without a hitch. Mobley shed tears when he talked about what Houssmann had disclosed about the child trafficking.

"There are no words to describe it," he told me. "'Inhumane' isn't nearly descriptive enough. 'Disgraceful?' 'Insane?' 'Unfathomable?' None of those convey what was going through my mind when Houssmann told me about it. I can't even imagine what it was like for Governor Latchey and his family knowing their young son was being held captive by a man who thought nothing of feeding children to sexual predators of the worst sort."

I wasn't sure how Eric Ryland and his superiors would feel about publishing that. It might be too much an invasion of the privacy of Latchey's family. It had not been publicly disclosed that fourteen-year-old Bobby Latchey had been one of Houssmann's captives. I argued that we should notify Harriet Latchey that it would come out and let it happen. The boy was the sword that Houssmann held over Latchey's head to keep the governor under control. As long as his son was in massive danger, Latchey would do what Houssmann told him to do. I would have to ask Mobley how Houssmann's employees and board members let it slide when they were subjected to coercion to contribute huge sums to the Latchey campaigns. Surely they saw something improper in it. So why did no one say anything? I refused to buy the ignorance-is-bliss excuse if anyone tried to offer it.

There would be a second interview the following Tuesday both to hear more elements of the story and to wrap up any matters not fully addressed on Sunday. Eric Ryland, Jonathan Bruckner, and I would spend Monday deciding how to parcel out the story. There was no question it needed to be a series. While the three of us hammered out a plan, a stenographer employed by the *Journal* transcribed the audio recording of the first interview. The process would make sure all the quotes were correct and help us find any holes in the story that needed to be filled.

Harriet Latchey gave her blessing to the use of the political-contributions aspect of the story and to disclosing Bobby Latchey's kidnapping. But she asked us to include the family's desire to be left alone as they tried to put their lives back together, to respect their privacy. When she and Bobby were ready to speak about the matter publicly, she promised, I would be the first—and the only—reporter she would reach out to.

I was exhausted by the time we finished up.

It was the beginning of the end of a nightmare that had consumed me for three months. It was time for me to get on with my life, too.

As soon as the stories were written and edited, Mark and I would have that conversation. Our future together depended on it.

72

———————

Honus Houssmann had chosen his hidey hole carefully during property research that spanned most of two years and seventeen trips overseas. He intended his next home to be his last, a long finale to a life lived too fast and too stressfully. It was time to relax and have fun.

He had a list of possible places where he would be welcome as an expatriate, The Maldives among them. Initially he rejected the nation of nearly 1,200 islands, largely because of its susceptibility to storms. The Indian Ocean tsunami of 2004 completely wiped out or severely damaged dozens of islands, including the capital, Malè. Further research disclosed that many of the islands that went undamaged or lightly damaged were out of the reach of the ferocious wave. Others were protected from it by atolls and coral reefs that sapped the tsunami's strength before it reached developed areas.

He found an estate he very much liked on one of the more isolated islands. The island had nine private, high-priced homes and two resorts from which the homes were isolated. The logistics of his move took time and money, beginning with the remodeling of the house to Houssmann's specifications. That had been completed, and the house was ready for him.

Houssmann's next move was to buy an amphibious Twin Otter turbo to *fly him around the islands as the need or the urge struck him. He bought the plane in Colombo, Sri Lanka, where he signed a long-term lease at the airport for a private hangar where the Airbus 320 could be housed until needed. He contracted with a company that could repaint the entire exterior of the 320 and apply a new, nonexistent tail number. The plane became untraceable. The two pilots who flew the arduous flight from Sacramento loaded boxes of cash from the Airbus to the Twin Otter and flew it to Malè. They all moved easily through customs and immigration with the help of complete sets of false papers, including drivers' licenses and passports, and compliant Maldavian customs officials. The sealed boxes on board? Personal effects and private papers, they were told. The officials accepted the explanation.*

Once at Houssmann's new house the plane was secured to a reinforced private dock. Its landing gear rested on the hard-pack sand below the tidal water line. Once the boxes of cash were transferred into the newly completed vault, the pilots would fly the Otter back to Malè and book flights for themselves back to Chicago, a multi-day trip. At least they didn't have to fly it themselves. Arrangements were made with several professional pilots in the islands to fly Houssmann's Twin Otter around the country when he wanted to sightsee and over to Colombo when he had business there.

That done, he settled into his new life.

N INE DAYS LATER H*OUSSMANN, now known as Peter Mason, met one of his neighbors, a man named Androsian. They got along well enough, but Houssmann knew they would never be friends. He had no friends. Friends were a breach of his strict security requirements.*

Four days after their meeting on the beach, which served as their only access to one another's property, Houssmann stepped out of his expansive salt-water pool where he swam laps twice a day. He leaned back on a lounge beside the pool. Something had been making him uneasy for several days, and he finally decided he would have to deal with it.

He would not be able to live comfortably, assured of his safety, until Deuce Mora and Drigger Morton were dead. He suspected Morton was dead already. Two reports from the site of the showdown at Red Twig reported that Morton had been very badly wounded, was bleeding heavily and unconscious when he was loaded onto a Medevac chopper and flown away from the scene. No one had seen him since. Houssmann had to find out what happened to him. If he was dead, fine. If not, Houssmann had people back in the States who could hunt him down and kill him in such a way that the bastard would be sorry he was ever born. Houssmann wouldn't feel completely comfortable in his new life until his twisted sense of justice was served.

He knew Deuce Mora remained alive and well, still working for the Journal *and peeling back the sordid details of the operations of Houssmann Health. It infuriated him that she wouldn't let well enough alone. She had run him out of the country. Why couldn't she just forget about him? If the publicity and sordid disclosures stopped, sooner or later the hunt for him would taper off, too. But how long that would take was anybody's guess. Besides, he wanted the satisfaction of knowing she was gone. Perhaps his crew could incorporate several days of torture and then kill her.*

A new satellite phone replaced the one he had been using. While sat phones are extremely difficult to trace, it's not impossible. So, he had ditched the old one over the Indian Ocean. The new one sat on a small table beside him. He picked it up and called a phone number he had memorized.

A man answered immediately using their agreed upon code.

"Kenosha," the voice said.

"Iroquois," he responded. "Listen, I've got a couple of jobs for you."

THE NEXT AFTERNOON Houssmann walked through the triple-paned sliders out to his poolside. There were five sets of sliders along the living room wall facing the pool and another in a spare guestroom Houssmann had planned to fix up as an office when all his U.S. business was complete. That included learning that Drigger Morton and Deuce were both confirmed dead. Houssmann hadn't thought of it when he talked with his contact the day before or he would have included the murder of Mark Hearst in the assignment, too. Perhaps the bastard would die with Deuce. He could only hope.

There had been no word on the progress of the lethal missions. But it had only been one day. If Drigger were alive it could take a long time to flush him out. Deuce Mora, on the other hand, should have been snatched up by now. The mental image of the bitch being raped and subjected to other repeated horrors aroused Houssmann, and he let it happen, using his right hand to help himself to completion. Thus sated, he dozed off.

WHEN HOUSSMANN AWOKE *the sun was beginning its daily trip toward the horizon. He wondered how long he had slept. He was surprised he had slept at all. He didn't remember ever napping in the middle of the day.*

He remained still on the lounge, allowing himself to enjoy the rich blue sky and the occasional fluffy cloud gradually changing shapes in the high-altitude winds. He checked his phone to see if he'd missed a call while he slept. He hadn't, and that annoyed him. He would swim it off in the pool.

He stretched as he walked to the pool. He looked around at his property and hoped he soon would be able to enjoy the peace and beauty without worry about unfinished business.

As he took the first step down into the water, the hairs on the back of his neck stood up. It was a feeling he never ignored. As he began to turn around, he might have heard a brief and vague popping noise in the distance. He had no chance to analyze it. Half of his head exploded out over the pool and the deck, blood, bone, and brain matter forming a gruesome fan shape as it blew into small pieces. Only half his head remained, and even it was grue-somely damaged. His right eye had been knocked out its socket and hung against his cheek on a rope of blood vessels and nerves. He fell backwards into the pool, its water now staining claret red.

Honus Houssmann was dead.

The sniper, who had hidden himself in some boulders at the edge of the beach, backed away as quietly as possible, though there was no one around to hear him. He disassembled the rifle and buried parts of in in the dunes and parts of it in public grounds around the island. If a storm exposed their resting places they could not be identified or traced because he had destroyed the identification numbers, and eventually the salt in the sand and air would corrode them beyond repair.

Houssmann's body rested on the bottom of the pool for nearly two days before the chest cavity filled with the gases of decay and floated him to the surface. That's where Androsian found him when tried to deliver a gift of some tuna caught the same morning.

Authorities were able to identify the body through DNA sent to Interpol. But since there was no one in the world willing to claim the body, Houssmann was cremated and his ashes committed to the sea.

73

The public reaction to my stories about Houssmann Health, based on interviews with Mobley, Emilio Martinez, Harry Conaway and, surprisingly, Harriet Latchey, were shock, horror, and disgust. Illinois's two U.S. senators convened bipartisan hearings in Congress on the whole sordid mess. There appeared to be strong sentiment on Capitol Hill for new federal legislation that would slam the door on trafficking of every sort. Such laws already existed, but obviously enforcement was severely lacking.

Harriet Latchey agreed to talk to me about what she knew of her husband's dealings with Houssmann. It wasn't much, but she had wondered where all the money came from that funded her husband's campaigns. Her first thought after Bobby disappeared was that he had been kidnapped. But when there were no demands for ransom, and the FBI found no evidence of an abduction, she decided he must have run away. She remained adamant that the boy, Bobby, stay out of the public eye since his return. He had been emotionally traumatized and would need a great deal of therapy to regain a normal life. He didn't need more pressure and stress.

The morning after, Eric Ryland and I sat in his office discussing all this and what, if any, future I had with the *Journal*. We had discussed it most of the morning and seemed to be coming to an agreement. I would resume my column and stick by what it was originally intended to be, a three-a-week commentary on local political and social issues. Not as exciting as the adventures I'd had in the recent past, but a lot safer and more acceptable to the newspaper and to Mark. He and I had discussed the matter the night before. He said he could live with those parameters if Ryland could and as long as I stuck with them. Mark feared that I wouldn't. I denied it, but I shared his concerns.

Jerry Alvarez knocked on Ryland's door frame. Ryland waved him in. He took a chair across from mine.

"Well?" Ryland said.

"I have news and a surprise," Alvarez said. "News first." He glanced at Ryland. "Positive ID. DNA."

I felt left out.

"Please don't forget I'm in the room, too," I said.

"Houssmann had been plotting his getaway for some time," Alvarez said. He then led Ryland and me step by step through what he knew about Houssmann's flight from the United States, about his offshore bank accounts, and about his dealings in The Maldives.

"Of course, without your work in tracking his plane to Sri Lanka, Deuce," he said, "we might have spent years scouring the world for him and never finding him. Great job."

"Amazing," I said. "So you know for sure where he is?"

"Scattered all over the Indian Ocean by now," Alvarez said. "He's dead. We made a positive identification through pieces of his head blown around his swimming pool. Nobody claimed the body, so it was cremated, and the ashes dumped at sea."

I felt my mouth drop open, and it suddenly felt easier to breathe.

Jerry continued. "Houssmann was shot by a skilled sniper while standing outside beside his pool. The combination of the devastating head shot and submersion in the warm water for a few days did nothing to help his appearance. His fingers were too bloated to get reliable prints. But the DNA was conclusive."

"Do you know who did it?"

"Not a clue, but we owe whoever it was a debt of gratitude. Houssmann had buried himself so deep in assumed names, forged IDs, and intrigue that it's doubtful we ever would have unearthed him. And even if we had, The Maldives has no extradition treaty with us. It's enough for me that he's dead."

"Not for me," I said. "I feel like I only know half the story."

"Well, let me add a little more. We know where his money is stashed. He put enough into offshore banks to pay off the U.S. national debt. And he took about $200 million in cash with him to The Maldives. All the money will be retrieved. It will be used to pay his debts, his taxes, and his fines and penalties. There will be plenty left over, and it will be distributed to his victims and their families."

"Are you absolutely sure the dead man is Houssmann?"

"Not a shred of doubt," Alvarez said.

Ryland and I both remained quiet for several minutes, trying to absorb news we never expected to hear.

Then I asked, "What about his goon squad?"

"Also dead. Houssmann apparently took care of most of them before he left. We have two in custody, the two who assaulted you at Mark's condo. They will never know freedom again. When it gets around their prison that they were party to a child trafficking ring, they'll probably be shanked in the recreation area or in their bunks."

"Wow." It was all I could think of to say.

"So, what's the surprise, Jerry?" Ryland asked. "As if that news isn't enough?"

Alvarez stood. "Can I close the blinds on these windows?" he asked, indicating those that overlooked the newsroom.

"I guess so," Ryland said.

He did, and then he opened the office door and nodded at Ryland's secretary. She looked at someone else and said, "You can go in now."

Drigger walked in. He had only a slight trace of a limp.

I got up and walked over to hug him. He returned the hug.

"God, it's good to see you again," I said. "I heard you were out of the hospital, and it almost hurt my feelings that you didn't tell me. How're you feeling?"

He hugged me tightly. "I love you to death, Deuce," he said, "but I couldn't call right away. I'm sorry."

"Well, you're here now, and from all appearances, you're doing well. Jerry said he had a surprise for me, and you're the best one I could imagine."

Drigger stepped back from me and held me at arm's length.

He said, "I think I've got a bigger one. You remember when we were down in Joe Pye you said I looked vaguely familiar."

"I think so," I said. "I don't remember why."

"And a couple of times you asked me why I was risking my life to save you."

"I never did get an answer."

"Well, let me show you."

He walked out of the office and returned moments later with two boys, one maybe twelve, and the other a few years younger. I recognized the older boy immediately. I ran to him and held him tight. I couldn't stop the tears—mine or his."

"Charles," I whispered. "Oh, God, Charles. I didn't think I was ever going to see you again. Are you okay? You look so good."

I had met Charles—though not his real name—during my first encounter with the child trafficking ring. He had been a street kid, and his younger brother, Joey, had been stolen off the street by the traffickers and used by heaven knows who. I had found him in a warehouse, hiding in a cabinet, his body just a shadow of the robust little boy hanging onto Drigger's hand now as if his life depended on it.

"Joey?" I asked. He pressed his face into Drigger's leg, casting a sideways glance in my direction. He was either shy or scared. Maybe both.

"Do you remember me, honey?"

He gave me the slightest nod, then buried his face in Drigger's leg again.

"Thank God they're okay," I said to the room. Then to Drigger, "I don't understand."

"These handsome guys are my sons," Drigger said. "The one you know as Charles is Alec Gerard. His little brother is Joey Gerard. My real name is Charles Gerard. Alec took his street name from me."

The memory returned. "You're the man who brought Charles—sorry, Alec—to my house that night to say goodbye. You broke my heart."

"Let's sit down, and I'll tell you the story," he said.

Ryland asked his secretary for a pitcher of coffee and two Cokes. He closed his office door behind him and nodded to Gerard. "Whenever you're ready."

Alec sat next to his dad, and Joey sat on his dad's lap, seeming to be mindful of which was the injured leg.

"These guys were growing up in a happy home," he started. "My wife and I adored them both. Then the Marines sent me off to Afghanistan—that part of my story was true. I was out of touch with my family for extended periods of time. My wife couldn't deal with two wild young boys by herself, especially since she was a dental technician, and her job didn't give her a great deal of time at home. In the end, she simply couldn't take it. She asked her sister to take the boys, and she did. She had no better luck corralling them, and they spent most of their time on the streets. Then my wife was killed in a car accident, and the kids had no adult supervision at all. They wound up in foster homes, which made matters worse. You know the rest of the story."

Ryland's secretary arrived with the coffee and Cokes on a big tray and set it in the middle of the conference room table. Each boy happily took a Coke and began sucking it down. Joey was watching me and gave me a tentative smile.

"Thank you," he said in almost a whisper.

Alec nodded. "Yeah, thanks."

Everyone who wanted coffee poured some, and Drigger returned to his story.

"When my wife was killed, it took a while for the Marines to locate me. I was deep under cover in the Hindu Kush, a part of the effort to run down Bin Laden. I came home on the first military flight I could find, but by then it was too late. Alec was in the wind, and Joey was gone. I spent a good deal of time trying to find them. Alec finally came home and decided to stay when he found me there. He told me about Joey, and about you, Deuce. I will be forever grateful for how you helped my boys. That's the debt I owe you."

I asked, "So it was you who stood on the sidewalk that night when Alec came up the steps to say goodbye to me?"

"Yes, though I looked quite a bit different that night compared to when I found you in Joe Pye County. The dreads were part of the act. I didn't own the old cabin. It belonged to the Forest Service, and they loaned it to us. I can't tell you how much I never want to use an outhouse again. Or live without electricity. But it was all part of the cover story."

"You actually frightened me that night on my stoop," I said. "I didn't know who you were or where you were taking Ch—uh, Alec. But I was pretty sure I'd never see him again. Saying goodbye to him was one of the hardest things I ever did. Mark and I had actually talked about adopting him."

"Be glad you didn't," Drigger said. "Or you'd have had all three of us living with you. I've promised both boys I'll never leave them again, and I intend to follow through."

I turned to Jerry Alvarez. "Did you ever figure out how Houssmann slipped out of town without anyone noticing? Your people had his whole life staked out."

"We didn't figure out, no," Alvarez said and glanced toward Drigger. Joey had been listening carefully and turned his face into his father's shoulder.

Drigger stroked the boy's head. "Joey's the hero there," he said. He chose his next words carefully so they wouldn't be too painful for the boy. "Houssmann had a penchant for 'test driving' the children that came to his operation, if you get my meaning."

I did and it made me sick.

"The kids came and went via the tunnel. Joey remembered it, and he remembered how to get to it from the house. When the judge issued the search warrant, the FBI only had to check out where Joey sent them."

He lowered his head so he could look Joey in the eye. "You know that helping makes you a hero Joey, right?" The little boy nodded and buried his head again.

The truth dawned on me. "That's why you went to Joe Pye." I said. "You had targeted Houssmann and Sparks. You intended to put a permanent end to the trafficking."

Drigger nodded. "Something like that," he said.

"You got Sparks, but Houssmann got away from everyone. So, you tracked him down again and finished the job in The Maldives."

"I followed your lead, that his plane was in Colombo. The manager of a flight service at the airport there told me the plane was in a locked hangar being refurbished. He didn't know how to reach the owner, but the foreman of the crew making the alterations had a satellite phone number. As you know, a satellite phone's a lot harder to track than a cell phone, but American intelligence was able to pull it off. Once I knew exactly where Houssmann was, well, the rest came easy. I did what I had to do. It didn't feel good, exactly, but I felt as though I had closed a really horrible book."

"You told me a couple of times that you owed me a debt," I said. "Is this what it was?"

"Yep."

"Why didn't you answer the question then? Why didn't you tell me the truth about Alec and Joey—and yourself?"

"I didn't want there to be any distractions," Drigger said. "I was afraid if I told you what happened to Alec and Joey, you'd be full of questions. They could divert our attention from the problems we had to resolve if we were going to get out of Joe Pye alive and with the world made a better place with the elimination of Sparks and his men."

Something else popped into my head.

"Grey Houssmann said somebody had suggested – I think he said someone ordered him to come to me to give up his father. He wouldn't tell me who. Was it you?"

Drigger just nodded.

"And what did Sally—whoever she really is—mean when she said Houssmann's activities were endangering the country?"

Drigger pursed his lip, then said, "I still can't discuss that. Sorry."

I sat in dumb silence until Alec left his father's side and came over to hug me again. Then he crawled into my lap and kissed my cheek. I felt tears coming.

"So, now you're going to find another line of work?" Ryland asked Drigger.

"Same organization. Desk job," he said. "Even if I didn't have the boys, my leg will never be strong enough for more situations like Bin Laden or Joe Pye."

I invited Drigger and the boys to dinner and called Mark so he could join us. I asked the boys what they liked to eat. Simultaneously they said, "Pizza."

"Giordano's is their favorite," Drigger said.

As we got ready to leave, I turned to Ryland.

"You want to join us?" I asked.

"No, but thanks," he replied. "I have a paper to publish."

"Thank you for everything," I said.

He took a deep breath. "Just don't forget our agreement. Tomorrow you restart the column. And no more Don Quixote missions. Right? Are we agreed on that."

"We are," I said.

When I arrived at work the next morning, I got my desk straightened up and sat down in front of the computer. I had to admit, it felt good to be out of danger and back to a columnist's assignment. I had made that commitment to Eric, and I was ready to make the change for Mark and myself, as well.

I was just about to power up the computer.

My phone rang.

Acknowledgments

If you want to write a book—or a novella or a short story—the first thing you need is a good story idea. Then come the folks willing to make room for you in their days to coach you on technical aspects of the story with which you are not sufficiently versed. You need them even before you type "Chapter 1" at the top of the first page to make sure the story will work. And when you're finished, you need outstanding editors. With BLACK MARSH I was incredibly lucky. I had all of the above. I came up with the story idea. I came up with the professional advisors. The editors took over from there. I need to publicly acknowledge and thank them all. I could not have done any of it without their help.

For one Deuce Mora book I asked the director of pharmacy at a major Florida hospital to help me find a drug that would kill someone quickly and then disappear from the body without leaving a trace. He looked at me strangely, then called his assistant to join the conversation and help him make sure I didn't have any murderous intent.

In another book I had to learn the details of how a modern high rise building works. The building manager and the chief of security spent most of a day showing me around "the dirty places" that most people never see, giving me very useful lessons along the way. As our day ended, the security chief asked me, "My character dies in this story, doesn't he?" As a matter of fact, yes.

A very good mystery writer and dear friend once spent two weeks researching what wine would have been served with a cassoulet in Paris in the 1920s. I asked him, "Who's going to know if you're right?" He replied, "Someone will know."

People who know "stuff" ("stuff" is a technical writing term) are my best friends. They're the ones who help me get my facts right. Because if you make a mistake, someone will know, and the trust that develops between a writer and reader will evaporate. Picking up a book is an act of trust by the reader that the author will make the effort worthwhile. Break that bond of trust and you lose the reader, perhaps forever.

There are several people to thank for help with BLACK MARSH. Alisa Kaplan is an official with the voting watchdog, Reform Illinois. She was so gracious with her time that I only hope I didn't mess up her extremely valuable information by paring it down to a manageable length. Illinois voting laws are hugely complex, sort of like knowing the difference, in lay terms, between nuclear fission and nuclear fusion. I hope I never have to explain that. Second, David Ehrman who, as always, is a master of "story." David, a television writer/producer in Hollywood, can take any scene and turn it into a cinematic gem that the reader can readily envision. And Judith Paul, an amazing editor who can sniff out typos, dropped words, syntax errors, and spelling issues. She did a remarkable job.

I am deeply indebted to you all, including those of you who took the time to read the book and, hopefully, to enjoy it.

jh